NOTES WAVERED, THEN DIED AWAY . . .

I bent and scooped up the sword.

In my hands, it burned.

"*Hoo*lies—" Flesh fused itself to steel. "Let go!" I shouted. "You thrice-cursed son of a goat— *let go of my hands!*"

Steel clung, caressed, absorbed. I thought again of melted eyes in a blade-riven skull.

"Hoolies take you!" I yelled. "What do you want, my *soul?*"

Or was it trying to *give* one?

—on my knees, now—

—hoolies, oh, hoolies—stuck to a sword . . . oh, hoolies, *stuck* to a sword—

—and for how *long?*

This book is dedicated to Donald A. Wollheim

SWORD-MAKER

JENNIFER ROBERSON

Acknowledgment

As any author with spouse or significant other can attest, no book is written completely independent of that person. There are things that person does: answers the phone, brings in the mail (telling you if there's a royalty check), goes out for more milk, gets the cat off the computer, tells the barking dog to be quiet, plus myriad other tasks. These things are all important; concentration is occasionally a very delicate thing. But this person also contributes a great deal to the actual creation of a book. He reads, rereads, re-rereads. Tells you what works, and what doesn't. Drives you completely bonkers. But he also improves the book.

Mark O'Green had much to do with *Sword-Maker*. Without him, it wouldn't exist. For this, and other things, I give him my gratitude.

Prologue

She is not a woman for idle conversation, having little patience for small talk, and even less for excuses and explanations. Including those dealing with life and death; mine, or her own. And yet I resorted to both: excuses, explanations. Somehow, I had to.

"It wasn't my fault," I declared. "It wasn't. Did I have any choice? Did you *leave* me any choice?" I snorted in derision. "No, of course not—not *you* . . . you leave no choice or chance to anyone, least of all me . . . you just stare me down across the circle and *dare* me to take you, to cut you, to chop you down with my blade, because it's the only thing that will make you admit you're just as human as anyone else, and just as vulnerable. Just as fragile as anyone, man or woman, made of flesh and blood . . . and you *bleed*, Del . . . just like anyone else—just like *me*—you bleed."

She said nothing. Fair hair shone white in firelight, but blue eyes were nothing more than blackened pockets in a shadow-clad face lacking definition or expression. The beauty remained, but changed. Altered by tension, obsession, pain.

Behind me, tied to a tree, the stud snorted, stomped, pawed a thin layer of slush away from winter-brown turf. Pawing again and again, stripping away even the turf until what he dug was a hole.

Horses can't talk, not like humans; they do what they can with ears, teeth, hooves. What he told me

now was he didn't want to eat. Didn't want to sleep.
Didn't want to spend the night tied to a bare-branched
tree, chilled to the bone by a Northern wind that
wouldn't—quite—quit. What he wanted was to leave.
To go on. To head south toward his desert homeland
where it is never, ever cold.

"Not my fault," I repeated firmly. "Hoolies, bascha,
you and that storm-born sword of yours . . . what did
you *expect* me to do? I'm a sword-dancer. Put me in a
circle with a sword in my hands, and I dance. For pay,
for show, for honor—for all those things most men are
afraid to name, for fear of showing too much . . . well,
I'm *not* afraid, Del—all I know is you left me no
choice but to cut you, coming at me like that with that
magicked sword of yours—what did you *expect?* I did
what I had to. What was needed, for both of us, if for
different reasons." I scratched angrily at the scars in
my right cheek: four deep-scored claw marks, now
white with age, cutting through the beard. "I tried like
hoolies to make you quit, to make you leave that
thrice-cursed island before it came to something we'd
both regret, but you left me no choice. You stepped
into that circle all on your own, Del . . . and you paid
the price. You found out just how good the Sandtiger
is after all, didn't you?"

No answer. Of course not; she still thought she was
better. But I had proven which of us was superior in
the most eloquent fashion of all.

Swearing at the cold, I resettled the wool cloak I
wore, wrapping it more closely around shoulders. Brown
hair uncut for far too long blew into my eyes, stinging,
and my mouth. It also caught on my short-cropped
beard repeatedly, no matter how many times I stripped
it back. Even the hood didn't help; the wind tore it
from my head again and again and again, until I gave
up and left it puddled on my shoulders.

"You and that butcher's blade," I muttered.

Still Del said nothing.

Wearily I scrubbed at brows, eyes, face. I was tired,

too tired; the wound in my abdomen ached unremittingly, reminding me with each twinge I'd departed Staal-Ysta far sooner than was wise, in view of the sword thrust I'd taken. The healing was only half done, but I'd departed regardless. There was nothing left for me in Staal-Ysta. Nothing at all, and no one.

Deep in the cairn, flame whipped. Smoke eddied, tangled, shredded on the air. Wind carried it away, bearing word of my presence to the beasts somewhere northeast of me in darkness. The hounds of hoolies, I called them; it fit as well as any other.

I waited for her to speak, even to accuse, but she made no sound at all. Just sat there looking at me, *staring* at me, holding the *jivatma* across wool-trousered thighs. The blade was naked in the darkness, scribed with runes I couldn't—wasn't meant to—read, speaking of blood and forbidden power too strong for anyone else to key, or to control, with flesh, will, voice.

Del could control it. It was part of her personal magic; the trappings of a sword-singer.

Sword-*singer*. More than sword-dancer, my own personal trade. Something that made her different. That made her *alien*.

Whose name was Boreal.

"Hoolies," I muttered aloud in disgust, and raised the leather bota yet again to squirt Northern *amnit* deep into my throat. I sucked it down, gulp after gulp, pleased by the burning in my belly and the blurring of my senses. And waited for her to say something about drink curing nothing. About how a drinking man is nothing more than a puppet to the bota. About how dangerous it is for a sword-dancer, a man who lives by selling sword and skill, to piss away his edge when he pisses liquor in the morning.

But Del said none of those things.

I wiped *amnit* from my mouth with the back of a hand. Glared at her blearily across the guttering fire. "Not my fault," I told her. "Do you think I *wanted* to cut you?" I coughed, spat, drew in breath too deep for the half-healed wound. It brought me up short, sweating, until I could breathe again, so carefully, meticulously measuring in- and exhalations. "Hoolies, bascha—"

But I broke it off, confused, because she wasn't there.

Behind me, the stud dug holes. And he, like me, was alone.

I released all my breath at once, ignoring the clutch of protest from my ribs. The exhalation was accompanied by a string of oaths as violent as I could make them in an attempt to overcome the uprush of black despair far worse than any I'd ever known.

I dropped the bota and rose, turning my back on the cairn. Went to the stud, so restless, checking rope and knots. He snorted, rubbed a hard head against me, ignored my grunt of pain, seeking release much as I did. The darkness painted him black; by day he is bay: small, compact, strong, born to the Southron desert.

"I know," I said, "I know. We shouldn't even be here." He nibbled at a cloak brooch: garnet set in gold. I pushed his head away to keep curious teeth from wandering to my face. "We should go home, old son. Just head south and go home. Forget all about the cold and the wind and the snow. Forget all about those hounds."

One day he *would* forget; horses don't think like men. They don't remember much, except what they've been taught. Back home again in the South, in the desert called the Punja, he would recall only the grit of sand beneath his hooves and the beating heat of the day. He'd forget the cold and the wind and the snow. He'd forget the hounds. He'd even forget Del.

Hoolies, I wish *I* could. Her and the look on her face as I'd thrust home the steel in her flesh.

I was shaking. Abruptly I turned from the stud and went back to the cairn. Leaned down, caught up the sheath and harness, closed my fist around the hilt. In my hand the cold metal warmed at once, sweet and seductive; gritting teeth, I yanked the blade free of sheath and bared it in firelight, letting flame set steel to glowing. It ran down the blade like water, pausing only briefly to pool in the runes I now knew as well as I knew my name.

I was shaking. With great care, I took the sword with me to one of the massive piles of broken boulders, found a promising fissure, wedged the blade into it. Tested the seating: good. Then locked both hands around the hilt, meaning to snap it in two. Once and for all, to break it, for what it had done to Del.

Samiel sang to me. A small, private song.

He was hungry, still so hungry, with a thirst that knew no bounds. If I broke him, I would kill him. Was I willing to run that risk?

I tightened my hands on the hilt. Gritted teeth— shut my eyes—

And slid the blade, ringing, very carefully out of the fissure.

I turned. Sat. Slumped, leaning against the boulders. Cradling the deadly *jivatma;* the one I had made my own.

I rested my temple against the pommel of the twisted-silk hilt. It was cool and soothing, as if it sensed my anguish.

"I must be getting old," I muttered. "Old—and tired. What am I now—thirty-four? Thirty-five?" I stuck out a hand and, one by one, folded thumb and fingers absently. "Let's see . . . the Salset found me when I was half a day old . . . kept me for—sixteen years? Seventeen? Hoolies, who can be sure?" I scowled into distance. "Hard to keep track of years when you don't even have a name." I chewed my lip, thinking. "Say, sixteen years with the Salset. Easiest. Seven years as an apprentice to my shodo, learning the sword . . . and thirteen years since then, as a professional sword-dancer." The shock was cold water. "I could be thirty-*six!*"

I peered the length of my body, even slumped as I

was. Under all the wool I couldn't see anything, but I
knew what was there. Long, powerful legs, but also
aching knees. They hurt when I walked too much,
hurt after a sword-dance. Hurt when I rode too long,
all thanks to the Northern cold. I didn't heal as fast as
the old days, and I felt the leftover aches longer.

Was I getting soft around the middle?

I pressed a stiff hand against my belly.

Not so you could tell, though the wound had sucked
weight and tone. And then there was the wound itself:
bad, yes, and enough to put anyone down for a couple
of weeks, but I'd been down for nearly a month and
still was only half-healed.

I scratched the bearded cheek riven by scars. Old,
now; ancient. Four curving lines graven deeply into
flesh. For months in the beginning they'd been livid
purple, hideous reminders of the cat who had nearly
killed me, but I hadn't minded at all. Not even when
people stared. Certainly not when women fussed, worried about the cause. Because the scars had been the
coinage that bought my freedom from the Salset. I'd
killed a marauding sandtiger who was eating all the
children. No more the nameless chula. A man, now,
instead, who named himself the Sandtiger in celebration of his freedom.

So long ago. Now the scars were white. But the
memories were still livid.

So many years alone, until Del strode into my life
and made a mockery of it.

I scratched the scars again. Bearded. Long-haired.
Unkempt. Dressed in wool instead of silk, to ward off
Northern wind. So the aches wouldn't hurt so much.

The sword, in my hands, warmed against my flesh,
eerily seductive. The blade bled light and runes. Also
the promise of power; it flowed up from tip to quillons, then took the twisted-silk grip as well. Touched
my fingers, oh so gently, lingering at my palm. Soft
and sweet as a woman's touch: as Del's, even Del's,
who was woman enough to be soft and sweet when the

mood suited her, knowing it something other than weakness. An honest woman, Delilah; in bed and in the circle.

I flung the sword across the cairn into the darkness. Saw the flash of light, the arc; heard the dull ringing thump as it landed on wind-frosted turf.

"I wish you to hoolies," I told it. "I want no part of you."

And in the dark distances far beyond the blade, one of the beasts bayed.

Part I

One

Only fools make promises. So I guess you can call me a fool.

At the time, it had seemed like a good idea. The hounds that dogged Del and me to Staal-Ysta, high in Northern mountains, were vicious, magic-made beasts, set upon our trail by an unknown agency. For weeks they merely stayed with us, doing nothing other than playing dogs to sheep, herding us farther north. Once there, they'd done much more; they attacked a settlement on the lakeshore, killing more than thirty people. Some of them were children.

Now, I'm no hero. I'm a sword-dancer, a man who sells his sword and services to the highest bidder. Not really a glorious occupation when you think about it; it's a tough, demanding job not every man is suited for. (Some may think they are. The circle makes the decision.) But it's a job that often needs doing, and I'm very good at it.

But it doesn't make me a hero.

Men, I figure, are pretty good at taking care of themselves. Women, too, unless they stick their pretty noses into the middle of something that doesn't concern them; more often than not it doesn't, and they do. But children, on the other hand, don't deserve cruelty. What they deserve is time, so they can grow up enough to make their own decisions about whether to live or die. The hounds had stolen that time from too many settlement children.

I owed nothing to Staal-Ysta, Place of Swords, which had, thanks to Del, tried to steal a year of my life in the guise of honorable service. I owed nothing to the settlement on the lakeshore, except thanks for tending the stud. But no one owed *me* anything, either, and some had died for me.

Besides, my time on the island was done. I was more than ready to leave, even with a wound only halfway healed.

No one protested. They were as willing to see me go as I was to depart. They even gave me gifts: clothing, a little jewelry, money. The only problem was I still needed a sword.

To a Northerner, trained in Staal-Ysta, a *jivatma*—a blooding-blade—is a sacred thing. A sword, but one forged of old magic and monstrous strength of will. There are rituals in the Making, and countless appeals to gods; being Southron, and apostate, I revered none of them. And yet it didn't seem to matter that I held none of the rituals sacred, or disbelieved (mostly) in Northern magic. The swordsmith had fashioned a blade for me, invoking the rituals, and Samiel was mine.

But he didn't—quite—live. Not as the others lived. Not as Del's Boreal.

To a Northerner, he was only half-born, because I hadn't properly keyed him, hadn't *sung* to forge the control I needed in order to wield the power promised by the blessing, by the rituals so closely followed. But then, clean, well-made steel is deadly enough on its own. I thought Northern magic redundant.

And yet some of it existed. I felt it living in the steel each time I unsheathed the weapon. Tasting Del's blood had roused the beast in the blade, just as her blade, free of the sheath, had roused the trailing hounds.

I did not leave the sword lying in dirt and turf throughout the night. Old habits are hard to break; much as I hated the thing, I knew better than to ignore it. So I fetched it, felt the ice replaced with warmth, shoved it home in its sheath. I slept poorly, when at all, wondering what the hounds would do once I caught up to them, and if I'd be called on to use the sword. It was the last thing I wanted to do, after what Del and others had told me.

She had said it so plainly, trying to make me see: *"If you go out there tomorrow and kill a squirrel, that is a true blooding, and your sword will take on whatever habits that squirrel possesses."*

It had, at that moment, amused me; a blade with the heart of a squirrel? But my laughter had not amused her, because she knew what it could mean. Then, I hadn't believed her. Now, I knew much better.

In the darkness, in my bedding, I stared bitterly at the sword. "You're gone," I told it plainly, "the moment I find another."

Unspoken were the words: *"Before* I have to use you."

A man may hate his magic, but takes no chances with it.

The stud had his greeting ready as I prepared to saddle him. First he sidled aside, stepping neatly out from under the saddle, then shook his head violently and slapped me with his tail. Horsehair, lashed hard, stings; it caught me in an eye, which teared immediately, and gave me cause to apply every epithet I could think of to the stud, who was patently unimpressed. He flicked ears, rolled eyes, pawed holes in turf. Threatened with tail again.

"I'll cut it off," I promised. "As far as that goes, maybe I'll cut more than your *tail* off . . . it might be the making of you."

He eyed me askance, blowing, then lifted his head sharply. Ears cut the air like blades. He quivered from head to toe.

"Mare?" I asked wryly.

But he was silent except for his breathing. A stallion, scenting a mare, usually sings a song loud enough to wake even the dead. He'd do the same for another stallion, only the noise would be a challenge. This was something different.

I saddled him quickly, while he was distracted, untied and mounted before he could protest. Because of his alarm I nearly drew the sword, but thought better of it. Better to let the stud run than to count on an alien sword; the stud at least I could trust.

"All right, old man, we'll go."

He was rigid but quivering, breathing heavily. I urged him with rein, heels, and clicking tongue to vacate the clearing, but he was having none of it.

It was not, I thought, the beasts I'd christened hounds. The stink of them was gone; had been ever since I'd left Staal-Ysta. Something else, then, and close, but nothing I could name. I'm not a horse-speaker, but I know a little of equine habits; enough to discard humans or other horses as the cause of the stud's distress. Wolves, maybe? Maybe. One had gone for him before, though he hadn't reacted like this.

"Now," I suggested mildly, planting booted heels.

He twitched, quivered, sashayed sideways, snorted. But at least he was moving; insisting, I aimed him eastward. He skittered out of the clearing and plunged through sparse trees, splattering slush and mud. Breathing like a bellows through nostrils opened wide.

It was an uneasy peace. The stud was twitchy, jumping at shapes and shadows without justification. Most times, he is a joy, built to go on forever without excess commentary. But when he gets a bug up his rump he is a pain in *mine,* and his behavior deteriorates into something akin to war.

Generally, the best thing to do is ride it out. The stud has been a trustworthy companion for nearly eight years, and worth more than many men. But his actions now jarred the half-healed wound, putting me decidedly out of sorts. I am big but not heavy-handed; he had no complaints of his mouth. But there were times he tempted me, and this was one of them.

I bunched reins, took a deeper seat, and slammed

heels home. He jumped in surprise, snorting, then bent his head around to slew a startled eye at me.

"That's right," I agreed sweetly. "Are you forgetting who's boss?"

Which brought back, unexpectedly, something I'd heard before; something someone had said regarding the stud and me. A horse-speaker, a Northerner: Garrod. He'd said too much of our relationship was taken up in eternal battling over which of us was master.

Well, so it was. But I hate a predictable life.

The stud swished his tail noisily, shook his head hard enough to clatter brasses hanging from his headstall, then fell out of his stiff-legged, rump-jarring gait into a considerably more comfortable long-walk.

Tension eased, pain bled away; I allowed myself a sigh. "Not so hard, is it?"

The stud chose not to answer.

East, and a little north. Toward Ysaa-den, a settlement cradled high in jagged mountains, near the borderlands. It was from Ysaa-den that reports of beast-caused deaths had been brought to Staal-Ysta, to the *voca*, who had the duty to send sword-dancers when Northerners were in need.

Others had wanted the duty. But I, with my shiny new Northern title, outranked those who requested the duty. And so it was given to me. To the Southron sword-dancer who was now also a *kaidin*, having earned the rank in formal challenge.

I tracked the hounds by spoor, though with slush dwindling daily there was little left to find. Prints in drying mud were clear, but snowmelt shifted still-damp mud and carried the tracks away. I rode with my head cocked sideways, watching for alterations, but what I saw was clear enough: the beasts cut the countryside diagonally northeast with no thought to their backtrail, or anything set on it. Ysaa-den was their target as much as Del had been.

We had come down from above the timberline, now

skirting the hem of upland forests, slipping down from bare-flanked peaks. Uplands, downlands; all terms unfamiliar to me, desert-born and bred, until Del had brought me north. Only two months before; it seemed much longer to me. Years, maybe longer. Too long for either of us.

The turf remained winter-brown and would, I thought, for a while. Spring in the uplands was soft in coming, tentative at best. I knew it could still withdraw its favor, coyly turning its back to give me snow in place of warmth. It had happened once before, all of a week ago, when a storm had rendered the world white again and my life a misery.

The trees were still bare of leaves, except for those with spiky green needles. The sky between them was blue, a brighter, richer blue, promising warmer weather. Beyond lay jagged mountains scraping color out of the sky. Pieces of the peaks lay tumbled on the ground, rounded by time into boulders scattered loosely here and there, or heaped into giant cairns like piles of oracle bones. Chips and rubble fouled the track, making it hard to read. The stud picked his way noisily, hammering iron on stone. Stone, as always, gave.

In the South, spring is different. Warmer, certainly. Quicker with its favors. But much too short for comfort; in weeks it would be summer, with the Punja set to blazing beneath the livid eye of the sun. It was enough to burn a man black; me, it baked copper-brown.

I lifted a hand and looked at it. My right hand, palm down. Wide across the palm, with long, strong fingers; creased and ridged with sinew. Knuckles were enlarged; two of them badly scarred. The thumbnail was spatulate, corroded by weeks in a goldmine when I'd been chained to a wall. In places I could see bits of ore trapped in flesh; my days in the North had bleached some of the color out, but beneath it I was still darker than a Northern-born man or woman. Sunburned skin, bronze-brown hair, eyes green in place of blue. Alien to the North, just as Del had been to me.

Ah, yes, Delilah: alien to us all.

Men are fools when it comes to women. It doesn't matter how smart you are, or how shrewd, or how much experience you've had. They're all born knowing just what it takes to find a way to muddle up your head. And given the chance, they do.

I've known men who bed only whores, wanting to make no better commitment, saying it's the best way to avoid entanglements. I've known men who marry women so as not to buy the bedding. And I've known men who do both: bed whores and wives; sometimes, with the latter, their own.

I've even known men who swear off women altogether, out of zeal for religious purity or desire for other men; neither appeals to me, but I'll curse no man for it. And certainly, in the South, I've known men who have no choice in the matter of bedding women, having been castrated to serve tanzeers or anyone else who buys them.

But I've known no man who, drunk or sober, will not, at least once, curse a woman, for sins real or imagined. *A* woman; or even women.

With me, it was singular.

But it wasn't Del I cursed. It was me, for being a fool.

It was me, for proving once and for all which of us was better.

Bittersweet victory. Freedom bought with blood.

The stud stiffened, snorted noisily, then stopped dead in his tracks.

I saw movement in the trees, coming down from tumbled gray rocks. Nothing more, just movement; something flowing through oracle throws made of stone instead of bone. I caught whipping tail, fixed eyes, teeth bared in a snarl. Heard the wail of something hunting.

Too late the stud tried to run. By then the cat was on him.

It took us down, both of us. It sprang, landed, sprawled, throwing the stud over. I felt him buckle and break, felt him topple. I had time only to draw my left leg up, out of the way; he'd trap it, landing on it. Maybe even break it.

I rolled painfully as the stud went down. Grunted, then caught my breath sharply as my abdomen protested. And ignored it, thinking of the stud.

I came up scrambling, swearing at the cat. A big, heavy-fleshed male. White, splotched with ash, like a man come down with pox.

I picked up a rock and threw it.

It struck a flank, bounced off. The cat barely growled.

Another rock, another strike. This time I shouted at it.

Teeth sank into horseflesh. The stud raked turf with forelegs, screaming in pain and terror.

My hand closed around the hilt. "Oh, hoolies, bascha—not a squirrel, a *cat*—"

And the sword was alive in my hands.

Two

Hungry. It was *hungry*.

And so very thirsty.

I had felt it before, in the sword. Felt *them* before: hunger and thirst both, with equal dominance. Nearly inseparable, indivisible from one another.

Felt them before, in the circle. When I'd run the sword through Del.

Oh, hoolies, bascha.

No. Don't think about Del.

Hot. It was *hot*—

Better than thinking of Del.

Was it?

Hot as hoolies, I swear.

Sweat broke from pores and ran down forehead, armpits, belly. Beneath hair and wool, it itched.

The cat. Think of the cat.

Hoolies, it is *hot*—

And the sword is so very thirsty.

Oh, bascha, help me.

No—Del isn't here.

Think of the cat, you fool.

Think only of the *cat*—

The sword is warm in my hands. All I can think of is thirst, and the need to quench it with blood.

Sweating, still sweating—

Oh, hoolies, why me?

Thrice-cursed son of a Salset goat—

Watch the cat, you fool!

In my head I hear a song.

Can the cat hear it, too?

Hoolies, it sees me now. Sees the sword. Knows what I want. Turns from the stud—poor stud—to me . . .

Oh, hoolies, here it comes—lift the sword, you fool . . . *do something,* sword-dancer—

But I don't want this sword. And this isn't a real circle—

Real enough, Punja-mite. Are you ready for the cat?

Am I ready for the *sword?*

It has happened before, the slowing. The near stoppage of motion in everything I look at, as if it waits for me. It happened now, as before, though this time the slowing was nearly a true *halt,* clean and pure, leaving me time and room to work, to pick and choose my method; to give the best death to the cat before he gave it to me.

It has happened to me before. But never quite like this.

I smelled blood, musk, extremity, as well as morbid fear. Felt nerves twinge in my belly as the half-healed wound contracted. I wondered, swiftly and uneasily, what the sword was doing. But as I heard the stud's screaming, fear bled away.

Slowly, oh so slowly, the cat looked up from the stud. There was blood in his mouth, blood in his claws, as well as gobbets of horsehair.

In my head, I heard a song. A small, private song, hinting at powerful things.

Beneath the cat, the stud was thrashing, legs flailing. I heard his grunts of extremity.

And the sword sang me a promise: the stud would be released if I gave it the power it needed.

Except I ought to be able to take the cat without using any magic. The sword was, after all, a *sword,* and effective enough on its own.

But the stud squealed and thrashed, and in my head

I heard the song. A soft, subtle song. Yet too powerful to ignore.

I didn't exactly give in to it. I just ignored it. I was
too worried about the stud to waste any more time on
the noise rolling around in my head. And so, impatiently, I let go of it altogether.

Not for long. Just long enough to think about something else. To stop suppressing it. To rescue my poor
horse.

And so, all unwittingly, I let it have its moment. I
let it have its lifetime in the shadow of an instant.

Noise rushed in even as I rushed the cat. No, not
noise: *music.* Something far more eloquent than anything so commonplace as noise. More powerful than
sound. And abruptly I recalled what I had heard on
the overlook by the lakeshore, kneeling with the sword.
When the music of the Cantéada had crowded into my
skull.

How they could sing, the Cantéada. A race born of
dreams, given substance by belief. Who had, Del told
me once, given music to the world.

Just as they'd given *me* some for the moment of the
Naming.

For the stud, I thought, it's worth it. The risk is
worth the taking for all the times he's saved *my* skin.

Only the thought, for a moment. And a moment
was all that was needed.

The cat flowed aside. The stud lurched up, staggered, ran.

The mouth curled back and opened to display impressive fangs. But slowly, oh so slowly; didn't he
know I sang his death?

White cat with gray-irised eyes, and dappled, silver-
splotched coat. The pelt would be worth a fortune; I'd
take it once he was dead.

—*the sword was alive in my hands*—

"What's mine is mine," I told him, so he would
understand.

The sword was *alive.*

The cat peeled back lips and screamed.

The sword invited him in. *Come closer,* it said. *Come closer.*

It made it all so *easy*.

The leap was effortlessly smooth. Smiling, I watched it, admiring his grace. Watched the hind legs coil up to rake; saw the front paws reach out, claws unsheathed; saw the mouth stretch open, the gleam of ivory fangs. Laughing aloud in anticipation, I let him think he'd win.

Then took him in the back of his throat and drove the blade through the base of his skull.

Elation. *Elation.* And a powerful satisfaction.

Not mine. Not *mine;* someone else's. Some*thing* else's—wasn't it? It wasn't me, was it?

Something inside me laughed. Something inside me *stirred,* like awareness awakening.

Oh, hoolies, what is it?

I smelled burning flesh. Thought it was the cat's. Realized it was my own.

I shouted something. Something appropriate. Something *explicit.* To release shock and rage and pain.

Wrenched my hands from the hilt as the metal burned white-hot.

Oh, hoolies, Del, you never warned me about *this*.

I staggered back, hands crossed at the wrists, mouthing obscenities. Tripped, fell, rolled, sprawled flat on my back, afraid to block with my hands. Hoolies, but they hurt!

I smelled burning flesh. Not my own, the cat's.

Well, that's something, at least. Except he's too dead to feel it.

I lay on my back, still swearing, letting the stream of obscenities take precedence over pain. Anything was welcome, so long as it blocked the fire.

Finally I ran out of breath, if not out of pain, and opened my eyes to look at my hands. It was easy to see them; they were stuck up in the air on the end of painfully rigid arms, elbows planted in the ground.

Hands. Not charred remains. *Hands*. With a thumb and four fingers on each.

Sweat dried on my body. Pain sloughed away. I breathed again normally and decided to stop swearing; there seemed no point in it, now.

Still on my back, I wiggled fingers carefully. Gritted teeth, squinting—and was immensely relieved to discover the flesh remained whole and the bones decently clad. No blisters. No weeping underskin, only normal, everyday hands, though the scars and enlarged knuckles remained. *My* hands, then, not some magical replacements.

I felt better. Sat up slowly, wincing at the protest in my abdomen, and wiggled fingers and thumbs yet again, just to be sure. No pain. No stiffness. Normal flexibility, as if nothing had ever happened.

Scowling, I peered at the sword. "What in hoolies are you?"

In my mind was a word: *jivatma*.

Oh, hoolies, bascha . . . what do I do now?

What I did was get up. Everything appeared to be in working order, if a trifle stiff. Through wool I massaged the sore scar below my short ribs, then forgot it immediately; the cat was worth more attention. The cat—and the sword.

I went over to both. I'd stuck the cat pretty good: through his open mouth and on through the back of his skull. He lay sprawled on his side, but the hilt, thrust into dirt, propped up his head so it was level with the ground.

Two sockets stared up at me. The eyes in them had melted.

For longer than I care to remember, I couldn't look away. Couldn't even move. All I could do was stare, remembering the heat of the hilt. I'd begun to believe it imagined; now I knew better.

Swords don't melt eyes. Nor do they singe whiskers or char lips into a rictus. Swords slice, thrust, cut open; on occasion they will hack, if the swordsman has no skill. But never do they *melt* things.

Something inside me whispered: *Maybe jivatmas do.*

I looked again at my hands. Still whole. Grimy and callused, but whole.

Only the cat had burned.

Well, parts of him. The parts the sword had touched.

Empty eyesockets were black. I realized there was no blood; the sword had swallowed it all.

Oh, hoolies, bascha, I've done what I swore I wouldn't.

In the distance, beasts bayed. Like a pack of hounds, they belled. As they had for Boreal whenever Del had keyed.

And in answer, the stud snorted.

Stud—

I left the cat and the sword and went at once to the stud. He hadn't gone far, just far enough to put distance between himself and the cat, and now he waited quietly, sweat running down flanks and shoulders.

Sweat mixed with blood.

"Oh, hoolies," I said aloud, "he got you good, didn't he?"

The stud nosed me as I came up to him. Grimly I peeled ragged dark mane off his withers—down South, we crop manes short; up North, they leave them long—and saw the cat had dug in pretty deep across brown withers, though the saddle had helped protect the stud a little. I found teeth and claw marks, carving gouges in his hide. There were more claw marks low on the stud's right shoulder from the cat's hind legs, and a few others here and there. All in all, the stud was lucky; the cat had been distracted, by me or the sword. I've seen half-grown sandtigers, in the Punja, take down larger horses much as this cat had done. But they finished the job more quickly by tearing open the jugular.

Then again, I—or the sword—hadn't given the cat the chance to finish the job properly.

Something like fear pinched deep in my belly. But I ignored it with effort, purposefully turning my attention to the stud. "Well, old man," I consoled him, "looks like we'll make a pair. You match my cheek, now—maybe I should name you Snowcat. To go with the Sandtiger."

The stud snorted messily.

"Maybe not," I agreed.

The death-stink of the cat—and the smell of burned flesh—made the stud uneasy, so I tied him to the nearest tree and unsaddled him there, taking weight off his sore hide. I knew I'd do no more riding for a day or two, so I set up camp.

When a horse is the only thing between you and a long walk—or death—a man learns to value his mount, and the stud's health and safety came first. If it slowed us down, too bad; the hounds, I knew, would wait, and the South wasn't going anywhere. So I picked up the remaining bota of *amnit*. I didn't dare risk infection; liquor leaches well enough.

I paused to pat the stud gently, and to check the strength of rope and knot. "Easy, old man. I won't lie—this'll hurt. Just don't take it out on me."

I aimed carefully and squirted, hitting every stripe and bite I could see. Ruthless, maybe, but sponging each wound gently would clean out only one, because the stud wouldn't let me near enough to do any more once he'd felt the bite of the *amnit*. At least this way I got almost all of them at once.

Squealing, he bunched himself and kicked. A horse—especially a stallion—cutting loose with both hind hooves is a dangerous, deadly creature capable of murder. Prudently I moved another pace away, just to be sure, and grinned as he slewed an angry eye around to find me. Once found, he tried a scooping sideways kick with a single hind hoof, hoping to catch me on the sly. When that one missed, he pawed testily, digging craters in the turf.

"You dig a hole, you stand in it," I told him. "I

know you're mad—I'd be, too—but it's better than dying, you know. So just stand there like a quiet old ladies' mare and think about what you'd be facing if I didn't have this stuff." I paused, checking the contents. "Good waste of liquor, if you ask me. Might as well drink the rest."

The stud blinked a baleful eye.

I relented. "Tell you what, old son—I'll give you extra grain. That ought to make you feel better."

I dug into one of the pouches and pulled out a fistful of grain, moving within striking range to offer it. But the stud wasn't hungry. He lipped listlessly at the grain, spilling most of it between slack lips. He didn't even want sweetgrass, which was beginning to show signs of life now that most of the snow was going.

Something pinched again inside my belly. "Better not sicken on me," I warned, "after all that *amnit* I wasted." While thinking instead of the sword.

But the stud made no answer.

It came swift and clear and sharp: *If he up and dies on me—*

No. I cut it off. No sense in borrowing grief.

The stud shifted restlessly, knocking stone against stone. I didn't want to leave him just yet, so I leaned against his tree and squirted *amnit* into my throat.

"You've just been out of the South too long, old man . . . like me. *Just* like me; you're a sandtiger drug out of his desert, swallowing snow instead of sand . . . best get yourself right back home before the cold stiffens all your joints."

Well, it already had stiffened some of mine. In the North, bones age faster. In the South, skin does.

Which means, I guess, I'm growing old inside *and* out.

Gack. What a thought.

I moved off the tree and rubbed a hand down the stud's backbone, smoothing coarse, thick hair. He quivered, expecting *amnit;* I soothed him with a few words.

Over his rump I stared at the cat with its alien steel tongue.

I recalled the emotions I'd felt. The *need* to quench the sword; how it had sung its private song. How I, too easily seduced in my moment of fear for the stud, had turned my back on self-made wards and let the song commence. Giving the blade its freedom.

For the stud.

Worth it? Maybe. For that moment. For that *particular* moment.

But what was I to do now? I didn't need it. I didn't *want* it. Not now. Not ever. I'd tasted too much of its power.

"Leave it," I said aloud. "You can get another sword."

Well, so I could. Somewhere. Someday. Meanwhile, I needed a weapon.

"Leave it," I repeated.

Hoolies, I wish I could.

Three

A *small, soft song. A private, intimate song. Powerful in its promise, weakened by neglect.*

Deep in sleep, I muttered.

A small, sad song; a trace of desire only hinted at, too shy to speak of need.

Memories of both.

The stud, stirring, woke me. I sat up, stared hard into darkness, oriented myself. Got up and went to the stud, who pawed listlessly at turf.

His head drooped, hanging heavily on the end of a slackened neck. He shifted from hoof to hoof. When I touched him, he barely took note.

I was, abruptly, afraid.

Singlestroke and this horse were all I'd ever had. And Singlestroke was gone.

A small, soft, seductive song, promising me companionship such as no one had ever known.

Companionship—and *power.*

Beneath my hand, he stiffened. I felt the tension in his body; heard it in his rattling snort, in the crunching of gravel beneath shod hooves. His ears lanced erect, then slapped back against his head.

"Hey—" But abruptly I shut it off.

I hadn't felt it for weeks. At first it was so alien I didn't recognize it, and then the strangeness slid away and familiarity took its place. A man doesn't forget what it's like to be sick.

Not *sick* sick. I've been that before, from wound

fever or the Northern malady called a "cold." And not sick from too much liquor; I've been that, too, more often than I care to recall. No. This sickness wasn't of the body but of the soul, all wrapped up like a nameday gift in a sash called fear.

And even that was different.

All the hair stood up on my arms. Tickled the back of my neck. Tightened scalp against skull. I shivered involuntarily, cursing myself for a fool, then felt nausea knot my belly.

Don't ask me what it is. Del called it an affinity for magic. Kem, the sword-maker, said I was sensitive to the *essence* of it, whatever that means. All I know is it makes me sick and uncomfortable, and very sour in my outlook. Being a conspicuously lighthearted, good-humored soul—or at least one lacking in personal demons—I don't much like having my sensibilities mangled by something as dark and erratic as magic.

If it just didn't make me feel *sick*.

Maybe it was the cat. I'd eaten too much cat. Too much Northern cat stuffed into a Southroner's belly.

But the stud hadn't had any, and he wasn't happy, either.

Or, more likely, the sword. Trust it to make my life miserable in more ways than one.

Then again—

"Ah, hoolies," I muttered, as I smelled the stink of the hounds.

I'd forgotten what it was to be up close, to see white eyes ashine in the darkness. To smell their stink. To sense the press of numbers crowding so close to me.

I had played tracker. Now they hunted me.

The stud knew the stench, too. He, like me, had killed, smashing furred bodies beneath cold Southron iron, but liked it no better than I. We weren't made for magic, either of us, being bred only to travel the sands beneath a Southron sun. *Without* benefit of magic.

The sword lay sheathed by the fire, set beside my bedding. It was, I thought grimly, a mark of decay in habits that I had left my weapon to go to the stud. It displayed an unaccustomed trend toward worrying, which has never been my vice, as well as pointing up my distinct dislike for the Northern sword. I mean, it *was* a sword, like it or not; it could save my life even if I disliked it. But at the moment it couldn't do anything, because I'd left it behind. All I had was a knife, and no horse to use for escape. Or attack, if it came to that; I'd have to do it on foot.

White eyes shone bright in darkness. In silence the hounds gathered, wearing shadows in place of clothes. Black and gray on gray and black; I couldn't count their numbers.

It crossed my mind that maybe the stud could be ridden after all, pain or no pain. Not far, not far enough to injure him, just far *enough;* enough to leave beasts behind.

But retreat wasn't what I'd come for. It wasn't the promise I'd made.

I sucked in a guts-deep breath. "Come on," I said, "try me."

Sheer bravado, maybe. Nothing more than noise. But it's always worth a try, because sometimes it will work.

*Some*times.

They crept out of the shadows into the red-gray glow of dying coals. Maned, gray, dappled beasts: part dog, part wolf, part nightmare. Without a shred of beauty, or a trace of independence. What they did was at someone's bidding, not a decision of their own.

The stud shifted uneasily. He stamped, breaking stone.

"Try me," I repeated. "Have I come too close to the lair?"

They came all at once, like a wave of slushy water. In spate, they swallowed the campsite, then ebbed back toward the trees.

But the tide had taken the sword.

Gaping in disbelief, I saw the glint of the pommel, a

flash of moonlight off the hilt. Saw teeth close on the sheath and shed it, leaving it behind; apparently the warding magic inherent in a named blade made no difference to equally magical beasts.

Which made me wonder why it existed at all, if it was useless against the hounds.

Two of them mouthed the sword awkwardly. One held the hilt, the other the blade, busily growling at one another like two dogs fighting over a stick. But this stick was made of steel. Magicked, gods-blessed steel.

The others surrounded them like a tanzeer's phalanx of guards. They headed for the trees, for the shadows I couldn't pierce.

Hoolies, they wanted the *sword*.

So much for my own value.

I very nearly laughed. If they wanted the thrice-cursed thing *that* much, let them have it. I didn't want it. It was one way of getting rid of it.

Except I knew better than that. The beasts could never use it, but the man who made them could. And that I couldn't risk, since he was the one I sought.

Very calmly I drew the ward-whistle from beneath my woolen tunic and stuck it between my lips. Such a tiny, inconsequential geegaw, but made by beings I still had trouble believing in, even though I'd seen— and heard—them myself. Cantéada. I recalled their silvery skin, feathery scalp crests, nimble fingers and froglike throats. And I recalled their music.

Music was in the whistle, as was power. And so I waited a moment, to build up false hopes, then blew an inaudible blast.

It did its job, as always. They dropped the sword and fled.

Grinning around the whistle, I went over and picked up the blade.

And wished I hadn't touched it.

Shame flooded me. Shame and anger and grief, that

I had treated the sword so poorly when it was deserving of so much better. What had it done to me?

In disbelief, I spat out the whistle. *I* hadn't thought those thoughts. And wouldn't; of that I was certain. But the thoughts had come from somewhere. The *feelings* had come from somewhere.

I threw the sword down again. It thumped dully against turf, glinting red-white in coals and moonlight. "Look, you," I said, "you may not be like any sword I've ever known, but it doesn't give you the right to tell me what to think. It doesn't give you the right to make me feel guilty, or ashamed, or angry—or *anything*, hear me? Magic, schmagic—I want nothing to do with you and nothing will ever change that. As far as I'm concerned, the hounds can have you . . . except I'm not about to let you fall into the hands of someone who can tap into whatever power you possess—"

I broke it off abruptly. I realized precisely how stupid I sounded, talking to a sword.

Well, talking to a sword isn't so bad; I think we all do it from time to time, before we step into a circle. But talking to a magicked blade made me most distinctly uneasy; I was afraid it might understand.

I wiped sweaty palms on my clothing. I hadn't imagined the feelings. I hadn't imagined the *shame*.

And, most definitely, I hadn't imagined the power demanding to be unleashed.

Coiling itself so tightly, like a cat before it springs.

In my head, I heard a song. A small, soft song, promising health and wealth and longevity, as if it were a god.

"*Jivatmas* die," I said hoarsely. "I've seen it before, twice. You aren't invincible, and you don't make *us* immortal. Don't promise me what you can't."

Notes wavered, then died away. I bent and scooped up the sword.

In my hands, it burned.

"*Hoo*lies—" Flesh fused itself to steel. "Let go!" I

shouted. "You thrice-cursed son of a goat—*let go of my hands!*"

Steel clung, caressed, absorbed. I thought again of melted eyes in a blade-riven skull.

"Hoolies take you!" I yelled. "What do you want, my *soul?*"

Or was it trying to *give* one?

—on my knees, now—

—hoolies, oh, hoolies—stuck to a sword . . . oh, hoolies, *stuck* to a sword—

—and for how *long?*

Sweat ran down my body. In the cold night air, I steamed. "No one ever told me—no one ever said—no one *warned* me about this—"

Well, maybe they had. I just didn't listen much.

Sweat stung my eyes. I blinked, ducked my head into a shoulder, rubbed wet hair away. I stank of sweat, old wool and grime, with the acrid tang of fear.

I drew in a ragged breath. "What in hoolies am I—"

Fire lit up the sky.

At least, I *think* it was fire. It was something. Something bright and blinding. Something that damped the moon and the stars with a delicate, lace-edged beauty.

And beauty it was, like nothing I've ever seen. Nothing I've ever dreamed. Kneeling with the sword clutched in my hands—or the sword clutching *me*—I stared, mouth open, and let my head tip back so I could see the glory of Northern lights. The magic of sky-born steel, rune-wrought by the gods, baptised in human blood.

Celebrated by song.

Dancing in the sky was a curtain of luminescence. The colors were muted magnificence, flowing one into the other. They rippled. Dripped. Changed places. Met and melted together, forming other colors. Bright, burning colors, like fire in the sky. The night was alive with it.

In my head I heard a song. A new and powerful song. It wasn't one I knew. It wasn't from my sword, too new to sing like that. From a sword with a little age. From a sword who understood *power,* being cognizant of its own, and how to guard the gift. A sword born of the North, born of ice and snow and storm; of the cold winter wailing of a keen-edged banshee-storm.

A sword who knew my name; whose name I knew as well.

Samiel fell out of my hands. "Hoolies," I croaked, "she's alive."

Four

I denied it. Immediately. Vehemently. With everything I had; I did not *dare* allow myself to believe it might be true, because hopes hauled up too high have that much farther to fall.

Oh, bascha. *Bascha.*

I denied it. Desperately. All the way down through the darkness, picking my way with care. All the way down through boulders, slipping and skidding on rubble. Through the shadows of looming trees.

Choking on painful certainty: Del is dead. I killed her.

Fire filled the sky. Such clean, vivid colors, rippling like Southron silks. Boreal's doing, no other: steel brush against black sky, with artistry born of magic.

Doubts, like smoke, blew away, leaving me empty of breath.

—Delilah is alive—

I stopped walking. Stopping sliding. Stopped cursing myself for a fool. And stood awkwardly, rigidly clutching a tree. Trying to breathe again. Trying to comprehend. Trying to sort out a welter of feelings too complex to decipher.

—Delilah is alive—

Sweat bathed me. I leaned against the tree and shut my eyes, shivering, releasing the air I'd finally gulped. Sucking it back in even more loudly. Nearly choking. Ignoring the knot in my belly, the cramping of my guts, the trembling in my hands.

41

Trying to understand.

Relief. Shock. Amazement. An overwhelming joy. But also compelling guilt and an odd, swelling fear. A deep and abiding despair.

Delilah is alive.

Gods of valhail, help me.

Colors poured out of the sky like layers of ruffled silks: rose, red, violet, emerald, a hint of Southron yellow, traces of amber-gold. The blush of burnished orange. The richness of blue on black and all the shadings in between.

I scrubbed sweat off my face. Took pains to steady my breathing. Then silently followed the brightness down and stepped out of a tree-striped, hollow darkness into frost and fog and rainbow, where a sword held dominance. Alien, rune-wrought steel, naked in Del's bare hands.

Delilah was alive.

She stood as I have seen her stand before, paying homage to the North, or to the sword herself. With legs spread, braced; with arms stretched wide above her head, balancing blade across flattened palms. Three feet of deadly steel, shining whitely in the night; a foot of knotted silver twisted carefully into a hilt. Ornate and yet oddly plain, with a magnificent symmetry. Simplistic in promised power, lethal in promises kept.

All in white, Delilah. Tunic, trews, hair. And the stark, ravaged face, devoid of all save desperation.

Thin fog purled down from the blade. Streamers licked Del's hands, face, clothing, frothed around her ankles, spilled out across the ground. Drops of moisture glistened, reflecting sword-born rainbows. All in white, Delilah; uncompromising white. A blank, stark canvas. Behind her was the night; uncompromising black. But arrayed above us both were the colors of the world, summoned by rune-wrought steel.

White on black, and light. A brilliant, blinding light that made me want to squint.

Ghost, I thought; wraith. A spirit made of shadows,

lent light by a playful demon. Nothing more than a
fetch, or a trick of imagination. It wasn't really Del. It
couldn't *really* be Del.

Gods, let it be Del—

I felt the touch of wind. It blew softly across the
clearing, shredding sword-born fog, and gently touched
my face. The testing fingers of a blind man; the subtle
caress of a lover's touch. A cold, winter wind, border-
ing on banshee. Letting me taste its strength. Letting
me sense its power.

Believe, it told me plainly. *I am born of Boreal, and
only one commands her. Only one can summon her
power. To key it, and control it. To make me substance
out of nothing; to give me life out of proper season.*

Winter was in the clearing. It numbed my ears, my
nose; stiffened aging joints. Lifted the hem and folds
of my cloak and snapped it away from my body,
stripping hair out of my face. Threatening beard with
frost-rime and my lungs with frigid breath.

Del sang on. A small, soft song. A song of infinite
power.

She had traded her soul for that song. As well as
humanity.

I turned my back on her. I turned my back on her
power. On winter and on the wind, fixing my eyes on
spring. Thinking of things to come, not on what had
passed.

Walked out of her light into darkness. Into things I
could understand.

Thinking: Del is *alive.*

Which meant I could be angry.

And so I was, when at last she came riding into my
camp. Hoolies, six weeks. And all that time: *alive.*

Me thinking her dead.

Me thinking I'd killed her.

All those days and nights.

Delilah is alive.

I squatted by the fire cairn and warmed hands over

the coals. I didn't really need to, since Del's sword-summoned winter was banished, but at least it was something to do. It gave me something to look at instead of staring at her.

Oh, I looked. I looked—and swallowed hard. Glanced away again in forced, false negligence, staring blindly at hands that tried repeatedly to tremble; they didn't because I wouldn't let them. It took all the strength I had.

She rode a dark dappled horse; roan, I thought, blue, though in the darkness it was hard to tell. A tall dark-eyed gelding stepping daintily through storm-strewn rubble.

The stud, less concerned with pride and appearances, peeled back his lip and squealed. He'd teach the gelding his place or know the reason why.

Moonbleached hair was white, scraped back from a too-pale face showing keen edges of too-sharp bone. The skull, now strongly visible, was flawless in its beauty, but I preferred more flesh on it. She had lost too much to the circle, and to its aftermath.

The fire was gone from the sky like so much wine spilled from a cup. The blade rode her back in its customary harness, slanting left to right. From the downward curve of ornate quillons to the carefully crafted pommel knot, nearly a foot of shining steel rose beside her head.

Boreal: *jivatma.* A sword-singer's blooding-blade.

With it, she'd killed the man who had taught her how to fight. With mine, I'd nearly killed her.

Delilah is alive.

The stud stomped, pawed, squealed, arching neck and raising tail. I was relieved to see it, because even though, for him, it was muted, the show of dominance nonetheless meant he was feeling better. Maybe I'd worried for naught.

About the stud *and* Del; here she was before me.

With customary prudence, Del reined in her gelding at the edge of the cairn's sphere of meager light. Not far enough to calm the stud, but enough to tell him the gelding offered no threat to his dominance.

Or did she do it to tell me the same?

Hoolies, that was done with. The circle had made its choice.

All in white, Delilah: in the South, the color of mourning; in the North, I didn't know. Belted tunic, baggy trousers. Heavy cloak, free of all adornment, save for the moonwashed silver of fur gaiters cross-gartered around her shins, and brown leather bracers warding most of her forearms. They shone with silver bosses, as did her belt; silver brooches clasped the cloak. Loose hair tumbled over her shoulders.

I thought: *I can't do this.*

And knew somehow I would.

"Well," I said lightly, "what do you offer a wraith?"

"Amnit," she said, "if you have it."

There was nothing in her tone except familiar quietude. No trace of emotion; I hoped mine showed the same.

"Oh, a bota or two." I pulled one up from the ground, let it dangle from my hand. The leather bag twisted on its thong, then unwound in the other direction in a slow, predictable spiral.

She sat silently in her saddle, watching the bota spin. In the poor light her eyes were black. Too black in a too-white face.

Oh, hoolies, bascha. What do we do now?

She watched the bota spin.

Wondering what to say?

No, not Del. She hones words as well as weapons, but uses them less often.

She finally looked at me. "I came because I need you."

Deep in my gut, something spasmed.

Del's voice was steady; she gives little away in speech. "No one will dance with me."

Of course. That. Nothing else, for her. Her needs are different from mine.

The wound ached afresh. I set the bota down, carefully exhaling. "Oh?"

"No one," she repeated. This time I heard it clearly: pain, anguish, grief. In Del, always muted. Nearly always hidden. Often not present at all.

Anger stirred. I suppressed it instantly, idly rubbing a bearded chin. "But you think *I* will."

The gelding stomped. Del sat it out, hands only loosely holding reins across the pommel of her saddle. Her eyes were very steady. "You are the Sandtiger. Southron, not Northern. My dishonor means nothing to you." For only a moment, she paused. "After all, you were the victor."

I made no answer at first, letting the words settle. Victor, was I? In a way; I had won the dance, and therefore won my freedom. But winning is often losing; the taste of victory, in this case, was decidedly bittersweet.

I stared hard at the glow of the cairn. Coals and color ran together, filling up my eyes. Quietly, I said, "I very nearly died."

Softly, when she could, "I traveled farther than you."

I looked at her sharply. The residue of fireglow overlay her face, hiding expression from me. And then it faded, slowly, and I saw the expression. Saw the determination.

I wanted to laugh. Here we were arguing over which of us had come closer to dying, and each of us responsible for the other's circumstances.

I wanted to laugh. I wanted to cry. And then both emotions spilled away. In their place was anger. "I nearly killed you, Del. I stepped into that circle hoping only to beat you, to *stop* you, and yet I nearly killed you." I shook my head. "It's different now. Nothing can be the same."

"Sameness remains," she countered quietly. "There are still things I must do before my song is sung."

"Like what?" I demanded. "Hunt down Ajani and kill him?"

"Yes," Del answered simply.

Rising so abruptly pulled the new skin around my wound. But it didn't stop me. It didn't stop me at all. I took the shortest route: straight across the fire cairn directly to her gelding, where I reached up and caught Del's left wrist before she could react.

It isn't easy to take Del unaware. She knows me well enough to predict much of what I will do, but not so well as to predict *everything* I will do. And this time, she couldn't.

I heard her blurt of shock as I jerked her down out of the saddle. Heard my grunt of effort mingled with her sound.

It was awkward. It was painful. She is tall and strong and quick, but now weakened by her own wound. She came free in a tangle of stirrups, cloak, harness and sword, arms and legs awry. I knew it would hurt; I *meant* it to hurt. But at least it hurt us both.

She came down hard. The gelding snorted and sidled away, leaving us room as he avoided further hostilities. I grunted again as my half-healed wound protested. Sweat broke out afresh.

Hoolies, this hurts.

But I didn't regret it at all.

The pommel knot of her sword knocked me in the chin, though not hard enough to do damage. Not hard enough to loosen my grip. Not hard enough to stop me as I dumped her on the ground.

Breathing hard, I stood over her, tucking down toward the right a little to ward the wound from more pain. "You stupid, sandsick, selfish little fool, haven't you learned *anything*?"

Del was sprawled on her back with the sword trapped under her. Instead she went for her knife.

"Uh-uh, bascha—I don't think so." I slammed her wrist down with my foot and put some weight on it.

Enough to hold it still. The knife glinted in moonlight but a handspan away. "What—are you going to kill me because I insulted you? Because I called you a fool? Or selfish?" I laughed at her expression. "You *are* a fool, bascha . . . a silly, selfish, sandsick girl feeding off dreams of revenge."

Fair hair slipped free of her throat. I saw fragile flesh move as she swallowed heavily. Tendons stood out tautly.

"*Oh,* no," I said sharply, and bent to snatch her from the ground.

It aborted her efforts entirely, if without any grace. Having felt the results of her brothers' teaching before, I wasn't about to allow her the chance again. I pivoted hips aside and took the kick she meant for my groin on the shin instead, which hurt, but not as much as it might have. Then I filled my hands with cloak, tunic and harness leather and yanked her up from the ground, half-dragging, half-carrying her thirty or forty feet, where I pressed her back against one of the tumbled boulders. I restrained her the only way I knew how, which was with all of my weight. Caught between me and stone, Del had nowhere to go.

No knife. No sword. Now all she had was words.

"You're *scared*," she accused. "Swear at me if you like—call me all the names you can think of, if it makes you feel better. It doesn't change a thing. I see it in your face, in your eyes . . . I feel it in your *hands*. You're scared to death, Tiger. Scared because of me."

It was not what I expected.

"Scared." Less vehemence, but no less certainty. "I know you, Tiger—you've spent the last six weeks punishing yourself for what you did . . . I *know* you, Tiger—you've spent every day and every night of the past six weeks scared I was dead, and scared I was alive. Because if I was dead, you couldn't live with it—with killing your Northern bascha?" Only once, she shook her head. "Oh, no, not you . . . not the

Sandtiger, who is not quite the uncaring, unfeeling killer he likes people to think he is. So you prayed—yes *you,* just in case—you prayed I was alive so you wouldn't have to hate yourself, and yet the whole time you've been scared I *was* alive. Because if I was, and we ever came face-to-face again, you'd have to explain why. You'd have to *tell* me why. You'd have to find a way to justify what you did."

I took my weight from her. Turned. Took two disjointed steps away from her. And stopped.

Oh, hoolies, bascha. Why does it always hurt so?

Her voice was unrelenting. "So, Tiger . . . we are face-to-face. There is time now for the explaining, the telling, for the justifying—"

I cut her off curtly. "Is that why you came?"

She sounded a little breathless, if no less definite. "I told you why I came. No one will dance with me. Not in Staal-Ysta, certainly . . . and I think nowhere else, as well. Women are freer in the North than in the South, but few men will dance against a woman, even in practice bouts. And I need it. Badly. I have lost strength, speed, fitness . . . I need you to dance with me. If I am to kill Ajani, I must be strong enough to do it."

I swung, intending to say something, but let it die as I saw how she clung to the boulder. There was no color in her face, none at all, even in her lips. She pressed one arm across her abdomen, as if to hold in her guts. She sagged against the stone.

Oh, hoolies, bascha.

"Don't touch me," she said sharply.

I stopped short of her and waited.

She drew in a noisy breath. "Say you will dance with me."

I spread my hands. "And if I don't, you won't let me touch you—is that it? You won't let me pick you up from the ground—which is where you'll be in a moment—and carry you to the fire, where there's food and *amnit*—"

"Say it," she said, "and we won't have to find out that you *can't* carry me, which would hurt your pride past repairing."

"Del, this is ridiculous—"

"Yes," she agreed. "But we've both been that before."

"If you think I'm going to step into a circle with you after what happened the last time—"

"Just say it!" she cried, and something at last broke. She crossed both arms against her ribs and hugged herself hard, standing only by dint of braced legs and sheer determination. "If I don't go after him—if I don't kill Ajani—if I don't honor my oath . . ." She grimaced, loosened hair hanging, obscuring much of her face but not the ragged tone in her voice. "I have to, I *have* to . . . there is nothing left for me . . . nothing at all left for me . . . no parents, no brothers, no aunts and uncles and cousins . . . not even Kalle is mine—not even my *daughter* is mine—" She sucked in a painful whooping breath. "Ajani is all I have. His death is all I have. It's all the honor that's left."

I wondered briefly who she was talking to: me or to herself? But I let it go, thinking of something else. "There's more to honor than that." I intended to explain thoroughly, but broke it off to catch her as her legs buckled and she slid down the boulder to huddle against cold stone. And discovered she was right: I couldn't pick her up. So the two of us sat there, cursing private pain, hiding it from one another behind sweaty, muttered curses and denials to half-gasped questions.

"Dance with me," she said. "Do you want me to beg?"

I gritted it out through tight-shut teeth. "I don't want you to beg. I don't want you to dance. I don't want you to do anything but heal."

Del curled one hand into a fist and thumped herself weakly in the chest. "It's all I have—it's all I *am* . . . if I don't kill Ajani—"

I turned toward her awkwardly, trying not to twist sore flesh. "We'll talk about that later."

Her voice was startled. "What are you doing?"

"Trying to peel back some of your layers so I can get a look at your wound."

"Leave it," she said, "leave it. It is healing without your help. Do you think they would have let me go if I was in danger of dying?"

"Yes," I answered bluntly. "Telek and Stigand? And all the rest of the *voca*? Stupid question, bascha . . . I'm surprised they didn't kick you out before this. I'm surprised they didn't kick you out the day *I* left."

"To do that would have dishonored Staal-Ysta," she said faintly. "I was the chosen champion—"

"—who was meant to die in the circle, dancing with me," I finished. "Telek and Stigand threw you to the sandtigers, bascha—no joke intended—and they had no intention of you surviving the dance. Your death would have satisfied the honor of Staal-Ysta, and my victory bought me out of the year you pledged me to. In the South we call it two goat kids for a single breeding . . . it's what the *voca* wanted. You dead and me gone. As it is, we're *both* gone."

"And Kalle stays behind." Her tone was bitter as she twisted away from me and sat up very straight, easing the layers of rucked up wool binding her sore ribs. "So, they got what they wanted. I have lost a daughter, who was perhaps not meant to be mine . . . but there is still her father. And Ajani I will kill."

"Which means we're back where we started." I drew in a deep breath, caught it sharply on a twinge, let it out slowly again. "What I started to say earlier—"

"I did not come for your advice." Del pushed herself up awkwardly, straightened with infinite care, walked very slowly toward the roan.

The abruptness of it stunned me. *"What?"*

She caught the gelding's reins, led him to a tree safely distant from the stud, tied him. "I did not come for advice. Only for your dancing."

So cool and clipped. So much like the old Del, with no time for other's feelings. Full circle, I thought. Back where it all started.

But not quite, bascha. I'm not the same man. Because—or in spite—of you, I'm not the same man.

Five

I sat on my bedding by the fire cairn, scratching sandtiger scars, drinking *amnit*, thinking. *Thinking;* what in hoolies happens now?

So, she wanted to ride with me. For a while. To dance with me in the circle, until she was fit enough to challenge Ajani. Which meant she'd intended all along to leave me, once she found me. Once she was fit again.

Which meant she was using me.

Well, we all use one another. One way or another. But Del was using *me*.

Again.

Without, apparently, considering my own feelings. Or else she *had* considered them, and thought I'd be happier without her. Once she was ready to leave.

Or else she was merely concocting a wild tale to cover up the real reason she'd tracked me down, which had less to do with Ajani and more to do with me.

No. Not Del. She's nothing if not determined.

Nothing if not *obsessed*.

Which meant Ajani was still the most important issue, and I was merely a means to make her fit enough to kill him.

Which came back to me being used.

Again.

A little part of me suggested it didn't matter, that having Del around was enough compensation. Because, of course, she would share my bed again, and that ought to be enough to make any man overlook certain things.

Maybe, once, it would've been. But not anymore. I could overlook nothing. Because a bigger part of me didn't like being reduced to a *means*. I deserved better.

And a still larger part reminded me with exquisite clarity that Del hadn't thought twice about offering me as bait to the *voca* on Staal-Ysta to buy a year off her exile.

Well, she might have *thought* twice. But she'd still offered easily enough without even consulting me.

And it rankled. Oh, it rankled.

I sat on my bedding by the cairn, scratching, drinking, staring. Waiting for Delilah.

She puttered with her gelding, unsaddling him, wiping him down, talking softly, settling him for the night. Wasting time? Stalling? Maybe. But probably not; Del knows what she does and why, and spends no time on what-might-have-beens after the fact.

I watched her: white wraith in the cairnglow, white specter against black trees; so white-on-white, Delilah: tunic, trews, hair, except for flashing silver. Bosses on belt and bracers. Two heavy cloak brooches weighting each wool-swathed shoulder.

And the twisted sword hilt, slashed across her back.

Hoolies, what do I do?

Hoolies, what *don't* I do?

Having no answer for either, I sat by the cairn and sucked *amnit*, waiting for Delilah.

Eventually, she came. With arms full of gear and bedding, she came at last toward the cairn. Toward me. And at last I could tell her.

"No," I said calmly.

In mid-step, she hesitated. Then halted altogether. "No?" she echoed blankly, clearly confused. Thinking about something else.

"You asked me to dance with you. Well, I can give it to you in Southron, in Desert, in Northern. Even in uplander." Humorlessly, I smiled. "Which 'no' do you want? Which one will you believe?"

Her face was white as ice. Only her eyes were black.

With exquisite care, I set aside my bota. "Did you think I was so well-trained that I'd lie down and show you my belly so you could feel good again?"

She stood very still, clutching blankets.

I kept my tone even. Perfectly expressionless, so she would know what it was like. "You came fully expecting me to agree. Not to ask, not to request—to *tell*. 'Dance with me, Sandtiger. Step into the circle.' " Slowly I shook my head. "I don't disagree with your reasons for wanting Ajani dead. I understand revenge as well as or better than anyone. But you forfeited your right to expect me to do anything just for the asking. You forfeited the *asking*."

Del said nothing at all for a very long moment. The meager light from the cairn carved lines into her face, but showed me no expression. No expression at all.

I waited. The circle teaches patience, many kinds of patience. But never have I felt the waiting so intensely. Never have I wanted it to end so badly. And afraid to know the answer, to know how the ending would be.

Her voice was very low. "Do you want me to leave?"

Yes. No. I don't know.

I swallowed painfully. "You were wrong," I told her.

Del clutched bedding.

"Wrong," I repeated softly. "And until you can see it, until you can admit it, I don't think I can help you. I don't *want* to help you."

Breath rushed out of her mouth. With it, her answer. Her explanation. Her *excuse*, for something requiring none because none could be enough. "It was for Kalle—"

"It was for you."

"It was for kin—"

"It was for you."

A painful desperation: "It was for *honor*, Tiger—"

"It was for you, Delilah."

The full name made her flinch. The movement made her wince. Her defenses were coming down: against pain, against truth, against me. The latter, I thought, was what counted. It might yet make her whole.

"Pride," I said, "is powerful. You threw mine away very easily. Will you do the same with your own?"

Her face was slack with shock. "How did I throw away your pride?"

I was on my feet, oblivious to the pain of a wrenched abdomen. Yanking her out of the saddle had taken its toll on us both. "Hoolies, Del, have you forgotten entirely? I was a *slave* for half my life! Not an innocent young Northern girl playing at swords and knives, well-loved by her kin, but a human beast of burden. A chula. A *thing*. Something with no name, no identity, no reason for being alive except to serve others. Except to *service* others—what do you think I did at night in the hyorts with the women?"

I saw the shock in her face, but it hardly slowed me down. "Do you think it was always for pleasure? Do you think it was always merely a man using a woman?" I shook hair out of my eyes. "Let me tell you, Delilah, it isn't always a woman who gets used . . . it isn't always a woman who feels dirty and used and without value other than what she offers in bed. It *isn't always a woman*—"

Oh, hoolies, I hadn't meant to say so much, or so brutally. But I finished it anyway, since it was begging to be said; since it *had* to be said, if we were ever to recover even a trace of the old relationship. Even that of the circle.

I steadied my voice with effort. "I won my freedom—and my name—through desperation and sheer dumb luck, Del, not to mention pain both physical and emotional . . . and yet you were willing to throw it all away again just to buy yourself some time. Is that what I was to you? A means to an end? The coin to buy your daughter? A body to barter away? Is that what I was, Delilah?"

She was strung so taut she twitched. And then, jerkily, she bent. Set down bedding and gear. Shuddered once, deeply, then caught the hilt of her sword in both hands and whipped it out of the sheath.

For a moment, for one incredulous, painful moment, I thought she meant to kill me. That I'd gone too far, though I'd barely gone far enough.

The moment passed. Del cradled Boreal. Vertically, and carefully, pressing blade between breasts. Briefly, oh so briefly, she closed her eyes, murmured something, then slowly, painfully lowered herself to one knee. Then brought down the other.

Del knelt before me in the dirt. She bent, placed Boreal flat on the ground, then crossed her arms across her chest, making fists of her hands. In deep obeisance, she bowed, resting forehead against the blade.

She held herself in perfect stillness for a moment of rigid silence, then raised herself again. Her eyes were black in the cairnglow, empty of all save the knowledge of need. Hers as well as my own.

With frequent checks and taut swallows, she spoke to me in Northern. It was a dialect I didn't know, probably born of Staal-Ysta and precise, required rituals meant to enhance the mystery of the *jivatma*. I've never been much impressed with the trappings of such things, preferring straightforward, unadorned talk, but I made no move to stop her. Clearly she needed it.

Eventually she stopped. Bowed again. Then straightened to look at me, and repeated it all in Southron so I could understand.

Appalled, I cut her off almost immediately. "That's not necessary."

She waited. Swallowed. Began again.

I spat out an oath. "I *said*—"

She raised her voice and overrode me.

"Hoolies, Del, do you think this is what I want? Abasement? Atonement? I'm not asking any such thing, you fool . . . I just want you to understand what it is you did. I just want you to realize—" But I broke it off in disgust because she wasn't listening.

She ran down eventually. All the forms were followed, the requirements satisfied. She was a true daughter of Staal-Ysta, no matter what anyone said; no matter that she was exiled. She completed the ritual.

She bowed over Boreal once again. Then picked up her sword, rose, turned awkwardly from me and walked toward the roan. Stumbling a little. Catching herself with effort. All of her grace was banished, yet none of her dignity.

She had thrown away her pride. Now both of us were even.

Six

She broke through, thrust, cut into me, just above the wide belt. I felt the brief tickle of cold steel separate fabric and flesh, sliding through both with ease, then catch briefly on a rib, rub by, cut deeper, pricking viscera. There was no pain at all, consumed by shock and ice, and then the cold ran through my bones and ate into every muscle.

Deep in sleep, I twitched.

I lunged backward, running myself off the blade. The wound itself wasn't painful, too numb to interfere, but the storm was inside my body. The blood I bled was ice.

I drew a knee up toward my belly, trying to ward the wound. Trying to turn the blade that had already pierced my flesh.

"Yield!" she shouted. "Yield!" Shock and residual anger made her tone strident.

I wanted to. But I couldn't. Something was in me, in my sword; something crept into blood and bones and sinew and the new, bright steel. Something that spoke of need. That spoke of ways to win. That sang of ways to blood—

I woke up sweating, breathing like a bellows; like the stud run too hard. The fire was reduced to coals with only the moon for light, and it offered little enough. I looked for Del in the darkness. Saw nothing but deeper shadows.

Hoolies, did I dream it? Did I dream the whole thing?

I sat up rigidly and immediately wished I hadn't. Deep inside, I ached. I'd twisted in my sleep and the half-healed wound protested.

My sword was screaming for blood.

Did I dream the whole thing? Or only part of it?

A twig snapped. Movement. Maybe I didn't dream it.

Hoolies, make it real.

I stared into darkness. So hard my eyes burned, trying to define the narrow line between dream and reality.

"I'll make you," she gasped. "Somehow—" And she was coming at me, at me, breaking through my weakened guard and showing me three feet of deadly jivatma. "Yield!" she cried again.

My sword was screaming for blood.

Del was gone. That I was certain of, hating it. Hating myself for the wash of fear, of anguish; the uprush of painful guilt. What I'd said to her needed saying. I didn't regret a word of it. But none of what I'd told her was intended to chase her away.

Only to give her a choice.

Del always makes her own choices, no matter how painful they are. No matter how demanding. She shirks nothing I am aware of, counting the finished task more important than the doing. For my angry, obsessed Delilah, the end was always more important than how it was accomplished.

Which meant she might well have left, since I'd given her my answer.

Had I? I didn't recall refusing to dance with her, so long as she admitted her wrongdoing.

She'd conducted an atonement ritual. Begged my forgiveness. Spoken freely of dishonor, and how hers had tainted me. But not once, not *once*, had she admitted she was wrong.

Hoolies, she is stubborn!

Cursing softly, I untangled blankets and pelts from legs, stood stiffly, cursed some more. Then heard the roan gelding blowing in the darkness and realized Del wasn't really *gone,* she simply wasn't present.

Well, a woman is due her privacy.

And then I saw the light.

Oh, hoolies, bascha, what are you doing now?

Boreal, of course. Del went nowhere without her. She didn't always use her, being disinclined to show off, but when she did it showed. Like now, with the light.

Del was up to something.

I am big, but I can move quietly. I learned in childhood, in slavery, how to stay motionless for long periods of time. How to be *invisible,* so no one notices you. It saved me from extra whippings, from cuffs and slaps and blows. It was something I cultivated out of a need for self-preservation, and it served me even in freedom. It served me even now.

Silently I moved, muffling myself in my cloak, and slipped easily through the shadows. Pausing now and then, emulating trees; some say I am tall enough. And at last I found Delilah kneeling in the darkness. Singing softly to her sword.

Regardless of what had happened with my sword while killing the cat, music is still alien to me. I don't understand it. And I didn't, really, now, though the words were clear enough, if sung in Northern instead of Southron. But the song was a private song, composed solely for Boreal.

Del sings to her sword a lot. Northerners do that; don't ask me why. In the South, we merely dance, letting movement speak for itself. But on Staal-Ysta I'd learned it was customary—no, *necessary*—for a sword-dancer to sing. A variation of the dance. Music for the circle.

For Del, it was more than that. It was music for the sword. With it she keyed the power and used it, depending on the song to harness Boreal's magic.

Del sang softly, and Boreal came alive.

I've seen it before. Drop by drop, bead by bead,

running the length of the blade from tip to hilt until the steel is aflame. But this time the light was dull, private, as if she purposely damped it down. Her song was barely a whisper, and the answer that came the same.

Guilt flickered. Clearly this was a private, personal ritual, meant for Del alone. But I didn't leave. I couldn't. Magic I've always distrusted; now I distrusted Del.

Deep inside, something spasmed. Something that spoke of unease. Something that spoke of fear.

Would it ever be the same? Or had we gone too far?

Del sang her song and the sword came alive.

"Help me," she whispered. "Oh, help me—"

It was Northern speech, not Southron, but I've learned enough to understand. Necessity had made me; this moment was no different.

Del drew in a breath. "Make me strong. I need to be *strong*. Make me hard. I *need* to be hard. Don't let me be so soft. Don't let me be so weak."

She was the strongest woman I knew.

"I have a need," she whispered, "a great and powerful need. A task that must be finished. A song that must be ended. But now I am afraid."

Light shirred up the sword. It pulsed as if it answered.

"Make me strong," she asked. "Make me hard again. Make me what I must be, if I am to end my song."

Easy enough to ask. Harder, I thought, to live with.

Lastly, softly, she begged: *"Make me not care what he thinks."*

Oh, hoolies, bascha. Don't do this to yourself.

But it was already done. Boreal was quiescent. Delilah had her answer.

And I had a sword to hate.

Seven

Something bad woke me. Something snatched me out of a dreamless sleep and forced me into wakefulness. Into an abrupt, unpleasant awareness.

Something bad that smelled. Something in my *face*—

I don't know what I shouted. Something loud. Something angry. And, I'll admit, something frightened. But then I don't know a man alive who wouldn't feel afraid if he woke up from a sound sleep to discover a beast standing over his head.

Even as I exploded out of my bedding, the hound lunged at my throat. I smelled its stench, felt its breath, saw the white glint of shining eyes. Flailed out with both arms as I tried to thrust it away.

The hound lunged again, still trying for my throat. Dimly I heard Del, on the other side of the cairn, crying out in Northern. She sounded startled *and* furious; I made no answer, having no time to make the effort, but hoped she'd do something other than shout. Which, of course, she did, with Boreal at her beck.

My own sword was buried beneath tumbled bedding. Now I lay on dirt, hard, cold dirt, with my head at the cairn stones. The hound might take my throat; the coals might take my hair.

No one wants to die. But least of all with no hair.

The beast made no sound. But Del did, and loudly, as she told me to flatten myself.

I tried. I mean, no man aware of Boreal's power risks himself so readily. But even as I kicked over and tried to dig myself into the dirt, the hound evaded the blade. Del's skill was better than that, but my head was in the way. So were my flailing hands, locking themselves at a furred throat. I wanted nothing more than to try for my knife, but dared not take a hand off the hound, or I'd lose my brief advantage.

I felt teeth at my own throat. Snapping, grasping, grabbing. The stench was overwhelming. It smelled of rotting bodies.

Something snugged taut against the back of my neck. Something like wire, or thong. And then I realized it was my necklet. My string of sandtiger claws.

Hoolies, it wanted my *claws?*

But I had no time to wonder beyond my initial surprised response. I heard Del's muttered order to watch my head, which I couldn't actually do since my eyes were *in* it, and ducked. But she missed again, though barely; I heard Boreal's whisper as steel sang past my head.

"Just *do* it—" I blurted.

And then the beast was lunging away, evading the blade yet again. It left me in the darkness and fled away into the trees.

I lay sprawled on my back, one hand at my throat busily digging through woolen wrappings to see if I was whole. To feel if my flesh was bleeding. I yanked wool away with some violence, then heaved a sigh of relief as nothing but skin met my fingers. No blood or torn flesh at all; only whole, unbitten skin.

Meanwhile, Del ignored me entirely and stepped across my body to follow the spoor of the beast. Just in case it might double back. Just in case it might have companions. Not a bad idea, but she might have thought of me. After all, for all *she* knew I could be bleeding to death right there on the ground, dwindling bit by bit—or bucket by bucket—before her eyes.

Except she wasn't looking. Which sort of ruined the effect.

I felt the thong at my neck, heard the rattle of

claws, felt relief wash quickly through me. Which meant
I was perfectly entitled to be testy, since there was
nothing wrong with me.

I let Del get four steps. "Don't bother," I said. "It
got what it came for."

She swung back, sword aglint. "What do you mean,
'what it came for'?"

I sat up slowly, still massaging the flesh of my throat.
It felt bruised; no surprise. "The whistle," I told her
hoarsely. "The Cantéada ward-whistle. That's what it
wanted." Not my claws after all, though I didn't tell
her that. I didn't think she'd understand why I'd worried about it at all.

Del glanced back into the shadows. I knew the beast
was gone; the stink of it had faded. But she waited,
sword at the ready, until her own suspicions died. And
then she came to me.

"Let me see," she said.

Finally. But I shrugged negligence as she knelt down,
setting Boreal close at hand. "I'm all right. It didn't
even break the skin."

Del's hands were insistent. She peeled back wrappings, shoved my hand aside, carefully examined flesh
in the thin light of the moon.

It was odd having her so close to me after so long a
separation. I smelled her familiar scent, felt her familiar touch, saw her familiar face; the faint frown between her brows. At moments like this it was hard to
recall just what had come between us.

And then there were other moments when I remembered all too well.

Ah, hoolies, bascha . . . too much sand blown out
of the desert.

If Del was aware of my scrutiny, she made no sign
of it. She simply examined my throat carefully, nodded slightly, then took her hands away. "So," she
said, "they have learned. And we are back where we
started."

"Not quite," I muttered. "Too much sand blown
out of the desert."

Del frowned. "What?"

For some reason, I was irritated. "We're not back where we started because too many things have changed." I shifted position, felt the pull of newly stretched scar tissue, tried to hide the discomfort from her. Just as she hid her own from me. "Go back to sleep, Del. I'll take first watch."

"You're in no shape for that."

"Neither of us are, but we'll each of us have to do it. I just thought I might as well start."

She considered protesting, but didn't. She knew better; I was right. And so she went back to her bedding on the other side of the cairn and wrapped herself in pelts. All I could see of her was the dim pale glow of her hair.

I sorted out my own tumbled bedding and made sense of it again. And then I settled carefully, snugging deep into cloak and pelts, and prepared to wait through the night. I wanted to give her till dawn; she'd done the same for me.

Trouble was, I couldn't.

It didn't take much. Just a glance at Del on the far side of the cairn, all bound up in pelts and blankets. The glow of the moon in her hair. The sound of her even breathing. And all the feelings recalled.

I sat there rigidly, half sick. Joints ached, my wound throbbed, the flesh of my throat complained. Even my head hurt. Because I gritted my teeth so hard my jaw threatened to crack.

Just tell her, you fool. Tell her the truth.

Across the cairn, she settled. Hurting at least as much as I, inside *and* out.

Deep in my belly, something tightened. Not desire. Something more powerful yet: humiliation. And more than a little discomfort. Of the spirit as well as the flesh.

Oh, hoolies, fool, just tell her the truth.

Just open your mouth and talk; it's never been very hard.

You made Del ask for atonement. She's at least due an explanation.

But that she hadn't asked for one made me feel even worse.

Something inside of me quailed. Guilt. Regret. Remorse. Enough to break a man.

But the woman was due the words.

I stared hard out into the darkness. The night was quiet, save for its normal song. It was cold—colder in bed alone—but spring promised warmer nights. Already the color was different.

You're avoiding the truth, old man.

The woman is due the words. The least you can do is say them out loud where she can hear them, instead of inside your head.

Easier thought than said.

I looked at Del again. And knew all too well that even though she was—and had been—wrong, I shared the responsibility of putting things to rights. Of admitting my own faults. Because when things have gone awry, it takes two to straighten them out.

I drew in a deep breath, so deep it made me lightheaded, then blew it out again. And finally opened my mouth. This time the words would be spoken instead of locked away.

"I *was* afraid," I told her. "I was scared to death. I was everything you accused me of earlier. And it was why I left Staal-Ysta."

I knew she was still awake. But Del said nothing.

"I left on purpose," I continued stolidly. "I wasn't driven out, or invited out, or even asked to leave; I was a *kaidin*, according to all the customs, and they had no right to ask it. I could have stayed. They would have let me stay, to see if you lived or died . . . but I couldn't. I saw you lying there in the circle, cut open by my sword, and I left you behind on purpose."

Del was very still.

I scraped a tongue across too-dry lips. "They put you in Telek's lodge—in *Telek's!*—because it was the

closest. Because they thought you would die, and that
your daughter deserved to watch. To hear the funeral
songs."

Her breath rasped faintly.

"They stitched me back together—you carved me
up pretty good—and gave me the gifts bestowed upon
a new *kaidin*. I had, they said, conducted myself honorably, and was therefore due the tribute as well as
the rank. They patched me up, gave me gifts, rowed
me across the lake." I swallowed painfully; it was
much harder than I'd imagined. "I knew you were
alive. When I left. I knew. But I thought you would
die. I thought you would *die*. I thought—I *did*—I just
. . . and I couldn't—I just *couldn't*—" I let it trail off.
The emptiness was incredible. "Oh, hoolies, Del . . .
of all the lives I've taken, I couldn't face taking yours."

Silence. It hadn't come out the way I'd wanted it to.
I hadn't said everything that needed saying, that I
wanted to say; I couldn't. How could I explain what
I'd experienced when I'd felt my own sword cut into
her body? How could I tell her what it was to see her
lying on hardpacked dirt like a puppeteer's broken
toy, bisected by my sword? How could I tell her how
frightened I had been, how *sickened* I had been? How
much in that moment I had wished myself in her
place?

How could I tell her I was absolutely *certain* she
would die—and I couldn't bear to watch it?

And so I had left her. While she lived. So I could
remember her *alive*.

For me, it was very important. It was necessary. It
was *required*, as so many things have been required of
me. Required by myself.

Silence, while I sat there waiting for her to say
something about my cowardice. My lack of empathy.
My willingness to leave her on Staal-Ysta before her
fate was known. I'd made her ask my forgiveness; now
I needed hers.

And then, at last, a response. But her tone was

oddly detached. "You should have killed me. You should have finished it. Blooding and Keying in me would have made you invincible." Del sighed a little. "The magic of the North and all the power of the South. Invincibility, Sandtiger. A man to be reckoned with."

I drew in a steadying breath. The worst, for me, was over. I think. "I'm already that," I said dryly. "I'm everything I want to be right now, this minute, here. I don't need magic for that. Certainly not the kind of magic that comes from killing people."

Del tightened wrappings, locking the cold away. Locking herself inside, as she did so very often. "You should have killed me," she said. "Now I have no name. A blade without a name."

There was grief. Anguish. Bitterness. The painful yearning of an exile for a land no longer hers. For a world forever denied, except in memories.

I stared blindly into the dark. "And a song that never ends?"

Clearly, it stung. "I will end it," she declared. "I *will* end my song. Ajani will die by my hand."

I let a moment go by. "What then, Delilah?"

"There is Ajani. Only Ajani."

She was cold, hard, relentless. Focused on her task. Her sword had answered her plea.

But how much of it was the sword? How much merely Del? How responsible are *any* of us for what we do to survive, to make our way in the world?

How hard do we make ourselves to accomplish the hardest goal?

Quietly, I said, "I'm not going South."

Huddled in bedding, Del was little more than an indistinguishable lump of shadow against the ground. But now she sat up.

The moonlight set her aglow as blankets fell back from her shoulders: pristine white against dappled darkness. Her hair, unbraided, was tousled, tumbling over her shoulders. Curtaining the sides of her face.

She stared at me, frowning. "I did wonder why they told me you were going to Ysaa-den. I thought at first perhaps they lied, merely to trouble me—it was far out of my way, and yours, if I was to go to the South—but then I found your tracks, and it was true." She shook her head. "But I don't understand why. You've been complaining about the snow and the cold ever since we crossed the border."

I listened to her tone, hearing echoes and nuances; her fight to maintain balance. "I don't like it," I agreed. "I didn't like it *before* we crossed the border. But there's something I have to do."

I also didn't like the look of her. The intensity. She was too thin, too drawn, too obsessed with Ajani. The sword had cut her flesh, but the man had hurt her more.

Del's tone was carefully modulated so as not to show too much. All the same, it showed enough. "I thought you'd go south at once."

"No. Not this time."

"I thought the Sandtiger roamed wherever he wanted, unbound by other desires." She paused. "At least, he used to."

I shut my eyes, waited a beat, answered her quietly. "It won't work, Del. You've pushed me this way and that way like an oracle bone for months, now. No more. There are things I have to do."

"*I* have to go south."

"Who's stopping you? Weren't you the one who spent five years apprenticing on Staal-Ysta just so you *could* go south all by yourself? Weren't you the one who went hunting the Sandtiger with only a storm-born sword for companionship? Weren't you—"

"Enough, Tiger. Yes, I did all those things. And I have done this thing: I have come to you asking your help in making me fit again. But if you are unwilling to give it—"

"I'll give it," I interrupted. "I said that already, after you did your little ritual. But I can't go south right away, which means if you really want my help, you'll have to come along."

"Something has happened," she said suspiciously. "Did Telek and Stigand force you to swear oaths? Did they give you a task? Did you make promises to the *voca* in exchange for tending me?"

"No. I have every intention of going home as soon as I've tracked them to their lair. It has nothing to do with oaths to Telek and Stigand, or promises to the *voca*. It's just something I want to do." I paused. "And if you don't like it, you don't have to come."

"Tracked *who*—?" She broke it off. "Those beasts? The hounds? Oh, Tiger, you don't mean—"

"I made a promise, Del. To myself. I intend to keep it."

Wide-eyed, she stared at me, which didn't make me feel any better. No man likes having it thrown in his face that he's lacked responsibility throughout much of his life; me making this promise exhibited a new side of the Sandtiger. Del didn't exactly *say* anything, but then she didn't have to. All she had to do was stare at me in exactly the way she was.

"Tiger—"

"It's why I'm out here in the middle of a Northern nowhere, Del; why else? I'm tracking those hounds. To Ysaa-den or wherever. To *who*ever—I intend to find the sorcerer who set them loose."

"And kill him," she clarified.

"I imagine so," I agreed. "Unless, of course, he's polite enough to stop on my say-so."

She hooked hair behind her ears. "So. You're tracking the hounds in order to kill their master, and I'm tracking Ajani with much the same end in mind. What is the difference, Tiger? Why are you right and I'm wrong?"

"I don't want to argue about this—"

"I'm not arguing. I'm asking."

"My reasons are a bit different from yours," I said testily. "Aside from hounding us for more months than I care to remember, those beasts have also killed people. And some were children."

"Yes," Del agreed, "as Ajani killed my kin . . . including all the babies."

"Oh, hoolies, Del—" I shifted position, wished I hadn't. "What you're after is revenge, pure and simple. I'm not saying it's *wrong*—what Ajani did was horrible—but I think you've lost sight of reality. What's driving you now is misplaced pride and utter obsession— and that's not healthy for anyone."

"You think I'd be better off in some man's bed, or in some man's house, bearing him fourteen sons."

I blinked. "Fourteen might be a bit much. Hard on the woman, I'd think."

Del bit back a retort. "Tiger, do you deny it? Wouldn't you rather see me in some man's bed instead of in the circle?" She paused delicately. "In *your* bed, maybe, instead of in your circle?"

"You've been in my bed," I answered bluntly, "*and* you've been in my circle. I don't know what the first one got you, but the second nearly killed you."

That she hurt was obvious; that I'd cut too deep equally so. "So it did," she sighed finally. "Yes, so it did. As for the first? I don't know. I don't know what it got me. I don't know what it *should* have—do we put a price on bedding?"

"I'm going north," I told her. "Or wherever it is the hounds go. You can come, or not. It's up to you. But if you do, we'll put a price on nothing. No bedding, Del. Will that make you happy?"

She stared back at me. "I thought that would be your price."

"For sparring with you?" I shook my head. "Once, yes. Back when we first met, and you promised me a bedding in place of coin you didn't have. And you paid, bascha. You paid very nicely, eventually . . . except by that time I wasn't exactly counting. Neither, I think, were you—so that debt we'll call forgiven." I shrugged. "If you want to come along with me now to get your practice in so you can face Ajani, that's fine with me. But things can't be the same, not after all that's happened."

"You won't last," she predicted. "This could take weeks, and you don't do days very well."

"Bet me," I said.

Slowly Del smiled. "I know you, Tiger. This isn't a fair wager. Not for you. I *know* you."

"Do you? Really? Then let me tell you why it *is* a fair wager." I held her eyes with my own. "When a man's been made a fool of, he doesn't much feel like going to bed with the woman who did it. When a man has been *used*—without his permission or knowledge —he doesn't much feel like going to bed with the woman who did the using." With effort, I kept my tone uninflected. "And when that woman, faced with the truth of what she did, adamantly refuses to admit she was wrong, he doesn't really care about the bedding any more. Because what he likes in that woman is more than just her body and what it can do for him in bed. What he likes in that woman is her loyalty and honesty and honor."

Del said nothing. I don't think she could.

"But then you've sort of set aside all those useless attributes in the last year, haven't you, Delilah? So I guess what I feel doesn't matter so much any more."

Del's face was colorless. "Tiger—"

"Think about it," I said. "And think about *me* for a change, instead of your oaths of honor. Instead of your obsession."

Shock receded slowly. I'd struck a number of chords within her, but clearly she was unprepared to deal with what I'd said. And so she returned to the original topic. "I still say—I *still* say—the bet is a waste of time."

I shrugged. "So let's test it."

Her eyes were assessive. "How much are you willing to wager?"

I stared hard at her for a moment. Then pulled my sword from its sheath.

It felt right. Warm and good and *right,* like a woman hugging your neck.

Like a fully quenched *jivatma* making promises to protect you.

All the hairs stood up on my arms. It took all the strength I had to put the sword down. In fitful, tarnished moonlight, the new-made *jivatma* gleamed.

Color drained from her face. I nodded confirmation of the question she wouldn't ask. "Now you know how serious I am."

"But—you can't. You can't wager your *sword.*"

"I just did."

She stared at the weapon lying mutely in front of my knees. "What would I do with it?"

"*If* you won—and you won't—anything you want. He'd be your sword."

"I have a sword." Her left hand went out to touch the harness and sheath lying at her side. "I have a sword, Tiger."

"Then sell it. Give it away. Break it. Melt it down." I shrugged. "I don't care, Del. If you win, you can do whatever you want."

Slowly she shook her head. "You have no respect for things you don't understand."

I cut her off. "Respect must be earned, bascha, not bought. Not even trained, as it is in Staal-Ysta. Because until tested, respect is nothing but a word. Emptiness, Del. Nothing more than that."

Still she shook her head. "That sword was made for you—made *by* you—"

"It's a piece of steel," I said curtly.

"You completed the rituals, asked the blessing—"

"—and stuck it into you." I shocked her into silence. "Do you really think I want a sword that tried to kill you?"

Del looked at Boreal, sheathed by her side. Remembering the circle. Remembering the dance.

Her tone was oddly hollow. "I would have killed you."

"You tried. I made you mad, and you tried. Fair enough—it was what I meant to do, to throw you out of your pattern." I shrugged. "But I didn't want to kill you. I didn't intend to do it. The *sword* wanted to do it . . . that bloodthirsty, angry sword."

"Angry," she echoed.

"It was," I told her. "I could feel it. *Taste* it. I could hear it in my head."

She heard something in my tone. "But—now it isn't angry?"

I smiled grimly. "Not so much anymore. Just like that hound, it got what it came for."

Del nodded slowly. "You killed someone, then. After all. You've quenched your *jivatma.*"

I squinted thoughtfully. "Not—exactly. Killed *something,* yes, but not what you might expect. And not in the way you told me."

Del, frowning, was very intent. "What have you done, Tiger?"

"Killed something," I repeated. "Cat. White, dappled silver." For some reason I said nothing about the pelt, which I'd tucked away into saddle-pouches. "But I didn't sing."

"Snow lion," Del said. "You didn't sing at all?"

"I'm a sword-*dancer*, Del. Not a sword-singer, or whatever it is you claim. I kill people with my sword. I don't sing to it."

Del shook her head thoughtfully. "It doesn't really matter if you didn't sing aloud. Even a mute can earn a *jivatma*. Even a mute can sing a song."

I scowled. "How?"

She smiled. "A song can be sung in silence. A song can be of the soul, whether anyone hears it or not. Only the sword counts, and it only requires the soul and all the feelings in it."

I thought of the song I'd heard on the overlook by the lakeshore. The song I'd heard in my head ever since I'd named the blade. Thanks to the Cantéada, I'd been unable to forget it.

And now it was my sword.

"I don't need it," I declared. "I don't *want* it, Del."

"No. But it wants you." She pointed to my sword. "To find you, I used my *jivatma*. I painted the sky with my sword—you saw all the colors. You saw all the lights. All from a song, Tiger—and you could do the same."

The questions boiled up. "Why *did* you do it? And how did you find me so fast? *Especially* with that wound . . . it should have put you down longer than my own did." A sudden chill touched a fingertip to my spine. "You didn't do anything—*odd*—did you? Make any promises? Any pacts? I know how you are about those things."

"What I do is my business."

"Del—what did you do?" I looked harder at the strain etched into her face. "What *exactly* did you do?"

Her mouth was flat and hard. "I have a *jivatma*."

An answer, of sorts. It told me more than enough. "So, you sang to it, did you? Begged more magic of it? Offered up even more of your humanity in exchange for arcane strength?"

"What I do—"

"—is your own business; yes, Del, I know, I know . . . you've always been at such pains to make certain I understood that." It was all I could do to keep my tone even. "How did you manage it? Magic?" I lifted eyebrows. "Is that how you caught up so fast?"

Her face was pensive. "There is no magic about that, Tiger. They told me you were bound for Ysaaden. I know the North well—I took a shortcut."

I waited. She offered nothing further. So I asked. "Why did you paint the sky?"

After a moment, she shrugged. "I thought it might bring you in."

It was something. From her, it was everything. "But you came to me," I said. "After I left you in the clearing. You came to *me*."

She touched the hilt of her sword. Very gently. "I realized, after I did it, and you came, that you wouldn't stay. That I'd have to go to you." Del smiled sadly. "A man's pride is a powerful thing."

I scowled balefully, disliking the twinge of guilt. "I've got no use for painting the sky."

She laughed a little. "Maybe not. But there are other things. Other magics available; you've seen my *jivatma*."

"Hunh."

Del shrugged. "You swore to me you'd never use it. You'd never kill, never blood it. But you *have* killed, Tiger, and you made your blade a song." She looked again at my sword. "Whether you like it or not, there's magic in your blade. There's *power* in your blade. And if you don't learn to control it, it will control you."

I looked at Boreal, so quiescent in her sheath. I knew what she could do. But only at Del's bidding. If left to her own devices—

No. Don't think about that. Think about something else.

"You," I said, "are sandsick. So now it's your turn to watch."

And as Del, disgruntled, glared, I bundled myself in bedding.

Eight

It's very easy to fall into old patterns. Del and I had been together long enough to develop certain rhythms in our day-to-day existence. Simple things, mostly: one of us built and tended the fire, another laid a meal; each of us tended our horses. We knew when to rest them, knew when we needed rest, knew the best times and places to stop for the night. Much of what we did required no conversation, for most was a reflection of things we'd done before.

It was easy to forget. Easy to recall only that we were together. And then something, some little thing, would crop up and remind me that for the space of six weeks we *hadn't* been together—and I'd remember the reason why.

We rode toward Ysaa-den, following hound spoor. Saying little to one another because we didn't know what to say. At least *I* didn't. What Del thought—or knew, or didn't know—was, as always, her own business, and always exceedingly private, unless she chose to share. For the moment, she didn't.

She rode ahead of me. The stud didn't like it, but I was pacing him. I didn't want him to overextend himself. So I made him stay behind the blue roan and content himself with second place. Trouble was, he wasn't.

Del's back was straight. She rides very erect anyway, but I knew some of her exceptional posture had to do with the wound. No matter what she said, or

didn't—or how much magic she had used—I knew it
was hurting her. And I knew what an effort it took for
her to keep on going.

Boreal cut her back in half from left shoulder to
right hip, as Samiel did my own. I glared at Boreal,
thinking bad things about it. Thinking also about my
own sword; what did it want me to do? What would it
force me to do?

And then I forgot about Samiel, looking again at
Boreal. Noting how quietly she rode in the leather
sheath. How meekly the weapon rested, hiding deadly
blade. Hiding alien, gods-blessed steel that sang a
song of its own, just as Delilah did.

And in cold, abrupt clarity, I wondered just how
much of Del's obsession was born of blade instead of
brain.

I knew little of *jivatmas* other than what Del and
Kem had told me. And even then, I hadn't put much
stock in what they said. It wasn't until my own new-
made sword had made his bloodthirst known that I'd
realized just how independent a *jivatma* could be.
Which meant it was entirely possible Del wasn't fully
responsible for her own actions. Hadn't she begged,
on more than one occasion, for Boreal's aid? For
power?

I glared at the hilt riding so high on her left shoulder. Had Del somehow willingly subjugated her own
personality to the demands of a magicked sword? Did
she need revenge so badly?

She had sworn oaths. I swear a lot myself, but
generally not oaths. At least, not the binding kind; the
kind that make you do something you'd really rather
not do. But Del was different. Del took vows and
oaths and swearing much more seriously. It was what
had driven her to become a sword-dancer. To give up
a child. It was what had driven her south, alone, to
search for a kidnapped brother.

It was what had driven her to seek out a sword-dancer called the Sandtiger, who knew people she didn't, and how to find them.

A man makes of himself many things, depending on his needs and the shaping of his life. Me, I'd been a slave. And then a free man seeking power to make a real life for himself. A life of his own choosing without demands from other people.

Well, yes, there *were* demands. If I hired on to a tanzeer, I was his to command. But only if what he wanted agreed well enough with my willingness to do it. And there were things I was unwilling to do. Killing people who deserved it, or who gave me no other choice, was something I'd come to terms with many years before. For a long time, killing was almost enjoyable, because it released some of my anger. After a while, having grown up a little, hostility was no longer so evident. I was free. No one could ever make me a slave again. I no longer had to kill.

Except it was the only thing I was good at.

Sword-dancing was my life. I'd freely chosen it. I had apprenticed formally and become a seventh-level sword-dancer, which made me very good. It made me what I was. A dangerous, deadly man.

Who hired out his sword to anyone with coin.

By nature, we are solitary souls. After all, it's hard for a hired killer to have a normal life. Whores don't mind sleeping with us so long as we pay them and they can brag about it—and sometimes our fame is payment enough—but decent women don't generally marry us. Because a man who sells his sword for a living always walks the edge of the blade, and a woman who wants to grow old with her man doesn't like to lose him young.

There are exceptions, of course. Sword-dancers do marry, or take a woman as their own without benefit of rites. But most of us don't. Most of us ride alone. Most of us die alone, leaving no woman or children to grieve.

There was a reason for it. Domestic responsibility can ruin a sword-dancer's soul.

And now here was Del. No longer the same Del. Forever a different Del. Not because of the girl she'd borne, though it did make me think of her differently. Not because we'd shared a bed so many times in the past. But because of what she had done and what *I* had done; because of what we'd become.

Loyalty is a sacred thing. A thing to be admired. A thing to be treasured. It isn't something two people in our profession, where loyalty is so often purchased, experience very often. Loyalty within a circle is very rare indeed, because too often someone dies, or sacrifices pride, which can destroy a relationship. But for a while we'd known it. For a while we had lived it.

But we'd both of us forsworn the virtue in the circle on Staal-Ysta.

Oh, hoolies, bascha, what I'd give for the old days.

But *which* old days? The ones with her, or without her?

Without was easier. Because with I'd nearly killed her.

Del turned in the saddle a moment, hooking hair behind an ear. It bared her face. A fine-drawn face of magnificent planes, and too many of them visible. Pain, oaths, and obsession had reshaped youthful flesh into a mask of brittle beauty. A cold, hard-edged beauty that made me think of glass.

Glass too often breaks. I wondered when she would.

Just after dawn I awoke, looking for Del. It was something I'd found myself doing each morning since we'd joined up together, and it irritated me. But each morning I did it anyway. For reassurance.

And each morning I said to myself: Yes, Del is alive. Yes, Del is here.

It isn't a dream after all.

Grunting, I sat up. Tried to stretch muscles and pop joints without waking her, because no man likes a woman to see how he's growing older, how the years are taking their toll. And then I stood up, slowly, and walked, equally slowly, over to the stud. I checked him every morning, just to be sure. The claw slashes were healing well, but the hair would come in white. Like me, he'd carry the scars to his death.

Still, he seemed in much better spirits—or maybe it was just that the gelding's presence made him take more of an interest in life. Whatever it was, he was more like his old self. His old, unpleasant self.

I ran my hand down the stud's shoulder, peeling winter hair. It *was* nearly spring; he was beginning to shed his fur.

"Tiger."

I glanced back and saw Del standing beside the fire. She had shed all her wrappings and faced me in white woolens, pale hair braided back from her face and laced with white cord. She took the sheath and harness into her hands and slid Boreal into dawn. Rune-worked steel gleamed. "Will you dance with me, Sandtiger?"

I turned from the stud to face her squarely. "You're in no shape to dance, Del. Not yet."

"I have to start sometime. It's been much too long."

For some strange reason it made me very angry. "Hoolies, woman, you're sandsick! I doubt you could hold a stance for more than a single eyeblink, and certainly not against any offense I might show you. Do you think I'm blind?"

"I think you're afraid."

Something deep inside twisted. "That again, then."

"And again, and again." She lifted the deadly *jivatma*. "Dance with me, Sandtiger. Honor the deal we made."

Pride made me take a step toward my sword. But only a single step. I shook my head at her. "Not this time, bascha. I'm older, a little wiser. You can't tease me into the circle. Not any more. I know your tricks too well."

The tip of her sword wavered minutely. And then

flashed as she shifted her grip and drove the blade straight down, deep into the earth. "Tease you?" she asked. "Oh, no." And before I could stop her, Del knelt before her sword. She tucked heels beneath buttocks and crossed wrists against her chest. The braid fell over her shoulder to dangle above the ground. "Honored *kaidin*," she said, "will you share with me some of your skill?"

I stared at the Northern woman offering obeisance to me, and all I felt was anger. A deep and abiding anger so strong it made me sick.

"Get up," I rasped.

All she did was bow her head.

"Get up from there, Delilah."

The full name made her twitch, but it did not force her up.

In the end, knowing from experience the strength of her determination, I crossed the clearing to her. She knew I was there; short of being deaf, she could not miss my string of muttered oaths. But she didn't rise. She didn't so much as lift her head.

I reached out a rigid hand. What I grabbed was Boreal.

"No—" Suppressing a cry, Del fell back. Illness and pain had taken her strength, stealing away her quickness. In my hands I held the proof.

"Yes," I said clearly. "We made a deal, bascha, and I will honor it. But not yet. Not yet. Neither of us is ready." I shook my head wearily. "Maybe it's just that I'm older. Maybe it's that I'm wiser. Or maybe it's just the blind pride of youth that makes you risk yourself." I scrubbed a hand across my brow, thrusting fallen hair aside. "Hoolies, I don't know—maybe it's just sword-dancers. I used to do the same."

Del said nothing. She half-knelt on the ground, pressing herself upright with one hand while the other clutched her ribs. Color stood high in her face. Flags of brilliant crimson against pearl-white flesh.

I sighed. Set Boreal's tip against the ground and

pressed her down, slowly, so she stood freely upright. Then I gingerly lowered myself to Del's level, kneeling carefully, and unbuckled my heavy belt.

Del's eyes widened. "What are you doing?"

"Showing you something." I dropped the belt, pulled up layers of wool. Exposed my rib cage. "There," I said. "See? Your handiwork, Del. A clean, perfect sword thrust. And it hurts. It hurts like hoolies. It will for some time to come, Del—maybe even forever. Because I'm not as young as I used to be. I heal slower. I hurt longer. I learn from my mistakes, because my mistakes are around to remind me."

Del's face now was dirty gray. She stared transfixed at the ugly scar. It was more vivid than it might be because, coming north, I'd lost much of my color. Livid purple against pale brown is not an attractive mix.

"I hurt, bascha. And I'm tired. I want nothing more than to go home, to go south, where I can bake myself in the sun and forget about Northern snow. But I can't until I'm finished with the job I said I'd do. And in order to finish the job, I have to stick around."

Del swallowed hard. "I only want to dance."

I tugged my tunic down. "I won't ask you to show me yours, since I've got a good idea what it looks like. It was me who did it, bascha—I know what the thrust was. I know what it did to you. If you went into a circle now, you wouldn't survive the dance." I picked up my own sword, still on the ground between us. "I almost killed you once. I won't risk it again."

"Too much time," she whispered.

With a grunt, I stood up. "You've got all the time in the world, my Northern bascha. You're young. You'll heal. You'll recover your strength. You'll dance again, Delilah—that I promise you."

"How old are you?" she asked abruptly.

I frowned down at her. "I thought I already told you."

"No. All you ever said was you were older than me." Surprising me, Del smiled. "That I already knew."

"Yes, well . . . I imagine so." Irritated, I scratched my sandtiger scars. "I don't know. Old enough. Why? Does it matter? After all this time?"

"*You're* the one making age an issue, Tiger. I only wanted to know how old the old man is."

"How old are *you?*" I countered, knowing perfectly well. But it's a question women hate.

Del didn't flinch. Nor did she hesitate. "In three more days, I will have twenty-one years."

"Hoolies," I said in disgust, "I *could* be your father."

Del's face was serious. "He was forty when he was killed. How close are you to that?"

"Too close," I muttered sourly, and went off to appease my bladder.

Nine

Del and I rode steadily northeast for two more days. We took it pretty easy on several counts: one, the stud; two, me; and three, Del herself. Neither of us is the kind of person who enjoys poor health. Neither of us is the kind of person who likes to talk about it, either, which meant we mostly kept our mouths shut regarding respective wounds.

But we did notice, of course. I noticed Del, she noticed me. But we each of us said nothing, because to say something meant admitting to discomfort, which neither of us was prepared to do. Call it pride, arrogance, stupidity; only the stud was completely honest, and he made no bones about it. He hurt. And he told us.

I patted his neck, avoiding healing claw scores. "I know, old man—but it'll get better, I promise."

Del, who rode in front of me amid bare-branched trees, twisted her head to mutter over a shoulder: "How do you know? You don't even know where we're going."

"We're going to Ysaa-den."

"And if you find no answers there?"

That again. It had briefly been a topic of discussion the day we'd set out. She was unconvinced I had made the right decision to follow the hounds to their origins. But since all of *her* decisions were governed by an insatiable need for revenge, I'd told her I wasn't so certain she could be trusted to give me an unbiased opinion regarding much of anything; she had retreated into haughty silence, as women so often do when the man catches them out, and had said nothing of it again.

Until now.

I adjusted my posture to the motion of the stud, trying to find a position that didn't pull at healing scar tissue. "Del," I said patiently, "you didn't know where *you* were going when you went south to find your brother. I don't notice that it stopped you, since before we met up we'd never heard of one another— well, maybe you'd heard of *me*—and here we are now, riding together in the North. All of which means you didn't much care that you didn't know where you were going. You just went."

"That was different."

I nodded wryly to myself; isn't it always different?

Del peered at me over her shoulder, setting her jaw against the pain of twisting her torso. "How will you know when you've found whoever—or *what*ever— you're looking for?"

"I just will."

"Tiger—"

"Del, will you just stop trying to grind me into the ground in hopes I'll give in to you? I've made up my mind, and I intend to carry out my promise." I paused. "With you or without you."

Silence. Del rode on. And then, mostly muffled, "Those beasts were never after *you*."

It was half challenge, half boast. Also truth; it had become fairly clear months before the hounds wanted Del's sword, or Del, or both.

But that was then. Things had changed. "They are now."

Del stopped her gelding. Turned more squarely in the saddle, which hurt her, but didn't stop her from staring back at me intently. "What?"

"I said, 'They are now.' Why do you think the one stole the ward-whistle?"

Del shrugged. "That was Cantéada-made. Magicked. Lure enough, I think, without thinking it was you."

The stud reached out to sample the gelding's bluish rump. I pulled him back, chastised him a bit, turned him off diagonally in hopes of interesting him in something else, like maybe a tree. "They came once before into my camp. All of them. And they tried to take my sword."

"*Take* it!"

"Steal it," I confirmed. "They weren't much interested in me, just in the sword."

Del's frown deepened. "I don't understand."

"What's to understand?" I wrestled with the stud, who was showing signs of reacquainting his teeth with the roan's rump. "Originally all they wanted was *your* sword, remember? And then mine . . . once I'd blooded it. Once I'd killed that cat." Memory was a spasming in my belly. "Even once—" But I cut it off.

Del's brows shot up. " 'Even once' *what?*"

Memory blossomed more fully. I stood on the overlook by the lakeshore, staring down at Staal-Kithra, Place of Spirits, where Northern dead lay entombed in Northern earth, honored by barrows and stone dolmens.

I stood by the overlook by the lakeshore, staring down at Staal-Ysta, Place of Swords, the island floating in water dyed black by winter's embrace. And I had thrust a naked blade into the earth.

Naked when it went in. Rune-scribed when it came out.

A chill pinched my spine. "They've known since I named it."

Del waited.

"The must have," I mused. "They were one large group originally—I followed the spoor for days . . . and then the group split up. Some tracks went on. Others circled back . . ." I frowned. "Those hounds must have known."

After a moment, she nodded. "Names are powerful things. With *jivatmas*, one must be careful. Names

must be closely guarded." And then her expression
softened. "But you know that. You would never tell
anyone the name of your blooding-blade."

"I told *you*."

Del was astonished. "Told *me!* When? You have
said nothing of it to me. Nothing of its name."

I scowled at the stud's ears. "There on the overlook, above the island. After I pulled it free. I just saw
the runes, read the name—and told you." I squirmed
slightly, knowing how foolish it sounded. "I didn't
really expect you to hear. I mean, I wasn't even sure
you were still alive—" I cut that off abruptly. "I just—
said it. There on the overlook . . . for you." I paused,
needing to explain. "You'd told me the name of *your*
sword. I thought I should do the same. So we'd be
even." I exhaled heavily. That's all. That's why. So
we'd be even."

Del didn't say a word.

The memory was so clear. "There it was," I told
her. "Spelled out. His name . . . in the runes. Just as
you and Kem had promised."

"Runes," Del echoed. "Runes you don't know how
to read."

I opened my mouth. Shut it.

It had not occurred to me. The runes had looked so
familiar I hadn't even thought about it. Not ever. I
had just looked at them—and *known*. The way a man
knows the shape and texture of his jaw when he shaves
every morning. The way his body knows the fit of a
woman's without requiring lessons.

Oh, hoolies.

Abruptly I unsheathed. Balanced the blade across
the pommel of my saddle and stared at alien runes.

Stared *hard*. Until my eyes blurred and the shapes
ran together. The shapes that had not existed in the
blade originally. Not when Kem had given it to me.
Not when I had dipped it in the water, asking, very
cynically, the blessings of Northern gods.

Not when I had sheathed it in Northern earth, at the
brink of the overlook.

Only after I had drawn it out.

Del sat next to me on her blue roan. Like me, she stared at the blade. But she was smiling, if only a little; all I did was glare.

"So," she said, "once again the Sandtiger walks his own path. *Makes* his own path, as you have made that sword."

My tone was curt. "What?"

"Do you recall when Kem nicked your hand and had you bathe the blade in blood?"

I nodded sourly; I hadn't liked it much.

"It is part of the Naming ceremony. Ordinarily the runes show themselves then. Mine did; all *jivatmas* do." She paused. "Except, of course, for yours."

I recalled Kem saying something of the sort. I also recalled him saying something about belief being a requisite; that until I fully believed in the magic of a *jivatma*, its true name could not be known. Which was why, at that specific moment, there had been no runes.

But there on the overlook, so frightened Del was dead, I had believed. Because it had been the sword, not me, that had tried so hard to kill her.

And so, in that moment of belief, the sword had revealed its true name. In runes I couldn't read.

I said something very rude. Very violent. It had to do with things I would like to do with the sword. Do *to* it; things that would give me great pleasure, great relief; things that would resolve all potential future problems because if I did them—one, or even all of them—there would *be* no future for the sword.

"Yes," Del agreed. "It is difficult to accept the second soul—especially when that soul was once cat, not man. But you will." She smiled; a bit smugly, I thought, which was altogether unnecessary as well as unappreciated. "It knows you, now. It has told you what it must be. What it wants most of all."

"To kill," I muttered.

Del's tone was even. "Isn't that what you do? Isn't that what you are?"

I stared at the blade. The runes remained. Familiar shapes. But nothing I could read.

I looked away from the sword into Del's face. "Samiel," I told her.

Del drew in a startled breath.

"Samiel," I repeated. "You couldn't hear me the first time. Now you can. Now you know what it is."

I saw her mouth the name. I saw her look at my sword. I saw her think of her own; of what the "honor" entailed.

She turned her horse and rode on.

At sundown, Del watched pensively as I tended the stud, feeding him handfuls of grain and talking to him quietly. I didn't think anything of it; people riding alone often talk to their horses. And she'd seen me do it before, though admittedly not as much. She had talked to her silly speckledy gelding during the ride north; now she had the blue roan, but I doubted she'd change her ways.

She handed me the bota when I returned to the cairn and arranged myself on my bedding, wrapping myself in cloak and pelts. Quietly, she said, "You care for him very much."

I sucked *amnit*, swallowed, shrugged. "He's a horse. Good as any other, better than most. He'll do in a pinch."

"Why have you never named him?"

I tossed the bota back. "Waste of time, names."

"You named your sword. *Both* of them; your Southron sword, Singlestroke, and then your Northern sword." But she didn't say the name. "And you have a name yourself, honorably won. After years of having none."

I shrugged. "Just never got around to it. It seemed sort of silly, somehow. Sort of—womanish." I grinned at her expression. "He doesn't really need one. He knows what I mean."

"Or is it a reminder?"

She asked it mildly enough, implying nothing by it other than genuine curiosity; Del isn't one to purposely ask for hostilities, in words or with weapons. But it seemed an odd question.

I frowned. "No. I have a couple of good reminders: these scars and my necklet." I pulled the leather cord from beneath the woolen tunic and rattled curving claws. "Besides, I got him years later, long after I was free."

Del looked at her gelding, tied a prudent distance from the stud. "They gave him to me," she said, "to encourage a swifter departure."

Her tone was even enough, but I've learned how to read the nuances. More than the wound hadn't healed, and wouldn't for a while.

I let my necklet drop. "You did the right thing."

"Did I?" Now bitterness was plain. "I deserted my daughter, Tiger."

I saw no sense in diplomacy. "You did that five years ago."

It snapped her head around. She stared at me angrily. "What right have you—"

"The one you gave me," I told her evenly, "when you pledged me to Staal-Ysta—without my permission, remember?—to buy time with Kalle. Even though you'd given her up five years before."

I didn't intend to criticize her for it; it had been her decision. But by now she was so defensive she considered any comment at all a questioning of her motives. Which meant, as before, she was questioning them herself.

It is not something Del likes to do.

"I had no choice." Her tone was implacable. "I had made oaths. Blood oaths. All oaths should be honored."

"Maybe so," I agreed patiently, "and you're doing a fine job . . . but losing Kalle was the price. It was the choice you made."

Del turned her head and looked at me. "Another thing," she said quietly, "worth killing Ajani for."

I think there is no way a man can fully share or understand a woman's feelings for her child; we are too different. Not being a father—at least, not as far as I know—I couldn't even imagine what she felt. But I had been a child without kin of any kind, trapped in namelessness and slavery, feeling myself unwhole. Del's daughter had a family, even if not of her blood, and I thought that relationship justified the price.

Even if the mother did not.

"It's done," I said quietly. "You've been exiled from Staal-Ysta. But at least you're alive."

Del stared hard into darkness. "I lost Jamail," she said, "when he chose to stay with the Vashni. And now I have lost Kalle. Now I have no one at all."

"You have you. That ought to be enough."

Del's look was deadly. "You are ignorant."

I arched eyebrows. "*Am* I?"

"Yes. You know nothing of Northern kin customs. Nothing at all of family. Yet so quickly you under-value things I hold very dear."

"Now, Del—"

Del's impatience was manifest. "I will tell you once. A last time. I will tell you so you know, and then perhaps you will understand."

"I think—"

"*I* think you should be quiet and listen to my words."

I shut my mouth. Sometimes you have to let women talk.

Del drew in a steadying breath. "In the North kin circles are very close. They are *sacred* . . . every bit as sacred as a circle is to a sword-dancer. Generations live within a single lodge, sometimes as many as four if the gods are generous in portioning out our lives." Briefly she nodded. "When a man marries, the woman comes into his lodge—unless he has no kin, and then he goes into hers—and so the circle widens. Children are born, and still the circle widens. And when sick-ness comes and the old ones die, or even the newborn babies, the circle grows small again, so we may support one another. So we may share in the pain and the grief and the anguish, and not try to withstand it alone."

I waited, saying nothing.

"Brothers and sisters and cousins, aunts and uncles and grandfolk. Sometimes the lodges are huge. But always filled with laughter. Always filled with song. Even when people die, so the soul departs in peace."

I thought back to the lodges on Staal-Ysta. Big wooden lodges overflowing with people. So different from what I knew. So alien in customs.

Del spoke very softly. "When anything of substance happens, kinfolk always share. Courtships, weddings, birthings. *And* deaths. The songs are always sung."

She paused, swallowing, frowning, then continued. "A father begins one for the lost child, and the mother takes it up, and then the brothers, the sisters, the aunts, the uncles, the cousins, the grandfolk . . . until the child is sung to sleep forever. If it is a husband, the wife begins. A wife, and the husband begins, and so on. The song is always sung, so the newly passed know a life beyond the world. So that there is no darkness, but only light. The light of a day, the light of a fire . . . the light of a star in the night, or the glint from a *jivatma*. Light, Tiger, and song, so there is no need for fear." She drew in an unsteady breath. "But now, for me, there will be no song. There is no one to sing it for me." She controlled her voice with effort. "No one for whom *I* may sing it; Jamail and Kalle are gone."

It called for something. Something of compassion. Something of understanding. But I found myself lacking the words, the tact, the necessary understanding, because I had known the need for revenge. The need for spilling blood.

And so I blurted the first words I stumbled upon because they were easiest. Because they required no *com*passion—only quiet, deadly passion. "Then let's rid the world of these hounds, bascha . . . let's rid it of Ajani.

Del blinked heavily. But her tone was very steady. "Will you dance with me, Tiger? Will you step into the circle?"

I looked at my sword, lying quietly in its sheath. I thought of its power. I thought of a man named Ajani, and the woman once called Delilah. "Any time you like."

Lips parted. I knew what she wanted. To say here, now, this moment. The temptation was incredibly strong, but she denied it. And made herself all the stronger.

"Not now," she said quietly. "Not even tomorrow. Perhaps the day after."

She knew as well as I even the day after was too soon. But by the time that day arrived, we could put it off again.

Or not.

I rolled forward onto my knees, pulled one of my pouches close, dug down into its depths and pulled from it the ash-dappled pelt. I tossed it gently at her.

Del caught it. Let it unfurl, exhibiting all its glory. And looked to me for an explanation.

"Your birthday," I told her. Then, feeling awkward, "*I've* got no use for it."

Del's hands caressed it. Much of her face was hidden behind loose hair. "A fine pelt," she said softly. "The kind used for a newborn's cradle."

Something pinched my belly. I sat up straighter. "You trying to tell me something?"

Del frowned. "No. No, of course—" And then she understood exactly what I meant. She tossed back pale hair and looked me straight in the eye. "No, Tiger. Not ever."

"What do you mean, not ever?" And then I thought about how some women couldn't have children, and regretted asking the question. "I mean—no, never mind. I don't know what I mean."

"Yes, you do." Del smiled, if only faintly. "*I* mean, not ever. Only Kalle. I made it so."

"What do you mean, you *made* it—" And, hastily, "No, never mind."

"A pact," she explained simply. "I asked it of the gods. So I could be certain of fulfilling my oath. Kalle had delayed me enough already."

I blinked. "That sort of thing isn't *binding*." I paused. "Is it?"

Del shrugged. "I have not bled since Kalle's birth. Whether it was that, or the gods answering my petition, I cannot say. Only that you need have no fear I will make you something you have no wish to be."

So. Yet another piece of the puzzle named Delilah clicking into place.

Only Kalle, forever, who was no longer hers. And never could be, now.

Thanks to me.

Thanks to my sword.

Oh, hoolies, bascha . . . what's to become of you? What's to become of *us?*

After a moment I reached out and touched her arm. "I'm sorry, bascha."

Del stared at me blindly, clutching the moon-silvered pelt. And, eventually, smiled. "Giving up on the wager already?"

It took me a moment because I'd nearly forgotten. "No," I retorted sourly, "I'm not giving up on the wager. But I'll make you wish I had."

She slanted me a glance. "I don't sleep with my father."

Hoolies, she knows how to hurt.

Ten

"Here," Del announced. "It is as good as anywhere else, and we may as well see if either of us is capable."

Having been lulled halfway to sleep by the rhythm of the stud and the warmth of the midday sun—well, maybe not *warmth,* exactly; at least, not the sort I was used to, but it was warm*er*—I had no idea what she was talking about. So I opened my eyes, discovered Del dismounting, and hastily reined in the stud.

"Good as anywhere else for *what?*—and what is it we're supposed to be capable of?" I paused. "Or not?"

"Probably not," she observed, "but that had better change."

I scowled. "Del—"

"It's been long enough, Tiger. Ysaa-den is a day away—and we have yet to dance."

Oh. That. I was hoping she hadn't noticed. "We could wait a bit longer."

"We *could* wait until we've ridden out of the North completely . . . but that wouldn't fulfill your promise." Del squinted up at me, shielding her eyes with the edge of a flattened hand pressed against her forehead. "I need it, Tiger. And so do you."

Yes, well . . . I sighed. "All right. Draw a circle. I've got to limber up a bit, first."

What I had to do was remind aching joints and stiffened muscles what it was to *move,* let alone to dance. We had ridden northeasterly for six days, and I

was beginning to think tracking the hounds to their
creator was not such a good idea after all. It hurt too
much. I'd rather be holed up in some smoky little
cantina with *aqivi* in my cup and a cantina girl on my
knee—no, that would probably hurt too much, too.
Certainly it would hurt too much if I did anything
more strenuous than hold her on my knee, which
meant why should I bother to hold her on my knee at
all?

Hoolies, I hate getting old!

Del tied her gelding to a tree, found a long bough
and proceeded to dig a circle into the earth, thrusting
through deadfall, damp leaves, mud. Pensively, I
watched her, noting how stiffly she held her torso.
There was no flexibility in her movements, no fluid
grace. Like me, she hurt. And, like me, she healed.

On the outside, if not on the inside.

Del stopped drawing, threw the limb aside, straightened and looked at me. "Are you coming? Or do you
want a formal, ritualized invitation?"

I grunted, unhooked foot from stirrup, slowly swung
a leg over and stepped down. The stud suggested we
go over to the gelding so he could get in a few nips
and kicks, but I ignored his comments and tied him
some distance from the blue roan, who had done his
best to make friends. It was the stud who was having
none of it.

Slowly I unhooked cloak brooches, peeled off wool,
draped the weight across the saddle. It felt good to be
free of it; soon, I hoped, I could pack it away for
good. I wouldn't feel truly free until we were across
the border and I could replace wool and fur with
gauze and silk, but ridding myself of the cloak was
something. It allowed me to breathe again.

My hand drifted to the harness worn over the tunic.
Fingers tangled briefly in beads and fringe, then found
their way to leather straps, supple and soft, snugged
tautly against soft wool. Across my back, slanting,

hung the sheath with its weight of sword. My hungry, angry sword.

"Tiger."

I shut my eyes. Opened them again, turning, and saw Del in the circle, all in white, glowing in the sun. It was a trick of clear, unblemished light unscreened by a lattice of limbs, but nonetheless it shook me. It reminded me of the night not so long before when she had stood in fire of her own making and all the colors of the world. Then I had thought, however briefly, she was spirit in place of woman. Looking at her now, blazing so brightly, I wondered if maybe I *had* killed her—

No. No.

You fool.

"Tiger," she said again. Unrelenting, as always.

You sandsick, loki-brained fool.

Del unsheathed. Light took life from Boreal.

She wouldn't sing. She wouldn't. And neither, I swore, would I.

Oh, hoolies, bascha . . . I don't want to do this.

Del's face was composed. Her tone divulged nothing. "Step into the circle."

A tremor ran through my limbs. Something pinched my belly.

Bascha, please don't make me.

Del began to smile. Bladeglow caressed her face. It was kind, too kind; she was older, harder, colder. The light gave her youth again. Boreal made her Del again. The one before exile. And Kalle.

Something tickled the back of my neck. Not an insect. Not a stray piece of hair, falling against bared flesh. Something *more*.

Something that spoke of magic, whispering a warning to me.

Or was it merely fear, setting my flesh to rising?

Fear of my sword? Or of Del?

Oh, hoolies. Bascha.

"Tiger," Del said. "Have you gone to sleep standing up?"

Maybe. And maybe I am dreaming.

I slipped out of my harness. Closed my hand around the hilt and drew the blade from its sheath. Hooked the harness over my saddle and walked toward the circle.

Del nodded, waiting. "It will be good for us both."

My throat tightened. Breathing was difficult. Something stirred in the pit of my belly. I bit into my lip and tasted blood. Tasted fear also.

Oh, bascha—don't make me.

"Gently, at first," she suggested. "We both have healing left to do."

I swallowed tightly. Nodded. Made myself step over the limb-carved line.

Del frowned slightly. "Are you all right?"

"Do it," I rasped. "Just—do it."

She opened her mouth. To comment. Question. Chastise. But she did none of those things. She simply shut her mouth and moved away, closing both hands on Boreal's hilt. Slipping smoothly into her stance. That it hurt showed plainly in the soft flesh around her eyes and the brief tensing of her jaw, but she banished pain. Spread her feet. Balanced. Cocked the blade up. And waited.

In a true dance we would put our swords on the ground in the very center of the circle, and take up our positions directly across from one another. It was a race to the swords, and then a fight. A dance. Combat to name a winner. Sometimes it was to the death. Other times only to yield. And occasionally only to show what dancing was all about.

But this was not a true dance. This was sparring only, a chance to test one another's mettle. To learn how fit we were. Or how much we needed to practice.

I needed it for the beasts. Del for Ajani.

One and the same, perhaps?

She waited quietly. I have seen her wait so before,

always prepared, never wavering; completely at ease with her sword. It no longer struck me as odd, as alien, that a woman could be a sword-dancer. That a woman could be so good. Del had made herself both; I had seen—and felt—the results.

Sweat ran down the sides of my face. Tension made me itch. I wished myself elsewhere, *any*where, other than where I was.

Del dipped her sword. Briefly. Slightly. Barely. A salute to her opponent. In blue eyes I saw concentration. And no indication of fear.

Did it mean nothing at all to Del that she had nearly killed me?

Did it mean nothing at all to Del that I had nearly killed *her?*

"Kaidin," she said softly, giving me Northern rank. Giving me Northern honor.

I lifted my sword. Shifted into my stance. Felt the familiarity of it, the settling of muscles and flesh into accustomed places. Felt the protest of scar tissue twisted into new positions.

Sweat ran into my eyes. Desperation took precedence over other intentions.

I lowered the sword. Swung around. Stepped out of the circle completely. And cursed as my belly cramped.

"Tiger?" Del's tone was bewildered. "Tiger—what is it?"

"—can't," I rasped.

"Can't?" She was a white-swathed wraith walking out of the circle, carrying Boreal. "What do you mean, 'can't'? Are you sick? Is it your wound?"

"I just—can't." I straightened, clutching at abdomen, and turned toward her. "Don't you understand? The last time we did this I nearly killed you."

"But—this isn't a real dance. This is only *sparring*—"

"Do you think it matters?" Sweat dripped onto my tunic. "Do you have any idea what it's like stepping into the circle with you again, two months after the last disastrous dance? Do you have any idea what it feels like to face you across the circle with this butcher's blade in my hands?" I displayed Samiel to her. "Last time it—*he*—did everything he could to blood himself in you . . . and now he's even stronger because I *did* finally blood him." I paused. "Do you want to take that chance? Do you want to trust your life to my ability to control him?"

"Yes," she answered evenly, without hesitation. "Because I know you, Tiger. I know your strengths, your power. Your *own* share of power, from deep inside . . . do you think I would ever doubt you?"

She should. *I* would.

I flung damp hair out of my eyes. "Del, I can't dance with you. Not now. Maybe never. Because each time I try, I'll see it all over again. You, on the ground . . . with blood all over the circle. With blood all over my sword."

Del looked at my blade. Then at her own. Recalling, perhaps, that Boreal had been bloodied also? That someone other than herself had left his share of blood in the circle?

She drew in a deep breath. Shut her eyes briefly, as if she fought some inner battle; then opened them and looked at me. "I'm sorry," she said softly. "I am—different. For a purpose. I put behind me what may be disturbing to others. Again, for a purpose; memories can turn you from your path. But—you should know it was not *easy* for me to cut you." She frowned a little, as if the words hadn't come out the way she meant them. "You should know that I was afraid, too . . . that *you* were dead. That I had killed *you*."

"I can't," I said again. "Not now. Not yet. Maybe never. I know I promised. I know you need someone to dance with, so you can face Ajani. But—well . . ." I sighed. "Maybe what you should do is head south. Go on to the border. Harquhal, maybe—you should find someone there who will dance with you. Sword-dancers will do anything for coin." I shrugged. "Even dance against a woman."

"It will pass," she told me. "Perhaps—if I made you angry?"

I grinned. "You make me angry a lot, bascha—it doesn't mean I want to settle it with swords."

"It will pass," she said again.

"Maybe. Maybe not. Maybe what—" I stopped.

Del frowned. "What is it?"

My belly rolled. All the hairs on my arms stood up. A grue rippled through flesh and muscle. "Magic," I said curtly. "Can't you smell it?"

Del sniffed. "I smell smoke." She frowned, assessing, identifying. "Smoke—and something else. Something *more*." She glanced around, brow creased. "It is gone now—"

"Magic," I repeated. "And no, it's not gone. It's there. It's there, bascha—I promise." It was all I could do not to shudder again. Instead I contented myself with rubbing fingers through wool to flesh, scrubbing a prickling arm. "Not the hounds—not *quite* the hounds . . . something different. Something more."

Del stared northeast. "We are but a day away from Ysaa-den—"

"—and in clear, cold air like this, smells travel; I know. But this is *more*."

"Smoke," she said again, musingly, and then moved away from the circle. Away from me. Like a hunting hound tracking prey, Del sifted through trees and shadows until she found a clearing open to the sky, unscreened by trees. "There," she said as I came up beside her. "Do you see?"

I looked beyond her pointing hand. There was not much to see other than the jagged escarpments of a mountainside, and the blade-sharp spine of the highest peak, all tumbled upon itself into bumps and lumps and crevices, some dark, some shining white in the sunlight.

"Clouds," I said.

"Smoke," Del corrected. "Much too dark for clouds."

I stared harder at the peak. She was right. It wasn't

a cloud I saw, rolling down from the heights to swath the peak, but smoke rising from the mountainside itself. Ash-gray, gray-black; it trailed against the sky like a damp cookfire in the wind.

"Ysaa-den," she murmured.

I frowned. "Then that little mountain village is a lot bigger than *I* was told. That's enough smoke for a city half the size of the Punja—"

Del interrupted. "No, not the village. The name. *Ysaa-den.*"

I sighed. "Bascha—"

"Dragon's Lair," she said. "That's what the words mean."

I scowled up at the mountain. "Oh, I see—now I'm supposed to believe in dragons?"

Del pointed. "You should. There it is."

"That's a *mountain,* Del—"

"Yes," she agreed patiently. "Look at the shape, Tiger. Look at the *smoke.*"

I looked. At the smoke. At the mountain. And saw what she meant: the shape of the mountain peak, so harsh and jagged and shadowed, did form something like the head of a lizardlike beast. You could see the ridged dome of the skull, the overhanging brows, the undulating wrinkles of dragon-flesh peeled back from bared teeth. Only the teeth were spires of stone, as was the rest of the monstrous beast.

A *mythical* monstrous beast.

"There's the mouth," she mused, "and the nostrils— see the smoke? It's coming out of both."

Well, sort of. There was smoke, yes, and it kind of *appeared* to be coming out of odd rock formations that did, in a vague sort of way, slightly resemble mouth and nostrils—if you looked *real* hard.

"Dragon," I said in disgust.

"Ysaa-den," she repeated.

I grunted.

Del glanced at me. Tendrils of hair lifted from her face. "Don't you hear it, Tiger?"

"I hear wind in the trees."

She smiled. "Have you no imagination? It's the dragon, Tiger—the dragon in his lair, hissing down the wind."

It was *wind,* nothing more, sweeping through the trees. It keened softly, stripping hair out of our faces, rippling woolen folds, blowing smoke across the sky. And the smell of something—*something*—just a little more than woodsmoke.

The back of my neck tingled. "Magic," I muttered.

Del made a noise in her throat that sounded very much like doubt and derision all rolled into one. And then she turned and walked past me, heading back toward the circle she had drawn in the damp, hard soil of a land I could not trust.

No more than my own sword.

Eleven

With a name as dramatic as Dragon's Lair, you might expect Ysaa-den to be an impressive place to live. But it wasn't. It wasn't much more than a ramshackle little village spilling halfway down the mountainside. There were clustered lodges like those on Staal-Ysta, but smaller, poorer. Not as well-tended. There was an aura of disrepair about the whole place; but then the villager who'd come to the island had said something about the inhabitants losing heart because of the trouble with the hounds.

I sniffed carefully as Del and I rode into the little mountain village. There was plenty to smell, all right, and not all of it good, but the stench had less to do with hounds than with sickness, despair, desperation. Also the odd tang I'd noticed back by the circle Del had drawn. Smoke—and something more.

It was midday. Warm enough to shed our cloaks, even this high in the mountains. And so we had shed them earlier, tying them onto our saddles, which left harnesses and hilts in plain sight. And that is what brought so many people out to watch us ride into the village: Northern swords in Northern harness. It meant maybe, just *maybe,* we were the sword-dancers sent from Staal-Ysta. The saviors Ysaa-den awaited.

I am accustomed to being stared at. Down south, people do it because, generally, they know who I am. Maybe they want to hire me, buy me aqivi, hear my stories. Maybe they want to challenge me, to prove

106

they are better. Or maybe they don't know me at all,
but want to meet me; it happens, sometimes, with
women. Or maybe they'd stare at any man who is
taller than everyone else, with sandtiger scars on his
face. All I know is, they stare.

Here in the North, my size is not so unusual, because Northern men are very nearly always as tall, or
taller. But here in the North I am many shades darker
in hair and skin. And still scarred. So they stare.

In Ysaa-den also, they stared. But I doubt they
noticed size, color, nationality. Here they stared because someone had loosed magic on the land, and it
was killing them. And maybe, just maybe, we could
do something to stop it.

By the time we reached the center of the village, the
lodges had emptied themselves, disgorging men, women,
children, dogs, chickens, cats, pigs, sheep, goats, and
assorted other livestock. Del and I were awash in
Ysaa-den's inhabitants. The human ones formed a sea
of blue eyes and blond hair; the others—the four-
legged kind—serenaded us with various songs, all of
which formed a dreadful racket. Maybe Del could
have found something attractive in the music, since
she was so big on singing, but to me all it was was
noise. Just as it always is.

We stopped, because we could ride no farther. The
people pressed close, trampling slushy snow into mud
and muck; then, as if sensing the stud's uneasiness and
their lack of courtesy, they fell back, shooing animals
away, giving us room. But only a little room. Clearly
they were afraid that if given the opportunity to leave,
we'd take it.

Del reined in the roan to keep him from jostling a
child. The mother caught the little girl and jerked her
back, murmuring something to her. Del told the woman
quietly it was all right, the girl was only curious; no
harm was done.

I looked at her sharply as she spoke, hearing nuances in her tone. She was thinking, I knew, of Kalle,

of her daughter on Staal-Ysta. And would, probably, for a long time. Maybe even every time she looked at a blonde, blue-eyed girl of about five years.

But Del would learn to live with this just as she'd learned with everything else. It is one of her particular strengths.

She glanced at me. "It was your promise." In other words, she was leaving the introductions and explanations to me.

Uncomfortable, I shifted in the saddle, redistributing weight. Down south I'm happy enough to talk with villagers *or* tanzeers, to strike bargins, suggest deals, invent solutions to problems—but that's down south, where I know the language. And also where they pay me for such things. Coin is a tremendous motivator.

The thing was, I wasn't south. I didn't know the people, didn't know the language—at least, not very well—didn't know the customs. And that sort of ignorance can make for a world of trouble.

"They're waiting," Del said quietly.

So they were. All of them. Staring back at me.

Well, nothing for it but to do the best I could. I sucked in a deep breath. "I'm hunting hounds," I began in Southron-accented Northern—and the whole village broke into cheering.

It was noise enough to wake the dead. Before all I'd heard was the racket of animals; now there was human noise to contend with, too. And it was just as bad.

Hands patted my legs, which was all anyone could reach. I couldn't help it: I stiffened and reached up for my sword; realized, belatedly, all the hands did was pat. It was a form of welcome, of joy; of tremendous gratitude.

Del's roan was surrounded. She, too, was undergoing the joyful welcome. I wondered what it felt like for her, since she hadn't come to Ysaa-den to help anyone. She'd come for her own requirements, which had nothing to do with hounds. Only with Ajani.

If anyone noticed I wasn't Northern, which seemed

fairly likely, it wasn't brought up. Apparently all that mattered was that Staal-Ysta had heard of their plight, answered their pleas, sent us to settle things. No one cared who we were. To them, we were salvation with steel redemption in our sheaths.

I looked out across the throng. Since they expected us to save them, I saw no point in wasting time. So I got right to the point. "Where are these beasts coming from?"

As one they turned to the mountain. To the dragon atop their world. And one by one, they pointed. Even the little children.

"Ysaa," someone murmured. And then all the others joined in. The world rolled through the village.

Ysaa. I didn't need a translation: dragon. Which didn't make any sense. There *were* no dragons. Not even in the North, a place of cold, harsh judgments. Dragons were mythical creatures. And they had nothing to do with hounds.

"Ysaa," everyone whispered, until the word was a hiss. As much as the dragon's breath, creeping down from the gaping stone mouth.

Then, having named it, they all turned once more to me. Bright blue eyes were expectant; clearly, they wanted something. Something to do with the dragon.

I glanced at Del. "This is ridiculous." In Southron, not Northern; I have *some* diplomacy. "I came here to find whoever was sending out the hounds, not discuss bedtime stories."

"Well," she said lightly, "if it *is* ridiculous, your task will be that much simpler."

"Why?" I asked suspiciously.

"Why do you think?" she retorted. "They want you to kill the dragon."

I peered up at the dragon-shaped mountain. It was a pile of stone, nothing more. "If that's true," I told her, "this job will be very easy."

All right, it was a stupid thing to say. If I have

learned anything in this business, it is never to under-
estimate your opponent. But the idea of a *mountain*
being an enemy was enough to irritate even me, even-
tempered as I am; people who allow religion or mythology to control their lives are begging for trouble.
It just doesn't happen that way. We're born, we live,
we die—gods don't have anything to do with it any
more than *dragons* do.

And I'd come hunting hounds.

Now, inside a lodge, Del shook her head. "It doesn't
matter," she said. "No other sword-dancers from Staal-
Ysta ever reached them. Only you. And so now you
can fulfill your promise, as you said." She paused.
"Isn't that what you told me? That you took on the
task of aiding Ysaa-den in the name of your new-won
rank?"

Well, yes. Sort of. I mean, I *had,* but all I'd been
after was a chance to track down the hounds. At the
time, it had provided a means of escape. A means of
putting behind me what I'd done to Del. Because the
only way I could deal with her death was to hide from
it in a job.

Trouble was—well, no, not trouble—Del wasn't dead.
Which meant I no longer needed the job, because
there was nothing to hide *from*.

The people of Ysaa-den—with all their animals—had
escorted us en masse to the headman's lodge. It was
the biggest, but also the emptiest; he'd lost half of his
family to, he told us, the dragon.

I sighed, hung onto my patience, went about my
business. Del and I settled our horses in the guest pen
behind the lodge—the stud didn't like it much, threatening the sapling fence with iron-shod hind hooves
until I told him to mind his manners—then joined the
headman inside, where I tried to bring up the hounds.
But he waved them off like so much unnecessary bag-
gage. What *he* wanted to talk about was the dragon.

I listened for a moment or two, knowing better than
to cut him off too soon—you always have to humor

people impressed by their own authority—then mentioned something about a long journey. He took the hint; he bowed himself out of the lodge, leaving us alone. To rest and refresh ourselves.

At least the empty lodge was quiet. The thought of living with multitudinous people and animals was not something I cared to consider.

The headman's dwelling, like the lodges on Staal-Ysta, was built of wood with mud, twigs, and cloth stuffed into the cracks between the logs. It provided shelter from the worst of the cold and wind, but nonetheless remained a bit chilly on the inside despite the fire laid at one end of the lodge, beneath the open smoke hole, which let air *in* as well as letting smoke out. An open corridor ran the length of the rectangle, lined on either side by wooden roof supports evenly spaced about ten feet apart. Beyond the supports were the compartments the inhabitants called their own; small, cramped spaces more like stalls than rooms. It was a place of enforced closeness. Del had spoken of kin ties and blood loyalties strengthened by living customs; I could see why. If they didn't learn to live *with* one another, they'd end up killing each other.

Del went into the first empty compartment she came to. No doubt the headman expected us to use another—his own well-appointed one, I'm sure, down at the far end—but Del has never been one for unnecessary ceremony. She untied her bedding, spread pelts over hard-packed earth, sat down. And took out her *jivatma*.

It was a ritual I had witnessed many times. For anyone who lives by the sword, the care of a blade is an important part of survival. Del and I had spent many an evening beneath the moon, cleaning, honing and oiling our swords, tending the little nicks, or inspecting and repairing harness and sheaths. But now, here, in this place, it seemed odd to watch her yet again tending her sword. I don't know why. It just did.

In the distance, beasts bayed. I heard the mournful howls, echoing in rocky canyons; the eerie keening of magic-made hounds drifting down from the dragon to thread its way throughout Ysaa-den, sliding through chinks in the lodges and ghosting down the smoke hole. I shivered.

"Hoolies," I blurted irritably. "How can you people live in a place this cold? I have yet to see a truly warm day, or a piece of ground without some kind of snow on it. How can you stand it, Del? All this cold and snow and drab, gray-white days? There's no *color* here!"

Her head was bent over her work. The laced braid swung, back and forth, gently, as she tended the blade. With abrupt discomfort, I recalled the wager we'd made regarding solitary nights in different beds.

And then recalled other things. Behavior I couldn't condone. Explanations I couldn't accept.

Del didn't even look up. "There is color," she said at last. "Even in winter. There are the subtle colors of snow—white, gray, blue, pink, all dependent upon sun and shade and time of day—and the richness of the mountains, the lakes, the trees. Even the clothing of the children." She flicked a glance at me. "There is color, Tiger. You have only to look for it."

I grunted. "I prefer the South. The deserts. Even the Punja. At least there I know what's what."

"Because there are no dragons?" Del didn't smile, just ran her whetstone the length of the blade. "But there are cumfa, and danjacs, and sandtigers . . . not to mention lustful tanzeers, murderous borjuni, and warrior tribes like the Vashni."

Standing wasn't accomplishing much except sore knees and tired back; I dropped my roll of bedding and perched my rump upon it, addressing her final comment. "They gave your brother a home."

"The remains of him," she said. The whetstone rang out more loudly than usual. "You saw what he was to that old man."

So I had. I am a man for women, having no desire for men in my bed, but I'd seen clearly what there was between Del's brother and the old Vashni chieftain who'd taken him in.

And had thought, at the time, that at least the boy had found someone to love after being stripped of manhood and tongue. Someone to love *him*.

"But you would have brought him back anyway," I said. "Isn't that what you intended, to get him out of the South?"

"Of course. And I would have. But—he chose otherwise."

"I don't think he had a choice, Del. I think he knew it was best for him to remain with the Vashni, where he was accepted for himself."

"Accepted because he *belonged* to the old man."

I knew what she meant by the emphasized word. In the South, where women are little more than brood mares or ornaments, men often seek more stimulating companionship with their own sex. In bed as well as anywhere else. And then, of course, there was the slave trade—

I broke off the thought. "Maybe so," I agreed. "And maybe, by then, it was what he wanted."

Del stopped honing. "But what happens?" she asked. "What happens when the old man is dead? Does Jamail become the slave of a new chieftain? Does he then serve the new man as he served the old?"

"I don't know," I told her. "Short of going back down there to find out, we never can know."

"No," she said sharply. Then, more quietly, "No. You are right: he made his choice. Just as I made mine with Kalle."

I expected something more. But she gave me nothing save the muted ring of whetstone on steel. Another kind of song.

One I understood.

We had privacy until sundown. And then the headman and several other villagers came into the lodge and very politely invited us to dinner. Since Del and I had nothing better to do—and both of us were hungry —we accepted.

Given a choice, I'd have preferred the meal inside a lodge; as a matter of fact, it was sort of what I'd expected. But apparently the Northerners took the first breath of spring as a promise of temperate nights as well as days; when dinner proved to be a village-wide gathering under the naked sky, seated on pelt-covered ground, I wrapped myself so close in my cloak it was next to impossible to move, though I left enough room for my eating arm to do its work.

One thing I'm good at is eating. And you never spit on a gift meal unless it's served by an enemy.

The headman, whose name was Halvar, was very aware of the honor our presence did Ysaa-den; he was also very aware of his own responsibilities in hosting us properly. While Del and I chewed roast pork, bread, tubers, and swallowed mugs of ale, Halvar entertained us with the history of the village. I didn't pay much attention, since I had trouble following his accent, *and* since I kept hearing references to the dragon, which told me mythology ran rampant in Ysaa-den. And I've never cared much for mythology. Just give me a clean sword made of true-honed steel—

"Tiger."

It was Del; no surprise. I glanced over, picking a string of pork rind from between my teeth. "What?"

Briefly, she frowned. Then made a graceful one-handed gesture that somehow managed to indicate the entire gathering. "Because we go tomorrow to face the dragon, the village of Ysaa-den would like to make a song in our honor."

"I don't sing," I answered promptly.

"They don't want to hear *you* sing, Tiger. They want to sing for us."

I swallowed the freed bit of pork and washed it down with ale. Shrugged a single shoulder. "If they want to. You know I'm not big on music."

Del changed languages adroitly, switching to accented Southron and smiling insincerely for Halvar's benefit. "It's considered an honor. And if you have any manners at all—*or* good sense—you will tell them how honored we are."

"They can sing us to sleep, for all I care." I swallowed more ale.

Del's smile fell away. "Why are you being so rude? These people believe in you, Tiger . . . these people are trying to tell you how much it means to them that you've come to save the village. You are the *Sandtiger*—someone out of Southron legends. Now perhaps you can become the man of Northern legends as well. Someone who cares for the troubles of others, who tends the helpless and weak—"

I had to interrupt before she got in any deeper. "Appealing to my pride won't work."

"It has before."

I ignored that. "Maybe because I just can't understand why a village full of adults persists in telling stories instead of discussing things rationally." I gestured with my head toward the looming mountain. "It's a heap of stone, Del; nothing more. If the hounds are up there, I'll go—but why keep telling me there's a dragon?"

Del sighed and set down her own mug. All around us the people stared; we spoke in Southron, not Northern, but undoubtedly the tenor of our discussion was obvious, even if the words weren't.

"Tiger, weren't you listening to anything Halvar told us about how Ysaa-den came to be?"

"I *heard* it, yes . . . but I didn't catch one word in ten, bascha. His uplander is all twisty, and I don't speak it that well anyway."

Del frowned a little. "Mountain dialect; yes, it might be difficult for you. But that doesn't excuse your rudeness—"

"—in not taking his story literally?" I shook my head. "I'm not here to waste my time on a storyteller's fancy, Del. They're all a bunch of liars anyway, if you

ask me—spinning tales for coin when they should be
spending their time doing real work. I mean, how hard
is it to make up stories? And then to be *paid* for it—"

"Tiger." Del's tone cut me short. "We are not discussing *skjalds*, who hold high honor in the North—
and how would you know if being a *skjald* is difficult
or easy? What does a man who kills other men know
of telling stories?"

I slanted her a glance. "Last time I looked, you
carried your own share of death-dealing, Delilah."

It shut her up for a moment. And then she looked
at Halvar, who waited patiently, and managed a weak
smile. But there was nothing weak about her tone of
voice. "This man and his village have offered to pay us
high honor, Sandtiger. You will listen to the song, and
you will wait quietly for its conclusion, and then you
will thank Halvar and everyone of Ysaa-den for their
kindness and graciousness. Do you hear?"

"Of *course*," I said, affronted. "What do you think I
am, anyway? Some fool who fell off the goat wagon
this morning?"

"No," Del said coolly. "Some fool who fell off one
thirty-eight or thirty-nine years ago and landed on his
head."

"Thirty-*six!*" I retorted, stung. And swore as she
smiled sweetly and informed Halvar we would be very
honored by the song.

At least, I think that's what she said. You never can
be too sure with uplander. It's hilly as the North itself.
But whatever it was she said pleased Halvar mightily;
he called out something unintelligible—to me—and
people scattered to lodges, returning moments later
with skin drums, pipes, tambors, finger-bells, wooden
sticks, and other things I didn't recognize.

Musicians, obviously. The rest, who had only their
voices, gathered children into laps or lovers into arms
and prepared to make us a song.

The sun was gone, swallowed by the mountains.
The dragon smoked sullenly in the dusk, emitting a

faint red glow from deep in its "throat." I scowled up at it, noting that darkness did not entirely alter its shape into a more sanguine beast, as expected—if anything, it looked more dragonlike than ever—and realized the odd smell remained. Much of it was covered by other aromas—roast pork, sour ale, unwashed bodies, babies who needed clean wrappings, animals too closely confined—but it remained underneath it all, drifting down from the dragon-shaped mountain to shroud Ysaa-den in a musty, malodorous pall.

Not woodsmoke. Woodsmoke has a clean, sweet scent, depending on the wood. And not dung smoke, either, goat, cow or otherwise—I have reason to know, having gathered dung in my days as a slave—which has a pungency all its own. This was different.

"Hounds," I said sharply.

Halvar broke off his introduction to the song. Del looked at me crossly.

"Hounds," I repeated, before she could say anything, or call me names again. "That's what it smells like. Or, better yet, that's what *they* smell like." I lifted my chin in the mountain's direction. "The smoke."

Del frowned. "Eggs gone bad?" she suggested.

I considered it. "A little," I agreed. Then, upon further reflection, "but more like rotting bodies."

I said it quietly, so only Del could hear. It made her curt with me anyway. And then she turned from me to Halvar again. Pointedly, and told him to begin the long-delayed song.

He was more than ready. Trouble was, he needed one more thing from each of us. And asked it.

Del's face changed. I saw the color go out of it, very slowly; how her eyes, equally slowly, dilated. She shook it off quickly enough, but the damage had been done. When she spoke to the headman it was in her clipped, sword-dancer's tone of voice, all business, with little personality in it. I have heard her use it before. I had not expected her to use it with Halvar, whom she seemed to like.

I stirred within the folds of my cloak. "What?"

Del waved a hand at me, as if it would be enough.

"What?" I repeated, with a bit more emphasis. "There are two of us here, bascha—what did he ask?"

She shot me a deadly glance. "Names," she answered curtly. "The names of living kin, so that should we fail tomorrow, and die, our kinfolk can be told. So funeral songs may be sung."

It was unexpected. Equally discomfiting. "Well," I said finally, "I guess that means less work for Halvar, then, if anything *does* happen. Since there's no one to tell for either of us."

Del didn't answer at once. And then when she did it was very quietly, with an odd lack of emotion. She spoke uplander to Halvar, explaining the truth of things. I didn't catch all of the words, but I did catch his expression.

He looked at Del. At me. Then drew in a breath and addressed the gathered villagers, adult and child alike.

I heard Del's hiss of shock. And then she was trying to override Halvar's little speech, telling him no repeatedly. But he was adamant; I heard the word for honor.

Trust him to hit on the right word. It shut her up immediately.

"What?" I asked irritably.

Del was tight as wire. "I told him." Her teeth were gritted. "I told him. That there are no names. There are no kin. Only the Sandtiger and Delilah, with blooding-blades for kinfolk and the circle for our lodge."

I waited a moment. "And?"

Del sucked in a deep breath, held it, released it. Slowly. Silently. "So," she said, "they will sing. They will make a song for all our lost ones, a song of farewell, because they had no kin to sing it to for them when they died, to guide them into the light." She swallowed visibly. "As you and I have no kinfolk to sing the songs for us."

I heard the first voice. Halvar's: the headman's privilege. And then a woman's voice: his wife's. And another and another, until all the village was singing. Voices only; no pipes, no drums, no sticks, no tambors, no chiming finger-bells. Only voices.

Voices were enough.

Wrapped tightly in my cloak, I sat beneath a star-blotched Northern sky and thought only of the South. Of the desert. Of the Punja.

Where a woman had borne a boy—a strong, healthy boy—and left him to die in burning sands beneath a blazing sun.

Twelve

The stench was worsening. Halvar, riding a little ahead of Del, who rode ahead of me, seemed not to notice, which told me either he had no sense of smell, or he'd grown so accustomed to the stink he no longer noticed it. To me, it seemed impossible, in view of the magnitude of the odor. Hoolies, I could *taste* it. It made me want to spit.

I leaned over in my saddle, making sure I didn't threaten the stud, and spat. Twice. He waggled an ear, shook his head, walked on.

We climbed relentlessly toward the dragon, which was making its presence known through smell *and* smoke. Both filled up nose and mouth, lingering unpleasantly in lungs, causing a tight, dull headache that made me irritable as well as impatient. There had been no sign of hounds since Del and I reached Ysaaden, though we'd heard them. And no sign of any dragon; as we climbed, our closeness to the rock formations and crumbling spires caused them to lose their eerie shapes and became nothing more than stone and earth, which is what I'd said the thing was all along. I felt suitably vindicated; unfortunately, no one wanted to share in my victory.

As we climbed, Halvar entertained us with stories about the dragon and Ysaa-den. Trouble was, I was too far behind the headman and Del to hear everything over the noise of hoof on stone; moreover, his mountain dialect rendered his uplander mostly unin-

telligible. Which didn't particularly bother me, if you
want the truth; I was content to match the rhythm of
the stud's steady climbing and spent my time looking
around watchfully. Part of me waited for hounds. Now
that I no longer wore the Cantéada ward-whistle, the
stakes were a bit different. But I still had a sword, and
so did Del.

So did Halvar, but it was an old, ill-tended bronze
sword, of no use to anyone, let alone a headman
untrained in fighting. I had the feeling Halvar would
be more hindrance than help, if it came to making a
stand. But you can't just pat the village leader on the
head when trouble arises and send him off to mother
and father; the hounds had eaten Halvar's, and anyway he was too nice a person to dismiss so easily.
There would have to be some show of dignity and
honor in the name of the headman's pride.

From the heights came a mournful wailing howl that
changed, midway, to a vicious growling snarl. Halvar
halted his mount.

"Far enough," he said, so emphatically even I understood it. "I am headman, not hero; such things are
for sword-dancers and sword-singers trained on Staal-
Ysta."

Which meant Halvar was more than a nice person;
he was also pretty smart.

We were two-thirds of the way up the mountain.
The track had changed to trail some time back; now it
began to resemble little more than a trough formed by
melting snow. I asked Halvar why, if they so feared
the dragon and its hounds, the villagers even bothered
to climb far enough to *make* a trail.

Halvar stared back at me blankly a moment. Then
he looked at Del.

She sighed. "He explained all that, Tiger. As we
climbed."

I didn't like being made to feel guilty. "I told you I
don't understood his lingo very well. And besides, *one*
of us had to keep an eye out for hounds."

Del didn't answer right away. She looked up the mountain toward the "mouth," which still spewed fitful drifts of smoke. "The hounds weren't always here," she said finally. "Halvar says the first one appeared about six months ago, maybe seven. Apparently it killed one of the villagers; no one is certain, because the man was never found. But after that, more and more of the beasts appeared . . . and more and more villagers disappeared. There is a track here because the village holy man suggested the dragon might be appeased with gifts, and so the villagers began to climb up to the dragon to make offerings. Unfortunately, the dragon was not appeased; more people disappeared. So they sent to Staal-Ysta and begged for help." She paused. "You are what they got."

I wanted to respond to her overly bland tone of voice, which is infuriating at times, but Halvar pointed up the mountain and said something to Del I couldn't understand. It sounded like a warning to me. Whatever it was, Del didn't much like it; she snapped out something to Halvar that made him redden. But he tapped the hilt of his useless bronze sword and repeated what he'd said before. This time I caught part of it. Something about *jivatmas*.

"What?" I asked, as usual.

Del looked at Halvar. "He says we would be wise to leave our swords sheathed. That the village holy man has decreed magic a danger to Ysaa-den because the dragon feeds on it."

"Oh?" It sounded suspicious to me. "And how does he know that?"

"He set wards when the hounds first appeared," she explained. "Or so Halvar says. And the wards, instead of protecting the village, drew the hounds. Who stole them."

"Stole what, the *wards?* Is he sandsick? What would hounds want with wards?"

Del didn't smile. "Maybe the same thing they wanted with the whistle."

And my sword? My newly-quenched *jivatma*? They hadn't been even remotely interested in the thing until I'd blooded it; only in Boreal, who reeked of blood and power.

I looked at Halvar with a bit more respect. "Tell him we appreciate the warning."

Del stared. "Tiger—"

"And ask him if he will send someone each day to feed and water the horses; we're leaving them here and going the rest of the way on foot. I'd send them back down with him, but I don't like the idea of being completely horseless; at least this way they're in range, if we need them." I looked again at the smoking "mouth," easily an hour's hike from where we were. "Sort of."

"Each day?" Del echoed. "How many do you plan to spend tromping around the mountains?"

"Two," I answered succinctly. "If I can't beat a mountain by then, hounds or no hounds, I'm not worth the coin they're paying me."

"They're not."

I frowned. "Not what?"

"Paying you."

I frowned harder. "What do you mean, not paying me? This is what I do for a living, bascha. Remember?"

"But you took on this task as a duty to your rank as a *kaidin*." Her expression also was bland, but I know that look in her eye. "They didn't hire the Sandtiger, nor did Staal-Ysta send him. A new-made *kaidin* answered the plea of a village in need, and swore to help in any way he could." She raised pale brows. "Isn't that what you told me?"

"Hoolies, Del, you *know* I'm a sword-dancer. I don't do anything for free." I paused. "At least, not anything *dangerous*."

"Then perhaps you should explain that to Halvar, who is headman of a village which probably has no coin at all—oh, perhaps one or two coppers, if you insist on counting—but survives against all odds be-

cause people make a living out of the ground and from
the livestock, in coin of wool and milk and pork . . .
except you would not consider that a living, would
you? If it isn't gold or silver or copper, it's not worth
the effort."

I sat the stud and stared at her, taken aback by the
vehemence of her contempt. This wasn't the Del I
knew . . . well, yes, I guess it was. It was the *old* Del,
the one who'd used words as well as a weapon as we'd
crossed the Punja on the way to Julah.

Was this the Del I'd wanted back, just so we could
reestablish some of the old relationship?

Was I sandsick?

Del reined back the blue roan, who showed signs of
wanting to nose the stud. "So, do we turn back now?
Do you explain to Halvar that this was all a big misun-
derstanding, so that he will be forced into offering
what little coin Ysaa-den has? Will you hold a village
for ransom, Tiger, in the name of your avarice?"

The dragon snorted smoke. One of the beasts bayed.

"Nice little speech," I remarked finally. "You really
know how to manipulate a person, don't you? Too
bad you're not willing to consider that I had no intention of asking for money in the first place—you just
jumped to the conclusion that I'm a no-good, low-
down sword-for-hire with no sense at all of humanity,
only a well-developed sense of greed." I smiled at her
with eloquent insincerety. "Well, I won't give you the
satisfaction of thinking you convinced me . . . I'm
going to do what I please, regardless of what you
think, and let you try to figure out the truth of my
intentions. I'm also going to suggest you take your
own advice: never assume anything. It can get you
into trouble."

I climbed down from the stud and led him off the
remains of the track to a stout young tree, where I tied
him and explained I'd be back in two days, if not
before.

He nosed me, then banged his head against my ribs,

which hurt, and which left me less regretful about leaving him. As a matter of fact, it left me downright displeased; I thumped him on the nose and told him he'd just lost his ration of grain for the day.

Of course, I didn't tell Halvar that, which meant the stud would get his share from whoever came to tend him, but *he* didn't have to know that. It would do him good to suffer until nightfall.

I glanced at Del, who still sat her roan. "Well? You coming?"

She tipped back her head and stared up at the crown of the mountain, frowning faintly. Her hair, still laced and braided, dangled against her spine. The line of her jaw cut the air like a blade. I saw her lips part; she said something to herself, mouthing it in silence, and I wondered what was in her mind. Ajani? Delay?

Or maybe a Southron sword-dancer who taxed her dwindling supply of patience.

Hoolies, she didn't have to stay. I wasn't forcing her to. She could turn around with Halvar and ride back down the mountain to Ysaa-den. Or ride clear to the South. To Harquhal and beyond, maybe even to Julah; or to the Vashni, who had her brother; hoolies, there was no place in the world Del couldn't go if she put her mind to it.

Except Staal-Ysta.

Del slid a leg over her saddle and stepped down carefully, sparing her midriff as much as she could. It would be days, possibly even weeks, before either of us could move freely again, without awareness of stiffness and pain. It was possible neither of us would ever fully recover fluidity of motion, since respective sword blades had cut muscle as well as flesh.

Then again, it was possible only *I* wouldn't; Del was twenty-one. The young heal faster, neater, better.

And maybe she needed it more.

I unpinned my cloak, rolled it, fastened it onto my saddle. No doubt come night I would regret leaving it behind, but its weight and muffling folds would hinder me during the climb. Hopefully the task could be accomplished before it got cold enough for me to need the warmth of its weight.

Hopefully.

Well, one can *always* hope.

Del tied off the roan—outside of the stud's reach—and chatted briefly with Halvar. Like me, she shed her cloak and put it away. Sunlight glinted off the hilt of her *jivatma*; I saw Halvar stare at it in something akin to reverence. No doubt any village full of people who believed in dragons also told bedtime stories about Northern blooding-blades and the men who bore them. Now they could add a whole new raft of tales about the pale-haired woman who summoned a banshee-storm with only a name and a song.

"Let's go," I said irritably. "We're burning daylight."

"So is the dragon," Del observed, as smoke issued from "mouth" and "nostrils." This time sound came with it: a low-pitched, hissing rumble, as if the dragon belched.

"Beware the fire," Halvar said, clearly enough for me.

I looked up the mountain. "If there's fire," I pointed out, "someone has to tend it. Which means there's more up there than rock and hounds . . . likely a man as well."

Halvar looked at me strangely.

"It makes sense," I said defensively; I hate it when I'm doubted. "Do you really think there's a *dragon* up there, fire-breathing and all?"

Still Halvar stared. And then he looked at Del as if hoping she could explain.

"No," Del said quietly, "he thinks no such thing . . . Tiger, I am sorry you have been so left out of the conversation—I didn't realize it was so hard for you to understand. No one in Ysaa-den belives there's a *real* dragon up there—no one is so foolish as to believe in a mythical creature—but a sorcerer. A specific one, in fact: Chosa Dei."

"Who?"

"Chosa Dei," she repeated. "He is a legendary sorcerer, Tiger; surely you must have heard of him, even in the South."

"No." Emphatically. "Del—

"He has not been seen for hundreds of years, ever since a fight with his brother, Shaka Obre—who is also a sorcerer—but Halvar tells me Ysaa-den has lain in his shadow for nearly ninety years. They believe it is Chosa Dei who troubles them now, awakening; *he* is the 'dragon,' not this pile of stone."

"Have *you* heard of this sorcerer?"

"Of course." Del was dead serious. "He was one of my favorite stories when I was a child. I know all about Chosa Dei . . . and all his fights with his brother, and how they spent all their magic trying to kill one another—"

"Are you *completely* sandsick?" I gaped at her inelegantly. "You're standing here telling me you believe a man out of childhood stories is living in that mountain, blowing smoke out stone tunnels just to pass the time?"

Del smiled. "No," she said in Southron. "But it would be rude to tell Halvar so, and ruin the history of his village."

I blinked. "Then why *are* we here?"

She slipped a thumb beneath a harness strap and resettled her sword. "Because a newly-named *kaidin* made a promise he's sworn to keep."

I opened my mouth to respond. Rudely, of course; she was throwing things I'd said back in my own face. But before I could say a word something interrupted.

A keening, rising howl, echoing eerily. And a gout of malodorous smoke, fanned by heated wind.

No matter *who* it was, someone—some*thing*—was killing people. And I was here to stop it.

"Come on," I said curtly.

Del fell in behind me.

*   *   *

Conditioning is important to a sword-dancer. Because if you lack stamina, speed and wind, you risk losing the dance. And, much of the time, if you risk losing the dance, you also risk losing your life.

Which means a sword-dancer worth his salt always stays in condition.

Unless he's been recently wounded, which changes things altogether.

I suppose two months isn't recent. But it felt like it. It felt like yesterday every step I took—no, let's make it today. Like maybe a moment ago. All I know is, it hurt to climb the mountain.

I knew I was a fool to go charging up a rockpile where there wasn't any air to breathe and I had no lungs to breathe it. I knew I was a fool to even *consider* taking on anything with my sword, be it human or animal. And certainly I was a fool to be doing it with Del, who was in no better shape than I. It's nice to have backup—it's *great* to have backup—but only if they're healthy.

We huffed and puffed and coughed and swore and muttered all the way up the mountain. We also slid, staggered, fell down, gagged on the stink of the dragon's breath. And wished we were somewhere else, *doing* something else; Del no doubt thought of Ajani, while I dreamed of a cantina. A cantina in the *South*, where the days are warm and bright. And there are no mountains to climb.

The dragon snorted smoke. A rumble accompanied it. And then a relentless hiss spitting wind into our faces. It ripped the hair from my eyes and inserted hot fingers into the weave of my heavy wool tunic.

I slipped, slid, climbed. Threw a question over my shoulder toward the woman who climbed behind me. "*Who* is this man again?"

"What man?—oh." Del was breathing hard. She spoke in brief, clipped sentences, sparing no breath for more. "Chosa Dei. Sorcerer. Supposed to be very powerful—till he lost an argument."

"With his brother."

"Shaka Obre." Del sucked in a breath. "There are stories about both of them . . . tales of great and powerful magic . . . also ambition. Chosa Dei is the example parents put up before greedy children. *'Look, oh look, beware of wanting too much, or you will become like Chosa Dei, who dwells in Dragon Mountain.'* " It faded into a cough.

"So now everyone in Ysaa-den thinks *their* mountain is Dragon Mountain, and that Chosa Dei dwells in it."

"Yes."

"Sounds like they're taking after the old man and his taste for ambition. I mean, saying their village lies in the dragon's shadow is an attempt to claim some fame, isn't it? Just like Bellin the Cat."

It was Del's turn. *"Who?"*

"Bellin the Cat," I repeated. "You know, that silly boy back in Harquhal who wants to be a panjandrum. Who wants to make a name." I sucked more air. "The kid with all the axes."

That, Del remembered. "Oh. Him."

"So, it seems to me Ysaa-den's a little like him—" I bit off a curse as a foot slipped and nearly deposited me on my face. "I mean, isn't it a little silly to adopt a story as truth just to gain a little fame?" I brushed dirt from my clothes and went on.

"If you lived in Ysaa-den, what would *you* do?"

I thought it over. "True."

Del slid, caught at rock, climbed upward again. "After all, what does it hurt? No one really knows where Dragon Mountain lies—there are countless maps with countless mountains called after Chosa Dei's prison—and no one really knows if Chosa Dei ever existed. He's a legend, Tiger. Some believe it, some don't."

"Which are you, Delilah?"

Del laughed once. "I told you, stories about Chosa Dei and his battles with Shaka Obre were favorites when I was young. Of course I want to believe. But it doesn't mean I do."

I wondered, not for the first time, what childhood for Del had been like. I knew bits and pieces only, because that was all she'd shared, but it wasn't hard to put a few of them together.

I imagined a pretty but strong-minded girl who preferred boys' doings to girls'. And who, as the only daughter, was allowed the freedom to *be* a boy, even symbolically, because it was probably easier for father and uncles and brothers. Easier for a mother who knew she was outnumbered. No skirts and dolls for Del; she'd been handed a sword in place of a cooking spoon.

I'd asked her once what she would be if she hadn't become a sword-dancer. And she had said probably married. Probably bearing babies. But it was impossible for me to think of Del in those terms, to even *imagine* her tending a lodge, a man, a child; not because I didn't think she could, but because I'd never seen it. All I had ever seen was a woman with a sword, tending to men in the circle.

For six long years, it was all Delilah had been. But I wondered. Even if she didn't, I did. I couldn't help myself.

What would become of Del once Ajani was dead?

Yet more importantly: what would Del *become* once Ajani was dead?

"Tiger—look."

I looked. Was too out of breath to speak.

"Almost there," Del gasped, nearly as winded as I. "Can't you feel the heat?"

Heat, yes, if you're a Northerner. To a Southroner, it was merely a gentle warming, like the breeze of a spring day. What *I* noticed was, it stank.

"Hoolies," I muttered, "if this man's that powerful a sorcerer, why can't he live in a place that *smells* better?"

"No choice," Del croaked. "It was a spell put on him by Shaka Obre."

"Ah. Of course. I forgot." I topped off the last bit of mountain and arrived at the dragon's lip. Heat and stench rolled out to bathe me in dragonish breath. "Hoolies, this place *stinks!*"

Del came over the edge and paused to catch her breath. I saw her expression of distaste as the odor engulfed her as well. It's hard enough trying to suck wind back into laboring lungs, but when it smells this bad the task is that much harder.

Smoke rolled out of the "mouth." I steeled myself and went over for a closer look.

From below, it *looked* like a dragon. The shape of earth and rock, the arrangement of the same—from below, it looked drago*nish*. But from up top, from the opening in the rock, it was only a large odoriferous cave extending back into the mountain. The spires of rock forming "teeth" were nothing more than stone columns shaped by ancient rain and the wind moaning incessantly through the cavern's entrance, bearing the stench of rotting bodies and a trace of something more.

Does magic have a smell?

"No hounds," Del observed.

No hounds. No dragon. No Chosa Dei.

"Wait a moment," I muttered, frowning down at the ground. I bent, squatted, looked more closely at turfy ground and the tracks pressed into it. "Pawprints," I said, "going straight into the cave."

Del took an involuntary step back, one hand drifting up toward the hilt riding above her left shoulder. "It couldn't be their *den*—" But she let it trail off.

"Leave her sheathed," I suggested, thinking of Halvar's warning, "and yes, I think it could be . . . if I believed they were really hounds. It's what I've called them—the Hounds of Hoolies—for lack of a better name, but I never believed they were. And I don't think beasts live in dens." I shrugged. "Although I suppose they *could*."

We stared at one another, not liking the idea. Not liking the vision I'd painted. I thought it pretty disgusting; Del didn't say anything.

She edged closer to the entrance. She didn't draw Boreal, but her right hand hooked in her harness as if to stay close *just in case*. And I didn't really blame her.

"Tiger, do you think—"

But I didn't hear her finish. A blast of malodorous wind came roaring out of the cavern; with it came an overwhelming presentiment of power.

I itched, because all my hairs stood up on my arms, my thighs, the back of my neck. Even my bones tingled; my belly climbed up my throat. It was all I could do not to vomit. "Del—oh, hoolies—*Del*—"

"What is it? Tiger, what *is* it?"

I staggered back from the opening, trying not to retch. I also tried to wave Del off, but she followed anyway. "Don't, bascha—wait—can't you *feel* it?"

Maybe. Maybe not. But Del unsheathed Boreal.

It drove me to my knees. "I said *wait*—oh, hoolies, bascha—I think I'm going to be *sick*."

But I wasn't. I couldn't be. There wasn't time for it.

I got up, staggered a step or two, swung back around toward the cavern. "In there," I gasped. "I swear, it's in *there*—"

"*What* is, Tiger?"

"The thing we've been chasing. Sorcerer. Demon. *Thing;* I don't know! I just know it's *in* there. It's *got* to be—and that's where we have to go."

Del looked at the cavern. Looked back at me.

"I *know*," I said testily. "Do you think I like the idea?"

Del's *jivatma* gleamed: pale salmon-silver. In answer, the dragon roared.

At least, it *sounded* that way; it was wind keening through the cavern, whining in cracks and crannies, then whooshing out of the opening to splatter our faces with stink.

"Come on," I said unhappily, stepping into the cave. "Let's get this over with."

The weight of rock was oppressive. I stopped dead on the threshold.

"What?" Del asked; it fell away into dimness.

I waited, saying nothing. The feeling did not go away.

Del opened her mouth, then shut it.

Behind me yawned the sky. I wanted nothing more than to spin away from the cave and go out into the sky. To take myself from the dark. To walk on the dragon's spine in the cold, clear air with the sun on my face. Even the Northern sun.

Still Del waited. Somewhere, so did the hounds.

I sweated. Shoved hair out of my eyes. Sucked a breath and spat, cursing myself for the weakness.

"Do you need light?" Del asked.

I looked at her sharply, saw comprehension in her eyes. She knew. She remembered, even though she hadn't been there. She recalled the result too well.

"No," I rasped.

"All I'd have to do is sing. My *jivatma* will give us light."

I glanced at Boreal: thin silver promise in dimness. Light spilled into the mouth of the cavern from the day beyond, but it died too quickly to gloom. It lent the cavern an eerie insubstantiality, a sense of things unseen. The walls were pocked with shadows.

Light would alter everything. But we couldn't afford it now. "No," I told her curtly. "Let's not offer any more magic to the hounds."

She waited a moment. "Do you really think—"

"I haven't the faintest idea." I was snappish in discomfort. "I just figure it won't hurt anything not to take any chances."

Breath boomed in the dragon's throat. The sound was deafening as air rushed by us toward the entrance. The roar sounded almost real, though both of us knew it wasn't. It was nothing more than wind and smoke being blown or sucked out of the cave into the vast freedom beyond.

"Will you be all right?" Del asked.

"Leave it alone," I snapped. I took a step toward the darkness, then came to an abrupt halt. "It's *gone*."

"Gone?"

"That *feeling* . . . it's faded. A moment ago I could almost taste it, and now it's faded away." I frowned, turning in a slow revolution. "It was here . . . it was *here*—" I stabbed a finger downward, "—filling up this place . . . it was like a cistern choked with sand, spilling through all the cracks—only what I felt was *magic*—" I shook my head, frowning. "Now it's all gone."

Wind whined through the cavern. With it came the stink, and the wail of a distant hound.

I shut my hand on my sword hilt and slid the blade into freedom. "To hoolies with those hounds." And led the way into darkness.

Thirteen

Down the dragon's gullet—or so Halvar might have said. The ceiling dropped, the walls closed in, the darkness was nearly complete. Except for a sickly red glow that crept out of the depths of the dragon to illuminate our way.

A lurid carnelian light that reminded me of new blood.

The fear, for the moment, was gone. Movement provided the opportunity to set it aside, to think about something else. But I couldn't quite forget it. It waited for me to remember so it could creep out again.

The throat fell away into belly; we left behind the gullet and entered a larger chamber. Del and I stopped short, then tightened grips on hilts.

"What in hoolies is *that?*"

Del shook her head.

I scowled blackly. "I thought you knew Northern magic."

"I know *about* Northern magic . . . but I don't know what that is."

"That" was a curtain of flame. A lurid carnelian flame that stretched from floor to ceiling across the width of the cavern. It resembled nothing so much as a curtain hung for privacy, dividing room from room. Opaque, yet oddly vibrant, it shimmered against the blackness. Sparks burned bright, then died, pulsing against a net.

But it wasn't hot. It was cold.

Suspicion bloomed. "You know," I said lightly, "what that reminds me of—what that reminds me of *a lot*—is the light from Bor—from your sword." I caught myself in time.

Del flicked me a narrowed glance; I was not forgiven. "I don't think it's the same thing."

"How do you know? You yourself said you don't know what that is. For all *you* know, it could be exactly the same."

"But not from the same source." Del edged closer. Red light shirred off her blade, altering its color. Salmon-silver was dyed amber-bronze.

I looked at my own sword. It had not, up till now, shown any inclination to take on a particular color. The phenomenon was familiar—I'd seen numerous *jivatmas* keyed, and all displayed a signature color, but mine never had. It was bright and shining silver, but so was every other sword save those born of Northern magic.

Which left me wondering suddenly if perhaps mine *wasn't* blooded. Wasn't really quenched.

And yet it had to be. It showed too many symptoms. Displayed too much of its power. Even the hounds knew it.

Del frowned at the curtain. "Maybe some kind of ward? Something to keep people out?"

"But why? What is there to hide? Why would wards be *here?*"

Del abruptly smiled. "Chosa Dei," she answered. "It's Chosa Dei's prison."

"Oh, right. Of course; I was forgetting." I squinted against the brilliance of the curtain, looking around, searching for some clue. "I don't suppose there's some way around this thing . . . some tunnel or passageway."

Del shrugged, saying nothing. Like me, she examined the chamber.

I heard the dragon rumble. Swung and stared as the curtain rippled. The glow intensified, and then the curtain parted. Hot smoke belched out.

Del and I, of course, ducked; flame—or whatever—licked toward us both. The curtain wavered in the wind, then shredded on a roar as the smoke was sucked out of the chamber into the tunnel beyond.

The stench drove me to my knees. I forgot all about flaming curtains or passageways and concentrated on holding my breath so I wouldn't lose my belly. Del, half-shrouded by smoke, sounded no better off; she hacked and gagged and swore, though only briefly, in her twisty Northern tongue. I helped out with Southron, with a dash of Desert thrown in.

Then wished I hadn't; swearing made me suck air.

"Agh, *gods*—" I spat. "This is enough to make a man sick."

"Coal," Del said intently. "I know it now: *coal* . . . and something else. Something more. Something that smells—"

"—like rotting bodies; I told you before." The curtain sealed itself as smoke died away. For the moment the dragon slept, or else merely held its breath. I stood up, wished for aqivi to wash away the foul aftertaste, yanked my now-filthy tunics back into place. And clutched my sword in one hand. "What's this 'coal' you mentioned?"

Del got up, brushed gritty dark dust from her no-longer-pristine white clothing, scowled at the curtain. "Coal," she repeated. "It's a fuel. It's sort of like rock, but it burns. We lived in the downlands, where wood is plentiful; I saw coal only once. It comes from high in the mountains, in the uplands above the timberline."

"Well, if it smells this bad, I don't see how *anyone* uses it."

"I told you, there's something more—"

The curtain flowed briefly aside and emitted another belch. Smoky wind rushed through the chamber in its way to the dragon's throat. I swore, waving madly, and tried to peer through the rent in flame.

In shock, I sucked a breath. "Hoolies, I saw *people!*"

Del looked at me sharply; no need for her to ask.

"I did," I declared. "Through the curtain—I swear, I saw people. Men, I think, doing something around a fire. A *real* fire, bascha—not this magical curtain." I strode to the "flame," tried to peer through it again. "When the smoke comes through, it thins. You can see right through it. All we have to do is wait—"

"—then walk right in?" Del's brows arched. "Are you so sure that's wise?"

"Of course I'm not sure. I can't foretell the future, bascha; how in hoolies am I supposed to know what is and isn't wise? But Halvar said there was no other way into the dragon; here we are with nothing better to do, and two magical swords. So we may as well get this thing finished before the place smells any worse."

"I'm not so sure—"

I thrust up a silencing hand. "Hear it? That's the rumble—any moment the curtain will part . . . just use your *jivatma*, Del. Isn't that what it's for?"

"This isn't a circle, Tiger . . . you don't know—"

"Shut up and use your sword . . . Del—*now*—"

I thrust a swordtip into the curtain of cold flame as it thinned and blew apart, and prodded gently, none too sure what sort of response I might get. The tip sliced through easily enough, as if the curtain was made of air. Colored, cold air, shaped to look like a flame.

I slid the sword a bit farther, risking myself carefully. Felt a prickling in fingers and hands; then it spread to encompass forearms. I took a single step forward, closed nose and mouth against stench, felt the curtain snap shut against flesh.

The sensation was odd, but not threatening. I moved forward carefully, aware of a dampening of sound, a dying of the light. Everything was red.

"You coming?" I asked it thickly around the breath I held.

Her tone sounded no better. "Yes, Tiger, I'm coming." She sounded exasperated. Like maybe she didn't think we were doing the right thing. Like maybe she thought I was being foolish.

As if she were humoring me; never her strong point. I wanted to retort, but I was much too busy.

Almost through—almost—

Something knew I was there.

"Tiger—*wait*—"

—oh—hoolies—

"Del!"

The dragon swallowed me whole.

Fourteen

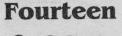

They had been beating me again. I could feel it clear to the bone.

I lay facedown on the stone, legs and arms asprawl. Cold, hard stone, biting into flesh. Bruising cheekbone and brow. Cutting into one hip.

They had been beating me again, just as the Salset had.

I twitched. Sucked air. Gagged. Tried not to throw up. Lay very, very still, to soothe my unhappy belly. To give it no reason to protest.

Hoolies, but I hurt.

Listened to the silence. Heard nothing in the darkness. Nothing save ragged breathing; I held it: the sound stopped. Began to breathe again and took comfort in the sound.

Awakening muscles spasmed. A leg jerked, then a hand. Beneath me, metal grated. The sound of iron fetters.

They had *chained* me again.

I surged up frantically, smashed my head against the low ceiling, sprawled on hands and knees. Then lunged backward against the wall and slid down it to land limply in a pile of flesh and bones. Squeezed my eyes tight-shut. Sat there breathing raggedly while I tried to find the Sandtiger and whatever will he had left.

Some, after all. It allowed me to deal with the fear. To push it back again, if only for a moment. It allowed me to open my eyes.

Saw the sword against the stone: dim glint in dimmer light.

Sword?

Astonished, I stared. Then scrambled for it, found it, dragged it chiming across the stone. Sat down awkwardly on uneven rock and held the sword in both hands.

Not Singlestroke.

Not Singlestroke?

And why do I have a sword if I'm in Aladar's mine?

The blade was ice in my hands. Vision blurred; I shook it off, then wished I hadn't tried. The motion jarred my head.

Hoolies, but I hurt.

I leaned against the wall and wiped the sweat from my eyes, shoving damp hair aside. Beard stubble caught on wool; on *wool,* not on flesh. Not on the nakedness of a slave.

All around me the rock waited with a vast complacency. Dim carnelian light washed the walls with illumination. It bathed the blade with blood.

I shifted, caught my breath, eased myself more carefully into another position. Even my ears hurt, filled with a stuffy ringing. I smelled something remarkably foul; also my own aroma, fear and exertion combined. What I needed was a bath. What I *wanted* was out of here.

Down the tunnel something whined.

I'm not in Aladar's mine.

Then where *am*—ah, hoolies.

I know where I am.

Claws scratched stone. Panting crept down the tunnel.

I think I don't want to be here.

Whining echoed in emptiness.

Hoolies—*where is Del?*

With Aladar, of course—no, no, you're not *in* Aladar's mine. You're not even in the South. Where you are is in the dragon with hounds hard on your trail.

Panting crept through the dimness. A snapping growl accompanied it.

Pick a direction and *go.*

I couldn't stand up straight because of the low tunnel ceiling. All I could do was scuttle, hunched half-way over, clutching a Northern sword and trying not to trip on steel too long for use in the confines of the tunnel. The tip scraped from time to time, screeching against stone; pulling it back from the wall usually resulted in a banged elbow, unless I was very careful.

It's hard to be very careful when you're running for your life. Careful can get you killed.

Oh, Delilah. Where are you?

Don't let her be dead again.

A howl pierced the dimness. I couldn't tell from which direction.

I smacked my head, bit my lip, spat out blood, and cursed. Felt the prickling on my neck; the pinch of fear in my belly. And lurched to a dead stop, having reached the end of the tunnel.

Hoolies, get me out of here. It's too much like Aladar's mine—

I broke it off abruptly. Smelled the stink of hounds.

—end of the tunnel—

But it wasn't the end of the world. The tunnel swelled into a hollow bulb large enough to stand up in. Wide enough for my sword. I straightened and struck a stance, cursing the tautness of scar tissue that pulled against my midriff.

I hadn't been in a circle since the one where I'd faced Del. I hadn't even *sparred* since the fight I'd danced with Del. Conditioning was a word that no longer applied to me.

But I'd been worse off before.

Of course, I'd also been *younger*—

A hound entered the bulb through the narrow neck.

At least, the hound *tried* to; I took its head with one blow.

There is something to be said for standing in an enclosed space while fighting vicious beasts. Because while I'd sooner be out of the mountain, in bright, clean sunlight again, I discovered there were advantages to fighting just as I was. Because each time I killed a hound, the body dropped to the floor. The pile was forming a plug against the beasts still in the tunnel. And it gave me a chance to breathe. To hoard my dwindling strength.

To wet my thirsty *jivatma*.

Eventually, they stopped. When they did, so did I. And I realized there were no more; at least, no more in the tunnel. The rest were somewhere else.

Winded, I stood sucking air, trying to clear my head. Sparks danced at the edges of vision, bursting like tiny flamelets. I leaned over, bracing forearms across bent knees, and tried to catch my breath. While beast-blood flowed over my boots.

When I could, I straightened, arched carefully backward, tried to unknot the kinks. Tried to stretch knurled scar tissue that threatened to crack with the strain.

Something echoed in the tunnel.

I snapped back into position, wincing, with *jivatma* at the ready. Before me was a piled blockade of bleeding bodies. Through the gaps I heard a voice, distorted by rock and distance; by the twists and turns of the dragon.

"—*long I have waited?*"

And Del's voice, softly: "*Six hundred and forty-two years.*"

A pause, and surprise. "*How can you know that?*"

"*They tell stories about you, Chosa.*"

Chosa. Chosa *Dei?* But he was only legend. A man made out of stories.

"*What else do they say about me?*"

"*That you are an ambitious, vengeful man.*"

Uh-oh, *bascha.* Not the best thing to say.

"*And what do they say about you?*"

"*That I am very like you.*"

I heard a hint of laughter. "*But I am not a woman, and you are not a man; yes?*"

"*Sword-dancer,*" she answered quietly. "*Sword-singer, as well. Staal-Ysta trained, Chosa . . . you do know of Staal-Ysta?*"

"Oh, I know; yes, of course I know; I know many things, yes? I know Staal-Ysta—I know of jivatmas—I know many things, yes? As I know what you are, yes? Exactly what you are. It's you I've been waiting for. I need you very badly, you and your jivatma—I've needed you for years—"

My cue, I thought. But my way was blocked by beasts.

Hastily I cleaned the blade on my dirty tunic and set the sword aside by the entrance. Without regard for the slime and putrid blood, I caught and dragged bodies aside, dumping them one on the other. Not all were in one piece; I kicked the bits aside. As soon as I cleared an exit, I caught up the sword and ran.

Trouble was, the moment I moved the voices faded, stolen away by tunnels and crannies. I stopped short, crouching to save my head, and listened. Heard nothing but my own breathing. No more Del. No more Chosa Dei.

It *couldn't* be Chosa Dei.

I swore and went on awkwardly, hating the size of the tunnel. Hating myself for my height. Wishing I had the kind of power that could blast the mountain apart, taking Chosa with it. Chosa and his hounds.

"—so I had to have the whistle, yes? I had to have the wards. I have to have all the magic. It's what I do: collect. And I have to have it all; of course, all, what else? There's no point to it, otherwise; the purpose is defeated, yes? There is no value to any magic if everyone has a little."

I stopped short, breathing hard, but Del made no answer. Or else I couldn't hear it in the maze of the dragon's entrails. I sucked breath and ran on again, bootsteps echoing in the tunnel.

"—were a means, nothing more. I have no particular liking for beasts; I'm not a man for pets. But I had to start somewhere, so I fashioned myself a—hound, I think you said, yes? Well, then, a hound. A good and loyal dog ready to die at my command. Of course, then I needed more; harvesting jivatmas is difficult. A single

*beast wasn't up to the task, so I had it bring me another
human. Who in turn could bring me another. Villagers
all, yes? Until I had enough, and sent them after
jivatmas."*

I took the left branch. Its ceiling was higher; I ran.

Hoolies, hoolies, bascha—what have you gotten yourself into?

The voice boomed by my side. *"—no, no, not
'make'—I do better than that. Making is very simple; I
unmake, yes? That is my personal gift; the magic of
Chosa Dei. I take what has been wrought and drain it
of its power. I unmake it most carefully, then reshape it
to personal needs."*

I stopped short as the voice died out, fading behind
me gently like a candle carried away. I spun in place,
sword tip scraping the wall. Nothing lay behind me.
Nothing but emptiness.

Oh, bascha. Bascha.

The voice echoed far down the tunnel. *"—know
what you are? Do you know what you are?"*

I listened as I ran, but heard nothing of Del's answer.

*"—think you have denied yourself the awareness,
afraid to admit the truth, yes? I can smell that sword; I
can taste it—I have tasted it all along. There is no
hiding it from me, in sheath or in a song. Nor can you
hide it now; I can unsing what you sing, unmake what
you make."*

This time I heard Del's voice: *"Why?"*

The sorcerer's tone was gentle. *"So I may unmake
the wards. So I may unmake my prison.* The tone
abruptly altered; Chosa Dei was angry. *"So I may
unmake my brother, who put me in this place!"*

The tunnel branched yet again. I started through it;
stopped. It branched yet again. The dragon was full of
tunnels, and Chosa was in them all.

Oh bascha, bascha. How in hoolies do I find you?

Fifteen

Rock bit into my knees. Blade clanged down. I realized I had fallen.

Behind me, the beast growled.

I lurched up, caught weapon, whirled. Spitted him as he leaped, then jerked the blade free and struck again as a second hound appeared, lunging out of ruddy shadows. Behind him was a third.

Blood sprayed freely as I scythed through rib cage and spine, shearing the third hound in half. I felt a flicker of pleasure; the jolt of victory.

And then I recalled Chosa's words: that the beasts had once been human. Villagers from Ysaa-den. Sword-dancers from Staal-Ysta.

Bile rose. Briefly, only briefly, the hilt slipped in my hand. And then I smelled the stink. Felt the blood crusting on my face. And knew if I had hesitated the unmade men would have killed me.

Chosa Dei had Del. He no longer needed me. He no longer needed my sword; he had the one he wanted. Had the one he *required* to set himself free of his prison so he could find his brother and unmake Shaka Obre, who had had the abiding good sense to put Chosa away in a mountain where he could harm nothing and no one.

For six hundred and forty-two years.

Six hundred and forty-*one;* for the last six months or so, Chosa Dei had been busy.

And where, I wondered fleetingly, is Shaka Obre *now?*

Chosa Dei's voice slipped through cracks. "*—and a woman is stronger, yes? A woman has greater needs. A woman has greater will. A woman, when she decides to be, is much more dedicated. Much more determined, yes? More* focused *on her need.*"

Del's voice echoed oddly. "*Some might say, more obsessed.*"

"*But yes—yes, of course! Obsession is necessary. Obsession is required. Obsession is the master when compassion undermines.*" I heard Chosa laugh. "*Now I understand. Now I comprehend. More than a jivatma. More than a blooding-blade. More than a sword-dancer's weapon; it is your second soul. It is a second you—*"

"*No!*" Del snapped. "*I'm more than just a sword. More than just a weapon.* More *than a need for vengeance—*"

Chosa sounded startled. "*What is greater than vengeance when it has brought you so far? It has shaped you; it has* made *you—*"

"*I made me! I made this jivatma. It didn't make me.*"

"*It unmade you,*" Chosa answered, "*to make you something else, yes? To make you what you required; vengeance is powerful.*" The sorcerer's voice altered subtly. "*Tell me the sword's name.*"

One thing she's not, is stupid.

"*Chosa Dei,*" Del answered promptly. "*Now go unmake yourself—*"

The voices faded again. Del and Chosa were gone.

Oh, hoolies, bascha—can't you sing out again? Just to give me a little clue?

Chosa's voice boomed loud; a trick of the tunnels again. "*You will tell me the name, yes? While you still have both feet, both hands? While you still have both your breasts?*"

I called him every name I could think of. But I did it silently.

Except for raspy breathing and echoing bootsteps as I ran.

Branch upon branch upon branch. But the light was growing brighter. The stench even more offensive. And Chosa Dei's threats were imperative; I heard the whine and snarl of gathering hounds. The wheezing of a bellows.

Bellows?

Light slashed briefly through a crack in the tunnel wall, glinting off my blade. I stopped short, muttered a curse as sore muscles complained, put out my hand toward the crack. Warm air and smoke wisped through; that, and ruddy light.

I pressed myself against the wall, jamming my face into the crack. I saw light and fire and smoke; all three made my eye water. Tears ran down my face.

I swore, changed eyes, tried to see specifics.

Saw men tending a fire. Men tending a *forge;* Chosa Dei was playing at smith.

Rock bit into my forehead as I slumped against the wall. I couldn't believe what I'd seen. Couldn't trust my eyes. But a second look confirmed it: Chosa Dei had a forge. Men were tending a bellows. He had been stealing *jivatmas*, and now he wanted Del's. So he could break free of the wards set by Shaka Obre.

Chosa Dei had more than a forge. He had a crucible. He was melting down *jivatmas*. Unmaking them, for their magic; to use for his own designs.

And now he wanted Boreal. Now he needed a banshee-storm and all the wild magic of the North in order to burst his bonds. To bring the mountain down so the dragon could fly again.

The voice came through the crack. *"—was powerful, once. I can be again. But I need the wild magic. I have to restore myself; to banish diminishment, yes? To make myself whole again, so I can unmake my brother."*

Del's answer was lost in the roar of newborn flame fanned into life by the bellows. I saw it sucked up, then out; saw it pass through the curtain that Del and I had faced. And at last I had my bearings.

Now all I had to do was find a way out of the

tunnels and into the second chamber on the far side of the curtain.

Where I would do—what?

Hoolies, I don't know. Cut Chosa's *gehetties* off—if sorcerers have *gehetties*—and give them to Del as a trophy.

If she was alive to receive them.

If she was in one piece.

Hang on, Delilah. The Sandtiger's on his w—

The hounds began to chorus.

Chosa Dei's voice rose above it. *"—can unsing any song. I can unmake any sword. Shall we try it, yes?"*

—don't let her die again—

Running. Stumbling. Swearing. Coughing in the smoke. Squinting against the light—*light* . . . hoolies, the tunnel floor was broken. The cracks were open fissures leading straight down into the chamber behind Shaka Obre's wards.

I threw myself to the tunnel floor and stuck my head into one of the fissures. Held my breath against odor and smoke as tears sprang into my eyes. Blinked my vision clear; saw, in the instant before tears returned, the glint of Del's *jivatma*. Saw the circle of beasts pressing close.

And Chosa Dei below me.

If I could drop my sword straight down, I could split his head like a melon.

Then again, I might miss. And give him another *jivatma*.

You can't tell much about a man when all you can see of him is the top of his head and shoulders. Eyes will tell you a lot; so will expression and posture. I could see none of those things. Only dark hair and dark-swathed shoulders.

But I could see Del clearly.

She was completely ringed by beasts. Within the circle, she stood umoving; carefully, utterly still. In her arms was Boreal: diagonal slash from left to right, cutting across her breasts. Forgeglow lighted the steel. Wardglow turned it red.

Del could change the color. She only had to sing.

But Chosa Dei could unsing her songs. Del had no weapon to use.

Leaving me with mine.

Hoolies, what do I do?

Chosa Dei spoke again. "Shall I show you how I unmake a man? How I remake him into a beast?"

Del said nothing.

"Yes, I think I shall."

Transfixed, I stared in disbelief. Del stood imprisoned by hounds, helpless to stop the sorcerer. Thus free to do as he wanted, Chosa Dei called over one of the men who tended the forge and dismissed the other three. The fourth one knelt, and Chosa put hands on his head.

Part of me screamed at the man to escape, to pull away, to get free of Chosa Dei. But he did none of those things. He just knelt in silence, staring blankly, as Chosa put hands on him.

"No," Del said quietly.

Chosa's voice was as quiet. "Oh, I think yes."

He unmade the man. Don't ask me how. All I know is the shape of the man altered somehow, *was* altered somehow, slowly and subtly, until the nose was thrust outward, the jaw pushed backward, the shoulders folded inward, hips rebent into haunches—the man was no more a man but a *thing* in bestial form.

Eyes shone whitely. A tail was pulled out of buttocks. He—it—the thing—bent upon the rock floor with the joints and hair of a hound, and nothing at all of humanity.

"No," Del repeated, but the tone was shaped by horror.

"Unmade," Chosa said. "Now he will join the others. And perhaps *he* will take your throat."

Oh, hoolies. Oh, *gods*—

I shut my eyes a moment, then forced myself to look.

Smoke gushed up from the forge. Most of it was

sucked through the curtain as the wards allowed it to go. The rest dispersed in the chamber, escaping through cracks, fissures, and holes.

Cracks, fissures, and *holes;* mouthing obscenities, I pressed my face more tightly against the fissure and looked for the proper sign. Saw it almost immediately; lunged up and ran down the tunnel all of twelve paces farther, where the hole greeted me. My entrance into the chamber.

It was the largest of them all; I knew from watching the smoke. The greatest amount had been sucked through here, but it wasn't saying much. Del couldn't get through, *maybe*, but I doubted I could. Unless I was stark naked and painted with alla salve.

Flesh quailed; so did spirit. The idea of dropping down unannounced—and bare-butted—to face a sorcerer was not a pretty thought. A lot of me didn't like it.

Especially my *gehetties.*

So, I'd compromise. *Half* of my clothes would come off.

I knelt by the hole and set the sword aside, then unhooked the wide leather belt with its weight of ornamental bosses, which could catch and scrape and grate. Then off came the harness itself, stripped over arms and head without undoing the buckles. And finally both tunics, which I dropped aside without thought. Cool tunnel air chafed bare chest and arms and set the flesh to rising.

First to test briefly: I eased boots and legs down into the hole punched through the rock, then braced forearms and elbows on either side and channeled my weight through shoulders. I lowered myself carefully. Felt hips catch briefly; a twist eased them through. But above them the spread of my rib cage and shoulder sockets promised to wedge me painfully if I didn't take steps to avoid it.

Hoolies, but it hurt—I pulled myself up again, blowing noisy breath between gritted teeth, and clambered out of the hole once more.

Chosa's voice drifted up: *"My beasts are growing hungry. Tell me the name of your sword."*

Come on, Del; hang on . . . I'm doing what I can.

A quick glance showed me jagged protrusions in the rock wall. I knew I'd have to jump when it came right down to it, but I wanted to shorten the distance. The easiest way was to use belt and harness to lower myself through the hole as far as I could go, then drop the rest of the way.

I'd risk breaking a leg. But I was risking so much anyway it didn't really matter.

I snugged the belt around the most promising stone protrusion, then buckled it firmly. I cut the sheath free of the harness, which left me with a crisscross affair of leather straps, and quickly severed the thong stitching. Then looped everything through the belt and dangled it down the hole.

Not very much. But something.

Meanwhile, there was the sword. I couldn't very well carry it down with me as I worked my way through the hole; the extra bulk would end the attempt. And I didn't dare tie it to my body with shredded bits of tunic; if I lost it by accident, Chosa would have a new *jivatma*. And I sort of wanted to keep it until I could stick it in him.

So I very carefully placed it beside the hole opposite my planned entry, and began to ease myself down.

In the tunnel, a beast bayed.

I froze. I didn't particularly relish the thought of being attacked while wedged in the hole; I prefer a fair fight. So I pulled myself up again, grabbed the sword, and made it as far as my knees as the hound leaped out of shadow.

I was getting tired of this. I'd just as soon not have to do it.

On knees, I battled the hound. My balance was off, and my leverage, but clean steel still parts beast flesh. The spray of blood slicked my chest and dribbled down my belly to the drawstring of my trews.

Which gave me an idea.

In the dimness, I saw eyes. The shine of white hound eyes. But this beast turned tail and ran, which was a welcome change.

Again I set the blade carefully beside the jagged hole. Then scooped up dripping handfuls of beast blood and slapped it all over my chest and sides, paying particular attention to the rib cage beneath my armpits, where the spread of bone and muscle was greatest, and to the shoulder joints themselves where they met my upper arms.

Hoolies, but I stink.

No more time to waste—

I slid boots over the lip, took an extra wrap in the harness straps around my left wrist, and lowered myself down.

Hips slid through again, though fabric snagged a little. And my waist, all slick with blood even though it didn't need it. And then my lower ribs. The upper ones stuck fast.

It is a particularly vulnerable sensation to be stuck like a cork in a bottle. From the waist down I was completely accessible, but I couldn't see past my rib cage.

There was still slack in the harness straps. I braced my right arm against the lip of the hole and pushed, trying to twist myself free. Layers of skin peeled away, stinging in protest. And finally I slipped free, leaving bits of me on stone teeth. My shoulder joints lost flesh also, then obligingly added my own blood to the slime already present.

It was enough to loosen the cork; I dropped, felt the straps tauten, winced as the loop snugged around my left wrist. All of my weight hung from it; I wished I weighed a bit less.

My head was level with the bottom of the hole. I peered down past my body and tried to judge the distance. It was still dangerously far from the floor— about seven of me hooked together—and the landing would be on rock. If I didn't break a leg, I'd probably break my head.

The sword still lay in the tunnel. Carefully I began pulling myself back up one-armed, sliding my right arm up through the hole. All I needed was a little lift; then I'd snatch the sword, hold it vertically, and drop straight down to the floor.

To get my bearings, I glanced down. And saw Chosa Dei with a hound.

Hoolies, he was *eating* it!—no, no he wasn't . . . he was—hoolies, I don't *know* . . . something, something disgusting . . . he knelt down before it and put his hands on its head . . . he said something to it, *did* something to it—and the hound began to change.

It melted. I have no better word for it. The beast melted from this known shape into something else. Something vaguely human, but without humanity.

He was *un*making the beast. Making the man again.

Hanging from my harness, I was very nearly sick. I had not, until that moment, realized the full implication of Chosa Dei's powers. If he was free, if he *got* free . . . once he unmade his brother, what would he do to others? By "collecting" all the magic, would he then remake the world?

Chosa Dei rose, leaving the half-made thing on the floor where it twitched and spasmed and died. "Someone is here," he said. "Someone *else* is here . . . hiding in the tunnels. Hiding in my mountain." He swept the chamber with a glance. "And he has a second *jivatma*, fully quenched and blooded."

Hoolies. Oh, *hoolies*—

"There!" Chosa cried, and pointed directly at me.

I saw Del's upturned face. I saw the mass of hounds. Knew what I had to do.

Unmake Chosa Dei.

Straining upward, I thrust my right hand up through the hole and scrabbled at the lip. Touched the blade, traced it back to the hilt, lurched up to lock fingers around it. Began to think of a song as I dropped back through the hole to dangle on my harness.

Beneath me swarmed the hounds, waiting for me to fall.

A song. Think of a song. Of something personal. Of something *powerful*. Of something no one but the Sandtiger fully comprehends.

I thought of the South. I thought of the desert. And then I thought of the Punja with its deadly simooms and sciroccos, the scouring wind-blast of sand that could strip a man bare of flesh, polishing his bones. I thought of the sun and the sand and the heat and the power of a storm blowing the Punja here and there, feckless as a goat kid, going where it was told. Because there is a greater power than merely heat and sand. There is also the desert wind. A hot dry wind. A wind composed of a violence equal to Chosa Dei's.

Scorching desert windstorm stripping everything down to the bone. Scirocco and simoom. But also called *samiel*.

Inside, I sang a song. Of blooding, of quenching, of keying. Of unmaking a sorcerer who thought only Del's *jivatma* was capable of great power.

Your mistake, Chosa. Now come grapple with *me*—

I sliced through the harness and dropped.

Sixteen

I landed in squirming bodies full of teeth and claws and foul breath. Thanked them for breaking my fall. Then disengaged myself, though my body remained where it was.

Heat—sand—sun . . . the blast of a samiel—

The blast of Samiel, loosed to cleanse the mountain of beasts and sorcerer.

Scorching, scouring sun—blistered, weeping flesh— cracked and bleeding lips—

Del and I had lived it. But Chosa wouldn't survive.

The chanting of the Salset, gathered to celebrate the changing of the year . . . the high-pitched whining of the shukar praying to his gods . . . the hoots and shrieks of desert borjuni, riding down a caravan . . . the clash and clatter of Hanjii with gold rings in nose and ears . . .

Music; all of it music; the song of desert life. The music of the Punja; the music of *my* life.

—dull chiming of the chains binding me into the mine—

—chink of chisel on rock; the crumble of falling reef thick with the promise of gold—

—squealing and snorting and stomping as the stud protests my wishes—

A personal, powerful song no one else can sing.

—the sobbing of a boy with a back afire from the lash, trying to hide his pain; trying to hide humiliation—

No one else knew these things.

—the song of a blued-steel blade; the song of

156

Singlestroke, gifting me with freedom; with life and pride and strength—

And the scream of an angry cat flowing down from a pile of stones.

Only I knew these things.

Only I could sing my life.

Only I could unmake Chosa Dei—

Scirocco. Simoom. Samiel.

Try your best, Chosa Dei—you can't unsing *this* song.

Dimly I heard the hounds. The whine of Boreal. The snatch of Delilah's song as she hewed through flesh and bone.

Dimly I heard Chosa Dei, but I couldn't make out his words. Everything in my head was part of my personal song.

Everything in my song was part of Samiel.

Take him. Take him. Take him.

Dimly, Del shouted.

Take him—take him—take him—

Del was shouting at me.

—take him—take him—

—*unmake him*—

"Tiger—Tiger, *no* . . . you don't know what you're doing—"

—*sing him into your song*—

"Tiger, it's *forbidden*—"

Samiel splintered ribs.

Flesh, blood, muscle and bone; Samiel wanted it all.

"Tiger—Tiger *no*—"

Samiel sang his song.

All I could do was listen.

Muscles spasmed. Arms and legs jerked; so did my head. I smacked it against the chamber floor.

Why is my head on the floor?

Why is *any* of me on the floor?

Opened eyes: saw chamber ceiling. Saw *several* chamber ceilings, until I could focus again.

Hoolies, what's wrong with me?

I sat up, wished I hadn't, lay back down again.

Hoolies. Oh, *hoolies*.

What have I been doing?

Much as I'm a man for keeping my aches to myself, I emitted a raspy groan. As well as a favorite obscenity, followed by a string of lesser favorites, until I ran out of breath.

By then Del was back.

"So," she said, "you survived."

I waited a beat. "Did I?"

Del's face was blood-spattered. Hair hung in ruddy ribbons. "I had my doubts at first when I saw you weren't breathing. But I punched you in the chest and you started right up again."

Thoughtfully, I rubbed a sore spot. It was right over my heart. "Why did you punch me?"

"I told you: you weren't breathing. It was your own fault, and I was angry." She shrugged. "It seems a valuable trick, this punching in the chest."

I explored my blood-crusted chest which seemed to be sore in more than one place. There were bite wounds and claw welts in addition to stinging scrapes. "Why wasn't I breathing?"

"Because you were a stupid, senseless, deaf, dumb and blind fool . . . a man so full of himself he has no time for others, and gives no *heed* to others when they're trying to save his life, since he seemed bent on losing it. And you nearly *did;* Tiger, you are a fool! What did you think to accomplish? Sacrificing yourself *or* your sanity is not a useful thing. *Not* a useful thing; did you spare no thought for me? Did you think I *wanted* you dead just to pay you back for nearly killing me?"

From the floor, I stared up at her. Her anger was truly awesome. "What did I do?" I asked.

"What did you do? What did you *do?*"

I nodded. "What did I do?"

Del pointed. "That."

It was hard to see from the floor. So I very slowly and very carefully levered myself up and leaned on one elbow. Looked at where she was pointing.

Someone—some*thing*—was dead. The remains were sprawled on the floor.

"I did *that?*"

Del lowered her arm. "You have no idea, have you? You truly don't know what you did."

"Apparently I killed someone. Or something; what *is* that?"

"Chosa Dei," she answered. Then, ominously: "Chosa Dei's *body*. His spirit is somewhere else."

"Hoolies, not here, I hope. I'd just as soon not tangle with him again any time soon." I sat up all the way. Glanced around the chamber. "I see you did in the hounds."

"I did. You did. What is important is that they are dead. I think all of them are dead." She shrugged. "Not that it matters now, since Chosa Dei is—gone."

I rolled shoulders gently, rubbed at tension in my neck. "Well, it's what we came to do. Now Ysaa-den is safe, and so are all the *jivatmas*."

"Oh?" Del asked. "Are you so certain of that?"

"He's *dead,* isn't he? Isn't that Chosa Dei?"

"His body," she repeated. "His soul is in your sword."

I stopped breathing again. "His soul is *where?*"

"In your sword," she answered. "What do you think you did?"

"Killed him." I paused. "Didn't I? I took him through the ribs. It *should* have killed him."

"Not that. I don't mean that. I mean what you did when you sang."

A chill washed across flesh. "What?"

Del's eyes sharpened. "You sang. Don't you remember? You dropped down from the roof of the chamber into a mass of hounds, and all the way you sang. You didn't stop once." She shrugged. "It wasn't very *good*—you have a truly terrible voice—but that doesn't matter. What matters is that you meant it. What matters is that it worked. You unmade Chosa Dei, but you also *re*made your sword."

"What?"

Del spelled it out. "You requenched, Tiger. Just like Theron did."

Theron. I thought back months and months and recalled the Northern sword-dancer who had come south hunting Del. He had a *jivatma*, as she did; a true-made, true-quenched *jivatma*. But he had addressed a new need and requenched his Northern blade in the body of a magician. It had given him an edge. It had nearly defeated Del. Nearly defeated me.

"Well," I said finally. "I didn't do it on purpose."

Del turned on her heel and walked away. I think she was still angry, though I didn't really know why. I had just saved her life. I had just saved the world.

I smiled wryly at that. Then worked my way to my feet and went over to the body.

Well, it was sort of a body. It was charred and shrunken and crisped, collapsed upon itself. It was half the size of me. It was smaller even than Del.

Does a soul take up that much room?

It was odd looking down on the remains of a man I'd never seen, but killed. There were no recognizable features, no normal hair, nothing that spoke of a man. He was a shape, nothing more; it left a bad taste in my mouth.

From the pile of loose cloth and crisped flesh gleamed the hilt of my requenched *jivatma*. Chosa Dei's new prison.

"I'll break it," I said. "I'll melt it." I glanced at the crucible. "I'll melt it into slag, then get me a Southron sword."

Del spun. "You *can't!*"

"Why not? I don't want to lug around a sword with *him* in it."

Del's face was white. "You have to lug it around. You have to carry it forever, until we find a way to discharge it. Don't you understand? Chosa Dei is *in* there. If you destroy the sword, you'll destroy his prison. You're his ward now. His own personal ward. Only you can keep him imprisoned."

I very nearly laughed. "Del, this is ridiculous. Are you really going to stand there and tell me that Chosa Dei is *in* my sword, and that if *I personally* don't guard him, he might get out again?"

Under the blood, she was white. "Always," she said, "always. Always you must doubt."

"You've got to admit it sounds pretty farfetched," I told her. "I mean, *you* were the one who told me Chosa Dei was only a legend, something someone made up for stories."

"I was wrong," she declared.

I stared at her. Here I'd been trying to get her to admit such a thing for the last two weeks with regard to her behavior on Staal-Ysta, and she still hadn't done it. But she was more than willing to say the three magical words when it came to Chosa Dei—or *who*-ever he was.

I itched all over from sweat and crusted, smelly blood. Thoughtfully, I scratched through my beard to complaining flesh beneath. "Let me see," I said. "You expect me to spend the rest of my life making sure Chosa Dei stays put."

"No, not your whole life. Only until the sword can be discharged."

I frowned. "How do we do that? And what exactly *is* it?"

Del lifted her own sword, still clasped in her right hand. "There is power in here," she said. "Wild magic, and controlled magic—the control comes from a proper blooding and keying, as well as strength of will. But there is a way of discharging the power, of channeling it elsewhere, so the sword is a sword again." She shrugged. "Magic is magic, Tiger—it has a life of its own. That's why, when Theron died, you could use his *jivatma*. The magic had been discharged."

That, I didn't much like. "So, you're saying if I died, my sword would discharge *its* magic—along with Chosa Dei."

Del's brows arched. "That is one way, yes. But then you would be dead; what sense is there in discharging a sword if you won't be alive to use it?"

I didn't even bother to reply to that. "Is there another way?"

"Yes. But it was not a thing taught on Staal-Ysta."

"Where *is* it taught?"

Del shook his head. "I think it would take someone who understood the magic of *jivatmas*. Someone also who understood Chosa Dei, and the threat he represents. Because Chosa Dei himself is powerful; if the discharging were not done properly, he might free himself."

"He'd have no body," I pointed out. "This one is sort of a mess."

Del shrugged. "He'd find another. It might even be yours, since by then he'll know you so well."

Flesh froze. "What?"

Del sighed, frowning, as if frustrated by my ignorance. "Chosa Dei is no longer *alive,* no more than Baldur is in *my* sword. But his spirit is there, and his soul; the things he most believes in. You will feel it, Tiger. You will feel *him.* After a while you will know him—you will *have* to—and he will know you."

I scowled. "Does he know he's in this sword?"

Del shrugged. "But even if he doesn't, it doesn't really matter. Chosa Dei unmakes things to reshape them to his desires. He will try the same with your sword."

"What if I gave it to someone else?"

Del smiled crookedly. "What blooded, named *jivatma* allows anyone else to touch it?"

"If I told him Samiel's name, he could."

One of her shoulders twitched. "Yes. You could. And then he could touch your sword. But not being you, he could hardly control the magic. Nor control Chosa Dei."

I said something brief and very explicit.

Del ignored it. "I wonder . . ." she murmured.

"Wonder? Wonder what? What are you nattering about now?"

Her face was pensive. "Shaka Obre."

"Chosa's brother? Why?"

"Because maybe, just maybe, he might be able to help."

"He's a *story,* bascha."

"So was Chosa Dei."

I scowled. Considered it. "I don't need any help from a wizard."

"Tiger—"

"I can handle this on my own."

Pale brows arched. "Oh?"

"Just give me a little time. I'll work something out. Meanwhile, let's get out of here."

I made it three steps. "Tiger."

I swung back. "What?"

Del pointed at my sword, still mostly buried in Chosa's remains.

"Oh." I went over, bent down, didn't quite touch the hilt. "What's supposed to happen?"

"I don't know."

"That's helpful," I told her. "I thought you knew all this stuff."

"I know *some* 'stuff,' " she agreed. "But you've done something no one else has ever done."

"No one?"

"No one. *An-ishtoyas* seeking the blooding-journey always take sponsors with them to prevent disasters like this."

"So what you're saying is, I'm on my own."

Mute, Del nodded.

Being best at something is often entertaining. But being *first* is a little different; it can be dangerous. And I've never been quite cocky enough to risk myself like that.

I sucked in a deep breath, stretched out my hand—

"May I suggest something?" Del inquired.

My hand jerked back. *"What?"*

"Make certain you are stronger. Now. This moment. If Chosa senses any weakness, he will use it for himself."

I cast her a baleful glance. Then straightened and *kicked* the sword out of the crispy, shrunken pile of cloth, bones, and flesh.

Steel clanged across the stone floor. Nothing happened. The sword just lay there.

Except the blade was dull.

Frowning, I stepped across the remains and stared down at the sword. The hilt was the same as always—bright, brilliant steel—but the blade was smudgy dull gray, almost black. The tip itself *was* black, as if it had been burned.

"All right," I said. "Why?"

Del stood next to me, sword in hand. She looked down at her own blade, which was a pale salmon-silver. When keyed, it burned richer and brighter. Nothing approaching black. No *jivatma* I'd ever seen had ever been this color.

"I don't know," she said. "No one knows what the color will be until the *jivatma* shows it."

"But you think this is it."

Del sighed a little. "I think so. It comes on the heels of quenching and keying."

"I don't like black or gray. I'd prefer something brighter. Something more desertlike."

Del stared at me in amazement.

Defensively, I shrugged. "Well, we all have our preferences. Mine isn't gray and black."

"Maybe it's what happens when you requench."

I stood staring down at the dull-bladed sword, hands on hips, chewing a bloody lip. Then, with an impatient twitch of shoulders, I bent and picked it up.

Nothing happened. Nothing at all. The sword felt cold and dead.

I frowned. "What's it supposed—"

"Tiger!"

This time I landed flat on my rump on the floor with my knees bent up, feet flat, bracing myself upright, and stared in astonishment at the sword lying but three feet away.

Still gray and black. But the black was a little higher.

Del's hand was over her mouth. After a moment, she spoke through her fingers. "Are you all right?"

"Did you have to punch me again in the chest?"

"No."

"Then I guess I'm all right." It hurt more this time to stand up, but I managed it with a minimum of fuss. And then I stood there for a moment or two, trying to banish disorientation, and scowled at the sword. "He's angry."

"Who?"

"Samiel. Chosa Dei is just shocked. He didn't realize he was dead—or whatever it is he is."

Del took a step forward. "Does *he* know?"

"Know what?"

"Where Shaka Obre is?"

"Oh, for hoolies—" I glared. "I said I'd handle this, bascha—*without* Shaka Obre's help."

"It was a thought," Del commented.

I walked to the sword. "Right now all I want to think about is leaving."

"How?" Del asked. "Don't you remember what happened the last time we tried to go through the wards?"

I remember very well. You don't often forget waking up in the middle of a tunnel in a mountain shaped like a dragon. "But now Chosa Dei is dead, so the wards are out of a job. Besides, I think if we used a piece of this Northern magic you're always talking about, we ought to be able to figure out a way."

"Only if you can figure out how to pick up your sword."

Basically, it was easy. All I had to do was show Chosa Dei who's boss.

Del and I crossed to the "curtain." Further study told us nothing more than we already knew: the thing was a ward set by Shaka Obre, intended to keep Chosa Dei imprisoned. It let out the smoke, let people in—though where they wound up was not quite certain, as I could testify—and prevented Chosa's escape.

Prevented *our* escape.

Sweat ran down my temples. "Now," I suggested, gripping the hilt with both hands.

Del frowned at me. "You don't look—"

The blade shook; *I* shook. "Now. Not tomorrow."

Del turned, raised her sword, glanced across at me. I mimicked her posture; together we sliced through the curtain as if it were nothing but silk.

Wards wisped into smoke. The prison was breached at last.

After six hundred and forty-two years, Chosa Dei was free of his mountain.

But until we found Shaka Obre, I'd never be free of Chosa.

Seventeen

We sat in the headman's lodge in Ysaa-den, repairing what we could of battered flesh and spirits. We were alone, as always, being honored with solitude. With one another's help we had washed blood and grime and stink off, replacing missing or ruined clothing with articles given us by Halvar and his wife. Now I sat on a warm pelt with eyes scrunched closed, legs crossed, gritting teeth as Del tended puncture wounds and tooth tears with herbal paste.

"Sit still," she commanded as my eyes snapped open.

"It *hurts*."

"I know it hurts. It will hurt worse if you let these bites get infected. Especially this one *here*."

She did it on purpose. I flinched, swore at her; swore at her harder as she merely smiled and smeared more salve into a bite very low on my belly. Del had peeled the loosened waistband of my trews away, baring scraped and bitten skin, and now took pleasure in poking and prodding.

"I can do it," I said. "For that matter, Halvar's *wife* can do it; she offered."

"Everyone in Ysaa-den offered, Tiger; you're a hero. They will give you anything you ask, if they can." Del sat back on her heels. "Am I to suppose you want their two copper pennies, now?"

She wore blue in place of filthy white, a cool soft blue that heightened the color of her eyes. Pale lashes, pale hair, paler skin; she was, no doubt, feeling every

167

bit as tired and battered as me. But somehow she didn't look it.

"No," I answered testily. "All I want is to be rid of this sword, so I can live in peace. Or, more immediately, a warm bed and a bota of aqivi; since this is the North, I'll take *amnit*."

"You'll get your *amnit*. You'll even get your bed. As to the warmth of it, that will depend on how many women you put in it."

I grunted. I was so full of bruises, bites, scrapes, scratches and claw scores I doubted I could provide much pleasure for a bedpartner. Especially since what I most wanted to do was sleep.

"The meal first," Del reminded, as my eyes drooped closed. "It's a celebration."

"Can't they celebrate without me?"

"No. Then they would have no one for whom to sing their song of salvation and gratitude."

I grunted again. "There's you."

"But *I* didn't kill Chosa Dei."

"You killed half the hounds."

"Who once were villagers." Del's tone was serious. "I think we need not tell that part of the story. Let them think the hounds simply killed their kinfolk, instead of being remade into beasts who killed more people, including kin and friends." She stroked hair from her eyes. "It would be a kindness."

It would also be a lie, but one I understood. "Give me the tunics, then, so we can go get some food. My belly's screaming at me."

Del handed me first the undertunic of soft-combed undyed wool; then, as I dragged it on, she presented the green overtunic. It rattled with intricate beadwork: bronze, copper, and amber.

"This is too much," I muttered. "He's giving away his best."

"A measure of his respect and gratitude." Del's tone, as it can be, was bland.

Frustrated, I glared at her. "I would have come anyway. It had nothing to do with Ysaa-den or their troubles; it had to do with the hounds. If they'd gone somewhere else, *I'd* have gone somewhere else."

"But they didn't, and neither did you." Del got up slowly, suppressing a wince of discomfort. She wore her sword as usual, hanging in harness across her back. "They're waiting for us, Tiger. We're the guests of honor."

I frowned, rising carefully. Little by little I was losing my links with the South. First Singlestroke, broken fighting Theron. Then my Southron silks and gauzes, traded for Northern leather and fur. And lastly my harness, discarded in Chosa Dei's mountain. Bit by bit by bit, scattered along the way.

I gathered up my *jivatma*, lacking sheath as well as harness, and followed Del out of the lodge. There was nothing, *nothing* about her even remotely Southron. Northern bascha to the bone, no matter where she was. I was being altered, while Del remained the same.

Time to go home, I said.

But I said it to myself.

Hot food, fiery *amnit*, and warm wishes all conspired to make it extremely difficult for me to stay awake during the celebratory meal. The evening air was growing chilly, but in addition to new wool clothing I also wore two pelts. I sat like a furry lump on yet a third pelt, managing to keep my eyes open a slit as Halvar regaled—in uplander—the village with my exploits.

Well, *our* exploits; Del was not left out.

"Stay awake," she hissed, sitting on the pelt next to mine.

"I'm trying. Hoolics, bascha—what do you expect? Aren't *you* tired after everything we did?"

"No," she answered cruelly. "I'm too young for it."

I chose to ignore that, since I knew very well she was lying. Maybe she wasn't yet *sleepy*, but certainly she was sore. It showed in all her movements. It showed when she sat very still. "How much longer do we have to sit out here?"

"Until the celebration is finished." Del watched Halvar, half-following his words even as she spoke to me. "We've eaten, and now Halvar's retelling the story. Once that's done, they'll all sing a song of deliverance. Then everyone will sit around retelling the story, marveling at the accomplishment, and drink to your health." She paused, observing me. "But since, from the look of you, I doubt you can manage that, you'll probably be able to slip away."

I nodded, stifling a yawn. It took all the strength I had.

Halvar said something to Del, glanced past her to me— Del had wound up beside the headman to translate— and repeated to me whatever it was he'd said to Del, just to be polite. I caught one word out of twenty: *song.*

I nodded. "Sing, then. I'm listening."

Del slanted me a disapproving glance, then spoke briefly to Halvar. In response the headman grinned, turned to the gathered villagers all wrapped in warmest furs, and announced something. Yet again I saw musical instruments brought out.

I sat there with a polite smile pasted onto my face and tried to look interested as Ysaa-den launched into song. My own bout with singing in order to defeat Chosa Dei had not resulted in improved comprehension or appreciation; it all sounded like noise to me, though admittedly with a pattern. I suppose it was even pretty, if you like that kind of thing.

Del apparently did. She sat all wrapped in white fur with her eyes fixed on distances, losing herself in the music. I wondered if it took her back to her childhood, when her kinfolk had gathered to sing. And I wondered, suddenly, if *she* had ever sung to anything or anyone other than her sword.

At the end of the song Halvar turned yet again to us and said something. This time Del looked surprised.

"What?" I asked, rousing.

"He's bringing the holy man out to throw oracle bones."

"So, the old man likes to gamble."

Del waved a hand. "No, no—to *really* throw the bones, as they were meant to be thrown. Before people began using them for wagering."

I wanted to say something more, but the old holy man had appeared. He stopped before us, bowed to us both, then sat down on the spotted pelt Halvar carefully spread. He was a *very* old man, as holy men often are, having stuffed so much ritual into a single life. With the Salset there'd been the shukar, sort of a holy man/magician; I wondered if Northern customs were the same.

The old man—white-haired, blue-eyed and palsied—seemed to be waiting for something. And then one of the younger men brought a low tripod and set it carefully before him. Onto the triple prongs was placed a platter of polished gold. Its rim, curving upward gently, was worked in Northern runes.

I blinked. "I thought you said Ysaa-den had only two copper pennies."

"In coin," Del agreed. "That's an oracle stand and platter. Each village has one . . . unless it's stolen, or traded away." She shrugged. "Some of the old ways die when the need to survive is greater."

The old man took a leather pouch from beneath his furs and carefully untied the drawstring. He poured the contents into one palm: a handful of polished stones. They were opaque but oddly translucent; pale, pearlescent white showing green and red and blue as the old man spread them in his hand. One was fiery black, but alive with so many colors I couldn't name them all.

I frowned. "Those aren't really bones. Those are stones. Oracle bones are *bones*."

"Bones of the earth," Del said. "They've been carefully carved and polished."

I grunted. "Maybe so, but they're not the sort of oracle bones *I'm* used to."

"These work," she agreed.

I opened my mouth to protest—yet *another* story—but didn't say anything. Even though I didn't believe in foretelling, I knew perfectly well what Del would throw in my face if I said anything rude about the old man and his stones. She'd mention Chosa Dei, whom even *she* thought was a story until he'd nearly killed her.

So I didn't give her the chance.

The old man threw his stones onto the golden platter. They rattled and slid, as expected, falling into random patterns. Only to the man who uses them to foretell, the patterns are never random. That much even I knew.

He threw seven times before he spoke. And then he said a single word.

This time Del frowned.

"Jhihadi," the old man repeated.

Del glanced at Halvar, ignoring me entirely. "I don't understand."

Halvar shook his head, mystified as Del.

"Jhihadi," the old man said, and swept the stones into his hand.

A great silence lay over the gathering. No doubt everyone had expected profound words of wisdom, or a promise of good health. Instead, the holy man of Ysaa-den had given them a word none of them knew.

"Jhihadi," I said quietly, "is a Southron word."

"Southron?" Del frowned. "Why? What has a Southron word to do with us?"

"Actually, it's Desert, not pure Southron . . . and it might have something to do with the fact that *I* am, after all, Southron." I smiled benignly. "Although, knowing the word, I doubt it indicates me personally." I grinned at her, then shrugged. "He must mean something else, or some*one* else; he is old, after all, and those are just pretty stones."

"Why?" she asked suspiciously. "What does 'jhihadi' mean?"

"Messiah," I said plainly.

Braids whipped as she turned instantly and faced the holy man. She asked him something courteously, but I heard the underlying doubt. The need for an explanation.

Obligingly, the old man threw the stones again. And again they fetched up into varied patterns, none of which I could read.

He studied them, then nodded. "Jhihadi," he repeated. And then added something in uplander, ending in yet another Desert word.

"Iskandar?" I said sharply. "What's Iskandar got to do with this?"

Del looked at me blankly. "I don't know what that *is*."

"An old story," I said dismissively. "Iskandar is a place, named after a man who was supposedly a messiah. I don't know how much truth there is to the tale—you know how stories can get all twisted up." We stared frowning at one another, thinking about Chosa Dei. "Anyway, Iskandar was where this supposed messiah met his death."

Del's eyes were intent. "Was he murdered? Executed?"

I grinned. "Nothing so romantic. His horse kicked him in the head; he died ten days later. Which is why there are questions about his identity, since a true messiah shouldn't be physically vulnerable." I shrugged. "I don't know much about it, really, since it's not the sort of thing I pay much attention to . . . I just know that on his deathbed he promised to come back. But since that was hundreds of years ago and Iskandar lies in ruins, I have my doubts about this jhihadi the old man's talking about."

Del still frowned, locking brows together. "He says we're going there."

"Iskandar?" I didn't bother to hide my amusement. "Then the old man must be sandsick."

Del chewed her lip. "If Ajani's there—"

"He won't be. I promise, bascha . . . Iskandar is a ruin; no one goes there. Not even Ajani would, unless he likes to talk with ghosts."

"Then why would the holy man say so?"

After a judicious glance around at the gathered villagers, I couched my words politely. "Shall we just say that sometimes people try to protect pronounce-ments by insisting they're true when they're not?"

"He isn't lying," Del declared.

I winced. Here I'd been so careful to speak diplo-matically, and now Del was being too blunt.

"No," I agreed. "Did I say he was?"

"You said—"

"I said perhaps he was mistaken. Now, are we done yet? Can we go to bed?"

Del turned back to the holy man and asked some-thing in uplander. Accordingly, he threw the stones once again. Then told her what he read.

"Well?" I prodded, when she didn't translate for me.

"Oracle," she said. "There is an Oracle."

"Those are oracle *bones*—"

"No, not bones—*oracle*. A man is foretelling the com-ing of the jhihadi." Del's expression was blank as she stared at me. "A man who is not a man, but neither is he a woman." Now she frowned. "I don't understand."

"You're not supposed to, bascha. That's what these people trade on; they make coin off interpretation." I smiled at the holy man, inclined my head respectfully, then did the same to Halvar. "*Now* can we go to bed?"

Plainly, Del was irritated. "Oh, Tiger, I swear—you have become an old man. What happened to the days when you would sit up all night swilling *amnit* or aqivi, trading lies in cantinas?"

"I met you," I retorted. "I joined up with you and got the hoolies beat out of me more times than I can count." I stood up slowly and rewrapped pelts around my shoulders. "Is that answer enough for you?"

Del, taken aback, said nothing in return. I went off to bed.

Some time later I sat bolt upright in the darkness. Beside me, the sheathless sword was glowing. It was red as wind-whipped coals; hot as a smithy's forge. Hot as Chosa Dei's fire in the entrails of the dragon.

"No," I said clearly, and wrapped hands around the grip.

Shock jerked me rigid. Then I began to shake. It wasn't the heat of the sword, but the power surging through it. Raw, angry power, totally uncontrolled.

"No," I said again, moving onto my knees. Pelts fell away until I knelt half naked, wearing nothing but borrowed trews. I'd learned it was warmer sleeping naked under fur, but while in Ysaa-den I'd altered the habit a little. It seemed the courteous thing, although only Del shared the lodge.

Power ran through my hands, then crept the length of my arms until elbows and shoulders ached. "Hoolies take you," I gritted. "I already beat you once. I can do it again."

It hurt. Hoolies, it *hurt* . . . but I wouldn't give in to it. I can be stubborn that way.

Chosa Dei wasn't pleased. I sensed him in the sword, testing the confines of his prison. I wondered if he knew what had happened, if he understood his plight; if he realized he was dead. For a man such as he, accustomed to stealing lives as well as magic, it would be a horrific discovery to learn *his* life had been stolen, along with his remade magic.

He tested the blade again. I exerted my own strength of will. Felt rising curiosity; felt a need to understand.

And also felt Samiel trying to reabsorb the magic the sorcerer had borrowed.

How long? I wondered wearily. How long will this go on?

Power hesitated, then abruptly ran out again, leaving my arms numb. Slowly I unlocked my hands from around the grip and set the sword down again. I trembled with reaction; sweat bathed face and ribs.

Chill came rushing in, the kind that eats at bones. Shakily I crawled beneath pelts again, seeking leftover warmth. I snugged fur around my chin, then tried to relax arms and hands. When the shaking wouldn't stop, I thrust my hands between drawn-up knees and held them tightly in place. Waiting for the reaction to diminish.

A hand touched my rigid left shoulder, though I

could only just feel it through the pelts. "Tiger—are you all right?"

I sucked in a gut-deep breath, then blew it out again. Trying to steady my voice. "I thought you were still out with Halvar and all the others."

"It's very late. Nearly dawn. I've been in bed for hours."

Hours. Then she'd seen what had happened.

"Are you all right?" she repeated.

"Just leave me alone," I told her. "Let me go back to sleep."

"You're shaking. Are you cold?"

"Go back to bed, Del. You're keeping me awake."

Shock reverberated. The hand went away. In a moment so did Del, crawling back beneath her pelts all of three feet away from my own.

I lay there sweating, shaking, trying to still my hands while my arms threatened to cramp. I felt the strain in shoulder blades, traveling down to tie up my back. I didn't want to cramp; *hoolies*, don't let me cramp . . . I'd almost rather be knifed. At least the pain is cleaner.

Concentrate—*concentrate* . . . slowly, the trembling subsided. I took my hands from between my knees and felt the tendons slacken. The ghost pain of threatened cramp flowed slowly out of back and shoulders; at last I could fully relax. The relief was overwhelming.

I let out a rushing breath of gratitude. Then rolled over onto my left side, resetting pelts, and saw Del watching me.

She sat cross-legged on her bedding, one pelt wrapped around her body. There was not much light in the lodge, only a little from the coals. But pale hair and paler face caught the light and magnified it; I could see her face fairly well. I could see the expression on it.

"What?" I croaked.

She didn't answer at first, as if caught in some faraway place. She just stared at me fixedly, focused solely on my face.

With more emphasis: *"What?"*

Something glistened in her eyes. "I was wrong," she said.

I stared back, speechless.

"I was *wrong*," she repeated.

I watched the tears spill over.

"Wrong," she said huskily. "All the reasons: wrong. All the excuses: wrong. For nothing other than selfishness, I betrayed your thrust."

Finally I could force something past my tight throat. "There was Kalle—"

"Wrong," Del declared. "A daughter is a daughter, and worth many sacrifices, but to *use* you as I did—to make you coin with which to barter—" Her voice failed her abruptly. She swallowed painfully. "What I did was no different, in its own way, than what Ajani did to me. He took away my freedom . . . I tried to take away yours."

Any number of responses jumped into my mouth. Each and every one of them was meant to diminish the truth of what she said, to somehow dismiss what she had done. So she would feel better. So she wouldn't cry any more. So I wouldn't feel guilty, even though I wasn't to blame.

I choked all of them back. To give in to the impulse was to dilute the power of her admission.

I took a deep breath. "Yes," I agreed. "What you did was wrong."

Del's tone was oddly empty. "I have done nothing I am ashamed of, save that. I have killed men. Many men. Men who got in my way, in the circle and out. I excuse none of those deaths; all were necessary. But what I offered Staal-Ysta, even for only a year, was not necessary. It was not my right to offer. It was not my life to give."

"No," I said softly.

Del drew in a noisy breath. "If you want me to go, I will. You have finished the task you set out to do. You have fulfilled your promise. It is left to me to finish mine; to end my song. Ajani is not your responsibility."

No. He never had been. But I know I hated the man at least half as much as Del, for what he'd done to her.

I thought about riding alone again. Just the stud and me. No female complications. No mission of vengeance. No obsession. Just riding through the South trying to scare up work. Trying to make a living. Growing older by the day, with nothing to show for it.

And no Northern bascha with whom to pass the time, in argument or in the circle.

I cleared my throat. "I've got nothing to do."

"After what I have done—"

"I'll get over it."

It was abrupt. Off-handed. Casual. It was also enough. We're neither of us good at putting feelings into words.

Del pulled furs into place and lay down on her bedding again. Her back was toward me, right shoulder jutting toward the roof. "I would like that," she said.

I lay there thinking about it, overwhelmed with new feelings. But I was exhausted from the sword, and it took too much effort to think about emotions. Del had made her admission. Del had fulfilled the task I required of her. So now all I had to do was just shut my eyes and let it go, sliding away. Tumbling into darkness. The pain was gone for good, and the lure of sleep beckoned. Beckoned. *Beckoned*—

It was pleasant drifting there, just at the edge of the eddy . . . at the point of dropping off—

"You're not old," Del said. Very low, but distinct.

Sleep retreated a moment. I smiled and yanked it back.

Going home, I thought, and slid off the edge of the world.

Part II

One

"Tiger," she said, "you're whistling."

"No, I'm not."

"Not now, no—but you were."

"I don't whistle, bascha—too much like music."

"Whistling *is* music," she pointed out, "and you were doing it."

"Look," I said patiently, "I don't sing, I don't hum, I don't whistle. I don't do anything even remotely connected with music."

"Because you're tone-deaf. But that doesn't mean you *can't* do any of those things. It just means you do all of them badly." She paused. "And you do."

"Why *would* I whistle? I've never done it before."

"Because, thanks to the Cantéada and your *jivatma*, you have a better understanding of what power music holds . . . and maybe because you're happy."

Well, I *was* happy. I'd been happy ever since Del had made her admission. Happier ever since we'd traded uplands for downlands and then downlands for border country; before an hour was up we'd be out of the North for good.

But I don't know that it made me *whistle*.

I drew in a deep breath, then exhaled in satisfaction. "Smell that? That's air, bascha . . . good, clean air. And *warm* air, too . . no more frozen lungs."

"No," she agreed, "no more frozen lungs . . . now we can breathe Southron air and have our lungs *scorched*."

I just grinned, nodded, rode on. It felt good to be aboard the stud again, riding down out of hills and plateaus into the scrubby borderlands between the North and Harquhal. It felt so good I didn't even mind Del's steadfast silences, or the dry irony of her tone when she *did* speak. All I knew was that with each stride closer to the border, I was closer to home. To warmth and sun and sand. To cantinas and aqivi. To all the things I'd known so well for the last twenty-some-odd years of my life, once I was free to know them.

"Hah!" I said. "See? There's the marker now." Without waiting for an answer, I booted the stud into a startled, lunging run and galloped the distance remaining between me and the South. I sent him past the stone cairn, then rolled him back, held him in check, watched Del negotiate the same distance at a much more decorous pace.

Or was it reluctance in place of decorum?

"Come on, Del," I called. "The footing's good enough. Let that blue horse run!"

Instead she let him walk. All the way to the cairn. And then she reined in, slid off, looped his reins around the pile of stones. Saying nothing, Del walked a short distance away and turned her back to me, staring steadfastly toward the north.

Oh. That again.

Impatiently I watched as she unsheathed, balanced blade and hilt across both hands, then thrust the sword above her head as if she offered it to her gods. It brought back the night she'd called colors out of the sky and painted the night with rainbows. It brought back the night I'd realized she wasn't dead; that I realized I hadn't killed her.

Impatience faded. Del was saying good-bye to her past and her present. No more Staal-Ysta. No more Kalle. No more familiar life. As much as I was pleased to see the South again, it wasn't the same for her. It never could be, either, regardless of circumstances.

The stud stomped, protesting inaction. I stilled him with a twitch of the reins and a single word of admonishment; for a change, he paid attention. Then he swung his head around as far as he could swing it, staring toward still-invisible Harquhal, and snorted. With feeling.

"I know," I told him. "Just a moment or two more . . . you can wait that long, even if you don't like it."

He shook his head, clattered bit shanks, slashed his tail audibly. It needed cutting badly; I knew almost instantly because the ends of coarse horsehair stung me across one thigh.

"Keep it up," I suggested. "I'll cut your *gehetties* off, too, and *then* where would you be?"

Del came back down to the blue roan and pulled reins free of the rock, leading him toward me. She still carried a naked blade, and showed no signs of putting it away.

I frowned. Reined in the stud as he seriously considered greeting the roan with a nip. Tried to ask a question, but was overridden by Del.

"It's time," she said simply.

Eyebrows rose. "Time?"

Sunlight glinted off Boreal. "Time," Del agreed, "to face one another in a circle."

It had been three weeks since the last time the subject had come up, just before reaching Ysaa-den. Del said nothing about sparring, and I'd been content to let the matter rest. I'd hoped it could rest forever.

I glanced down at the hilt of my own *jivatma*, riding quietly next to my left knee in a borrowed sheath buckled onto my saddle. Halvar had been generous enough to give me the sheath he'd used for his old bronze sword; it didn't really suit me, since it was only a scabbard and not the sheath-and-harness as I preferred, but I'd needed something to carry the weapon in. I couldn't lug it around bare-bladed.

"I don't think so," I told her.

Del's brow furrowed. "Are you still afr—"

"You don't know this sword."

She looked at the hilt. Considered what I'd said. Sighed a little and tried valiantly to hang onto waning patience. "I need to practice, Tiger. So do you. If we're to earn a living while we try to track down Ajani, we've got to get fit again. We've got to spar against one another to recover timing, strength, stamina—"

"I know all that," I said, "and you're absolutely right. But I'm not stepping into a circle against you so long as Chosa Dei's in this sword."

"But you can control it. You can control *him;* I've seen you. Not just that night in Halvar's lodge, but all the other times on the way here—"

"—and it's all those other times that make me refuse now," I told her plainly. "This sword wasn't exactly easy to control *before* I requenched it in Chosa Dei . . . do you think I really want to risk losing whatever control I've learned while you and I spar?" I shook my head. "Chosa Dei wanted your sword. He wanted to drain the magic, to reshape it—re*make* it—for his own specific needs. As far as I can tell, I think he still does."

Del was plainly startled. "How can he still—?" She shook her head, breaking it off. "He's in a *sword,* Tiger."

"And do you, not knowing what he's capable of, really want to risk letting him make contact with Boreal?"

"I don't think—" She stopped. Frowned. Stared pensively at Samiel's hilt poking up beside my knee. Then made a gesture of acknowledgment. "Maybe you're right. Maybe if your sword and mine ever met, he'd steal my *jivatma's* magic. And then—" She broke off again, staring at me in realization. "If he bound your magic and mine together, what would that make him? What kind of man would he be?"

I shook my head. "There's no way of knowing what could happen. Your *jivatma* is different from others, bascha. You've known that all along, though you say little about it. But it's become obvious even to me, now that I've seen a few others. Now that I know how they're made, and what goes into them." I shrugged. "You blooded her in Baldur and completed your rituals, sealing all your pacts with those gods you revere so much, and then you sang your own personal song of need and revenge." I looked down at her steadily. "I think it gave your *jivatma* a more intense kind of power."

Del said nothing; silence was eloquent.

I spread both hands, reins threaded through fingers. "When I requenched—when I keyed the way you're supposed to, *finally*—I sang of specific, personal things, just like you did. And my sword, like yours, is different, only it's because of Chosa Dei, not any special pacts." I shook my head. "I don't understand it yet. Maybe I never will. But I do know that heat and cold don't mix. One always has to win. And I think it's the same with our swords."

Del was clearly troubled. "It was a mistake . . . it never should have happened . . . in Staal-Ysta, we are taught never to requench—"

"I didn't have a whole lot of choice, now, did I?"

"No, no—I am not blaming you." But still she frowned. "I am thinking of the reason why requenching is forbidden. I am thinking about a sword-dancer who, whenever he desires, requenches his *jivatma*. And how he himself can 'collect' the enemy's personal power, just as Chosa Dei collected magic by unmaking things." Del looked at my sword. "I am thinking about a man—or a woman—who forgets honor and promises and becomes addicted to power. Addicted to requenching."

"Are you saying nothing stronger than *custom* keeps sword-dancers with *jivatmas* from requenching each time they kill?"

"Custom," she answered, "and honor."

I made a sound of derision. "*That's* some kind of control! What you're telling me is a sword-dancer sick

and tired of all these customs and honor codes could
become a renegade. Ride all over the North and South
requenching as he goes."

"No one would do—"

"Why not?" I interrupted. "What's to keep him
from it? What's *really* to keep him from it, if habit
isn't enough?"

"A sword-dancer who did such a thing would be
formally denounced by the *voca* and declared outlaw,"
she said. "A blade without a name. He would owe
swordgild to Staal-Ysta and be subject to discipline by
any sword-dancer who challenged him."

I triple-clucked my tongue at her in mock sorrow.
"Such a frightening prospect, bascha. Enough to make
me go to bed and pull the covers over my head."

Color bloomed in her face. "Just because no one in
the South has an honor at all, or assumes responsibility—"

"That's not it," I told her. "That's not my point.
What I'm saying is, these swords are dangerous. Whatever magic turns a normal sword into a thing laden
with the power to suck a soul from a person is nothing
to take lightly. In the wrong hands a *jivatma* could
become a devastating weapon." I smiled sardonically.
"And yet the *an-kaidin* on Staal-Ysta continue to hand
them out." I shifted in the saddle. "Don't know as
how that's very wise, Delilah."

"No one except a *kaidin* is gifted with a *jivatma*. Or
the one who chooses instead to be a sword-dancer."
She shrugged, spreading a hand. "By the time of choice,
the *an-ishtoya* has proven his or her honor; that is
what rank is for. It is a selection process, a way of
enforcing the honor codes of Staal-Ysta. It isn't undertaken lightly, Tiger; they don't give a blooding-blade
to anyone unless it's quite certain he—or she—knows
how to invoke the magic properly, and that he is fully
committed to upholding the honor systems."

"Del," I said patiently, "*I* have a *jivatma*."

It sank in. Del stared at me wide-eyed. And then

waved a dismissive hand. "Yes, of course, but it's because you were worthy of one."

"Was I? Haven't I requenched?"

She opened her mouth to reply, then closed it slowly. Frowned more deeply, pulling smooth, creamy forehead into lines of tension and concern. It's never easy to come face-to-face with the weakness in lifelong beliefs. I know; I used to disbelieve in magic altogether.

"Del," I said quietly, "I'm not intending to requench again, if that's what you're worried about. I'd just as soon never key this thing again—I'm *sword-dancer*, not sorcerer. All I'm saying is, it seems kind of odd that this kind of power is given away freely with very few restraints. Honor is one thing, bascha—and I don't doubt it counts for something on Staal-Ysta—but not everyone in the world understands the value in such a thing. Certainly most people—everyone *I* know—would be more than willing to use any advantage at hand, if it meant the difference between living and dying."

Del stared up at me from the ground. "Are you telling me you believe I will cast off my honor and defeat Ajani unfairly?"

I grinned. "I believe you will do whatever it takes to kill him. Because what you're doing is in the *name* of honor, which sort of balances out the effort."

She shrugged one shoulder slightly. "Perhaps. Perhaps not. But how I kill Ajani has nothing to do with your unwillingness to meet me in a circle."

I sighed. "It does, but I guess you can't see it right now. So let's just say that I, being a Southroner and entirely lacking in honor *or* scruples, don't have the slightest understanding of what this sword is capable of. And that's why, in addition to other things, I don't want to dance with you."

"Chosa Dei," she murmured.

I tapped the pommel knot. "Right here, bascha . . . and growing angrier by the moment."

Del looked down at the sword in her hand. "I have to dance," she said. "It's why I went looking for you."

It cut deep. Right through flesh, muscle, belly wall, into the hidden places. For four weeks I had mostly put aside thoughts of personal things because we were busy hunting hounds, but now it was fresh again. Now it hurt again.

It was especially painful in view of the things she'd told me in Halvar's lodge.

"Well, then," I said finally, "why don't you head on down the road to Harquhal, all of twenty miles south or so, where I'm sure you'll find someone there who can give you a proper match."

Del stared up at me for a long moment. Her expression was unreadable. For a woman with only twenty-one years to her name—and that just barely—she was very good at hiding what she felt.

Abruptly she resheathed, turned to her roan, stepped up into the stirrup. Swung a leg over and settled, gathering loose rein.

Hoolies, I thought, she's going. After all this—after settling things at last, she's really going to go—

Del walked her horse to mine. "I lied," she said plainly.

Oh, hoolies, bascha . . . now you've got me confused.

"From the beginning, I lied."

"About what?" I asked warily.

"About the dancing. About why I came looking for you."

"Oh?"

Del nodded. "You are the kind of man—or were—who would take lightly a woman's devotion. A woman's admission of admiration. A woman's need for you. You would take it lightly, and hurt her, because she would have offered something of value—the truth of what she felt—and you would see nothing of value in it."

"*I* would?"

"Men," she said. "You, once, certainly; I recall what you were like."

"But I wouldn't any more?"

Her face was oddly expressionless. "Not around me. Not in reach of my sword."

I grinned, then hid it away behind an arch expression. "So, you're saying—I think—you didn't come looking for me just because of my dancing."

"No."

It brought me up short. I frowned. "No, you didn't come looking for me just because of my dancing; or no, that's not right?"

Del smiled. She *smiled*. "I came looking for you because of your dancing, yes—you are the Sandtiger— but also because of you. Just you, Tiger; now, I have said it aloud. I hope you treat it kindly."

It meant something. It meant a *lot*—but I couldn't show anything of it. Some things are just too private. "So, am I to take this to mean you're devoted to me? That you *need* me?"

Del turned her horse southerly. "Don't assume anything, Tiger. It can get you into trouble."

Two

It was warm in Harquhal. A faint afternoon breeze blew sand at our faces, lodging grit in our teeth. For once I didn't mind the crunching; it meant I was home again.

Del, however, did. She rode her roan in through the gates and blew her lips free of dust, brushing at blue woolen tunic and muttering in uplander. Something to do with dust and sand. Something to do with dislike. And something, I think, with a bath.

But a bath would have to wait. "Harness," I said briefly, and headed off down the street.

Harquhal is the kind of place that attracts sword-dancers. It's a border town, which means two cultures come together, and not always peaceably. *This* means there is often work for those of us who hire on to protect, retrieve, or bestow, depending on circumstances, and depending on the employer. Which means where there are sword-dancers, there are also swordsmiths and craftsmen dedicated to the art.

The man I went to see had been recommended by three different sword-dancers in three different cantinas. There is nothing at all accomplished by being hasty about accoutrements that can possibly save a life. I took my time, asked around, downed a few cups of aqivi just to reacquaint my tongue. Del made no complaint, but I could feel her growing impatience. She wanted to ask about Ajani, but I'd talked her out of it. First I wanted a proper harness and sheath, so that if we ran into trouble I'd be better prepared.

Although she did comment, eventually, that with all the aqivi in me I'd be lucky to remain standing, let alone dance.

"I don't want to dance," I told her. "I'd just as soon avoid dancing altogether, if I can; there's no need to be hostile."

"We want to kill a man. I don't think we can avoid it."

"*You* want to kill him. Ajani's not my problem. My problem, right now, is finding a man who can give me exactly what I want in the way of a proper harness."

Which had led me to ask yet a third sword-dancer, who gave me the same name. So we went to see him.

He was a typical Southroner: brown-haired, brown-eyed, burned dark by the sun. He wore the plain clothing of the tradesman—gauzy tunic, baggy trews, robe—and no ornamentation. Which meant he didn't take an inordinate amount of pride in his appearance, unlike some gifted men, but, more likely, in his craftsmanship.

He stood behind a table. The shop was small, jammed with flats of skins, racks of wood, trays full of wire, thong, tools. He watched Del and me come in through the curtained doorway and nodded greeting. It was very brief to Del, intended mostly for me; the man, the Southroner. Nothing much had changed while I'd been North.

I stopped at the table and looked the man dead in the eye. "It's a very special sword."

Juba smiled. Undoubtedly he had heard the exact same words before, uttered by countless sword-dancers intent upon the blade that earned them a living. Only in this case, what I said was understatement.

"Very special," I repeated, "and in need of precise attention." I set the sheathed sword on the table in front of Juba. "Don't touch," I said.

Again, Juba smiled. It was not a condescending smile, or one of disbelief—he was too professional to let his thoughts show so plainly—but it was a smile of subtle acknowledgement: *Let the customer say what he will. Juba will be the judge.*

Only the hilt was visible above the lip of Halvar's sheath. It was bright, twisted-silk steel devoid of excess ornamentation. The sword was simply a sword.

"*Jivatma*," I said, and Juba's brown eyes widened. "What I want," I continued, "is a true sword-dancer's harness, cut to my size, and a diagonal scabbard as well. Split sheath, of course—six-inch cut at the lip—so when I hook it out of the scabbard the blade rides free. While sheathed I want it snug—I can't abide rattling—but I need it to come to hand easy. No snags or awkward motion."

Juba nodded slightly. "Cadda wood," he said. "It's light, but very strong. And suede lining inside. Outside I will encase it in danjac hide, then lace and wrap it with thong, with a bit of wire for strength." He paused. "Do you want ornamentation?"

Some sword-dancers like to hang coin or rings or bits of jewelry from their sheaths, to prove they've been successful. Some even like to take something from the loser—dead or alive—as a kind of trophy. Me, I've always kind of thought that sort of thing was asking for trouble. While it's true not too many thieves want to tangle with a man who earns his living with a sword, I've never known a bandit yet who wouldn't do whatever he could to separate a man from his wealth. Which meant that a sword-dancer who got drunk, or fell in with a scheming cantina girl, or who simply lost track of his wits, was asking to be robbed.

I started to shake my head.

"Yes," Del said. "Can you copy this?"

She had waited so quietly behind me, saying nothing to Juba or me, that I'd nearly forgotten she was there. But now she came forward, asking Juba for clay slate and stylus. He set the slate out on the table, passed her the stylus, watched in pensive silence as she scraped out the design.

"There," she said at last. "Can you work those into

the leather? From top to bottom, like so—twisting
around and around and around . . . can you do this?"

Juba and I stared at the slate. Del had painstakingly
carved elaborate runes into the unbaked clay, then
blown the dust away. The shapes were intricate and
precise, and like nothing I'd ever seen.

Except on Samiel's blade.

Juba frowned, then looked at me. "Do you want
those?"

His tone expressed doubt; he was, after all, a
Southroner, and Del a Northern woman . . . but his
job was to please the customer. He'd let me decide.

I glanced sidelong at Del. She offered nothing save
silence again, but I felt the tension in her body. She
wouldn't ask me to say yes, because it had to be my
choice. But clearly she wanted me to let Juba put in
the runes.

What the hoolies . . . "Put them on."

Juba shrugged and nodded. "I must measure you,"
he said, "and also measure the sword. But if you
won't allow me to touch it—"

"I'll help," I told him. "Measure me first, then we'll
get to the sword."

He worked quickly and competently, wrapping thong
this way and that way around me, then tying knots on
it to mark his place. When he was done, all I saw was
a leather thong full of knots, but Juba knew the
language.

Then he looked at the sword.

I slid it clear of Halvar's sheath, dropping the scabbard aside. Now the blade was naked. It was black at
the tip, a smudgy dull black extending three fingers up
the blade, as if it had been dipped. Runes caught light
like water.

Juba sucked in a breath. Desire darkened his eyes. I
saw his fingers twitch.

"*Jivatma*," I repeated. "Did you think the Sandtiger
lies?"

I did it on purpose. Not to brag, although there's

always a little of that; but to make certain he under-stood who he was making the harness for. If a sword-dancer like the Sandtiger was pleased by Juba's work, it could improve his reputation and increase business one hundredfold. If he *didn't* like the workmanship, Juba might be finished.

But I did it also because I knew there was a chance that Juba, left alone, might yet touch the sword. Might try to pick it up. And I recalled much too well the pain of Boreal before Del had told me her name.

"Measure it," I said. "If you need it moved, I'll do it."

Swiftly Juba drew out yet another leather thong and measured the sword, tying knots here and there. I moved it as instructed, holding the thong for him when he needed to make contact. When he was done, he nodded. "It will fit. I promise. It will be as you have said."

"And the runes," Del said intently.

Juba looked at her for the second time. This time he *looked* at her, and saw what she was. Saw past the Northern beauty. Saw past the independence. Saw beyond the cool demeanor to the woman who lived inside.

And looked away again, being a Southron fool. "How soon?" he asked.

I shrugged. "As soon as you can. I don't like carry-ing my sword by hand, and I can't abide a belt or baldric."

No, of course not; no true sword-dancer carried his weapon in anything but harness-and-sheath. I wasn't about to change the custom and risk looking like a fool.

Juba thought about it. He might ask for better pay-ment if I wanted it so quickly; then again, my name ought to be enough. "Two days," he offered.

"Tomorrow evening," I said.

Juba considered it. "Not enough time," he explained. "There is much work for me, with so many going to

Iskandar. I would be honored to make by best harness and sheath for the Sandtiger, but—"

"Tomorrow evening," I said. "What's this about Iskandar?"

He shrugged, already digging through piles of leather. "They say the jhihadi is coming."

I grunted. "They say the same thing every ten years or so." I sheathed my sword and picked it up. With Del on my heels, I went out the curtained doorway.

"You heard him," she said as soon as we were outside. "He mentioned Iskandar and the jhihadi . . . are you going to pretend it's nonsense when a *Southroner* brings it up."

"Iskandar is a ruin," I said yet again. "There's no reason for anyone to go there."

"Except maybe if the messiah is coming."

"All sorts of rumors get started, bascha. Are we supposed to believe them all?"

Del didn't answer, but her mouth was set firmly.

"And now," I began, "suppose you tell me what these runes are all about."

She shrugged. "Just runes. Decoration."

"I don't think so, bascha. I know you better than that. You were too precise, which makes me nervous. I want to know what *kind* of runes—what do they say?—and what they're supposed to do."

Del didn't offer an answer. We were just outside Juba's shop; I stopped dead, swung to face her, very nearly stepped on her toes. She looked into my face and probably saw how serious I was; she took a step back and sighed.

"A warning," she told me. "Wards against tampering. Also your name, and who you are . . . and your Northern rank."

"I'm a Southroner."

She took it in stride. "Southron rank, as well," she continued evenly. "Seventh-level, as you have said; I have forgotten nothing."

"You forgot to ask me if I wanted such things on my scabbard."

Del was plainly troubled. "You yourself told me how dangerous a *jivatma* can be in the wrong hands. You pointed out that even a Northerner, if he felt strongly enough, might reject the teachings of Staal-Ysta to gain additional power."

"But what has that to do with *my* sword?"

"Protection," she said quietly. "If an unscrupulous sword-dancer wanted power for himself, he could not do better than to steal your *jivatma*."

"You mean—" I stopped. "Do you mean the runes are to protect *me?*"

"Yes."

"No one can even touch my sword without knowing his name, Del. Isn't that protection enough?"

She didn't avoid my gaze. "You drink," she said. "You have begun to drink already, and you will drink more before the night is through, to celebrate your homecoming. I have seen you do it before." She shrugged. "A man who drinks often does and says foolish things."

"And you think I might tell someone the name of this sword, thereby allowing him—or her—to touch it. To use it. Possibly even to requench it, if he or she knew the proper way."

Del's eyes were bleak. "Chosa Dei is no longer a story," she said. "He is a truth, and others will come to know it. You yourself have said you don't know what the sword is capable of; would you have an enemy gain your sword *and* Chosa Dei all at once? Do you know what that would mean?"

"It would free Chosa Dei," I said grimly.

"And more." Creases marred her brow. "A man wanting skill and strength could do worse than to quench a blade in *you.*"

I hadn't thought about it, to tell the truth. But now I did. I thought about it hard, scowling down at the scabbarded *jivatma*.

Me, at risk. Me, a source of skill and strength. The kind of "honored enemy" others might find attractive.

Hoolies, I was *the Sandtiger* . . . whatever anyone really thought of me no longer mattered. I had a reputation for being very good—well, I am—and anyone who wanted to improve a blooding-blade might indeed seek me out.

"But by putting on these runes, aren't we telling everyone who might be interested that I'm a good target?"

Del shook his head. "They say your name and who you are, yes; they also serve as wards. A man would be a fool to tamper with your sword."

I wasn't convinced.

Del tried again. "Chosa Dei will do everything he can to free himself. Anyone who tried to use this sword would be asking for death . . . or worse. Asking for possession."

"Like the loki. Isn't it?" I shook my head. "I thought we were free of that sort of thing forever, since the Cantéada entrapped them in the circle . . . and now there's *this* to face."

Del stroked a strand of fair hair behind her left ear. "It is well that only Northerners trained on Staal-Ysta understand the power of the *jivatmas* and how they can be used . . . a Southroner has no knowledge of such things. It is therefore unlikely a Southroner will try to steal your sword."

True. It made me feel like a little better. "So—you think Northern runes will warn away unscrupulous Northerners." I grinned. "I thought you once told me all Northerners are *honorable* people."

Del didn't see the humor. "Ajani is Northern," she said.

"But he isn't a sword-dancer."

"Nor is he an honorable man." Del's tone was intensely bitter. "Do you think he has become what he has become through ignorance and stupidity? Do you think he has no way of learning things he considers important? And wouldn't you consider the habits and training of a sword-dancer important, if you knew your life could be threatened by such?"

"Del—"

"Do you think he would be so foolish as to *ignore* a story of how a named blade is blooded? Or to ignore the chance to steal one from someone like the Sandtiger, who is a seventh-level sword-dancer in addition to a *kaidin*? Do you think—"

"*Del.*"

She shut her mouth.

"All right," I said soothingly, "all right; yes, I understand; no, I don't disagree. He's not stupid and he's not ignorant. All right? Can we go on now?" I plucked at heavy wool. "Can we go see someone about trading all this weight in on dhoti and burnous?"

"You don't know him," she said steadfastly. "You don't know Ajani at all."

No, I didn't. And I couldn't. Until Delilah found him.

I sighed, closed a big hand on her shoulder, aimed her down the street. "Come on, bascha. Let's shed this wool. *Then* we can set about finding people who might know where Ajani's been keeping himself."

"No more delays," she said. "*No more* delays."

It had taken six years. Del was, finally, at the end of her patience. And I couldn't really blame her.

"I promise," I told her. "We'll find him."

Del looked me in the face. Her eyes were something to behold. Bluest blue, and beautiful, but also incredibly deadly.

And I recalled, looking at her, something Chosa Dei had said to her in the chamber. Something even Del had agreed with, speaking of herself; thinking of her oath.

Obsession is necessary. Obsession is required. Obsession is the master when compassion undermines.

Three

She sat herself down on my knee and traced out the scars on my cheek. "Soooo," she purred, "you came."

I opened one eye. "Was I supposed to?"

"Oh, yes. Everyone said you would. And now you are here."

I opened the other eye. It didn't change the view: black-haired, brown-eyed woman, perching her rump on my thigh. Leaning up against me to show off abundant charms, hardly hidden by loose, gauzy blouse.

"Kima," she told me, smiling. "And you are the Sandtiger."

I cleared my throat. "So I am." I shifted a little, trying to find a more comfortable position. Kima was no lightweight, and I was still a bit sore from my travail in Chosa's mountain. "*Who* said I would come?"

Kima waved a hand. "Everyone," she said. "All the other girls and I had a wager as to which of us would get you."

Cantina girls are notorious for wagering, and for vulgarity. But then, when you're a man in dire need of a woman after too long alone in the Punja, you don't really care. It used to be I'd just nod at whatever they said, not being particularly interested in anything other than physical charms; now I frowned at Kima.

"*Why* was I coming?"

"Because all the sword-dancers are." She snuggled up next to my chest, butting the top of her head against my chin. "I know your kind, Sandtiger . . . the lure of coin is powerful. It brings you all out of the desert."

Yes, well, occasionally. Actually, *more* than occasionally; it's sort of part of our lifestyle. Hard to live without coin.

I reached past Kima, managed to snag my cup, carried it carefully to my mouth. Downed three swallows, then lost the cup to Kima. "How much did you win because you managed to 'get' me?"

Her giggle was low and throaty. "Haven't won yet. Have to take you to bed."

I sat—and Kima sat—in a corner of the cantina, snugged into a little alcove. I've never been one for sitting plop out in the middle of the place, since it's hard to keep an eye on everyone in the cantina. But give me a corner table, or one pushed into an alcove, and I'm a happy man.

I was not unhappy now, although I've been happier. I couldn't help thinking of Del, gone off to reserve a room at an inn up the street. What would she think of Kima?

Kima traced scars again, sliding fingernails through my beard. The other hand slid lower, then lower still; I sat upright so suddenly I nearly dumped her on the floor. "Sorry," I murmured as she spilled aqivi down her blouse.

She considered being affronted. Then took note of the fact the wet blouse displayed still more of half-hidden charms in a rather unique way. She leaned against me again. "First the son, and now the father. He might be younger, but you're bigger."

I grunted inattentively, trying to reach around her so I could pour more aqivi into the recovered cup. And then her words sank in. *"What?"*

She smiled, applied tongue tip to scars, pouted prettily as I pulled away. "Your son," Kima said. "He was here, too."

"I don't have a son."

Kima shrugged. "He said he was your son."

"I don't have a son." I tipped her off my knee. "Are you sure he said *my* name?"

She stood over me, hands on hips. Breasts strained against wet gauze. "Do you mean to take me to bed or not?"

Del's cool voice intruded. "Don't keep her waiting, Tiger. She might get out of the mood." She paused. "Then again, probably not; do cantina girls *have* moods?"

Kima swung around and came face to face—well, no, not *exactly* face to face; Del was a head taller—with the cold, hard truth: when Del is in the room, no other female exists. It's height, coloring, sword. It's also grace and danger. Plus a lot of their things.

Clearly, Kima knew it at once. She decided to fight *her* way, since she couldn't compete with Del. "He's taking *me* to bed! *I'm* going to win the wager!"

Del smiled coolly. "By all means."

"Wait a minute," I said, scenting trouble. "Right now I don't much care about who's taking who to bed—that can wait till later . . . what *I* want to know—"

Del interrupted. "You never could wait before."

I smacked down the brimming cup. Aqivi ran over my hand. "Look, bascha—"

Kima looked Del up and down. "You don't belong in here. What are you doing here? There's no room for another girl. And you *can't have him.*"

Del's smile widened. "I already have."

Women can be *nasty* . . . I stood up, scraping my stool so hard it fell over against the wall, and looked Del dead in the eye, which isn't a problem for me. "Can you just wait a minute? I'm trying to find out something."

Del assessed Kima. "Five coppers, perhaps."

"No, *no*—" I began, but Kima was swearing in outrage.

By this time the turmoil was of interest to the rest of the cantina. I overheard wagers being laid on which of the women would win. Or if either would be worth it.

Which made me want to swing Del around bodily so all could see what she was; the wager would be ended before it was properly begun. Then again, putting Del on display was not a thing I wanted to do, since it was hardly a compliment to treat a woman as an ornament.

Besides, she'd probably kill me.

I turned back to Kima. "You said—"

"*Go* with her!" Kima cried. "Do you think I care? Do you think you're worth it? I've had sword-dancers better than you. I've had sword-dancers *bigger* than you—"

"How do you know?" Del asked.

I swore. "Will you just—? Del, wait . . . *Kima!*" But she was gone, flouncing across the cantina. It gave me leave to turn back to Del. "Do you have any idea what you just did?"

"If you want her that—"

"That's not *it!*" I scraped a hand through my hair, attempting to control my tone. "What I was *trying* to find out was what she meant about a man claiming to be my son."

"Your son?" Del's brows rose as she hooked a stool with a boot and pulled it out from under the table. "I didn't know you had a son."

"I *don't*—oh, hoolies, bascha, let's just forget about it. Let's just sit here and drink."

Del eyed my mug. "You've been doing that already."

I righted my stool and sat down. "Did you get us a room?"

"Two rooms; yes."

I blinked. "Two rooms? Why?"

"To make it easier for you. So you can win your wager."

"To hoolies with the wager." I was a bit put out. I was feeling a bit kindlier toward Del of late, since she'd finally admitted she was wrong, and wasn't of a mind to make the wager stick. It really was a silly sort of thing, anyway, and I didn't see the sense in continuing the farce. After all, we were both healthy people with normal appetites, and it had been quite some time since we'd shared a bed.

Del smiled. "Giving up so easily?"

"I figure we've taken that wager about as far as we can go with it."

Del's tone was very solemn. "It was undertaken properly."

"I don't care. I don't *care*. Let's forget the wager."

Now her face matched her tone. "We can't. I think two rooms would be best. And not just for the wager . . . I need the time alone. I need the time to focus."

"Focus?" I frowned. "I don't quite understand."

"For the kill." Del's attitude was matter-of-fact.

"So? You'll just kill him. It's what you've come to do. It's what you've been meaning to do for six whole years."

Del frowned. "Before, it would have been easy. But now . . ." Her voice trailed off. She looked at the table, picked at knife and sword scars, flicked bits of wood away with a grimace of distaste. "I'm different now. The task is the same, but I'm a different person." She didn't look at me. "I've *been* changed."

"Del—"

Pale-lashed lids lifted. Blue eyes stared at me. "There was a time when it would have taken no effort at all, my task. When it was my whole world. When it was all I thought of. And the doing would have been sweet, because it was all I wanted."

I waited in silence, transfixed by her intensity.

"But you have changed me, Tiger. You have blundered into my life and changed the way I think. Changed the way I feel." Her mouth tightened slightly. "It's not what I wanted. It was *never* what I wanted. But now you are here, and I find myself confused. I find myself *distracted*—and distraction can be dangerous."

Distraction could be lethal.

"And so I will ask the gods and my sword to aid me in this. To help me focus myself, so I can complete my task without additional confusion. Without the distraction."

I stared at her intently. "Didn't you try that before? The night we met up again?"

Color came and went in her face. "You *saw?*"

"I saw." I wasn't proud of it. "Del, I didn't know what to think. I didn't know what you were doing, out there in the trees with that magicked sword. So I went to see for myself."

She wasn't pleased. "And I will ask it again. Again and again, if need be. I must regain my focus."

"If you mean to strip all the humanity away just to make yourself capable of killing Ajani, maybe it's not worth it."

Blue eyes flickered minutely. The mouth went hard and flat. "I have sworn oaths."

I sighed. "All right. I give up. Do what you have to do." I eyed her askance, assessing her commitment. "But if distance is what you want, don't play games with me. I hate women who play games."

"I never play games."

She never *had;* that was true. It didn't mean she couldn't.

I shoved the jug across the table. "Drink."

Del appropriated my cup. "Do you really have a son?"

"I told you before, bascha: not as far as I know."

"Yes, I remember . . . it's not something you think about."

"And I don't plan to *talk* about it—at least, not with you." I recaptured the jug and drank straight out of it, gulping aqivi down.

Del sipped her share. "But you *could,*" she observed.

I scowled. "I could, yes. I could have several sons. I could have *many* sons; why? Do you want to go find them all?"

"No. But they—or even just he—might want to find you." She glanced across at Kima, now sitting on another man's knee. "He obviously knows who you are, if he's bragging about you in cantinas."

I thought about it. Maybe if I had a famous father

I'd brag about him, too—but I wasn't so sure I liked being the subject. It's one thing to be bragged about; it's another thing having a total stranger claim himself close kin. The *closest* of kin.

Del sipped delicately. "The innkeeper asked a fortune. When I threatened to take our business elsewhere, he gave me leave to go, saying the inn was nearly full, and it was the same all over Harquhal because of the Oracle. That everyone's coming here."

Still thinking of my "son," I shifted attention with effort. "What?"

"The Oracle," she repeated. "Do you recall what the holy man in Ysaa-den foretold?"

"Oh. That." I waved a dismissive hand. "There's no reason for us—or anyone else—to go to Iskandar. Oracle or no."

Del studied her cup. "People are going," she said.

"I thought you just said people are coming *here*."

"First," she agreed. "Do you know where Iskandar is?"

"Someplace off over there." I waved my hand again: northeasterly.

"A little more *that* way." Del mimicked my gesture, but indicated a slight shift in direction to north-northeast. "The innkeeper said Harquhal is the last true settlement before Iskandar, so people are stopping here to buy supplies."

"Iskandar is a *ruin*."

"That's why they're buying supplies."

I upended the jug and drank more aqivi. Then thumped the jug back down. "And I suppose this chatty innkeeper believes in this Oracle. Believes in this messiah."

Del shrugged. "I don't know what he believes. I know only what he told me, which is that people are going to Iskandar."

I couldn't hide my disgust. "Because the jhihadi is coming again."

She turned her cup in circles, watching her fingers

move. "People need things, Tiger. For some it is religion, for others it is the dreams born of huva weed. I say nothing about what is good and bad, or right and wrong—only that people *need* in order to survive." Her voice was very quiet. "For me, after Ajani's attack, I needed revenge. That need helped me to live." Now her gaze left the cup and came up to meet my own. "You have needed, too. It's how you survived your enslavement. It's how you survived Aladar's mine."

I didn't answer for a long moment. And then when I did, I said nothing about myself or the months spent in the mine. "So, you're saying that people need this Oracle to be right. Because they need a jhihadi."

Del lifted a shoulder. "A messiah is a very special kind of sorcerer, is he not? Can he not do magical things? Can he not heal the sick and cure the lame and make rain to replenish a land sucked dry by years of drout?"

I grunted. "Is that what he's supposed to do?"

Del shifted on her stool. "When I walked to the inn, I heard talk on the street of the Oracle. When I came back the same way, I heard talk of the jhihadi." She shrugged. "The Oracle has foretold the coming of a man who can change sand to grass."

"Sand to grass? Sand to *grass?*" I frowned. "What for, bascha?"

"So people can live in the desert."

"People *do* live in the desert. *I* live in the desert."

Del sighed a little. "Tiger, I am only telling you what I heard. Have I said I believed any of it? Have I said I believed in Oracles or jhihadis?"

Not exactly. But she sounded halfway convinced.

I shrugged, started to say something, was interrupted by an arrival. A man stood by our table. Southroner, by the look of him; dark-haired, dark-eyed, tanned skin. About forty or so, and showing all his teeth. Some of them were missing.

"Sandtiger?" he asked.

I nodded wearily; I wasn't in the mood.

The smile widened. "Ah, so I thought! He described you very well." He bowed briefly, flicked a glance at Del, looked immediately back to me. "May I have more aqivi sent over? It would be an honor to buy you a jug."

"Wait," I suggested. "*Who* described me so well?"

"Your son, of course. And he was quite complimentary—" He frowned minutely. "Although he said nothing of a beard."

I wasn't concerned about the beard. Only about my "son." Evenly, I asked. "What was his name? Did my 'son' give you a name?"

The man frowned briefly, considered it, then shook his head. "No. No, he didn't. He said merely he was the Sandtiger's cub, and told us stories about your adventures."

"Adventures," I echoed. "I'm beginning to wonder about them myself." I pushed back my stool and rose. "Thanks for the offer, but I have an appointment. Perhaps tomorrow night."

The man was clearly disappointed, but made no protest. He bowed himself out of my way and went back to his friends at another table.

Del, still seated, smiled. "Does the girl win her wager, then?"

"What girl—oh. No." I scowled. "I'm going to the inn. Do you want to come?"

"Tired already? But you've only had *one* jug of aqivi." Del rose smoothly. "It was like this in Ysaaden, too . . . perhaps age has slowed you down." She shoved her stool back under the table. "Or is it knowing you have a son?"

"No," I said testily, "it's carrying this sword."

Del went out of the cantina ahead of me and stepped into the dark street. "Why should carrying that sword make you feel tired?"

"Because Chosa Dei wants out."

Del gestured. "This way." Then, as we walked, "It's getting worse, then."

I shrugged. "Let's just say, Chosa has finally realized what sort of prison he's in."

"You have to be stronger, Tiger. You have to be vigilant."

"What I have to be, bascha, is rid of Chosa Dei." I sidestepped a puddle of urine. "Where is this inn with the chatty innkeeper?"

"Right here," Del answered, turning away from the street. "I told him you would pay."

"*I'd* pay! Why? Don't you have any coin?"

Del shook her head. "I paid *swordgild* to Staal-Ysta. I have nothing at all."

It silenced me. I'd forgotten about *swordgild*, the blood-money owed Staal-Ysta if a life were ended unfairly. The *voca* had taken everything from Del: money, daughter, lifestyle. I'd nearly taken her life.

We went inside the inn and called for the innkeeper, who came out from behind a curtained divider. He took my coin, nodded his thanks, then welcomed me warmly. "It is an honor having the Sandtiger as a guest."

I muttered appropriate things, then added an extra coin. "I want a bath in the morning. And I want the water hot."

"I will see to it myself." Then, as I turned toward the curtain, "I have given you the same room I gave your son. I thought it might please you. And he liked hot water, too."

I stopped dead in my tracks.

"Never mind," Del said.

"I don't have—"

"*Never mind*, Tiger." And pushed me through the curtain.

Four

With knees doubled up nearly to chin, I sat gingerly in hot water. It wasn't particularly comfortable—the innkeeper's cask was too small—but at least I could get wet. Part of me, anyway; the rest would have to be hand-washed instead of soaking clean.

Del came in without knocking, carrying a bundle. "A pretty sight," she observed. And then, half-hiding a smile—but only half-heartedly—she suggested a larger cask. "You don't really fit in this one."

I scowled at her blackly. "I'd like a bigger cask. I'd *love* a bigger cask. This is all there is."

She perched herself on the edge of my fragile bed, observing my cramped position. "If you had to get out of that quickly, I don't think you could."

"I'm not going anywhere quickly. What I'm doing is taking a bath." I scratched an itching ear. "What are you doing here? I mean, didn't you rent two rooms for the express purpose of being apart?"

Del ignored the gibe. "I brought you some clothes," she said, and dumped out the bundle she carried.

I tried to straighten; couldn't. "What clothes?" I asked suspiciously, envisioning more wool. "What have you done, Del?"

"I bought supplies," she answered. "Including Southron garb. Dhoti—here—and burnous. See?"

I saw. Suede dhoti, as mentioned, a russet-colored robe with leather belt, and a dull orange silk burnous to wear over it all. Also a pair of soft leather riding boots. "How do you know my size?"

"I know you snore, I know you drink, I know you like cantina girls . . . I know many things about you." Del allowed the silk to slide out of her hand. "You're going to shave, aren't you?"

"I'd planned on it, yes. Why? Do you want me to *keep* all this hair?"

She tipped her head to one side. "You've worn a beard for so long I've forgotten what you look like without one."

"Too long," I muttered. "Too much time, too much hair, too much wool." I tried to reposition myself in the cask, barked my shin on sharp wood. "I thought you said you had no money. How did you buy all this stuff?"

"I told them you would pay." Del shrugged elegantly as I sputtered a protest. "The shopkeepers know you, Tiger. They are honored by your business. They said they would be most happy to wait for you to pay them—so long as it was later today."

"I don't exactly have a whole lot of money, bascha . . . and less, now, than before." I crammed buttocks against wood, hissed as a splinter bit. "You can't go all over Harquhal promising people coin in my name. I might not have any."

Del shrugged. "I'm sure you can win more. Other sword-dancers are arriving daily . . . I think most if not all of them would be happy to meet the Sandtiger in a circle."

"I'm in no shape to meet anyone in a—*ouch*." I swore, worked a splinter free, shifted position. Eventually pulled my legs out and draped them over the rim. Cooling water sloshed across my belly.

Del surveyed my posture. "You're dripping water on the floor."

"I can't help it—my knees were cramping up." More comfortable now, I ran a string of brown soap across my chest, loosening wool-bound hair. "So, you think we can win some coin, do you? Even though we're both out of condition?"

"We wouldn't be out of condition if you'd get *in* a circle." Del smiled blandly. "I've asked you how many times?"

"No." I scrubbed more vigorously and snagged a hair beneath a fingernail, snapping it right out of my chest. "Ouch—Del, do you mind? Can I have my bath in private?"

She stood up, slid out of her harness, set Boreal on the bed. "If you're going to shave," she said, "let me do it. You'll cut your own throat."

"Never have before . . . and I've been shaving this face longer than you've been alive."

Del lifted one shoulder. "I used to shave my father. He wasn't much older than you." Without my permission —and ignoring my muttered oath—she came over to the stool beside the cask and picked up my knife, freshly honed to scrape a jaw clean of beard. "Soap your face," she suggested.

Hoolies, it's not worth arguing . . . I dutifully lathered up, then tipped my head back as ordered. Tried not to screw up my face as Del set blade to flesh.

"Hold still, Tiger." Then, as I held still, "Do these scars hurt any more?"

"The sandtiger scars? No, not any more. Not for a long time." I paused. "But if you cut them, I think they might."

"I'm not going to cut them." Del sounded absent-minded as she concentrated on shaving between the claw welts, which didn't go far toward making me feel any safer. "They're getting whiter and thinner with age," she observed. "But they must have hurt badly when the cat first striped you."

"Like hoolies," I agreed. "Then again, I was in no shape to really notice. He got me other places, too, and his claws weren't budded. The poison made me pretty sick for a couple of weeks. I was lucky to survive."

"Which you did because of Sula."

Yes, because of Sula. Because of the Salset woman who wouldn't let me die. She had gone against the suggestion of the shukar and the rest of the tribe that the troublesome chula be allowed to die. Because they all knew that in killing the sandtiger, I'd also gained my freedom.

I stirred. Sula brought back memories I preferred to forget. "Are you done?"

"Not even half begun."

Her laced braid hung forward over one shoulder, swinging as she worked. The ends of it brushed my chest.

It was, rather suddenly, intensely difficult to breathe. I shifted, sat a bit more upright, shoved myself down again. "Del, do you think—"

"Just hold still."

She had no idea how difficult that was, in view of the circumstances. "You said you wouldn't play games."

She blinked blue eyes. "What?"

"Games," I said in frustration. "What do you think *this* is?"

"I'm *shaving* you!"

"Give me back my knife." I leaned forward, caught her wrist, stripped the knife free with my left hand. "If you think I haven't lived thirty-five or thirty-six—or however many years it is!—without learning a few female tricks, you're younger than I thought."

Which, once said, didn't make me much happier. I sat in cool water and glared, holding a wet knife dripping soap and bits of beard.

Del stood with hands on hips. "And if *you* think I would tell you I wanted two rooms, and then tease you like this—"

Frustration made me testy. "Women do that sort of thing all the time."

"Some women, perhaps. Not all of them. Certainly not *me*."

I scratched violently at my scalp. "Maybe not. Maybe not on *purpose,* but it doesn't disguise the fact—"

"—that you have no self-control?"

I glared. "You *could* take it as a compliment."

She thought about it. "I could."

"So? Can I shave my own face?"

Someone knocked on the door.

"Go *away,*" I muttered, but Del turned her back on me and went to open the door.

A stranger stood there. A Southroner. He wore a sword in harness. "Sandtiger?" he asked.

Warily, I nodded. Wishing I had my sword in hand instead of on the stool; feeling foolish for wishing it. But a naked man *often* feels foolish. Or at least vulnerable.

He grinned, showing white teeth in a swarthy face. "I am Nabir," he said. "I'd like to dance with you."

Nabir was young. Very young. Maybe all of eighteen. And I'll wager his knees didn't ache.

"Ask me tomorrow," I growled.

A frown creased his brow. "I won't be here tomorrow. In the morning I leave for Iskandar."

"Iskandar. Iskandar! *What's in Iskandar?*"

Nabir appeared somewhat taken aback by my outburst. "The Oracle says the jhihadi—"

"—is coming to Iskandar; that I know. I think *everybody* knows." I scowled at the boy. "But why do *you* care? You don't look religious."

"Oh, I am not." He made a quick, dismissive gesture. "I am a sword-dancer. That's why I'm going."

I scratched idly at my scars, now bare of beard. "Why is a young, admittedly nonreligious sword-dancer going to Iskandar? There's nothing to *do* there."

"Everyone's going," he said. "Even the tanzeers."

I gazed blankly at Del. "Tanzeers," I echoed.

"Ajani," she said intently.

Frowning, I looked back at Nabir, waiting so patiently. "You said everyone is going . . . sword-dancers, tanzeers—who else?"

He shrugged. "The sects are going, of course, even the Hamidaa and *khemi*. And they're saying some of the tribes as well: the Hanjii, the Tularain; also others, I think. They want to see the Oracle foretell in the flesh."

"Power shift," I murmured. "The tanzeers'll never let him survive, unless he works for them." I straightened in the cask and waved a hand at Nabir. "Go down to the nearest cantina—I forget its name—and have a drink on me." I arched a brow. "And tell Kima I sent you."

"Will you meet me?" Nabir persisted. "It would be an honor to dance with the Sandtiger in the circle."

I looked harder at his face—his young, still-forming face—and also at his harness. His new, stiff harness, squeaking as he moved.

"In a year," I told him. "Now go have that drink."

Del closed the door behind him, then turned to me. "He's young. New. Untried. He might have been worth it for the practice. And at least you wouldn't hurt him; some other sword-dancer might, just to initiate him."

"I can't take the risk, bascha. If I step into a circle, it will be against someone good. Someone up to the challenge of dancing against Chosa Dei."

Del's unspoken comment was loud in the little room. I shook my head. "Someone who isn't *you*."

"There *will* have to be someone," she said. "*Several* someones, in fact. You are badly out of condition. If you had to dance to the death—"

"I'm not stupid enough to hire myself out to kill anyone at the moment. And besides—"

"Sometimes you have no choice."

"—*and besides*—" I smiled "—you're out of condition, too."

"Yes," Del agreed. "But I intend to dance just as soon as I find an opponent."

I watched her move toward my bed. "What—right *now?*"

"It makes no sense to waste time." Del retrieved

harness and sword and slipped it on as she headed to the door. "Perhaps Nabir will do . . . no, don't get up—you've still got half your face to shave."

"He's a *boy!*" I shouted, sloshing awkwardly in my cask.

Del's tone was bland. "Not so much younger than me."

Five

Del was right: she knew me very well. The suede dhoti fit in all the right places without chafing, as did the soft horseman's boots—I've always been partial to sandals, but these were very comfortable—and the dull orange burnous poured into place like water over the belted desert robe. I was a Southroner again.

But I didn't waste much time admiring the clothing. I grabbed up my sword in its borrowed sheath and left the inn quickly, calling back over my shoulder to the innkeeper that someone else could have the water now. By the time he started to answer, I was out of the door.

It's not hard to find a sword-dance, especially in a border town like Harquhal that thrives on competition. All you have to do is look for the largest gathering of people—particularly men in harness—and you will find what you're looking for.

I found Del very easily, since she's the kind of woman who draws attention. She waited quietly within the human circle, the gathering of men and women waiting to see the dance. Someone was carefully drawing a circle in the dirt, taking pains to make the line uniformly deep. It didn't really matter—in a sword-dance, the true circle is in your mind since lines are quickly obscured by displaced dust and dirt—but it was all part of the ritual.

Her expression was unaggressive, as was her posture. But Del is very tall for a woman—tall even for

Southron men—and her posture is very erect. Even standing quietly by the circle she invited shrewd assessment from everyone waiting to watch. Especially with a Northern sword riding in harness across her back.

I looked for Nabir and found him waiting across the circle from Del. All his hopes were in his face as was his Southron arrogance. He had no doubt he would beat the Northern woman; I was only surprised she'd gotten him to agree.

Then again, when you're young and proud and new, any dance is welcome. No doubt Nabir thought it worth the trouble to dance against a woman since he was assured of a victory before so many watching sword-dancers, some of them his heroes.

I almost felt sorry for him.

I did a rapid, precise assessment. He was shorter than Del by four fingers, which probably didn't please him, and he lacked the hard fitness that would come with maturity and experience. He wasn't soft, but neither was he mature. He still had some growing to do. He was, I judged, seventeen, eighteen, maybe nineteen. Which meant many things, all of them important to a sword-dancer, particularly one with a vested interest in the opponent.

I am a seventh-level sword-dancer, which translates, in my case, to seven years worth of apprenticeship. But the seven years—with accompanying rank—is never a sure thing. Only those apprentices showing a certain amount of promise are even passed to the fourth level, let alone the seventh; Nabir, by age alone, couldn't be much more than a second year apprentice, possibly a third. Because the rank, though denoted by the term *year*, has little to do with time as measured by the seasons. An apprentice's "year" is completed only when particular skills are learned, and that can take much longer than twelve months.

I had finished seventh-level in seven years. It was very symmetrical. A source of pride. Something for the stories, for the legend. But now, looking at Nabir, I wondered what *his* reasons were for becoming a sword-dancer. Unlike mine, I thought, fueled by hatred and a powerful need for freedom. That need had been more than physical. It had also been emotional. Mental. And it had been enough to make me the Sandtiger.

Whom Nabir had wanted to meet.

Not for the first time I wished for a true harness-and-sheath. I stood there holding a scabbarded sword in the midst of other sword-dancers properly accoutered, feeling oddly out of place. Lacking, somehow. But it wasn't just the style, which was a badge of our profession. It was also *convenience;* I'd rather carry a blade across my back than have to lug it around by hand.

The circle was finished. I considered stepping up beside Del to tell her she was being a silly, sandsick fool; decided against it when I realized it might throw off her concentration and contribute to her loss, if she lost. And she might. No matter how much she crowed—albeit quietly—about youth being an advantage in the healing process, she still wasn't completely recovered from the wound I'd dealt her. Hoolies, her conditioning was terrible! She'd be fortunate if she lasted long enough to put on a decent showing.

Then again, she wasn't precisely on her own. She did have Boreal.

Someone moved close beside me. Male. In harness: sword-dancer. Smelling of huva weed and aqivi; also a satisfactory visit to Kima's bed, or to another very like hers.

"So, Sandtiger," he said, "have you come to see the debacle?"

I knew him by his voice. Low, raspy, half-throttled, catching at odd times and on odd consonants. It wasn't affectation. Abbu Bensir had no choice in the matter of his voice, since a sword-shaped piece of wood had nearly crushed his throat twenty-some-odd years before. He had lived only because his shodo—swordmaster—had cut open flesh and windpipe to let air into his lungs.

While that same shodo's newest apprentice looked on in horror at what he'd done to a sixth-level sword-dancer.

"Which debacle?" I asked. "The one about to begin in the circle, or the dance you'll ask of me?"

Abbu grinned. "Are you so certain I will ask you?"

"Eventually," I answered. "Your throat may have recovered—mostly—but your pride never will. It was your own fault I nearly killed you—the shodo warned you I was awkward—but you ignored him. All you wanted to do was knock the former chula on his buttocks so he'd remember what he'd been."

"What he *was*," Abbu said plainly. "You were a chula still, Sandtiger . . . why deny it? It took you all of your seven years to rid yourself of the shame—if you've managed it yet." He pursed weed-stained lips. "I hear you got caught by slavers last year and thrown into a tanzeer's mine . . . has that worn off yet?"

I kept my tone even. "Did you come to watch this dance, or simply to breathe huva stink in my face?"

"Oh, to watch the dance . . . to see the boy humiliate the woman who has no place in a Southron circle." He shrugged, folding arms across a black-swathed chest. "She is magnificent to look at—she would fill a man's bed—but to pick up a man's weapon and enter a man's circle is sheerest folly. The Northern bascha will lose—not too badly, I hope; I would not want to see her cut—and then I will commiserate with her." He grinned at me, dark brows arching suggestively. "I will show her a few tricks with the sword—in bed *and* out."

I had been in the North four, maybe five months. I'd also spent a year or so with Del. Enough time to discover I'd learned a thing or two about myself. Enough time to realize I didn't much like the ignorance of Southron men. More than enough time to feel my own share of disbelief at Abbu's bland certainty that a woman good enough for bedding wasn't good enough for the circle.

Then again, not every woman was Del. *No* other woman was Del. She'd chosen the circle and the sword for things other than equality.

Which didn't make her wrong.

I looked out at Del. She wasn't fit. Wasn't ready. But she was still distinctly *Del.*

I glanced sidelong at Abbu Bensir. "Care to make a little wager?"

"On *this?*" He stared at me in unfeigned disbelief, then narrowed pale brown eyes. "What do you know about the boy? Is he that good?—or that bad?"

No question regarding the woman. Good enough for the wager.

I lifted a single shoulder. "He came to me this morning and begged a dance. I refused; he accepted the woman instead. That's all I know."

Abbu frowned. "A woman in place of the Sand-tiger . . ." Then he shook his head. "It makes no difference. Yes, I will wager on this. What do you offer?"

"Everything in this." I tapped the coin-pouch dangling from my belt. "But you've caught me between jobs, Abbu. There isn't much left."

"Enough to equal a Hanjii nose-ring?" Abbu reached into his own pouch and drew forth a ring of pure Southron gold, hammered flat into a circular plate.

It brought back memories: Del and I, in a circle, but only to the win. We'd danced in front of the Hanjii, a tribe who believed in eating the flesh of enemies. Also a tribe which placed great emphasis on male pride and honor; Del's subsequent defeat of me—thanks to a well-placed knee in a very vulnerable area—had resulted in the two of us becoming guests of honor in a religious ritual called the Sun Sacrifice. Left in the Punja without food, water or mounts, we'd very nearly died.

But did I have anything in my pouch equal to a

Hanjii nose-ring? "No," I answered truthfully; I never lie about money. People can get hostile.

Abbu pursed his lips, then shrugged. "Ah, well, another time—unless you still have that bay stud—?"

"The stud?" I echoed. "I still have him, yes—but he's not part of the stakes."

Light brown eyes assessed me. "Growing sentimental in your old age, Sandtiger?"

"He's not part of the stakes," I repeated quietly. "But I will offer you something of value . . . something you've been wanting for more than twenty years." I smiled as color crept into his swarthy face. "Yes, Abbu, I'll meet you in a circle—*if* the woman loses."

"If the woman *loses*—" He very nearly gaped. "Are you sandsick? Do you want to *give* the wager away?" Eyes narrowed in suspicion. "Why do you bet on the woman?"

I nodded toward the circle, where Del and Nabir were bending in the center to place blades on the ground. "Why don't you watch and find out?"

Abbu followed my own gaze. As I had, he assessed Nabir as a potential opponent. But he didn't assess Del as anything but a potential bedmate.

All to the good for me.

Abbu flashed me a glance. "We are not friends, you and I, but I have never thought you a fool. Yet you wager on a woman?"

I smiled blandly. "Someone has to, or there would be no bet."

Abbu shrugged. "You must want to meet me very badly."

I didn't answer. Nabir and Del had stripped out of footwear and harness, positioning themselves outside the circle directly opposite one another. It was to be a true dance, a dance of exhibition; a dance of bladeskills matched for the joy of competition. There was no need for anyone to die, which is the true nature of the dance. Shodos taught no one to go out in the world and kill. They taught only the grace and skill necessary to master a Southron sword; that most of us later hired ourselves out was a perversion of the true dance. It was also one of the few ways of earning a living in a land comprised of hundreds of tiny domains ruled by hundreds of desert princes. When power is absolute, you find your freedom—and a living—any way you can.

Abbu Bensir was right: we had never been friends. When I had been accepted as an apprentice, he was a sixth-level sword-dancer already hiring himself out. He had agreed to spar with wooden swords as a favor to the shodo, but he had been stupid enough to be careless, believing too implicitly in skills learned years before. He was older than I and complacent; he had nearly died of it.

Since then we had met from time to time, as sword-dancers do in the South. We had behaved very much like two dogs who recognize strength and determination in one another; we had circled each other warily, repeatedly, judging and testing by word and attitude. But we had never entered the circle. He was an acknowledged master, if unimaginative; I had, after seven years of apprenticeship and more than twelve of professional sword-dancing, established a reputation as a formidable, unbeatable opponent. Bigger, stronger, faster in a land of quick, medium-sized men. And I hadn't yet lost a dance that required someone to die.

Of course, neither had he

Which meant he wanted me badly. Now I was worth the effort.

"She is magnificent," Abbu murmured.

Yes, so she is.

"But much too tall."

Not for me.

"And hard where she should be soft."

Strong instead of weak.

"She is made for bedding, not for the circle."

I slanted him a glance. "Preferably *your* bed?"

"Better mine than yours." Abbu Bensir grinned. "I'll tell you if she was worth it."

"Big of you," I murmured. "*In* a manner of speaking."

He might have replied, but the dance had begun. He, like me, watched attentively, assessing posture, patterns, styles. It's something you can't avoid when you watch others dance. You put yourself in the circle and judge how *you* would have done it, criticizing the others. Nodding or shaking your head, swearing under your breath, muttering derisively. Occasionally bestowing praise. Always predicting the victor and how badly the other will lose.

My belly clenched as I watched. There was no doubt in my mind whatsoever that Del was the superior sword-dancer—*far* superior—but she was, to me, all too obviously out of condition. She was slow, stiff, awkward, employing none of her remarkable finesse. Her blade patterns were open and sweeping, which is alien to the woman whose true gift is subtlety. Her stance lacked the lithe, eloquent power so often overlooked by men accustomed to brute strength in opponents. She gave Nabir none of the Del I knew, and yet she would beat him badly. It was obvious from the start.

Which gave me grounds for relief.

Abbu was glowering. "The boy is a fool."

"For dancing with a woman?"

"No. For giving in too easily. See how he defers to her? See how he allowed her to direct the dance?" Abbu shook his head. "He's afraid to hurt her, and so he has given her the circle. He has given her the dance. And all because she's a woman."

"You wouldn't?" I asked as blades clanged in the circle. "Are you telling me you could ignore her sex and simply fight her, dancer to dancer?"

Abbu glowered more darkly.

I nodded. "So I thought."

"And you?" he challenged. "What would the Sandtiger do? He was a woman himself for half his life—"

I closed my hand on his wrist. "If you are not very careful," I began, "our dance will be right now. And this time I will open your throat with steel instead of wood."

A roar went up from the crowd. It had nothing to do with Abbu and me, but with the outcome of the dance. Which meant Del had won. They'd have cheered for Nabir; for her, they'd award only silence once they were over their shock.

Abbu, swearing, jerked his wrist free. "You are soft," he accused. "Do you think I can't see it? Your color is bad, your bones too sharp, the look in your eye is dull. You are not the Sandtiger I saw dance eighteen months ago. Which means you are old, sick, or injured. Which is it, Sandtiger?" He paused. "Or is it all of them?"

I showed him all my teeth. "If I am sick, I'll get better; injured, I will heal. But if I am old, you are older; look in a mirror, Abbu. Your life is in your face."

I didn't exaggerate. His swarthy face was sharply graven at mouth and eyes, and there was gray in his dark brown hair. The nose had been broken at least once, retaining a notch across the bridge that had, in my apprenticeship, boasted a Punja-bred hook. He was, I knew, past forty; in our profession, old. And he looked every year of it.

But then, so do I. The desert is never kind.

Del, in the circle, said something to Nabir. Knowing her, it was something diplomatic. Something to do with victory in the future; she is not a woman to grind a man's pride in the dirt unless he demands it. And Nabir hadn't, not really. Oh, he'd been certain of his victory, but then I'd known a certain other young sword-dancer who'd felt much the same upon receiving his blued-steel, shodo-blessed sword. And who'd lost his first dance to an experienced sword-dancer who had no time to humor the whims and pride of an arrogant young man; I'd deserved to lose. And I had.

Now, so had Nabir.

He took it badly, of course. So had I. It remained to

be seen if Nabir would learn from the loss or let it
fester in his spirit. Admittedly he had more to flagel-
late himself with—he'd lost his first dance to a *woman*—
but if he was smart he'd think twice about underestimating
his opponent. Too many variables entered into a dance,
certainly more than sex. And if Nabir didn't learn how
to deal with them, how to adapt, he'd be killed the
first time he entered a circle to dance to the death.

When the boy refused to answer Del, she turned
away and walked out of the circle. She still wore blue
wool tunic and trews, now stained with sweat; she
needed to switch to Southron clothing. A lifted arm
scrubbed dampness from her face and stripped it free
of loosened hair. Her movements were stiff, lacking
grace. She bent, scooped up harness and boots, let the
crowd fall back from her. She was flushed, a little
shaky, obviously tired. But she hid the magnitude of it
from everyone save me.

I was so glad to have the dance over I didn't think
about anything else.

"The boy was a fool," Abbu declared.

"Yes."

"And I a fool for risking so much on him."

I smiled. "Yes."

Abbu pulled the Hanjii nose-ring from his pouch. "I
pay my debts, Sandtiger. I won't have it said I don't."

"Now I don't need to, Abbu."

He glared at me sourly as he handed over the nose-
ring, then stared past at Del's retreating back. "There
is much she could learn, if a man took the time to
teach her."

A man had. *Men* had, Northerners all, *an-kaidin*
from Staal-Ysta. And a bandit named Ajani. But I
said nothing of it to Abbu Bensir, who wouldn't
understand.

"Oh, I don't know, Abbu—seems to me she's already learned a lot."

"She could be better. Faster, smoother . . ." He
flicked an expressive hand. "She is a woman, of course,

with a woman's failings, but there *is* talent in her. Promise. And she is tall enough and strong enough . . ." Then he shook his head. "But it would be folly to teach a woman. To *attempt* to teach a woman."

"Why?"

He was very sure of himself. "She would cry the first time her shodo spoke to her harshly. She would give up the first time she was cut. Or she would meet a man and lose all interest. She would cook his food, keep his hyort, bear his children. And she would set aside the sword."

I raised eyebrows in nonchalant challenge. "Isn't that what a woman's for? Cooking food, keeping a hyort, having a man's children?"

Still frowning, Abbu glanced at me impatiently. "Yes, of course, all of those things—but have you no eye, Sandtiger? Or do you see nothing but the woman, instead of the woman's skill?" His gaze was very level. "When I saw you dance the first time—your first *real* dance, not when you nearly killed me—I knew what you would be. Even though you lost. And I knew there would be two names spoken in the Punja, instead of just mine." He hitched one shoulder. "I was willing to share, and so I do. Because I am not a blind fool. Because I acknowledge talent when I see it, even in a woman. So should you."

This was not the Abbu Bensir I remembered. He had always been supremely certain of his talent, technique, presence. But then, he *was* an excellent sworddancer. He *did* have superb technique. And certainly he had presence, ruined nose and all; shorter than I, and slighter, with more distinctly Southron features, Abbu Bensir nonetheless still claimed the unspoken ability to dominate those around him.

But he'd never been known for his humility or fairmindedness. Certainly not when it came to his dealings with women. He was, after all, Southron, and the women he knew were cantina girls, or silly-headed serving-girls in the employ of various tanzeers or merchants.

He certainly didn't know any woman worth the time to instruct in the ways of handling a sword. I doubt the idea had ever occurred to him, any more than it had to me—prior to meeting Del. But I had met Del, and I'd changed. Would Abbu Bensir do the same?

Not if I had anything to say about it. Better to let him remain the arrogant Southron male.

"I recognize talent when I see it," I told him. "I acknowledge it. Are you forgetting I wagered on *her?*"

"You did it to provoke me," Abbu declared. "We are oil and water, Sandtiger . . . it will always be so between us." He stared past me, watching the crowd slowly disperse. Then his eyes flickered back to me. "You have the nose-ring, Sandtiger. Now I will have the woman."

He brushed by me easily as he turned, black gauze underrobe rippling. He wore a harness and blade, Southron blade, glinting in the sunlight. An old, honorable sword, attended by many legends.

I watched him go, striding away in the fluid gait of a man well-content with his life. A man who, I was certain, entertained no doubts of himself.

Or of the woman he followed.

Six

By the time I reached the cantina, Abbu Bensir had already cornered Del. Well, not cornered *exactly;* she was sitting in a corner, and he was sitting with her.

She sat with her back to the wall, just as I always did. This allowed her to see me as I approached, although she gave no indication of it. It also allowed me to approach without Abbu knowing, since his back was to me. So I took advantage of it, pausing just behind him. Listening to *his* approach.

"—you could become much better," he said confidently. "With my help, of course."

Del didn't answer.

"You must admit," he went on, "it's unusual to find a woman with your potential and dedication. Here in the South—"

"—women are treated as slaves." Del didn't smile. "Why should I be yours?"

"Not my slave, my student."

"I've already been an *ishtoya.* I've already been *an-ishtoya.*"

Now he was confused. "I am Abbu Bensir. Any Southron sword-dancer can tell you who I am, and what I am capable of. *Any* Southron sword-dancer . . . all of them know me."

For the first time since my arrival, Del looked at me. "Do you know him?"

Abbu sat upright, then twisted his head around.

Saw me, scowled, sent me a silent message to leave, then turned back to Del. "Ask anyone but him."

I grinned. "But I *do* know you. And what you're capable of."

"Which is?" Del asked coolly.

Abbu shook his head. "He will not give you a fair answer. He and I are old rivals in the circle. He will not bespeak me well."

"And you're a liar," I said pleasantly. "I'd tell her the truth, Abbu: that you're a superb sword-dancer with much to teach anyone." I paused. "But I'm more superb than you."

Del very nearly smiled. Abbu merely glared. "This is a private table."

"The lady was here first. Why don't we ask *her?*"

Del made an impatient gesture; she has no tolerance for such things.

I hooked a stool over, sat down, smiled disarmingly at Abbu. "Have you told her your scheme yet?"

"Scheme?" he echoed blankly.

I glanced at Del. "He plans on flattering your skill, since women are gullible creatures . . . he'll tell you what he thinks you want to hear, even if he doesn't agree . . . and then he'll take you into the circle, just to keep you interested—" I grinned, "—and then take you straight to bed."

Abbu's pale eyes glittered.

"It won't work," I told him. "I already tried."

"*And* failed," Del declared.

Abbu, who is not stupid, frowned. He looked at Del. At me. Then demanded his nose-ring back.

"Why?" I asked.

"Because it was won under false pretenses. You and the woman know one another."

I shrugged. "I never said we didn't. It didn't come up, Abbu. I offered a wager. You accepted a wager. The nose-ring was fairly won." I smiled. "And I need it to pay *my* debts."

Del was staring at me. "You bet on the dance?"

"I bet on you."

"To win."

"Of *course* to win; do you think I'm a fool?"

Abbu swore under his breath. "*I* am the fool."

"For wanting to teach a woman?" Del's tone was cool again. "Or for betting on the wrong person?"

Kima arrived with a jug. "Aqivi," she announced, and smacked it down on the table.

Abbu Bensir stared across the lip of the jug at Del in obvious challenge. I have seen it before—Abbu, much as I hate to admit it, has success with women— but I didn't consider it much of a risk. He wasn't the type of man who would interest Del. He was too arrogant, too abrupt, too certain of superiority based solely on his gender.

He was, most of all, too *Southron*.

"What can you teach me?" Del asked.

I kicked her under the table.

Abbu considered it. "You are tall," he said, "and strong. You have as good a reach as any Southroner— except perhaps the Sandtiger. But you would do better to make your patterns smaller. More subtle." He reached across the table, tapped Del's left wrist. "You have the necessary strength here—I saw it—to support the smaller patterns, but you don't use it. You were much too open earlier. It slowed your response time and left opportunities to defeat you. That you won had less to do with your better skill than with the boy's inexperience." He smiled briefly. "I would not do the same."

It was an accurate summation of Del's dance. That he also suggested smaller blade patterns did not please me, because it showed me he'd judged her very well. Del usually *does* employ smaller, tighter patterns, but she was out of condition and hadn't employed her usual techniques.

And if anything would impress Del, it was a man judging her on her merits instead of by her gender.

"Here," I said abruptly, "no need to let good aqivi

go to waste." I grabbed the jug, started splashing liquor into the cups Kima put down.

Abbu watched me sidelong. In profile, his nose was a travesty—but it lent him the cachet of hard-edged experience. Unlike Nabir, he was not a boy on the threshold of manhood; Abbu Bensir had stepped across many years before. He had the lean, lethal look of a borjuni, though he was sword-dancer instead of bandit.

What he thought of me, I couldn't say. I was considerably taller and heavier, also younger—but Abbu Bensir was right. I hadn't quite recovered strength, stamina, or health from the wound Del had given me, and it showed. Certainly it showed to an experienced sword-dancer who knew very well how to judge what counted.

He eased himself back on his stool and tipped aqivi down his throat. "So," he said idly to Del, "has this big desert cat told you of our adventures?"

"Adventures?" I echoed blankly; Abbu and I had not, to my knowledge, ever shared much more than a cantina.

Predictably, Del said no.

Of course it was what he wanted. With an adroit flick of fingers, Abbu slipped the neck of his underrobe and let it fall open. His throat was now bared, showing the pale scar left by the shodo's knife. "My badge of honor," he said. "Bestowed on me by none other than the Sandtiger."

Del's brows rose.

Abbu's tone was expansive. "It was quite early in his career, but it was a dramatic signal to the South that a new sword-dancer was about to be born."

"There was nothing 'about to be' about it," I said sourly. "It took me seven more years."

"Yes, but it served notice to those of us able to judge such things as talent and potential." He paused. "To those *few* of us."

"Did it?" Del asked coolly.

"Oh, yes," Abbu said. "He was a clumsy seventeen-

year-old boy with hands and feet too big for his body—
and his brain—but the potential was there. I knew
what he would become . . . so long as his inborn
submissiveness and all his years as a chula didn't
destroy him before he truly began."

Del's lids didn't flicker. "Abbu Bensir," she said
softly, "be careful where you walk."

He is not a stupid man; he changed tactics instantly.
"But I am not here to talk about the Sandtiger, whom
you undoubtedly know much better than I do." There
was a glint in his eyes. "I came to offer my services as
a shodo, even briefly. I think you could benefit."

"Perhaps I could," Del said. And then looked me
dead in the eye. "If you kick me one more time—"

I overrode her by raising my voice and talking to
Abbu. "Won't you be going to Iskandar like everyone
else?"

"Eventually. Although I think it is nonsense, this
talk of a jhihadi." Abbu shrugged, swallowed aqivi.
"Iskandar himself, the stories say, promised he would
return to bring prosperity to the South, to turn the
sand to grass. I see no signs of that." He shook his
head. "I think it is nothing more than a foolish man
who fancies himself an oracle . . . a zealot who requires
attention before he dies. He will rouse the tribes,
undoubtedly—that, I hear, is begun—but no one with
any sense will pay mind to it."

"Except the tanzeers." I shrugged as Abbu frowned
over his tankard. "They won't believe the Oracle's
foretellings, but if they have any intelligence at all
they'll recognize that this Oracle—and the proclaimed
jhihadi, if one ever appears—could siphon off some of
their power."

"An uprising," Abbu said thoughtfully, "couched in
the name of religion."

"People will do amazing things in the name of faith,"
I remarked. "Wrap it in the trappings of holy edict,
and even assassination is revered."

"I don't understand," Del interjected. "What you

say of religion, yes—that I have seen myself—but how would it affect the South?"

I shrugged. "The South is made up of hundreds of desert domains ruled by any man strong enough to hold it. He comes in, establishes his dominance, names himself tanzeer to gain a little glitter—and rules."

She blinked. "So easily?"

"So easily," Abbu confirmed in his broken voice. "Of course, any man who decided to do it would require a large force of loyal men . . . or a large force of *hired* men loyal to his coin." He grinned. "I myself have engaged in establishing several such new reigns."

Del's tone was bland. "But you yourself have never attempted to set up your *own* domain."

He shrugged. "Easier to take the money and leave, then move on to the next desert bandit who has notions of naming himself tanzeer."

Del glanced at me. "Have you done it as well?"

"Never from the beginning," I told her. "I have hired on to protect the tanzeer already in place, but I've never gone in and set up a brand-new domain."

She nodded thoughtfully. "So a tanzeer is not born . . . he becomes a prince only through force of arms."

I shook my head. "A tanzeer is born if his family has held the domain long enough. And some of these desert 'princedoms' have been in existence for centuries, handed down to each heir—"

"—who must himself be strong enough to hold it," Del finished.

"Of course," Abbu rasped. "There have been many newly proclaimed tanzeers, inheriting at an untimely age, who simply could not muster the forces needed to defend against usurpers." He smiled. "That is the easiest way of enlarging a domain."

"Stealing from someone else," she said.

"*All* of the domains were stolen," Abbu countered. "Once, surely, the South belonged to no one, it simply *was*—and then men strong enough to do so selected for themselves the domains they wanted . . . and so on and so on until the land was sectioned off from the sea to the Northern border, and to the east and west as well."

"Sectioned off," she echoed. "Is there no free land left at all?"

Abbu shrugged. "Domains exist where the land is worth having. There is water, or a city, or an oasis, or mountains—a place worth having becomes a domain. What no one wants is free."

"The Punja," I said. "No one rules the Punja. Except the tribes, maybe . . . but they have more respect for the land. They don't divide it up and sit on it. Nor do they give in to the rule of any man proclaiming himself a tanzeer. They just go with the wind, blowing here and there."

"Much like a sword-dancer." Del turned her cup on the table. "So, the Oracle—who gains disciples among the tribes—offers threat to the tanzeers."

"By rousing the tribes, yes," Abbu agreed.

"But the Oracle is only a mouthpiece," I said. "It's the jhihadi who offers the true threat. Because if the stories were to come true—that sand will be turned to grass—it means *all* of the South would be worth having. Each man would be a tanzeer unto himself, and the authority of those petty princes holding the present domains would collapse."

"So they will try to kill him." Del's tone was matter-of-fact. "No matter who he is, no matter why he's come; even if it's all a lie—the tanzeers will have him killed. Just in case."

"Probably," I agreed.

Abbu smiled a little. "First they would have to find him."

"Iskandar," Del said. "Isn't that where he's supposed to appear?"

Abbu shrugged. "That's what the Oracle says."

"*You're* going," she pointed out.

Abbu Bensir laughed. "Not for the Oracle. Not for

the jhihadi. I'm going for the dancing. I'm going for the coin."

Del frowned. "Coin?"

Abbu nodded. "Where there are people gathering, there will be wagering. Where there are *tanzeers*, there will be employment. Easier to find both in one place rather than scattered across the South."

"In uplander, a *kymri*," I explained. "We don't have many here in the South . . . but Abbu is right. If this Oracle rouses enough people, they will all go to Iskandar. So will the tanzeers. And so will sword-dancers."

"And bandits?" she asked.

"Borjuni, yes," Abbu agreed. "Even whores like Kima."

"I want to go," Del said.

I sighed. "Seems as good a place as any to learn something of Ajani's whereabouts."

But Del wasn't looking at me. She was looking at Abbu. "And I want you to teach me."

I nearly choked on aqivi. "*Del—*"

"Tomorrow," she declared.

Abbu Bensir merely smiled.

Seven

"**W**hy?" I asked, standing in the doorway. "What are you trying to prove?"

Del, inside her tiny room at the inn, barely glanced at me as she sat down on the edge of her slatted cot to pull off boot and fur gaiter. "Nothing," she answered, unwrapping leather garters.

"Nothing? *Nothing?*" I glared. "You know as well as I do you don't need Abbu Bensir to teach you anything."

"No," she agreed, peeling gaiter from boot.

"Then why—"

"I need the practice."

I stood braced in the doorway, watching her tug off the boot. She dropped it to the floor, then turned to the other boot. Once again, she started with the gaiter. Her bare right foot was chafed at the edges; the rest of it was white.

"So," I said, "you're using him for a sparring partner."

Del unlaced the garter. "Is he as good as he says he is?"

"Yes."

"Better than you?"

"Different."

"And *was* it you who put that scar on him?"

"No."

She tilted her head slightly. "So, he is a liar."

236

"Yes and no. I didn't give him the scar itself, but I did provide the reason for making it necessary."

Del looked up at me. "He doesn't hate you for it. He could—another man might—but he doesn't."

I shrugged. "We've never been enemies. Just rivals."

"I think he respects you. I think he knows you have your place in the South—in the pecking order of sword-dancers—and he has his."

"He is an acknowledged master of the blade," I said. "Abbu Bensir is a byword among sword-dancers. No one would be foolish enough to deny him that to his face."

"Not even you?"

"I've never considered myself a fool." I paused. "You're really going to spar with him?"

"Yes."

"You could have asked—"

"—you?" Del shook her head. "I did ask you. Several times."

"I'll spar," I said defensively. "Just not with my *jivatma*. We'll go find some wooden practice swords—"

"Steel," Del said succinctly.

"Bascha, you know why I don't want—"

"So you don't have to." She stripped gaiter free of boot. "So I'll use Abbu Bensir instead."

"But he thinks he's *teaching* you."

"He may think whatever he likes." Del tugged at her boot. "When a man won't do what you want him to in the *way* you want him to, you find new names for the same thing. If it satisfies Abbu Bensir's pride to believe he is teaching the gullible Northern bascha, let him. I will still get my practice. I will still improve my fitness." She looked at me squarely. "Which is something *you* need, too."

I ignored that; we both knew it was true. "How long is this to go on?"

"Until I am fit."

Frustration boiled up. "He only wants to get you into his bed."

Del rose, began to unhook her harness. "I am having a bath brought for me. If you truly believe I would be the kind to tease you, you would do well to leave."

On cue, one of the innkeeper's sons rolled the cask from out of my room. It was empty, of course, which meant Del had paid extra for clean water. But she had no money.

Frustration rose another notch. "Am I paying for this, too?"

Del nodded.

I glared. "Seems like I'm paying for an awful lot, yet getting nothing for it."

"Oh?" Pale brows rose. "Is courtesy and generosity dependent upon how soon and how many times I will go to bed with you?"

I moved aside as the boy rolled the cask through the doorway. I waited impatiently for him to drop the cask flat and depart; once he had, I turned back to Del.

I stood directly in front of her now, halting as she turned from the cot to match me stare for stare. Barefoot, she gave up an extra finger's-worth of height to the five additional I always claimed. But it didn't diminish her.

I drew in a steadying breath. "You're not making this any easier."

Del shut her teeth. "I'm not trying to *make* it anything. I'm trying to end my song."

I tried to keep my tone even. "How many men have you killed?"

Del's eyes narrowed. "I don't know."

"Ten? Twenty?"

"I don't know."

"Guess," I suggested.

She opened her mouth. Shut it. Then gritted between her teeth: "Perhaps twenty or so."

"How many in a circle?"

"In a circle? None. All have been in defense of myself." She paused. "Or in defense of others. Even you."

"And some for plain revenge. Ajani's men; you've killed some of them, haven't you? A few months ago?"

"Yes."

"And did each of those deaths require such intense focus?"

Del's mouth flattened. "I know what you are saying. You are saying I am wrong to require such behavior, such *focus;* that if I have already killed, one more death will be no less difficult."

I shook my head. "I'm saying I think you might be punishing yourself. That by demanding such rigorous behavior of yourself, you think you can make up for the deaths of your kinfolk."

The innkeeper's son banged the bucket of water as he brought it through the door, slopping water over the rim. Whatever Del might have said died before it was born, and I knew nothing would come of it now. The moment was gone.

"Soak well," I suggested flatly. "I have to go pay all your debts."

Mutely, Del watched the boy pour water into the cask. If she looked after me, it was too late. I was out of the room. Out of the inn. And very much out of temper.

It took me three cantinas to find him. Maybe he was embarrassed. Maybe he was shy. Or maybe he just wanted to do his drinking in a quieter, smaller place, lacking the huva stink and clamor of the cantina Kima worked.

But I did find him. And, having found him, I stood in the dimness of dusk inside the door and watched him from afar.

Nabir was, I decided, a handsome, well-set-up boy. In time he would grow into his potential and offer decent skills to anyone in the circle. Probably decent company, too, although at the moment he was plainly black of mood. More out of sorts than I'd been, if caused by the same woman.

He slouched on his stool at a table in the back of the common room, hitched up against the wall. His head was thrown back indolently, but there was nothing indolent about him. He was scowling. Black hair framed a good if unremarkable face; thick black brows met in a self-derisive scowl over the bridge of his nose. It was a straight, narrow nose, with only the suggestion of a hook. More like mine, in fact, than Abbu's, which displayed—or had once—the characteristic hook of a bird of prey. In some desert tribes, the hook of a man's nose denotes greater prowess as a warrior; don't ask me why. One of those fashions, I guess, like the Hanjii with their disfiguring nose-rings, or the Vashni with their necklets of human finger bones.

Before him on the table lay the harness and sword. It was at that he scowled so fiercely. Next to it sat a jug of liquor and a cup, but he drank nothing. Just sat and scowled and sulked and considered giving up his new profession.

I made my way through the tables and paused as he glanced up. I saw the recognition, the acknowledgement, the dilation of dark brown eyes. He sat up so hastily he nearly overset his stool, which would have damaged his pride even more.

I waved him down when he would have risen, and sat down on another stool. "So," I said, "quitting already?"

Anger flared, died; was replaced by humiliation. He couldn't meet my eyes.

I kept my tone conversational. "It's difficult, getting started. You don't know if anyone will dance with you, so you don't ask. And then when you summon up enough courage to ask an acknowledged master, a seventh-level sword-dancer—because, you think, losing to him will be expected, and therefore easier—he refuses. You leave wondering if anyone will *ever* dance with you—anyone other than another former apprentice only just getting started—and then a woman comes to you and says *she* will dance with you." I shifted on the stool. "At first you are insulted—a *woman!*—and then you recall that she was the woman with the Sandtiger; a woman who carries a sword and goes in harness, just as you do. You see she is tall and strong and foreign, and you think she should be in a hyort somewhere cooking food and nursing a baby; and you think you will put her in her place. In the name of your hard-won sword and your prickly Southron pride, you accept the woman's invitation." I paused. "And you lose."

"I am ashamed," he whispered.

"You lost for one reason, Nabir. One." I leaned forward and poured liquor into his cup: aqivi. "You lost because she won."

Lids flickered. He stared briefly at me, then looked back at his rejected sword and harness.

I drank. "You lost because you could not divide yourself from the arrogance of your sex, and from the knowledge of *hers.*"

He frowned.

I put it more plainly yet. "She won because she was better."

Color swept in to stain his swarthy desert face. "How can a woman be better—"

"—than a man?" I shrugged. "It might have something to do with her training, which began before yours. *Formal* training, that is; but she, like you, played with wooden swords when she was a child."

His jaw clenched. "I am a second-level sword-dancer."

I sipped. Nodded. "Something to be proud of. But I ask you this: why did you leave before you accomplished the other levels? There are seven, you know."

Dark eyes glittered. "I was ready to leave."

"Ah. You wearied of the discipline." I nodded. "*And* you kept hearing the song of coins going to other sword-dancers instead of yourself."

Black brows dove between his eyes. "There is no dishonor in leaving when I did. There are those who leave after a *single* year."

I nodded. "And most of them are dead."

His chin came up. "Because they accepted an invitation to dance to the death."

"So will you."

He shook his head. Black hair caught on the dropped hood of his indigo burnous. "I am not so foolish as to think I am good enough for that."

"But that's where the real money is." I shrugged as he stared intently. "Tanzeers always pay handsomely when they want someone killed."

"I'd rather—"

"—avoid it; I know. But what happens when a sword-dancer is hired to kill *you?*"

Eyes widened. *"Me?"*

"Of course. If you serve this tanzeer—" I flicked my left hand, "—then *that* tanzeer—" my right hand, "—will eventually desire you to be put out of his way. And so someone like me, or someone like Abbu Bensir—or someone like Del—will be hired to invite you into a circle where the dance will end in death."

"I can refuse." But his certainty was fading.

"You can refuse. Several times, in fact. But then you will get the reputation of a coward, and no tanzeer will hire you for anything." I shrugged. "Kill or be killed."

Nabir frowned. "Why are you telling me this?"

"Oh, maybe because I'd hate to see you quit a profession you might be suited for." I sipped again. "All you need is a little practice."

He blinked. "With—you?"

"With me."

"But—I'm not good enough for you."

At the moment, he probably was. But I didn't tell him that. "You were good enough to ask me to dance, weren't you?"

"But I knew I would lose. I just thought—" He sighed. "I just thought that if I was seen in a circle with the Sandtiger, it might help my name a little. I knew I would lose, of course, but I'd lose to the *Sandtiger*. Everyone loses to you."

"And you'll lose in practice, too," I pointed out. "But at least you'll learn a little something." And I'd get my conditioning back. "So, shall we begin tomorrow?"

Slowly, Nabir nodded. "What about—" He broke it off, thought about it, began again. "What about the woman? Is she truly a sword-dancer?"

I grinned. "If you're concerned your reputation—and pride—has been dealt too harsh a blow to survive, I wouldn't worry about it. Del's beaten me."

"You?"

"Only in practice, of course." I rose, put down his cup. "Thanks for the aqivi. I'll see you first thing in the morning."

He pushed himself to his feet. "Sandtiger—"

"Oh, yes—you won't be needing that." I pointed to his blade. "We'll be using wooden swords."

He blinked. "Wooden? But I haven't sparred with wooden blades since my first year."

"I know; me neither—and it's a considerably longer time for me than for you." I shrugged. "I'd hate to get carried away and cut your belly open. At least with a wooden sword, all I can do is break a few ribs." I grinned at his stricken expression. "Now go find yourself a woman—maybe that pretty little cantina girl across the way who's been eyeing you so much—and forget about Northern baschas."

"She's beautiful," he blurted.

I didn't need to ask which woman he meant; I've seen that expression before. "First lesson," I said. "Forget about such things. When you're in the circle, even against a woman—" I paused, "—even a woman like Del—you have to think about the dance. And *only* about the dance."

"It isn't a woman's place to be in a circle."

"Maybe not." I didn't feel like giving him any of Del's arguments against that line of reasoning; it would take too long. "But if you meet one there, are you willing to die just because she has breasts instead of *gehetties*?"

"*Gehett*—" He figured it out. It was enough to startle him into thinking about it. After a moment he nodded. "I will try not to think of the woman. I will try not to *see* the woman. I will try to do as you."

Hoolies, I wish when I was in the circle with Del I *could* only see the woman. Like Abbu Bensir. Like Nabir. Like all the other men who'd seen—or met—her in a circle.

Because then I'd forget the blood.

Eight

We met out in the open, away from the center of town. I wanted privacy for the boy's sake, and for my own; one needn't tell the competition one isn't what one should be.

"Draw the circle," I told him.

Nabir's dark eyes widened. "Me?"

I nodded solemnly. "The privilege of rank," I said, "is that you can have others do tedious things like digging in the dirt."

He waved a hand. "No, no—I only meant . . . I thought you would do it to make certain it was right."

"It's not too terribly difficult to draw a circle," I said dryly. "I think a second-level sword-dancer can manage it."

Which reminded him, as I meant it to, that he had some status of his own; as a matter of fact, if there was a first-level apprentice here, Nabir could assign the task to *him*.

But there wasn't. So Nabir took wooden sword in hand and asked me what size circle I wanted.

"Practice," I answered. "No sense in dancing our legs off yet." Especially since even a practice circle seven paces in diameter would test me. "We'll move to a sparring circle next, and then a full-fledged dancing circle once I think you're ready."

He opened his mouth. "But—" And broke it off. So, his discipline wasn't completely eroded.

"I know," I said. "You were going to tell me you

245

danced in a dancing circle yesterday. So? You lost.
We'll do it my way."

Nabir flushed, nodded and proceeded to draw a
meticulous circle in the dirt. He knew the dimensions
as well as I—seven long paces in diameter for a practice circle, ten for sparring, fifteen for a full-fledged
dancing circle—and had a steady hand, which meant
his line didn't waver very much. It's one of the things
a first-year apprentice learns: how to draw a clean
circle. It helps to fix the confines in the mind, which
is where the true circle must exist if an apprentice is to
succeed. It sounds easy. It isn't.

Nabir finished and looked at me expectantly, dusty
blade in hand.

"Sandals," I suggested. "Or were you going to give
me yet another advantage?"

Again he colored. I knew what he felt—couldn't he
remember *anything* in front of the Sandtiger?—but
holding him by the hand wouldn't help him one bit.
He had to get over being too impressed by me, or it
would hurt his concentration.

Although, I'll admit, the boy's regard made me feel
good. It's always nice to know *someone* is impressed
by what you've accomplished.

Even if Del wasn't.

Nabir stripped out of his sandals and dropped them
outside the circle, along with his indigo burnous, cream-
colored underrobe, belt. In leather dhoti he was mostly
naked suddenly, showing a lean Southron frame beneath dark Southron flesh. Tendons flexed visibly as
he moved, since every bit of skin was stretched taut.
Lean as he was, there was still an undulating section of
muscle between shortribs and the top of his dhoti.

I frowned thoughtfully. "What tribe are you?"

He stiffened visibly. Color moved through his face,
staining cheekbones, setting dark eyes aflame. "Does
it matter?"

There was belligerence in his tone. I shrugged. "Not
really. I was only curious . . . you just don't fit any of

the tribes I know. And yet there is tribal blood in you—"

"Yes." He cut me off. "I have no tribe, Sandtiger . . . none that will have me." Jaws clenched tautly. "I am a bastard."

"Ah, well, some of the best people I know are bastards." I grinned. "Myself included—maybe. Hoolies, at least you know."

Nabir stared at me across the circle he'd drawn so carefully. "You don't *know* if you're true-born or bastard?"

"It happens," I said dryly. "Now, shall we get about our business?"

Nabir nodded. "What's first?"

"Footwork."

"Footwork! But I learned footwork nearly two *years* ago!"

"Didn't learn much, did you?" Then, more kindly, "Or maybe you've just forgotten."

It did exactly as I expected. It shut the boy up.

Practicing something as rudimentary as footwork was good for us both. It's one of the basics in sword-dancing, part of the foundation that must be laid down if you're to learn anything, or progress. Clumsiness makes for a sloppy sword-dancer and little future; it also makes for a dead one, and no future at all. There just isn't any sense in skimping on the essentials when a few extra hours a day spent practicing footwork can mean the difference between survival and death.

But it had nonetheless been a long time since I had broken the practice routine down far enough to include footwork techniques. Del and I, prior to the dance on Staal-Ysta, had sparred together every day, or very nearly; footwork was not one of the things we practiced because, for us, it came naturally after so many years. It was all part of the sparring. But Nabir required a new attitude, and one way of developing one is to start all over again.

Well, in a manner of speaking. I couldn't spend *that* much time with him. I'm a sword-dancer, not a shodo; I didn't have the years to invest. Hoolies, I didn't even have the *days*. Del would be pushing to move on to Iskandar as soon as she felt sparring with Abbu no longer necessary

Which meant I needed to get as much out of the practice sessions with Nabir as I could. And *that* meant working a lot harder than I was used to, even in good health.

By the time I called a halt, both of us were dripping. Harquhal is a border town, not a desert town; it was only just spring, even in the South, and the temperature was still mild. But we sweated, and we stank; I'd need another bath.

He stood in the center of the circle, nodding weary satisfaction. Hair was pasted to his scalp, except where it curled damply against his neck. "Good," he gasped. "Good."

Well, maybe for him. I hurt.

"I am remembering some little things the shodo taught very early. The sort of things he said could mean the difference between a thrust through the ribs or a cut on the side."

Good for him, I thought ironically. I'd had both nearly three months before. And from the same sword.

Speechless, I nodded. I stood hands on hips, wooden sword doubled up in one fist, trying not to pant.

"So Sandtiger, is this the new—*ishtoya*?"

Broken male voice, not Del's. I turned abruptly and wished I hadn't. Saw Abbu Bensir standing outside the circle. Next to my clothes, and the Northern *jivatma* sheathed in cadda wood, leather, and runes.

So, he'd learned a Northern word between yesterday and today. No doubt he expected me to react. So I took great care not to.

"New sword, new harness," I said lightly.

"Poor old Singlestroke . . ." Abbu shook his head. "It must have been a great blow. After all, it isn't often a chula wins his freedom, let alone a shodo-blessed sword. And then to have it *broken* . . ." Again he shook his head.

From the corner of my eye, I saw Nabir stiffen as he heard the word chula. I lifted a single eloquent shoulder. "The new sword's better."

"Is it?" Abbu glanced down at the hilt, exposed above the lip of the danjac hide sheath. "Northern, from the look of it. And here I thought a desert-bred Punja-mite like yourself would never carry a foreign sword."

"We all change," I said offhandedly. "We get older, a little wiser . . . we learn not to judge people and things by homelands, language, gender."

"Do we?" Abbu grinned. "So we do. Yes, Sandtiger, the woman is much better than I expected. But there is still much I can teach her."

"Wait till she warms up." I showed him my teeth. "Better yet, wait until she sings."

Abbu wasn't listening. He was staring thoughtfully at my midriff, bared by the shedding of underrobe and burnous. Like Nabir, I wore only a dhoti. It hid nothing at all of the knurls, nicks, and scars gained from nineteen years of dancing. Nothing of the lash marks from sixteen years of slavery. And nothing at all of the stripes earned from a dying sandtiger who had, in that dying, given me my freedom.

But Abbu Bensir had seen all of it before, since a sword-dancer wears only a dhoti in the circle. My story was no secret, nor was the evidence hidden, since I wore it in my skin.

No, he'd seen all that before. What he looked at now was something he *hadn't* seen: the ugly, livid scar tissue left behind by Boreal.

He flicked a quick glance at my face. "I see," he remarked thoughtfully.

"Let me guess," I said dryly. "Now you plan to invite me into a circle."

Abbu shook his gray-dusted head. "No. When you

and I meet, you will be the man I saw eighteen months ago. I want no unfair advantage because you are recovering from—*that*." He frowned, locking black brows together. "I've seen men dead of less."

I arched brows. "Big of you."

It was Abbu's turn to display teeth. "Yes." Then the frown came back. He looked again at the healing wound. "You went north," he said. "I heard you went north."

"To *the* North; yes." I shrugged. "Why? I don't know a sword-dancer yet who stays put in one place."

Abbu flipped a dismissive hand. "No, no, of course not. But I have heard stories about Northern magic . . . about Northern swords . . ." He scowled at me in consideration. "Steel *cuts*," he said quietly. "It doesn't burn. It doesn't blister. It doesn't eat skin away."

It hadn't burned. It had frozen. In a way I'd been very lucky. Boreal's banshee-bite had eaten away enough outer flesh to leave a depressed knot the size of a man's fist, but the icy steel had also frozen blood and inner tissue, preventing significant blood loss. The *jivatma* had missed anything vital, thank valhail. But had Del cut into me with a Southron blade, even missing the vitals, I'd have bled to death in the circle.

"Does it matter?" I asked. "It's healing."

"Don't you understand?" Abbu persisted. "If a sword could do that in the *circle*—"

"No." I said it flatly, leaving no room for doubt. "It's best if the circle is left as we learned it."

"A sword-dancer with a blade capable of doing that would be worth his weight in gold, gems, silks . . ." Abbu shrugged. "He could name his price."

"Maybe found a domain of his own?" I grinned. "Believe me, Abbu, you don't want to pay the price of lugging around a Northern *jivatma*."

He looked down at my belongings once more: at the visible hilt of a foreign sword. At the alien runes looping the sheath from split lip to brass-footed tip.

"*Jivatma*," he breathed, pronouncing the syllables

oddly. "I heard her say that word. Only once. But once said, it was loud." Abbu looked away from the sword and back at me with effort. "As one sword-dancer to another—as a student who shared the teachings of your shodo—I ask permission to make the acquaintance of your sword."

It was stilted, formal phraseology. It was also a ritual performed by every sword-dancer who wanted to touch another sword-dancer's weapon. Killers we may be, more often than not, but the true dance is founded in elaborate courtesy. A few of us remember.

Nabir, who had, out of his own sense of courtesy, remained in the circle and left the two experienced sword-dancers to their conversation, now came closer. He had, after all, met the bared steel of Del's blade. I figured he had as much right to ask me about it as Abbu.

"Did you and Del spar with steel? With your own blades?"

Abbu frowned. "Of course."

"Then you saw her *jivatma*."

"Saw. Didn't touch." His smile was twisted. "Something about her—forbade it."

I glanced sidelong at Nabir. His eyes were fixed on the hilt glinting brightly in the sunlight. The blade itself was hidden in rune-warded sheath.

Sighing, I walked the rest of the distance and dropped the wooden practice blade beside the puddle of silk and gauze. Scooped up the harness, beckoned Nabir closer, slid Northern steel out into Southron moonlight. Shed harness and sheath, then displayed the sword in its entirety, resting blade in left hand while the other balanced the hilt at the quillons.

Sunlight poured across runes like water. The pristine brilliance was blinding.

Except for one thing.

"What's the matter with it?" Nabir asked. "Why is the tip all charred?"

Charred. I hadn't put it like that. But it was true:

the blade looked like about five inches of it had been thrust into a conflagration.

Well, in a way it had. Only the fire had been Chosa Dei.

"It's like hers," Abbu said intently. Then nodded slowly. "So, it's true. There *is* magic in Northern swords."

"Only some of them. Del's, yes; trust me. But this one—well, this one isn't quite sure what it wants to be yet. Trust me on that, too."

"May I?" Abbu put out a hand.

I grinned. "He wouldn't like it."

Abbu frowned. "He who? *Who* wouldn't like it?"

"Him. The sword."

Abbu glared. "Are you telling me your sword has *feelings?*"

"Sort of." I pulled the hilt away as Abbu's hand threatened imminent capture. "Unh-*unh*—I didn't give you permission." Quickly I bent, scooped up the harness, resheathed the sword. Tucked it into the crook of my left arm. "Take my word for it, Abbu—you don't want to know."

He was red-faced. Pale brown eyes turned black as pupils dilated. "You offend me with this idiocy—"

"No offense intended," I countered swiftly. "Believe me, Abbu, you *don't* want to know."

"I know too much," he snapped. "I know you went to the North and got the sense frozen out of your head, along with the guts removed from your belly." He flicked a disdainful glance at my still-naked midriff with its sword-born scar. "And I have better things to do than stand here listening to your babble."

"So don't," I suggested mildly, which didn't please him any more.

Abbu said something beneath his breath in Desert, which I understood—and spoke—as well as he, then turned on his heel and marched away, black underrobe flapping.

I sighed. "Ah, well, no harm done. We're no *less* fond of each other than we were before."

Nabir's expression was unreadable as I reached down to gather up wooden blade, boots, underrobe, and belt. He waited until I was finished tucking things here and there.

"Is it true?" he asked.

"Is what true?"

"That." He nodded toward my sword. "Is it alive?"

I didn't laugh, because it would offend his dignity. And I tried very hard not to smile. "There's a wizard in here," I said solemnly.

After a long moment, he nodded. "I thought there might be."

I opened my mouth. Shut it. Swallowed the hoot of laughter trying very hard to escape. Not because there *wasn't* a wizard in my sword, but because of Nabir's reaction.

Finally I managed an inoffensive smile as I turned away from the circle. Away from Nabir. "Don't believe everything you hear."

"I don't have to," he said. "I *saw* it."

It stopped me dead in my tracks. Slowly I turned back. "Saw it?"

Nabir nodded. "You were making Abbu Bensir think you lied. You knew he would disbelieve you. And he did. He went away thinking you a fool, or sandsick . . . a man who says his sword is *alive*." He shrugged. "I heard the words, too—but I saw what you did." His youthful mouth twisted. "Or what you *didn't* do."

Now he had *me* intrigued. "What didn't I do?"

Nabir's tone was calm. "Let him touch the sword."

I passed it off with a shrug. "I just don't like others touching my sword."

"May I?"

"No—and for the same reason."

Nabir's dark eyes were steady. "Student to shodo, I respectfully request—"

"No," I said again, knowing I was trapped. "We're not *really* student and shodo, so the forms don't apply."

His young features were almost harsh. There are tribes in the South very feral in nature, and it shows in the flesh. Bastard-born, maybe, but Nabir had more than a splash of Punja-bred fierceness. It altered him significantly.

"If the forms do not apply," he said quietly, "I have no desire to dance with you."

"No?"

"No. And you *need* me to dance with you." Nabir smiled in beguiling innocence. "You aren't helping me, Sandtiger. You're helping yourself. You are slow and stiff and awkward from that wound, and you're afraid you won't get your fitness back so you can dance against men like Abbu Bensir. And if you *can't*—"

"All right," I said, "all right. Yes, I'm out of condition. I'm slow and stiff and awkward, *and* I hurt like hoolies. But I *earned* the pain, Nabir . . . I earned the slowness, the stiffness, the clumsiness. Yours may be inbred."

It wasn't nice. But he'd cut too close to the bone in shedding his awe of me.

"So," he said softly, "you put the dull blade against the newborn whetstone and fashion an edge again."

"Does it matter?" I asked. "You'll be better for it yourself."

Nabir nodded. "Yes. But you might have asked me."

I sighed wearily. "I might have. But you'll learn when you get to my age that pride can make you do and say strange things."

"You are the Sandtiger." He said it with an eloquent simplicity that made me ashamed.

"I was a slave," I said flatly. "You heard the word when Abbu said it: chula. And I was very nearly your age before I gained my freedom. Believe me, Nabir, all those years of the past don't make for an easy future, even when you're free."

"No," he agreed, very softly.

I sighed heavily and scrubbed at my forehead beneath still-damp, itchy hair. "Look," I said, "I can't tell you his name. So you can't touch him. I'm sorry, Nabir—but like I told Abbu, you're better off not knowing."

"That is the answer, then? His name?"

"Part of it," I agreed. "The rest is better left unexplained." I started to turn away. "Are you coming? I'm for a jug of aqivi."

Solemnly, he came. And then, "Am I really slow and stiff and clumsy?"

I considered lying. Discarded the idea; he was worth the truth. "Yes. But that will change." I grinned. "A few more circles with me, and you'll be the Sandtiger's heir-apparent."

Nabir smile was slow, but warm. "Not so bad a thing."

"Only sometimes." I slapped him on his back. "How was the little cantina girl?"

Nabir forebore to answer. Which meant either he liked the girl too much to say, or he hadn't had the courage.

Ah, well, give it time . . . young manhood can be awkward.

Nine

Across our wooden blades, Nabir's face was stiff. "She won't marry me."

As interruptions go, it was terrific. I straightened out of my crouched stance and lowered my sword, frowning. "Who won't—" I blinked. "The little *cantina girl?*"

Nabir, nodding, lowered his own blade-shaped piece of wood. His eyes were very fierce.

It was, I thought, an interesting time to bring it up. We were in the middle of a sparring session, having progressed from the practice circle after two days. "Why do you *want* her to?" I asked.

Nabir drew himself up. Sweat ran down his temples. "Because I love her."

I opened my mouth. Closed it. Thought over how best to discuss the situation with the boy, whose prickly tribal pride—bastard-born or not—sometimes required diplomacy. Not that he could have harmed me, if it went so far; but I had no desire to hurt his feelings.

I scrubbed a forearm across my brow, smearing hair out of my eyes. "Don't take offense, Nabir—but is she your first girl?"

His entire body went stiff. "No," he declared. "Of course not; I have been a man for many years."

I waited patiently. Eventually his gaze shifted.

"Yes." The word was muffled.

So. Now I understood.

"Water break," I suggested.

He followed me out of the circle, took the bota as I slapped it into his hands, sucked down several swallows as I folded myself onto my gauze and silks, nestling buttocks into sand. I set aside the wooden blade and hooked elbows around crooked-up knees.

"So," I said lightly, "you slept with the girl. And you liked it. You like it very much."

Nabir, still standing, nodded. He clutched the bota tightly.

"Nothing wrong with that." I squinted up at him. "But you don't have to *marry* her."

"I want to."

"You can't marry every girl you sleep with."

Obviously, it had not occurred to him that other women might enter into it. He had discovered the magic in a woman's body—and in his own—and thought it was supposed to be that way—with *this* woman—for the rest of his life.

Poor boy.

"She won't have me," he said tightly.

A blessing, undoubtedly. But I asked, since he expected it. "Why not?"

Muscles twitched in his jaw. "Because I am a bastard. Because I have no tribe."

Better yet, because he had little coin and fewer prospects. But I didn't say it. "Look at it this way, then," I said. "It's her loss, not yours."

"If I could rejoin the tribe—" Abruptly, he altered his sentence. "If I could prove myself worthy, they would overlook my birth."

"Who would?"

Nabir scowled, handed down the bota. "The elders."

"Which tribe?"

Nabir shook his head. "I shouldn't speak of it. I have said too much."

I didn't really want to spend too much time trying to decipher Nabir's past, or foretell his possible future. I scratched at sandtiger scars. "Well," I said finally, "it's their loss, too. Meanwhile, we have a lesson to finish."

"If I could be worthy of the tribe, I'd be worthy of her," he persisted. "She said so."

More likely she'd said anything she could think of, just to put him off. It also might be true; a cantina girl hoping for a better life would fix her dreams on someone of greater stature, not a bastard-born halfbreed with nothing to offer but himself. For a girl who sold herself nightly to men of all ilk, Nabir's regard—and his presence in her bed—would not be enough. She'd have to know there was more.

Right now, there wasn't.

I sucked water, replugged the bota. "A sword-dancer really shouldn't think about marriage, Nabir. It dulls the edge."

"We have no edge at all." He grinned, lifting his blade. "See? Only wooden."

I smiled. "Still after me to use real swords, are you?"

"My shodo told me wood was useful for only so long. That to develop a true understanding of the dance, a true sword is required. Because without the risk, nothing is learned."

Yes, well . . . Nabir's shodo had never known my *jivatma*. "Maybe so," I agreed, "but right now I prefer wood."

Nabir looked beyond me. "It's her," he said obscurely.

The cantina girl? I turned. No. Del.

She had, at last, traded Northern wool for Southron silks. Rich blue burnous rippled as she walked, hood puddled on her shoulders. Already the sun had bleached her hair a trifle blonder, and her skin was pinker than normal. In time, it would turn creamy gold. The hair would pale almost to white.

Del crossed the sand smoothly, hilt shining behind her left shoulder. Her sessions with Abbu Bensir had removed some of the tension from her body, as if she understood she was doing something definite toward reaching her goal, since she needed to be fit to meet Ajani. I was glad to see her moving better, feeling better, but I wasn't pleased by the source. If she'd been willing to meet me with wooden blades, like Nabir, I could have done the same. Hoolies, I could have done more.

Del stopped beside the circle. "Tiger is the only sword-dancer I know who practices his dancing by sitting on the ground."

Nabir's eyes widened; how could I stand for this?

"Not true," I replied equably. "Nabir can tell you I've thwacked him upside the head more times than you can count—I'm giving him a breather."

Nabir frowned; it wasn't true. Del, who saw it, smiled crookedly, interpreting it easily. But she said nothing, looking critically at the wooden blade the boy held. "Do you *ever* plan to use steel?"

Nabir opened his mouth.

"No need," I answered for him. "You know as well as I the fundamentals are better taught with wood than with steel."

"He doesn't *need* the fundamentals . . . at least, not independent of steel. There is no risk with a wooden blade, and nothing is learned without risk."

I glared at her sourly as Nabir snapped his head around to stare at me. "I told you why," I said. "As long as we're speaking of risk, what about the kind of risk the boy would face if I *did* use my sword?"

"What of it?" Del returned. "It's as much for you to learn control as for him to learn technique."

Nabir cleared his throat. "I would like to face steel."

"Then face me." Del slipped the burnous easily and left it lying in a puddle at her feet. Beneath it she wore a soft cream-colored leather tunic, cap-sleeved and belted, that hit her mid-thigh. She'd worn something similar the first time I'd seen her. Though there was nothing indecent about the tunic—it was completely unrevealing—it was still considerably less than Southron women wore. Even in bed.

Nabir, who had seen her in Northern tunic and trews and boots, stared. There was a lot of limb showing, since she is long of legs and arms, and therefore a lot of flesh. A *lot* of creamy Northern flesh stretched over exquisite Northern bones.

I, who also had seen her in nothing less than tunic and trews and boots for longer than I cared to recall, stared, too. But with less shock than Nabir; she is very impressive, yes, but also exceedingly frustrating.

Nabir swallowed heavily. "I've already danced against you."

"And lost," she said. "Shall we see what Tiger has taught you?"

I watched her unhook her harness, preparing to add it to her pile once she'd unsheathed. I got up. "I don't think so, Del."

She was unsmiling. "His choice."

"Yes," Nabir said instantly

I ignored the boy, staring instead at Del. "You're doing this to force my hand. To *make* me use my sword."

"You can't spend your life being afraid of it," she said. "I don't deny it's worth your concern, but you have to learn to control it. Best to do it now rather than in a dance to the death, or in a dangerous situation where hesitation might kill you."

Nabir frowned. "I don't understand."

"You shouldn't," I said curtly. "This has nothing to do with you."

"Then what *does* it—"

"This." I bent, scooped up harness, stripped the sheath from my sword. "This is what it has to do with, Nabir: Blooding-blade. Named blade. *Jivatma*. And one more thing: Chosa Dei. Whose soul is in this blade."

"So is yours," Del said steadily. "Do you think only Chosa Dei went into that sword when you requenched? You sang yourself into it, Tiger, as much as Chosa Dei. That, coupled with your determination and strength, will overcome any attempt he might make to steal the power from you."

"Chosa Dei," Nabir echoed.

I looked at him sharply. "Do you know Chosa Dei?"

"Of course." He shrugged. "In stories about how the South became the South."

My turn to frown. "What?"

Again he shrugged. "I heard as a child that once the North and the South were the same. That there was no desert, only grasslands and mountains. And then Chosa Dei grew jealous of his brother—I forget his name—and tried to steal what his brother had."

"Shaka Obre," I muttered.

Nabir, cut off, blinked. "What?"

"His brother." I flapped a hand. "Go on."

"Chosa Dei grew jealous. He wanted what his brother—Shaka Obre?—had. And when his brother would not give it up, Chosa tried to steal it."

"*What* did he try to steal?"

Nabir shrugged. "The South. Chosa already held the North, but he wanted the South, too, because he always wanted whatever his brother had. He tried many magics, but none of them worked. Until he learned how to collect the power in things, and how to reshape it." Nabir frowned. "It was a true threat. So Shaka Obre set wasting wards around the land, knowing Chosa wouldn't dare destroy what he wanted so badly—only he was wrong. Chosa *was* willing to risk destroying the land. He thought if he couldn't have it, his brother shouldn't, either."

"But it didn't work." Del, sounding reflective; did she know the ending, too?

I decided to forestall them both. "Oh," I said, "I see. Chosa tried to take the South, and Shaka Obre's wasting wards kicked in. Which laid waste to the land and turned it into a barren desert—most of it, anyway." I didn't believe a word of it. "But if that's all true, why didn't Shaka Obre transform the ruined South back into what it was?"

Nabir took up the tale again. "He wanted to. But Chosa was so angry that he put a spell on his brother and locked him away somewhere."

"*Chosa* was the one locked away," I declared, as if it refuted the story.

"I don't know," Nabir said testily. "I only know what I heard, which is that Chosa Dei's brother built wards to imprison his brother inside a dragon. But that by the time the spell was tripped, Chosa's magic finally succeeded. Shaka Obre was also imprisoned."

I looked from him to Del. They wore identical expressions. "Why is it," I began again, "that everyone knows these stories but me? Northerner, Southroner—it doesn't seem to matter. Who *told* you these tales?"

"Everyone," Del answered. "Mother, father, uncles, brothers . . . everyone just knew."

I looked at Nabir. "What about you?"

"My mother," he answered promptly. "Before—" But he cut it off abruptly.

I let it go. "No one ever told *me*."

Del's voice was soft. "No one tells stories to slaves."

No. So they don't.

Another thing I'd lost.

I pushed by Nabir and walked into the circle. "All right," I said, "all right. If you want true steel so much, I'll give you true steel. But you're putting your life at stake."

Nabir hesitated only a moment. Then he reached down, traded wooden blade for steel, straightened erect again. And walked into the circle.

His quiet faith was implicit. "You're the Sandtiger."

I'm a fool, I thought. An aging, sandsick fool.

Who doesn't know any stories except the ones he makes up himself.

Ten

The sword knocked me to my knees. Not Nabir's; mine.

"See?" I shouted at Del, who waited quietly by the circle.

Nabir, who had backed away instantly the moment my blade had delivered its somewhat dramatic message, stood at the very inner edge of the circle. That he wanted to step out was obvious; that he wouldn't, equally so. Habits die too hard.

"I see," Del observed. "I see also that you *let* it do that."

"Let it! Let it? Are you sandsick?" I rose awkwardly, off-balance, muttering curses about sore knees, and stared at her belligerently. "I didn't *let* it do anything, Del. One moment I was sparring with Nabir, the next I'm in the sand. I didn't have a whole lot of choice."

"Look at it," she said.

I looked. It was a sword. The same old sword it had always been; at least, since I'd requenched it inside the mountain.

Then looked more closely. The sword *was* different. The black discoloration had moved up the blade. Nearly half of it was swallowed.

I didn't want a black sword.

I shut hands more tightly around the grip. "No," I said flatly, and sent every bit of strength I could muster flowing through arms, hands and fingers into the

263

sword itself. I would *make* the sword change by forcing my will upon it.

I felt like a fool. What good would it do to *envision* myself overcoming a Southron sorcerer imprisoned in my sword? What kind of power was that? I couldn't summon demons or create runes; couldn't collect magic from men and things. All I could do was sword-dance.

"Sing," Del said quietly.

"Sing," I blurted in derision.

"Singing is the key. It's always been the key. It's how you defeated him."

I had also thrust a blade into him. But things were different, now. I couldn't very well stab a sword.

In my head, I muttered. But I also made up a little song; a *stupid* little song. Don't ask me what it was. I can't even remember. Just some silly little thing about a Southron sandtiger being fiercer than a Northern sorcerer . . . at any rate, it worked. The black receded a little. Now only the tip was charred.

"It's something," Del said, as I swayed on my feet. "For now, it should be enough."

I squinted, rubbed at my eyes, tried to focus clearly. "I'm dizzy."

"You invoked power." Her tone was matter-of-fact. "You can't just *do* it without expecting to pay some price. Do you come out of a circle as fresh as when you went in?"

Not hardly. I could smell myself. "Dizzy," I repeated. *"And* thirsty, and hungry."

Nabir still stood at the very edge of the circle. He was staring at the sword. "Can it do anything? Anything at all?"

I looked down at the blade. "One thing it *can* do is make you feel pretty sick. Hoolies, I need a drink!"

Del tossed me my harness. "You *always* need a drink."

I sheathed, scowling at her, and hooked arms through the loops. The new leather was still stiff. I'd have to spend some time working oil into the straps. "Put some clothes on," I told her crossly. "Let's go get some food."

Del looked past me to Nabir. "Are you coming?"

He shook his head. "I want to go see Xenobia."

"His light o' love," I told her quietly, as Del looked blank.

She watched Nabir gathering his things as I gathered mine. "I didn't know he had one."

"Since two days ago. Cantina girl. He wants to marry her."

"*Marry* her!"

"That's what I said." I stuffed silk, gauze, bota, and practice sword beneath arms and turned toward Harquhal. "But she's his first girl, and he fancies himself in love." I grinned as Nabir departed at a trot. "Why is it so many boys and girls fall in love with the first one who takes them to bed?"

Del's tone was deadly. "I didn't."

No. Not with Ajani.

"Come on, bascha," I sighed. "You need a drink, too."

The cantina was crowded and noisy. Greenish-gray huva smoke eddied in the beamwork, trailing malodorous tails. The place also stank of sour wine, pungent aqivi, mutton stew, and spiced kheshi, all bound together with the acrid tang of Southron sand, dusty bodies; a trace of cheap perfume. The place was packed with men, making the cantina girls happy. Also overworked—in both modes of employment.

Every table was filled shoulder-to-shoulder by burnous-clad men. I saw swords hanging from belts, swords hanging from baldrics, swords strapped on by harness. If a tanzeer desired an army, he need go no farther than here.

"No room," Del murmured.

"There's room. Just no tables." I pushed through a knot of men next to the door, aiming for a deep-cut window. They ignored me mostly, moving apart only slightly, but when Del started through I heard silence abruptly descend. Not over the entire room—it was too packed for that—but the group by the door most decidedly stopped talking.

I shot a glance over my shoulder. Sure enough, five mouths hung open inelegantly. And then closed, smiling broadly, as Del slid through the stirring knot.

You'd have thought they'd step aside. Southroners have *some* manners—only apparently this bunch didn't. As Del arrived in their midst, on the way to me, they closed ranks around her.

Oh, hoolies, bascha, can't you go *anywhere?*

I doubt they intended much. Maybe a pinch here, a tweak there; a stroke or a fondle or two. But whatever it was they expected to receive in return, Del didn't offer. She had something else in mind.

I heard, in the blink of an eye, several curses, a blurt or two of pain, a breathy hiss of shock. And then Del was through. She joined me at the window.

I noted the merest glint of steel as she returned her knife to its sheath. Beyond her, two of the men bent to rub shins. One inspected sandal-bared toes; Del was wearing boots. All of them glared at her.

"Here?" Del asked at the window.

"Deep ledge." I stuffed clothing, bota, and wooden sword back into the space. "We can use it for a table."

We could. The adobe walls of the cantina were nearly a man-length thick, with the windows cut into the slabs. As deep as the ledge was, a man could sit on it.

Del glanced around at the crowd. "We should have gotten food and drink up front. Now we have to fight our way through again."

"No, we don't. This little girl will be glad to help us out." I caught the elbow of a cantina girl perching on someone's knee, dragged her up, pulled her over. "Aqivi," I said succinctly. "Also kheshi and mutton stew." I glanced at Del. "And wine for the lady; she has refined tastes." Before the girl could protest, I slapped her on the rump and sent her off through the crowd.

Del's expression was curiously bland. "If you ever do that again, I'll send you to stand with the others."

"What others?"

"The men by the door."

I glanced over, saw she meant the men who'd accosted her, scowled. "What did *I* do?"

"You treated her like dirt."

I nearly gaped. "All I did was send her to do her job. *One* of them, anyway."

Del's mouth was hard. "There are ways of doing the same without degrading the girl."

"Oh, Del, come on—"

"Perhaps this will make more sense: you treated her like a slave."

It got my back up; after all, I'd been a slave. "I did no such—"

"Yes, you did," she said. "And if you can't see it, you're blind."

"All I did was—" But I never got to finish. Someone came up behind me and slapped me on the back.

"Sandtiger!" he cried. "When did you get in?"

Hoolies, that hurt. I turned to scowl at him, then blinked in astonishment. "I thought you were *dead*."

"Hoolies, no," he said, "though it felt like it, even to me." He grinned, glanced past me at Del, elbowed me in the ribs. "I'd show you the scar, Sandtiger, but the bascha might be offended."

"I'd probably even swoon." Del's tone was perfectly bland.

Belatedly, I recalled introductions. "Del, this is Rhashad. Old friend of mine. Rhashad, this is Del. New friend of mine."

"I can see why." He bestowed his best smile on her, displaying big, very white teeth framed by heavy red mustaches drooping just past his jaw. "Northern-born, are you? I'm half Northern myself."

And it showed. Rhashad was a Borderer, born in

the foothills near the ruins of Iskandar. His hair was reddish blond, his eyes dark blue. To go with the hair his skin was tanned an odd yellowish red, with a generous sprinkling of sunspots. He was big; his height nearly matched mine. Del was only a finger's-width shorter. He packed more weight than me, though, especially through the shoulders.

"So," I said dryly, "I suppose you're heading home, since home is near Iskandar. No doubt you'll make a side-trip, if only to check out the action."

Rhashad grinned. He has a nice grin. He kept showing it to Del. "It's in my blood, Tiger. And I don't dare go home poor. My mother would throw me out of the hut."

Rhashad's mother was a long-standing joke among sword-dancers who knew him. She was, he claimed, a giantess, able to knock him silly with only the flick of a finger. But someone who'd met her once said she was a little bit of a thing, hardly reaching her son's elbow. Rhashad is known to exaggerate, but it's all part of the package. So far it hasn't killed him, though he came close some time before.

I glanced at Del. "His mother's the Northern half. That's where he gets his color."

Del arched her brows. "That's where he gets his *charm*."

Which promptly set Rhashad to braying for a cantina girl to reward Del's prescience. I told him a girl was on the way; he settled back into the window, hooking elbows on the sill.

"I'm up from Julah," he said. "New tanzeer down there, now that Aladar's dead. I picked up a little work, then the Vashni got too active and I decided to head back home. No sense in giving up my life just to let their black-eyed women make jewelry out of my bones."

I knew all about Aladar; I'd been present when Del killed him. "What's stirred up the Vashni?"

Rhashad shrugged. "This Oracle fellow. He keeps

telling everyone the jhihadi is coming to reclaim the
South for the tribes. The Vashni have always been
superstitious. So now they're beginning to think maybe
they ought to help out the foretelling by making it
come true. They've been killing a few people here and
there; nothing serious yet, but it's been the obvious
foreigner. You know—anyone blond, red-haired, blue-
or green-eyed . . . whoever they *think* looks non-
Southron. I guess they feel that if they're to reclaim
the South, they've got to rid it of foreigners." He
shrugged, stroking one half of his mustache. "I look
too Northern, I'm thinking, so I made my way back up
here."

"Jamail," Del said blankly.

Rhashad frowned. "Who?"

"Her brother," I explained. Del's face was white.
"He's living with the Vashni."

The frown deepened: two lines met between his
eyes. "What's a Northerner doing with Vashni?"

"Never mind," Del said grimly. "Are you certain
they're killing all foreigners?"

"That's what they've *been* doing. Whether they still
are, I can't say. All I know is, this Oracle fellow's got
them all stirred up." His blue eyes were solemn. "I'll
be frank, bascha—if your brother's with the Vashni,
his chances aren't worth much. They take matters of
religion seriously."

"They'll kill him," she said bitterly, "because this
loki-brained Oracle tells them to."

Rhashad lifted a negligent shoulder. "Take it up
with *him*, then; he's heading to Iskandar."

"The Oracle?" I frowned. "How do you know that?"

"Rumor. Makes sense, though. This Oracle fellow's
been predicting the jhihadi will show his face at
Iskandar; don't you think he might want to be there?
Sort of to prove his point?"

I didn't answer. The cantina girl arrived, at last,
carrying bowls of stew and kheshi, also a jug each of
wine and aqivi. She balanced all with great care and

concentration, gritting out Southron "excuse me's" as she fought her way through the throng. Del saw it and reached out at once to relieve her of the jugs and cups.

"Pay her extra," Del commanded as I reached for my pouch.

I scowled as I dug deep. "*You're* awfully free with my money."

"Women are," Rhashad observed cheerfully. "You should see how quickly my mother spends the coin I send home."

Del thanked the girl, then arched an eyebrow at Rhashad. "You send money home to your mother?"

"If I didn't, she'd have my ears. Or worse: my mustaches." Rhashad grinned. "You should come meet my mother. She'd like a bold bascha like you."

"Or not," I said hastily, seeing interest in Del's eyes. It might have been for the mother; I wouldn't risk it being for Rhashad. "Here, have some aqivi. Del prefers wine."

Del preferred not drinking. "Do you know a man named Ajani? He's Northern, not a Borderer, but he rides both sides."

"Ajani, Ajani," Rhashad muttered. "The name sounds familiar . . . Northerner, you say?"

"Very much so," she said flatly, "in everything but his habits. He is blond, blue-eyed, very tall . . . and he likes to kill people. If he doesn't sell them to slavers."

Rhashad's eyes sharpened. He looked at her more closely. This time he really saw her. Saw her *and* the sword.

The note in his voice was odd. "Have you ever been to Julah?"

Say no, I warned her mutely.

Del said yes.

Hoolies, he'll put it together.

Rhashad nodded slowly. His look on me was shrewd. "Eighteen months—or so—ago, Aladar ruled in Julah. Rich man, Aladar: he traded in gold and slaves. And would be to this day, if a slave hadn't killed him." He didn't look at Del. "Nobody knows any names. Only that one was a Northern woman, the other a Southron man. A man with scars on his face, who was a slave in Aladar's mine."

I hunched one shoulder. "Lots of men are scarred."

Rhashad spread four fingers and scraped them down one cheek. "Lots of men are scarred. Not all of them quite like this."

"Does it matter?" Del asked roughly.

Rhashad dropped his hand. "Not to me," he said evenly. "I don't betray my friends. But other people might."

A coldness touched my spine. "Why? If Aladar's gone, what does the new tanzeer care about how it happened?"

"The new tanzeer is Aladar's daughter."

"Aladar's *daughter?*" I gaped. "How did a *woman* inherit the domain?"

"Thank you," Del said dryly.

I waved it off. "Not now; this is important."

Rhashad nodded. "Indeed, it is. And the reason she holds the domain is because she was rich enough to buy men, and strong enough to hold them." He smiled a little. "Too much woman for me."

"A woman," I mused. "Hoolies, things are changing."

"For the better," Del remarked, then sipped her sour wine.

"Maybe not, bascha." I scowled into my bowl of rapidly cooling kheshi. Then I shrugged. "Ah, well, it won't last. They may be taking her money now, but it'll wear off. They won't put up with taking orders from a woman for long. Rhashad didn't, did he? And he's a Borderer. A man afraid of his mother."

"I *respect* my mother. And you should, too; she's a better man than you."

"They'll overthrow her," I said thoughtfully. "They'll change loyalties. They'll sell it to a man, or else one will steal it for himself. And then another will try to steal it from *him*." I shook my head. "Julah will run with blood."

"See why I left?" Rhashad asked. "First the Vashni begin killing, and now there will be war for control of Julah. I'd rather go see my mother."

"With Jamail in the middle, if he's not already dead." Del sighed and scrubbed at her brow. "Oh, Tiger, how much longer? First there is Ajani to think about, and now Jamail as well. What am I to do?"

"Go to Iskandar," I said. "It's the only logical choice."

Del's mouth was twisted. "There is no logic to feelings."

Which was, I thought, about the truest thing she'd ever said. Especially when applied to *her*.

Eleven

Something landed on my head. "Come on," the voice said. "We're going to Iskandar."

I lay belly-down on my precarious cot, mashing my face into the lump of cloth pretending to be a pillow. My left arm was under the lump. *I* was under a gauzy sheet, trying to recapture sleep.

The thing on my head did not go away. Without opening my eyes I reached up, felt the saddle-pouches, dragged them off my head and over the side of the bed. "Who's keeping you?" I mumbled.

Del was not amused. "I have no time for this. Ajani could be at Iskandar."

"Ajani could be anywhere. Ajani could be in hoolies." I freed my left arm. "I *hope* Ajani's in hoolies; then we can forget about him."

Del scooped up the pouches. "Fine," she declared. "I'll go there with Abbu."

Del never threatens. Del does. She was about to do now.

"Wait—" I levered myself up, squinted through too-bright daylight at her, tried to remember my name. My mouth tasted like an old dhoti. "Give me a moment, bascha."

She didn't give a moment. "Meet me at the stables." And thumped the door behind her.

Oh, hoolies.

Hoolies.

Why does she always do this on the morning after the night before?

I swear, the woman plans it. She plans it, and she waits. She knows what it does to me.

With effort I turned all the way over and sat up. Sure enough, the door was still shut. Del was still gone.

I sat on the edge of the bed and buried my face in my hands, scrubbing at sleep-creased flesh. I needed food and a taste of aqivi; Del would give me neither. Nor would she give me time.

"You could always catch up," I suggested.

Yes. I could. I knew where she was going.

And I knew who'd be going with her.

Hoolies, hoolies, *hoolies.*

I hate men like Abbu.

I used the nightpot. Then, in an effort to wake up as much as wash myself, I splashed water all over my face and soaked most of my hair. Wet tendrils straggled down my neck. Droplets broke free and rolled, tickling shoulders, chest, belly.

I didn't feel any better. Just wetter.

I glowered at the door as I reached for underrobe, harness, burnous. "What do you expect? I sat up with Rhashad all night."

Del, being gone, didn't answer. Which was just as well with me. She'd say something back. Then *I* would be required to respond. And we would waste too much time bickering over nothing in an attempt to prove dominance.

Which struck me as pretty stupid.

I bent over to pull on the boots Del had found me. "You *are* stupid," I muttered. "You could be sitting in a cantina right about now with a warm and willing little Southron beauty in your lap and a jug of aqivi at your elbow. Or you could be hiring on with some rich tanzeer to protect his dewy-eyed daughter—some cushy job like that. Or sitting over the oracle bones with Rhashad, stealing all his money. *Or* you could be sleeping." One boot was on. I turned to the other. "Instead, what are you doing? Getting ready to ride to

Iskandar on a mission of revenge with a cold-hearted, hot-tongued bascha—"

—whom I very badly wanted back in my bed.

I glared at the door. "Message for you, Ajani: if *she* doesn't kill you, I will."

Del was waiting at the stables. With the blue roan. Out in front. In the street. Which told me a little something.

"It'll be there," I told her. "It's been there for hundreds of years."

She frowned.

"Iskandar," I clarified.

Del's frown deepened. But she spoke about something else. "I'd have had him waiting for you, but no one can get near him."

Him. She could only mean one thing. "That's because they don't have the proper technique." I went by her into the lathwork stable, gathered up bridle, went over to the stall. At least, it was sort of a stall; there wasn't much left of it. "All right," I said, "what have you been up to?"

The stud, who was tied to a thick piece of timber sunk in the ground, answered by pawing violently. More bits of stall came down. The ground around him was littered.

"Ah," I said, "I see."

So did the stableman. He came running when he realized the stud's owner was back. I listened to his diatribe for much longer than I liked, but since I had to bridle, saddle and load the stud anyway, I didn't lose any time. Only my waning patience.

"How much?" I asked.

The stableman took the question as an invitation to start all over again with complaints. I cut him off in mid-stride by drawing my knife.

He went white. Gaped. Then changed from white to red as I bent over the stud's left forehoof to check for stones or caked dirt, cleaning the frog of the hoof with my knifetip.

"How much?" I repeated.

The stableman named a price.

"Too much," I told him. "That would buy you a second stable; he didn't do *that* much damage."

He named another price.

I let the stud have his left hoof back and moved to work on the right. "I could *leave* him here . . ."

A third—and better—price. I nodded and gave him money.

Del was mounted and waiting as I led the stud out of doors into daylight. Her roan snorted. The stud curled back his upper lip and trumpeted his dominance, meanwhile stomping on my heels as he raised his tail and danced. A stallion dancing around on the end of an all-too-human arm is rather disconcerting. So between being momentarily deafened by his noise and having my bootheels tromped on, I was not in a good mood.

But then, neither was Del. "Nice technique," she observed as I bashed his nose with a fist.

"Have to get his attention."

"You did," Del said. "Now he's trying to bite you."

Well, he was. But horses have bad moods, too.

I put my left foot in the stirrup and started to pull myself up. The stud bent his head around and missed getting a hunk of me only because I saw it coming and slapped him in the mouth. He tried twice more; I slapped him twice more. Then I gave up on the leisurely mount and swung up all at once, coming down into the saddle with toes hooking stirrups.

"*Now* try," I suggested.

He might have. He has. This time he didn't. For which I was very grateful, since I had the feeling he'd win.

"Are you done?" Del asked.

Before I could answer—though nothing was expected—the stableman stepped forward. "I couldn't help noticing your scars—are you the Sandtiger?"

I nodded, gathering rein.

The man showed me a gap-toothed grin. "I sold a horse to your son."

"My *son*—" I scowled down at him. "What kind of horse, where was he going, and what does he look like?"

Del's tone was dry. "One at a time, Tiger. You'll confuse the poor man."

The stableman knew horses best. "Old gray mare," he said. "Splash of white down her nose, and three white legs. Very gentle. A lady's mare, but he said that's what he wanted."

"Where was he going?"

"Iskandar."

Where else? "What does he look like?"

The man shrugged. "Not tall, not short. Eighteen or nineteen. Brown-haired, blue-eyed. Spoke Southron with an accent."

"What *kind* of accent?"

He shrugged, shaking his head.

"But he told you he was my son."

"Son of the Santiger; yes." He grinned. "Hasn't got the scars, but he wears a necklet of claws."

"And a sword?" I asked grimly.

He frowned. Thought back. Shook his head. "A knife. No sword."

"A necklet, but no sword. And riding an old gray mare." I glanced at Del. "If he's really going to Iskandar, at least we know what to look for."

She was startled. "You'll *look?*"

"Shouldn't be hard to find him. He's obviously not shy of boasting about his parentage—even though it's a lie."

Her tone was a little odd. "How do you know it's a lie?"

"He's too old," I told her. "If I'm thirty-six, and he's eighteen—or even *nineteen*—it means I was all of—" I stopped.

"Eighteen," Del supplied. "Or maybe seventeen."

Not too old after all. "Let's go," I said curtly. "No sense in staying here."

* * *

By the time we were out of Harquhal, most of my bad temper was gone. It was too hard staying out of sorts when the Southron sun was shining on my face, warming the place where the beard had been. It felt odd to be clean-shaven. It felt odd to wear gauze and silk. It felt odd to be so carefree.

But it felt *good* to feel so odd.

"You know," I remarked, "you might have warned me last night you wanted to leave. I could have said good-bye to Rhashad, told Nabir there'd be no more lessons—"

"Nabir knows. *I* told him."

"Oh? When?"

"Last night. You and Rhashad were full of aqivi and too busy trying to win one another's money . . . Nabir came in, and I told him." She shrugged. "He said he would come, too, if he could convince Xenobia to quit her job and go with him."

"Xenobia," I murmured.

"And I told Abbu, who also came in last night."

I looked at her. "He did? I didn't see him. When did he come in? Last night? In our cantina?"

"I said you were full of aqivi." Del waved a fly away. "Not long before I left."

"Left," I echoed. "You *left?* When? Why?" I frowned. "With him?"

"Aren't *you* full of questions today."

"I think I have a right."

"Oh? Why?"

"I just do." I scowled, disliking her tone. "Who knows what kind of trouble you might have gotten yourself into, going off with Abbu like that. You don't know what kind of man he is, bascha."

"One very much like you." She raised a hand to forestall my protest. "No—like you *were.* I'll admit, you've changed. You're not the arrogant fool you once were."

"So comforting," I said dryly. "And was he like me in bed, too?"

"You have no right to ask that."

"Hoolies, you mean you *did?*" I jerked the stud up short. "I was only joking, after all your natter about needing focus . . . do you mean to tell me you went off with Abbu last night?"

Del's tone was deadly. "I did not lie to you about requiring a focus. And if I have told you plainly I desire solitude, would I then go to bed with Abbu?"

It slowed me down only a moment. "Maybe. I'm not sure any more."

"No."

I felt a little better—I felt a *lot* better about Abbu's lack of success—but was still a trifle disgruntled about her accompanying him. "You've got to admit, I've got a right to be concerned."

"No," Del retorted. "It's not your place."

That got my back up. "Why is it not my place? We've spent the last—what, eighteen months?—together, *in* bed and out, and you say it's not my place?"

"It's not your place to ask whom I choose to sleep with," Del declared, "any more than it's *my* place to ask the same of you."

"But you *can* ask," I said. "You've been the only woman in my bed since—since—" I frowned. "Hoolies, see what you've done? I can't even remember."

"Elamain," she said dryly.

Elamain. Elamain—oh, *Elamain.*

Del saw my expression. "Yes," she said, "Elamain. *That* Elamain."

How could I forget? How could *any* man forget? Her appetite was insatiable, her skill beyond belief, her stamina unbelievable, her imagination unparalleled—

"Of course," Del remarked, "she did nearly get you killed."

The dream evaporated. "Worse," I said—with feeling.

"What could be worse than—oh. Oh. Yes, I remember. She almost got you gelded."

I shifted in the saddle. "Let's not talk about that.

Besides, what did you expect? *You* weren't giving me anything. Why shouldn't I sleep with Elamain—"

"—especially since she didn't give you much choice." Del smiled. "Tiger, you may think other women don't know, but we do. I know very well what kind of woman Elamain is—or was; Hashi probably had her killed—and how she worked her magic on you. Women like that have power. Men can never withstand it." She tossed loose hair behind her shoulders. "You can be sidetracked so easily . . . you can lose sight of what you intended just because a woman—"

"—tells me a story about how a Northern borjuni killed her family and sold her brother into slavery." I smiled. "Sound familiar, bascha?"

"That's not what I meant, Tiger."

"No. You meant women like Elamain luring poor fools into their beds. I know. I won't even deny it hasn't worked on me other times, either." I shrugged. "You used a different method, but the end result was the same."

Del didn't say anything right away. She'd turned her blue roan to face me, and now she had to rein him back to keep him from nosing the stud. Once she had him settled, she met my gaze stare for stare. Then tilted her head a little.

"What would you have done?" she asked. "What would you have done with your life if I hadn't found you in that cantina?"

"Done?"

"Done," she repeated. "You said I'd sidetracked you as much as Elamain might have—sidetracked you from what? Made you lose sight of—what?"

"Well, if you *hadn't* found me in that cantina, I wouldn't have been left as a Sun Sacrifice by the Hanjii. I wouldn't have been thrown into Aladar's mine. I wouldn't have lost Singlestroke and gotten stuck with this Northern sword, or sucked up Chosa Dei."

"That's not what I asked."

"Those things *wouldn't* have happened."

"Tiger, you're avoiding my question."

"No, I'm not." I shrugged. "Hoolies, I don't know. I'm a sword-dancer. I hire on to do things. I'd probably be *doing* things; does that answer your question?"

"Yes," she said, "it does." She waved away another fly. Or maybe the same one. "You asked me once what I'd do when Ajani was dead. Once I'd ended my song."

"Yes, I asked. As I recall, you didn't have an answer."

"Because I refuse to look past that. To look beyond Ajani's death is to lose focus. To dilute the vision. And I can't afford that." Del flicked a hand in the air. "So, I don't look. But you don't have the same restrictions. You *can* look. What I ask now is, have you?"

"No sword-dancer wastes much time thinking about next year, next month, next week. Hoolies, sometimes not even next *day*. Only the next dance. He looks to the dance, bascha. Because that's what he lives for."

Del's eyes were steady. "When will your dance be ended?"

"I can't answer that," I said crossly. "I don't even know what it means."

"You do. Oh, you do. You're not a stupid man. You're not a foolish man. You only pretend to be when you don't want to deal with truths."

I didn't say a word.

Del smiled a little. "It's all right, Tiger. I do the same thing."

"You don't pretend to be stupid. And you never pretend you're a fool."

"No." Her mouth was oddly warped. "Instead, I make myself cold and hard. I make myself dead inside, so I don't have to face those truths."

There are times when I hate this woman.

This was not one of them.

Part III

One

Del's voice was distant. "Tiger—what's wrong?"

It didn't make any sense. Just a jumble of words. No, not words; *sounds.*

"Tiger? Are you all right?"

I felt—odd.

"Tiger!"

Oh, hoolies, bascha . . . something's wrong—something's wrong with *me*—something's *wrong* with—

I stopped the stud. Got off. Dragged the sword from its sheath. Then walked across the trail to a tumbled pile of rocks. Found a fissure. Wedged the sword into it.

Wedged the *hilt* into it, leaving the blade stuck up into air.

"Tiger—?" And then she sent her roan plunging between the blade and my body.

It knocked me backward. It knocked me flat on my rump. I sat there on the ground trying to figure out what had happened.

Del reined the roan around. Her expression was profoundly frightened. "Have you gone loki?" she cried.

I didn't think so. What I was, somehow, was sitting on the ground instead of in the saddle.

Silence: Del said nothing. Her gelding pawed, digging pebbles and dust. I heard the clack of rock on rock, the scraping of hoof in hard ground, the clink of bit and bridle.

Saw the sword sticking up from the fissure.

"Hoolies," I muttered hoarsely.

Del said nothing. She watched me get up, watched me slap dust from my burnous, watched me take a step toward the sword. Then put the gelding between.

Brought up short, I stuck out a hand to ward off the roan. "What are you trying to—"

"Keep you from killing yourself," she said flatly. "do you think I couldn't tell?"

"I'd *never*—"

"You just did. Or would have."

I stared up at her in astonishment. Then across the roan's bluish rump to the waiting sword jutting patiently into the air.

I couldn't have. I *couldn't* have. It's not something I would do. I've survived too much travail in my life to end it willingly, let alone by my own hand.

"Let me go," I said.

Del didn't move the gelding.

"Let me go," I repeated. "I'm all right now, bascha."

Her expression was unreadable. Then she moved the gelding out of my way. I heard the hiss of a blade unsheathed. I was visited by an odd thought: would Del try to kill me to keep me from killing myself?

Somehow, I didn't laugh. Not looking at my sword. I approached it carefully. Felt nothing. No fear, no apprehension, no desire to do myself injury. Just a mild curiosity as to what the thing had wanted.

It didn't say a word.

I bent. Closed one hand around the exposed portion of the hilt, avoiding the blade itself. Worked the sword from the fissure and turned it right side up.

Black crept up the blade. This time it touched the runes.

"It doesn't want to go," I blurted.

Del's voice: *"What?"*

"It—*he*—doesn't want to go." I frowned down at the sword, then wrenched my gaze away to meet hers. "Chosa Dei wants to go south."

Del's mouth flattened. "Tell him we're going north."

"Northeast," I corrected. "And he knows exactly which way we're going—it's why he pulled this stunt." I paused. "One of the reasons, anyway; he also wants out of the sword. Killing me is a way of succeeding."

Del sheathed Boreal and edged the gelding closer. "It's black again."

"Some of it." I turned the blade from edge to edge to show both sides. "What do you suppose would happen if the whole thing went black?"

Del's tone was odd. "Do you really want to find out?"

I glanced at her sharply. "Do you know?"

"No. But *I* wouldn't run the risk."

"Neither will I," I muttered. "Time to show him who's boss again."

As before, I shut both hands around the grip, locking fingers in place. It had taken a song last time, a snatch of a little song sung to put Chosa Dei in his place. I summoned it again and let it fill my head. Thought briefly of nothing else other than proving my dominance. Like the stud with Del's blue roan.

I was sweating when I opened my eyes. The song in my head died away. The runes were free of charring, but not the entire blade. "Only a little," I rasped. "Each time, more of the black remains."

"You must be vigilant," Del declared.

"Vigilant," I muttered. "*You* be vigilant."

Her face wavered before me. "Are you all right?" she asked.

I staggered toward the stud, who, bored, lipped idly at dirt. His muzzle was crusted with it. "Am I all right, she asks. I don't know; *should* I be all right? Every time I have this little argument with my sword, I feel like I've aged ten years." I stopped short of the stud and swung around. "I haven't, have I?"

"What?"

"Aged ten—or *twenty*—years."

Del appraised me critically. "I don't think so. You look the same as before—about sixty, I would say."

"That's not funny," I snapped, and then realized how I sounded. "All right, all right—but do you blame me? Who knows what Chosa Dei can do, even in a sword!"

"True," Del conceded. "No, Tiger, you do not look like you have aged ten or twenty years. In fact, you look better than a week ago; sparring agrees with you. You should do it more often."

"I would if I could," I muttered. "Maybe at Iskandar."

I turned back to the stud, who greeted me with a bump of his muzzle against my face, followed by a snort. His snorts are bad enough any time; this time it included dirt. Dirt and mucus make mud.

I swore, wiped slime from face and neck, called him a dozen unflattering names. He'd heard them all before and didn't even flick an ear. So I caught reins, dug a foot into the left stirrup, dragged myself up with effort, plopped rump into saddle. Peered over at Del.

"All right," I said, "all right. I give up. The sooner I get Chosa Dei out of this sword, the happier I'll be . . . and if that means finding this Shaka Obre, then that's what we'll do."

Del's expression was odd. "It could take months. Maybe years."

I gritted teeth. "I know that," I told her. "What in hoolies *else* am I supposed to do? Fight this thing for the rest of my life?"

Del's tone was quiet. "I just think you should realize what sort of commitment you're making."

I glared at her. "This sword just tried to make me kill myself. Now it's *personal*."

Her smooth brow creased. "Shaka Obre is little more than a name, Tiger . . . he will be difficult to find."

I sighed. "We found Chosa Dei. We'll find Shaka Obre, no matter what it takes."

Del's smile was oddly abrupt.

"What?" I asked warily.

"Only that you sound very like me."

I thought about it. About Del's quest to find Ajani, and the sacrifices she'd made.

Now it was my turn.

She brought her roan up beside me. "How much farther to Iskandar?"

"According to what Rhashad told me, another day's ride. We should make it by tomorrow evening." I peered down the track winding through scrub trees and webby grass. "You know, maybe it wouldn't be so bad if there *is* a jhihadi due. Maybe he can cure my sword."

Del sounded cross. "There's nothing wrong with your sword that you can't cure yourself. All it takes is control. And the willingness to *try*."

I looked at her a long moment. Then shifted in my saddle. "You know," I said lightly, "I'll be glad when Ajani's dead."

It caught her off guard. "Why?"

"Because maybe then you'll remember what it's like to be human again."

Her mouth opened. "I *am*—"

"*Some*times," I agreed. "Then again, other times you're a coldhearted, judgmental bitch."

I turned the stud and went on. After a moment, she followed.

Silence is sometimes noisy.

Iskandar, I knew, had been very old even before Harquhal was born. Which meant the track between them was very new, beaten into the ground only in answer to the Oracle. In time the track would fade, washed away by wind and rain, and the land would be true again, lacking the scars put on it by pilgrims gone to see the new jhihadi. Until then, however, the track would become a lifeline.

Rhashad had been explicit in his instructions, but it wasn't necessary. It was easy to see the way. Easy to see the people leaving Harquhal behind on the way to Iskandar. Harder to avoid them.

We avoided them eventually by riding off the track. It was dusk, growing chilly, and my belly was complaining. Del and I went over a hill and found a private place for a campsite, not desirous of company. On the road you can never be sure.

"No fire," I suggested as I climbed down from the stud.

Del, saying nothing, nodded. She pulled off saddle, pad, pouches, the roll of pelt and blankets. Dumped everything in one spot and went back to tend the roan.

It took no time at all. We settled mounts, spread bedrolls, ate a journey-meal out of our pouches and drank water out of botas. By the time the sun was down there was nothing left but bed. But neither of us sought it.

In the white light of a full moon I sat on my pelt, blankets draped around my knees, working oil into my harness. The leather was stiff from newness and needed softening. In time the oil, my sweat, and the shape of my body would coerce the harness to fit. Until then, I'd tend it every night. It was ritual.

Del performed her own even as I completed mine. But it was not her harness she tended. It was Boreal's blade. Whetstone, oil, cloth. And exquisitely tender care.

She had braided back her hair. It left most of her face bare. In the moonlight, the angles were harsh. The planes were cut from glass.

Down the blade and back again: seductive sibilance. Then the whisper of silk on steel.

Her head was bent, and tilted, as she looked down the length of blade. White-lashed lids were lowered, hiding the eyes from me. Thick, pale braid fell over a silk-clad shoulder, swinging with her motion. Down the blade, then back again: slow, subtle seduction.

Abruptly I had to know. "What are you thinking about?"

Del twitched minutely. She had been very far away.

Quietly I repeated it: "What are you thinking, bascha?"

The mouth warped briefly. Then regained its shape. "Jamail," she said softly. "Remembering what he was like."

I'd only seen him once. Never as she had.

"He was—a boy," she said. "No different from any other. He was the youngest of us all, at ten—five years younger than me. Trying so hard to be a man when we wanted to keep him a boy."

I smiled, seeing it. "Nothing wrong with that."

"He thought so. He would look at my father, my uncles, my brothers, then look at me. And swear he was as brave . . . swear he was as strong . . . swear he was as capable as any man full-grown."

I had not had a normal boyhood. I couldn't say how it should have been. Couldn't feel what Jamail had felt. Couldn't say the words I might have said if I had been Jamail, wanting to soothe my sister.

"They took us together," she said. "We hid beneath the wagon, trying to make ourselves small, but the borjuni fired the wagon. There was no place left to hide. We ran—Jamail's clothing caught fire—" She broke off a moment, face twisted oddly. "They caught fire, but he wouldn't scream. He just stuffed his fists in his mouth and bit them until they bled. I had to throw him down. I had to trip him and throw him down so I could smother the flames . . . and that was when they caught us."

My hands stilled on the harness. Del's continued to work her blade. I doubt she even knew it.

"He was burned," she said. "They didn't care. He was alive, he would mend; he would still bring a pretty price. That was all they thought of: what the Southron slavers would pay."

No, it was not all they thought of. There was Delilah as well—fifteen-year-old Northern beauty—but Del wasn't speaking of her. Jamail was the topic. Jamail was all that counted, and the fate of her family.

Del didn't count herself worthy enough to warrant the obsession.

Oh, bascha. Bascha. If only you knew.

"But he survived it," she said. "More than I, surely: slavery, castration, losing a tongue. He survived all of that only to fall to the Vashni." Del drew in a breath. "So now I am left to sit here, wondering if he's dead."

"You don't know that he is."

"No. No, I don't. Not knowing is what hurts."

Her hand continued its task, never faltering in its stroke. Boreal sang a song, a song of promises.

"Don't borrow grief," I told her. "Jamail could be perfectly safe with the Vashni."

"They're killing foreigners. He's all too obviously Northern."

"Is he? Was he?" I shrugged as she glanced up. "By the time we found him, he'd spent five years in the South. Two years with the Vashni. For all we know, they might consider him one of their own. The old man loved him; that should carry some weight."

"*Old* men," she said quietly, "often lose their power."

"And sometimes they don't."

"But all old men die."

I shook my head. "I can't make it any easier for you, Del. Yes, he could be dead. But you don't *know* that."

"And I wonder: will I ever? Or spend the rest of my life not knowing if there is anyone left of my blood."

"Believe me," I said roughly, "you can learn to live with that."

Del's hand closed over the blade. "And do you say *that* because I am a coldhearted, judgmental bitch?"

I looked at her sharply, startled by the question. More startled by the raw tone. "No," I answered honestly. "I say that because it's what *I've* done."

"You," she said blankly.

"Me," I agreed. "Are you forgetting the circumstances? No mother, no father for me . . . no brothers or sisters, either. I haven't the vaguest idea if there is anyone left of *my* blood, since I don't know what blood it is."

"Borderer," she said. "Borderer, or foreign."

I straightened. "That's what you think?"

Del shrugged. "You have the size of a Northerner, but your color is mostly Southron. Not as dark, of course, and your features are not as harsh. You are a little of both, I think, which might make you a Borderer." She smiled a little, assessing. "*Or* a foreigner. Have you never imagined it?"

That, and more. Everything. Every day of my enslavement. Every night in my bed of dung. Admitting it to no one. Not even to Sula, or Del. Because the admitting could make me weak. The weak do not survive.

"No," I said aloud, driving the weakness away.

"Tiger." Del set the sword aside. "Did it never occur to you that the Salset might have lied?"

"Lied?" I frowned. "I don't understand."

She sat cross-legged. Fingers curved around her knees. "You have spent your life believing you were left in the desert to die. Abandoned by mother, by father . . . that's what you have said."

"That's what I was told."

"Who told you?" she asked gently.

I frowned. "The Salset. You know that. What is this all about?"

"About lies. About deception. About pain inflicted on purpose, to make the foreign boy suffer."

Something pinched my belly. "Del—"

"*Who* told you, Tiger? It wasn't Sula, was it?"

My answer was instant. "No. Sula was never cruel. Sula was my—" I stopped.

Del nodded. "Yes. Sula was your salvation."

In my hands I clutched the harness. "What of it?" I asked. "What has Sula to do with this?"

"When were you first made aware you weren't Salset?"

I had no real answer. "I just always knew."

"Because they told you."

"Yes."

"*Who* told you? Who told you first? Who told you so young that you would never think otherwise?"

"Del—"

"Was it the adults?"

"No," I said crossly. "The adults completely ignored me until I was old enough to be useful. It was the children, always the children . . ." I let it trail off. Recalling all too well the painful days of my past; the nightmare of childhood.

Recalling and *wondering*.

Could it have been a lie?

I sat very still. Everything was suddenly, oddly, clear, the way it is just before a sword-dance. When you walk the edge of the blade, knowing an instant can make the difference.

All my senses sharpened. I knew who and where I was, and what I had become. And I knew it was hard to breathe.

In perfect stillness, Del waited.

"The children," I repeated, feeling the abyss crack open below.

Del's face was taut. "Children can be cruel."

"They said—" I broke it off, not daring to say it aloud.

After a moment she took it up. "They said you'd been left for dead in the desert by parents who didn't want you."

"They all said it," I murmured vaguely. "First one, then all the others."

"And you never questioned it."

I couldn't sit there anymore. I couldn't sit at all. How could I just *sit*—?

I thrust the harness aside and stood up stiffly, then walked away four paces. Stopped. Stared blindly into darkness.

Swung back numbly to challenge. "There was no one *to* question. Who was I to ask? What was I to say? I was a chula . . . chulas don't *ask* questions . . . chulas don't talk at all, because to talk invites a beating."

"There was Sula," she said gently.

Something stirred sluggishly. Anger. Desperation. A kind of pain I'd never felt because I'd never cared before. Not the way she made me care. "I was *fifteen.*" I didn't know how to explain it; not so she could see, could understand, could comprehend. "Fifteen when I met Sula. By then I knew better than to ask. By then I didn't care. By then there was nothing in me to even wonder who I was."

"That's a lie," she said.

Despair cuts like a blade. "Oh, hoolies . . . oh, bascha, you just don't know . . ." I scraped stiff fingers through my hair. "There's no way you *can* know."

"No," she agreed.

I stared at her in the moonlight. It hurt to look at her. To think about what she'd said. To wonder if she was right.

"You were wrong to do this," I said. "You shouldn't have done it, bascha. You should have left it alone— should have left *me* alone . . . don't you see what you've done?"

"No."

"*Before,* I knew what I was. I knew what had happened. It didn't make me happy—who would be happy knowing he was abandoned?—but at least I had an idea. At least there was something to hate. At least I didn't wonder if it was falsehood or truth."

"Tiger—"

"You took it away," I said. "And now there's nothing at *all.*"

Del's face was stricken. She stared at me blindly a moment, then drew in a noisy breath. "Wouldn't you rather know you *weren't* abandoned?"

"Do you mean would I *rather* know my parents were murdered by borjuni? Or maybe murdered by the Salset, who then took me for a keepsake?"

She flinched. "That's not what I—"

I turned my back on her again. Stared very hard into darkness, trying to sort things out. She had changed everything. Altered the stakes. I had to regain my footing. Had to find a new way of playing.

My turn to suck a breath. "What do I do now? What do I do, Del? Drive myself sandsick wondering about the truth?"

"No," she answered harshly. "What kind of life is that?"

I swung around. "Your kind," I told her. "You punish yourself with *your* life. Shall I punish myself with mine?"

Del recoiled. Then swallowed visibly. "I only meant to give you a little peace."

All the anger died out of me. With it went the bitterness, leaving emptiness in its place. "I know," I said. "I know. And maybe you have, bascha. I just don't know it yet."

"Tiger," she whispered, "I'm sorry."

The moonlight was on her face. It hurt me to look at her.

"Go to bed," I said abruptly. "I've got to check on the stud."

The stud was tied all of four paces away. He was fine. He was asleep. He needed nothing from me.

But Del didn't say a word.

Two

Iskandar was a child's toy: a pile of unfired clay blocks left too long in the sun and rain. There were no corners left on the buildings, only rounded, slump-shouldered shells being transformed slowly to dust. Into the dirt and clay and piles of shale from which the city had come.

"This is stupid," I said. "All these people, on the word of an unknown zealot, are leaving behind their homes to come to a ruined city. And for all anyone knows, there isn't even any water."

Del shook her head. "There's water; too much green. And don't you think the jhihadi will provide if this is where he plans to return?"

Her tone was dry, ironic. A reflection of my own. Del believes in religion more than I do—at least, in the worth of faith—and she had not, up to now, shown any intolerance for the predicted return. If anything, she had admonished me for my cynicism, saying I should respect the beliefs of others even if they didn't match my own.

But now, faced with Iskandar, Del wasn't thinking of faith. Nor even of religion. She was thinking of Ajani. She was thinking of killing a man.

And of the oaths to her own gods, far from Iskandar.

"Where's the border?" I asked. "You know all these things."

Which she did, better than I. Part of Del's training on Staal-Ysta was something she called *geography*, the

297

study of where places were. I knew the South well
enough, particularly the Punja, but Del knew all sorts
of different places, even those she'd never been to.

"The border?" she echoed.

"Yes. The border. You know: the thing that divides
North from South."

She slanted me a glance that said precisely nothing.
Which meant it said a lot. "The border," she said
coolly, "is indiscernible."

"It's what?"

"Indiscernible. I can't tell where it is. The land is
too—odd."

The stud stumbled. I dragged his head up, steadied
him, let him walk on again. "What do you mean:
odd?"

Del waved an encompassing hand. "Look around
you, Tiger. One moment we are in desert sand, the
next in Northern grassland. Then another step into
borderland scrub; a fourth into wind-scoured stone."

"So?"

"So. It is one thing to ride from Julah to Staal-Ysta
and see how the land changes . . . it is entirely another
to see the same changes in the space of ten paces."

I hadn't really thought about it. But now that she
mentioned it, the land did change a lot. So did the
temperature. One moment it was hot, the next a tad
bit frosty. But one melted into the other and made it
mostly warm.

We skirted, as did the track, the edge of a broad
plateau. On our left rose the foothills of the North; to
our right, beyond the plateau, stretched scrubby borderlands that, if the eye could see so far, would flatten
into desert. Below us, directly northeast, was another,
smaller plateau. In the center, on the top, stood the
city of Iskandar.

It could not be characterized as a hilltop fortress, or
even a desert city. There were no walls, only buildings, with dozens of alleys and entrances. Most were
cluttered with fallen adobe blocks, crumbling away

into dust, but shale walls marked foundations, mortared together with dried, grassy mud.

Once, the ruins might have been majestic, markers of human pride. But humans had returned, and the majesty was destroyed.

Iskandar was a warren overrun by desert vermin. There were carts, wagons, horses, danjacs, and countless human beasts brought to carry in the burdens. Most had moved into the city, filling in all the chinks, but many had staked out hyorts around the edges, creating little pocket encampments of desert dwellers unwilling to mix with city rabble.

We halted our mounts at the edge of the plateau. The trail wound down, but we didn't look down. We looked across at the city.

"Tribes," I said succinctly.

Del frowned. "How can you tell? They look like everyone else."

"Not when you get up close; do I look much like a Hanjii?" I nodded toward Iskandar. "The tribes don't build cities. They won't live in them. Most of them travel in carts and wagons, staking out hyorts when they stop a while. See? That's what all those tents are, skirting the edges of the city."

"But they've just made their *own* city by all settling in one spot."

"Special circumstances." I shrugged as she glanced at me. "You don't find this many tribes gathered together ever—at least, not without bloodshed. But if this Oracle's got all of them stirred up, it will change things. They'll suffer one another until the jhihadi question is settled."

Del looked down at the ruined city. "Do you think the Salset are there?"

Something tickled inside my belly. "I suppose it's possible."

"Would they come for the jhihadi?"

I thought about the shukar. The old man's magic had been failing, or *he'd* have killed the cat and left me with no escape. Among the Salset, magic is religion-based; when magic doesn't work, the gods are looking away. They'd looked away from the shukar. Otherwise how could a mere chula kill the cat in the shukar's place?

I thought about Del's question. Would he bring them to Iskandar? If he thought he needed to. If he thought it would bring him honor. If the old man was still alive.

He had been a year before.

"Maybe," I said. "Maybe not. Depends on how things are going."

"You could see Sula again."

I gathered up my reins. "Let's go. There's no sense in staying here just to gaze across the landscape."

Well, there wasn't. But I might have put it better.

Del turned the roan and headed down the trail winding off the plateau rim. Down, across, then up. And we'd be in Iskandar.

Where she might find Ajani at last.

The stud topped the final rise and took me onto the plateau where Iskandar jutted skyward. The trail, instead of narrow, was wide and well-rutted, showing signs of carts and wagons. It wound around trees and close-knit bushes, then split into five fingers. Five smaller tracks leading toward five different parts of the city, where they fractured yet again. Most didn't enter Iskandar. Most stopped at clusters of hyorts; at knots made of wooden wagons.

Which told me a thing or two.

"What is it?" Del asked as she put her roan next to me.

I frowned bemusedly at the hyorts. There were tens and twenties of them staked between the plateau's edge and the city. It changed the look of the place. Softened Iskandar's perimeter. Altered the lay of the land in more ways than one.

"Tribes," I said at last. "Too many, and too different."

"They have as much right here as anyone."

"I'm not questioning that. I'm wondering where it will lead."

"If there really is a jhihadi—"

"—he could be dangerous." I reined the stud around a goat standing in the middle of the track. "Too much power held by a single man."

Del also passed the goat. "And if he used it for good?"

I make a noise of derision. "Do you know anyone who holds that much power and uses it for *good?*" I shook my head. "I don't think it's possible."

"Just because you haven't seen it doesn't mean it can't exist. Maybe that's why he's coming."

"*If* he's coming," I muttered.

Hyorts lined either side of the track. I smelled the pungent aroma of danjac urine. The tang of goat's milk and cheese. The almost overwhelming stench of too many people—of too many customs—living too close to one another.

And this was outside of the city.

Del and I were hardly noticed. I didn't know how long some of the tribes had been camped here, but obviously long enough so that the sight of two strangers was no longer worth comment. In the Punja, half a dozen of the tribes gathered would have killed us on the spot, or taken us prisoner. But no one bothered us. They looked, then looked away.

Looked away from *Del.*

I frowned. "There must be Northerners here."

"Why do you—oh. Oh, I see." Del glanced around. "If any *are* here, they must be inside the city."

"It's where we're going," I said. "We'll know sooner or later, bascha; sooner—we're almost in."

And so we were. We passed through the last cluster of hyorts and wagons and entered Iskandar proper. No walls, no gates, no watch. Only open roads, and the city.

The city and her new people.

Southroners, most of them. Fewer Borderers. A handful of towheaded Northerners, head and shoulders above the rest. And goats and sheep and dogs and pigs running loose through the streets of Iskandar.

I couldn't help grinning. "Doesn't much look the kind of place a long-awaited jhihadi might come back to."

"It smells," Del observed.

"That's because no one actually lives here. They don't care. They're only *borrowing* it for a while . . . they'll leave with the jhihadi."

"If the jhihadi leaves."

I guided the stud through a narrow alley. "Wouldn't make sense for him to stay. Iskandar's a ruin. He might prefer a livable city."

"It could be *made* livable . . . Tiger, where are we going?"

"Information," I answered. "Only one place to get it."

Del's tone was dry. "I don't think there is a cantina."

"There probably *is*," I remarked, "but that's not where we're going. You'll see."

So she did, once we got there. And it wasn't a cantina, either. It wasn't one thing at all, but two: the well, and the bazaar.

In every settlement, the well is the center of town. It is where everyone goes, because it is a necessity. Also an equalizer, especially in Iskandar where no tanzeer reigned. It was the only place in the city where all paths would cross.

Thus it becomes the bazaar. Where people go, they buy. Others had things to sell. Even in Iskandar.

"So *many*," Del exclaimed.

More than I expected. Stalls filled much of the central square and spilled into adjoining alleys. There were vendors of all kinds, shouting at passersby. The whine of dij-pipes filled the air, keening in ornate Southron style, while street dancers jangled finger-bells and beat taut leather heads of tambor-drums.

They wound their way through the crowds, trying to scare up a coin or two, or lead customers back to the stalls of the merchants who'd hired them.

"It is," Del said. "It's just like a *kymri*."

But this was the South, not the North. We don't have *kymri*.

I reined in the stud. Before us lay the choked square. "No sense in riding through there," I said. "We'd do better to walk—*hey!*" The shout was to stop a boy trying to squeeze by the stud. "You," I said more quietly. "Have you been here long?"

"A six-day," he answered, in Desert.

I nodded. "Long enough to know a little something about the place, then."

The boy smiled tentatively. Black-haired, dark-skinned, light-eyed. Half-breed, I thought. But I couldn't name the halves.

"How do we go about finding a place to sleep?" I asked.

The boy's eyes widened. "All around," he answered. "There are many, many rooms. Many more rooms than people. Stay where you want." His eyes were on my sword hilt. "Sword-dancer?" he asked.

I nodded confirmation.

"Then you will want the circles." He waved a hand. "On the other side of the city. It's where all the sword-dancers are."

"All?"

"All," he repeated. "They come every day. That's where they all stay, to challenge one another so they can impress the tanzeers."

"And where are the tanzeers?"

The boy's quick smile flashed. "In the rooms that still have roofs."

Ah. Of course. In a ruin as old as Iskandar, timber would have rotted. Dwellings would be roofless, except for those with more than one story. Which was where the tanzeers would go.

So. The division of power began.

Boys often learn things other people don't. "How many?" I asked. "How many tanzeers?"

He shrugged. "A few. Not many yet. But they have brought sword-dancers with them . . . the rest they are hiring." His eyes were very bright. "You'll have no trouble finding work."

It didn't ring quite true. "And do you know *why* they're hiring so many of us?"

The boy shrugged. "Protection against the tribes."

It made sense. The tribes and tanzeers didn't mix much; didn't see eye to eye when they did. And if the promised messiah was appealing primarily to the tribes, which is what it sounded like, the tanzeers would want to know.

I dug a copper out of my pouch and flipped it at the boy. He caught it, grinned again, glanced past me toward Del. Said something quickly in Desert, then turned and ran into the square.

Grinning, I kneed the stud out. We'd cut straight across the bazaar to the outskirts directly beyond. Where the boy had said there were circles.

"What did he say?" Del asked. "And you know which part I mean."

I laughed, then twisted my head to glance back. "He complimented me on my taste in baschas."

"That boy must have been no more than twelve!"

I shrugged. "In the South, you start young."

It wasn't easy cutting directly across the square. There was no organization to the tangled walkways between stalls. Some turned, some stopped, some doubled back. Twice I got turned around, then finally found the way. Through the cheek-by-jowl crumbling buildings, then out onto the plateau.

We were, I judged, directly opposite the hyorts, with Iskandar in between. But here there were no hyorts. Here there were no wagons. Only horses, bedding, and circles.

"Looks more like a war," I observed, "than a gathering for the jhihadi."

Del halted her gelding beside me, gazing upon the scene. "Many wars," she agreed. "Are there not many tanzeers?"

Slowly I shook my head. "It doesn't feel right."

"What doesn't?"

"The tanzeers *are* hiring an army . . . an army of sword-dancers. They only do that on an individual basis—feuding tanzeers hire men to fight one another, so they can destroy one another—never as a group. The *nature* of desert domains is each man for himself . . . it just doesn't seem right that so many are here together, and all are hiring men."

Del shrugged. "Does it matter?"

"Maybe," I said uneasily. "Maybe it does."

And then I thought about what Abbu Bensir had said concerning going to a single place to win coin and find a job. It wasn't the Southron way, but I saw certain advantages. No doubt so did the others; it was why so many were here.

"We could get rich," I said thoughtfully. "If we hired on with the right tanzeer, we could get *very* rich."

"I didn't come to get rich. I came to kill a man."

"*If* you find him," I said, "what do you plan to do? Challenge him to a dance?"

"He's not worth the honor."

"Oh. So, are you just going to walk up to him and gut him?"

Del's expression didn't change. "I don't know."

"You think you might want to consider it?"

Now she looked at me. "I have considered it for six years. Now is the time for doing."

"But you can't *do* without thinking it through." I shifted in the saddle, taking weight on locked arms braced against the pommel. "He's not a popular man. Others will want to kill him. I doubt he walks alone. And if he's done all the things you say, I doubt he *pisses* alone."

Del's tone was steady. "I will find a way."

I sat back down in the saddle. "Can we at least get a meal first? And maybe a place to stay?"

Del extended a hand, indicating the plateau. "*There* is a place to stay."

"I kind of thought we might go find a room. It might not have a roof, but then neither of us is a tanzeer. And it doesn't look like rain."

Automatically, Del glanced up at the sky. It was a clear, brilliant blue, without a cloud apparent. But this was border country. This was *odd* country; it just didn't feel right. Too many bits mixed together: vegetation, temperature, people.

"Sandtiger! Tiger! *Del!*"

I glanced around. Frowned. Peered at the circles, but saw no one I knew. Only men in the circles with swords in their hands.

"There." Del pointed in the other direction. "Isn't that—Alric?"

Alric? "Oh—*Alric.*" The Northerner who'd helped us in Rusali, the domain just before Julah. I squinted. "Yes, I think it is."

Alric approached, waving. With him walked a short, fat woman. Two little girls preceded them; in one arm he carried a third. At least, I think it was a girl; sometimes it's hard to tell.

Del slid out of her saddle. "Lena had her baby."

I stayed in mine. "And, from the look of it, is expecting yet another."

The little girls, upon arrival, hurled themselves at Del, who bent down to receive them. I was privately astonished they even remembered her; they were all of three and four—or maybe four and five; at this age, who can tell?—and they'd only spent a week or so around us when Alric had taken us into his home after I'd gotten myself wounded. But Del is very good with children, and the girls had adored her. Obviously their opinions hadn't changed.

I watched her as the girls competed for her hugs. She was smiling, laughing with them, exchanging

Southron greetings. I almost expected pain, expecting Del to see Kalle in their faces, but there was only happiness. I saw no trace of anguish.

About then Alric arrived with his heavily pregnant wife. The last time I'd seen her she'd also been heavily pregnant. And since the older girls were but a year apart, I began to suspect Lena and Alric enjoyed active nights together.

Lena was Southron, and looked it; he was clearly Northern. The girls were a little of both. They had their mother's black hair and dark skin, but their father's bright blue eyes and high-arched cheekbones. They'd be beauties when they were grown.

Alric was grinning. "I thought so!" he said. "I told Lena it was you, but she said no. She said by now Del would have come to her senses and looked for a Northern man instead of a Southron danjac."

"Oh?" I looked down at Lena, who showed white teeth at me. "I suppose you think she'd be better off with another Alric."

Lena patted her swollen belly. "A strong, lusty Northerner is good for a woman's soul." Black eyes glinted. "And other things as well."

Alric laughed aloud. "Although so far all this lusty Northerner makes is girls." *He* patted Lena's belly. "Maybe this one will be a boy."

"And if not?" I asked.

Alric's grin widened. "We'll keep trying until we get one."

I waited for Del's comment; surely she had one. But the girls were chattering at her and she had no chance to speak.

Lena waved welcoming hands. "Come, come . . . we have a house in the city not far from here. You will come and stay with us; there are plenty of rooms. We can wait for the jhihadi together."

I glanced at Alric. "Is that why you came?"

He shifted the baby in his arms. "Everyone else was coming to Iskandar. Even the tanzeers. I thought it might be worthwhile to come up myself and see how the dancing was." He gestured with his head in the direction of the circles. "And, as you can see, there are sword-dancers aplenty. There will be coin as well. Or a tanzeer who'll hire me. With all these little mouths to feed, extra coin would be welcome."

Three little mouths to feed, and a fourth on the way. No wonder he'd come to Iskandar, but I thought it odd for Lena. She couldn't be far from delivering.

Lena sensed my thought. "A child born in the presence of a jhihadi will be blessed throughout his life."

"Or hers," Alric said affably; the possibility of yet another daughter did not appear to trouble him.

He hadn't changed much. Still big. Still Northern. Still a sword-dancer. But it seemed odd to look at him now—smiling, cheerful, openly friendly—and recall how I had felt when I'd first met him. How I'd thought he was after Del. I hadn't trusted him at all until we'd sparred in an alley circle. You learn a man that way. Learn what he is made of.

"Alric," I said suddenly, "how is your dancing these days?"

His brow creased. "Well enough. Why?"

"How'd you feel about going a few matches? For old time's sake."

He grinned, displaying big teeth. Alric was big all over. "You always beat me," he said. "But I've been practicing. Now maybe I can beat you."

I glanced across at the circles. "Shall we go find out?"

"Not *now*," Lena said. "First you will come to our house. You will eat. Rest. Give us the news you have. And we will give you ours." She slanted a glance at Alric. "Time for dancing and drinking later."

Del came forward with a girl on either arm. The roan trailed behind them. "We are grateful for your offer. Your news will be welcome."

I was a little surprised. I expected Del to want to go haring off after news of Ajani, trying to track him down in Iskandar, or find out if he was expected. But apparently she'd thought about what I'd said. If she was to kill the man, it would have to be carefully planned.

"Come," Lena said. She turned and waddled away.

Alric looked at Del over the black-fuzzed head of the baby. He smiled, said something in Northern dialect, slanted an oblique glance at me.

Del's chin came up. She answered briefly in the same dialect, then told the girls to show her the way to their quarters. Tugging on her arms, they led her toward the city. The roan trotted behind.

"And what was that?" I asked Alric.

He grinned. "I asked her if a Southroner was enough man for a free-hearted uplander woman." Blue eyes glinted. "Speaking as an older brother looking out for a sister's welfare."

"Of course," I agreed dryly. "And what did the sister *tell* the older brother?"

"There is no Southron translation. It was a Northern obscenity." Alric's grin stretched wide. "Which says something all on its own."

Well, I suppose it does. But he didn't tell me what.

"Let's go eat," I said sourly.

Alric's eyes were guileless. "Would you like to hold the baby?"

Which gave me an opportunity to use an untranslatable *Southron* obscenity.

The toothy grin widened. "And here I heard you were a father."

The stud walked onto my heels. Since I'd stopped moving, it wasn't surprising. "A father—? Oh. That." In disgust, I elbowed the stud in the nose and pushed him back a step. "Have you see him?"

Alric hitched the baby higher on a big shoulder and headed for the city. "Your son? No. Just heard there was a boy here—young man, really—who says he's the Sandtiger's son."

"He isn't," I muttered, matching my pace to his. "At least, not as far as I know."

"Does it matter if he is?"

I thought about it. "Maybe."

"Maybe? *Maybe?* What an odd thing to say." The baby caught a handful of blond hair and tugged; Alric freed it gently. "Don't you want to have a son to carry on your blood?"

What blood? And whose? For all I knew, it could be the blood of borjuni killers. "I figure I'm doing a good enough job carrying it all on my own."

Alric scoffed, but gently. "A man should have a son. A man should have a family. A man should have kinfolk to sing the songs of him."

"Northerner," I muttered.

"And if you meet him in the circle?"

I stopped short. "He's a sword-dancer? My s—this young man?"

Alric shrugged, frowning a little. "I heard of him at the circles. I assumed he was a sword-dancer, but perhaps he isn't. Perhaps he's a tanzeer."

My son, a tanzeer. Which meant he could hire me.

"No," I said, "I don't think so."

"Well, it doesn't matter. He is whatever he is." Alric lengthened his stride and led me into the city.

Three

The building Alric had claimed for Lena and the girls was large—four rooms—but lacked a roof and half of a wall on one side. Into the room lacking most of one wall he put the carthorse and his own mount, a bald-faced bay gelding. It left two rooms vacant: he offered one to Del and me.

I've never been one for sharing close confinement, preferring privacy, but in some situations it's good to have folk around. I thought it possible this might become one of them. As the city filled with strangers, trouble would inevitably break out. There would be thieves, certainly, come to prey upon worshipers, and feuds between hostile races. And if the promised jhihadi never arrived—which I believed was likely—frustration would drive impatient people to do things they might not otherwise think about. Like starting fights, and killing. All things considered, I thought Alric's offer generous. Del and I agreed.

Lena sent the two little girls—Felka and Fabiola; don't ask me which was which—off to help Del with settling our belongings in one of the other rooms. I briefly considered lending a hand, then decided against it; Del looked pleased to spend time with the girls, even though they'd be little help, and I felt more like sitting with Alric by the fire, sharing a bota of aquivi. Lena prepared food.

Alric wiped his mouth. "Did you ever find Del's brother?"

311

I accepted the bota. "We found him. We left him."

"Dead?"

"No. With the Vashni."

Alric grimaced. "Good as dead, then. They're not a hospitable tribe."

I cocked an eyebrow in his direction. "It was a Vashni you got your sword off of, wasn't it? The blade with human thighbone hilt?"

Alric nodded. "But I put it away and got a Southron sword. I decided it was a bit too grisly to use a sword with a hilt made out of the bone of a man I never knew—or maybe a man I *did* know."

"New swords," I reflected. "A lot of that going around."

"I noticed." Alric's eyes were on the harness next to my leg. "No more Singlestroke?"

I accepted a flat, hot loaf from Lena, blew on it to cool it. "Got broken in a sword-dance after we left Julah." I blew some more, then bit. The steaming loaf was nutty, flaky, delicious. "Like you, I've got another."

"But yours is a *jivatma*."

Alric's tone was odd. I glanced at him, glanced at the sheathed sword, then looked back at him. Recalled it was Alric who'd first told me about *jivatmas*. About Northern blooding-blades, and how rank in the North was reckoned.

"*Jivatma*," I agreed. "Del took me to Staal-Ysta."

Blond brows swooped up. Then down. "Since you have a blooding-blade, I'm assuming you are a *kaidin*."

"I'm Southron," I said. "I'm a seventh-level sword-dancer. I don't need a fancy name."

"But you carry a *jivatma*."

Irritably, I swallowed hot bread, then washed it down with aqivi. "Believe me, Alric, I'd give it to you if I could. But the thrice-cursed thing won't let me."

Alric smiled. "If you enter a circle with a blooding-blade at your beck, no one will defeat you." He paused thoughtfully. "Except maybe Del."

"No," I blurted.

"But she has a *jivatma*, too—"

I shook my head. "That's not what I meant. I meant, Del and I have done it once. We'll never do it again."

Alric grinned. "You lost."

It stung, but only a little. "Nobody lost. Nobody won. Both of us nearly died." I drank, then continued before he could ask any questions. "And as for taking my sword into a circle—no. Not *here* at any rate—this is exhibition. I just don't think it's fair."

Alric shrugged. "Then don't sing. An unkeyed *jivatma* isn't much more than a sword."

"It isn't like that." I accepted a second loaf. "You don't understand. This sword wasn't quenched properly, the first *or* second time."

"Second!" Alric's eyes widened. "You requenched your blade?"

"No choice," I muttered, biting into the second loaf. "The thing's a pain in the rump, and I plan to replace it. I'll put this one away and use a Southron sword."

"There's a swordsmith here," he said. "With so many sword-dancers present, a smith would be a fool to ignore such a windfall. His name is Sarad, and he's set up a smithy out by the circles."

"I'll see him tomorrow," I said, as Del came back with the girls.

A faint frown puckered her brow, though she gave nothing away in behavior. The girls joined their mother in preparing the meal, and Del came over to sit near Alric and me.

"What's up?" I asked.

The puckered brow didn't smooth. "Can't you feel it? The weather is changing. It doesn't feel right."

Alric and I both glanced around, assessing daylight and temperature. The way the day *tasted*, odd as it sounds.

"Cooler," Alric remarked. "Well, I won't complain. After living so long in the South, I could use some Northern weather."

"This is the border." I shrugged. "Sometimes it's cool, sometimes hot."

"It *was* hot," Del said, "all of an hour ago. But now it's cooler. Significantly cooler; it just doesn't feel right."

I glanced up at the roof, which wasn't really a roof. A few spindly timber rafters remained, but most had rotted and fallen in, supplying wood for Lena's cookfire. All four rooms were in similar shape, which left them mostly open to the elements. No proper shade, but no cover, either. Alric had strung up a couple of blankets to provide a makeshift roof, but it wouldn't do much if the weather did turn chancy.

Del just shook her head. "I feel something in my bones."

I arched unsubtle brows. "Getting along in years?"

She slanted me a glance. "One of us certainly is."

"Here." Lena handed clay bowls around with bread and mutton stew. "With the tribes coming in, we should have mutton enough to spare. And all the merchants, too; we could live here for months."

I thought it unlikely they'd have to.

"I could set snares," Del offered, and instantly Felka and Fabiola wanted to accompany her.

It reminded me of something. For a moment I was swept away somewhere familiar, and yet unknown; abruptly the feeling died, and I realized what I remembered. Del offering to set snares while a towheaded Borderer boy asked to help her. Massou, Adara's son, who had hosted a Northern demon and nearly destroyed us all.

Loki. It was enough to make me shiver. Thank the gods for the Cantéada, who had sung them into a trap-circle and freed the Borderers.

"Later," Del promised the girls. "We'll see first if it's going to storm."

Lena cuddled the baby against her breasts. "At least this little one need not concern herself with where her meals are coming from."

Alric's eyes glinted. "Nor I, if it comes to it."

A gust of wind blew into the room, scattering handfuls of dust. A cool, damp-tasting wind, hinting at coming change. After months spent in the North, I knew the promise well.

Del looked at me. "Rain."

Well, it *was* the border. A day's ride south of here and rain was almost an unknown thing.

"Maybe." I drank *amnit*.

"Rain," she said again, mostly to herself.

Alric looked overhead. Two blankets tied to rotting timbers, and the weather tasted of rain.

Lena shifted uneasily. Southron-born and bred, rain was not to be trusted, or understood very well. "Maybe we should look for a house with a roof."

Alric's blond hair swung against shoulder blades as he shook his head, still staring into the sky. "No roofs for people like us . . . the tanzeers have claimed them all."

"All?" I asked. "There aren't *that* many people here—and there can't be that many tanzeers. Not yet."

Alric shrugged. "I looked. All the decent dwellings were claimed. We took the best we could find."

I set the bota aside. "Tell you what . . . I want to take a little walk anyway, just to check things out. I'll see what I can find in the way of better shelter. If there *is* to be a storm, we might as well be prepared."

Alric rose. "I'll go to the merchants and buy more blankets, some skins . . . we can put up a makeshift roof."

Del shook her head as I glanced her way. "I'll stay and help Lena."

It surprised me a little. Del is not a woman for women's things, as she has so often been at such pains to tell me. But neither is she a woman to ignore the needs of others; Lena had her hands—and belly—full with four children. Del never shirks assistance if she can offer any.

Well, it was fine with me. I didn't think Del would

approve of me talking to a swordsmith about another
blade.

I left them all behind and headed out toward the
circles. More wind kicked up as I walked, gusting
down through narrow alleyways and curling around
corners to snatch at my burnous. Grit stung my face; I
blinked to clear my eyes.

"Sandtiger? *Tiger!*"

I stopped, squinting, and turned. From out of a
broken doorway stepped a Northerner, blond braids
hanging to his waist. And a scar across his top lip.

"Garrod," I said, on a note of disbelief.

He grinned as he approached, blue eyes bright. "I
never thought to see you again, once you and Del left
the Cantéada and went north." He sobered, recalling
the reasons. "Did Del settle her trouble?"

"Yes and no," I answered. "What are you doing
here? Iskandar isn't exactly Kisiri."

He shrugged, hooking thumbs into a wide belt. His
braids swung; dangling colored beads rattled in the
wind. "We started for Kisiri. Got about halfway there—
but then we heard about Iskandar; that people were
coming here. I didn't know anything about any Oracle, or this promised messiah—at least, not right away—
but I'd picked up a string of horses along the way.
Since trading is my business, I wanted to go where I
could buy or sell. Only a fool would ignore such an
opportunity, and I've never been a fool."

Not lately, maybe. I hadn't been so sure before,
when we'd briefly ridden together. Garrod was a horse-
speaker, a man who had a knack with horses. He
called it a kind of magic. He claimed he could *talk* to
them, understand them, the way a man understands a
man. I wasn't so certain that was true, but he did have
a way with them. I'd seen it in the stud.

"So, you didn't go on with Adara and her children
after all." It surprised me a little. Garrod had sworn
he'd take them to Kisiri, but a man can change his
mind.

Garrod grinned. "Oh, I went with them . . . by then I had no choice. The girl didn't give me any." And he shouted for Cipriana.

She came. So did Adara, her mother. And so did her brother, Massou.

I blinked in dull surprise, surrounded on the instant. They were clearly as startled, and certainly more pleased. I felt a little awkward: the last time I'd spent any time with them, they'd been hosting hostile demons.

Bronze-haired, green-eyed Adara was flushed with color, which didn't quite agree with her hair, but set her eyes aglint. She was oddly reserved, almost shy; I recalled, with a twinge of discomfort, she had hoped for affection from me. But it was Del who had it all; Adara had surrendered the field, but obviously recalled it.

Massou, blond and blue-eyed like his sister, was taller than I remembered. Now eleven, in place of ten; Cipriana was sixteen.

Cipriana was also *pregnant.*

Now I knew what Garrod meant about not having any choice. Women can do that to you.

Like her mother, she was red-faced, but for a different reason. It didn't take much to figure it out, either; she stepped up next to Garrod and twined fingers into his belt. Pale hair was tied back from a face delicately rounded from pregancy. I saw again the Northern features that had reminded me of Del. A younger, softer Del. The Del before Ajani.

Garrod dropped an arm around her shoulder. "We're kinfolk now."

"So I can see," I said dryly.

"Is Del here?" Massou demanded.

"Del's here," I agreed. "We're a couple of streets over."

The boy's eyes lighted. "You could come *here*," he asserted.

Adara nodded. "You could. We have enough room. See?" She gestured toward the building.

"We're with friends," I explained.

Garrod shrugged. "Bring them."

"They have three small girls, and another on the way."

The horse-speaker grinned again. "*We* have one on the way." Which made Cipriana blush.

"There is room," Adara said quietly. "I understand if you have no wish to share, but there is room for you all."

Her manner was a mixture of emotions. Clearly she recalled how I had proved uninterested in her availability: a widow whose husband had been unable because of bad health. It had taken courage for her to speak at all; I'd let her down gently, but no doubt it had been difficult. And then the loki had invaded her body, and her children, forcing them all into bizarre behavior.

She recalled it all, was embarrassed, and yet wanted my company, which embarrassed her yet again.

I looked past her at the building, thinking of the others. "Do you have a roof?"

Garrod shook his head. "The tanzeers have all the buildings with proper roofs."

"So I keep hearing." I glanced up at the graying sky. "I think there's a storm brewing."

"But it's warm," Cipriana protested.

Massou disagreed. "Cool."

Garrod sniffed the wind, and frowned. "It smells almost like snow."

"Snow!" Adara was astonished. "Are you forgetting we come from a place not far from here? We know the weather. It never snows on the border."

"It smells like *something*," I said. But nothing like the hounds.

Garrod still frowned. "I think I will see to the horses."

Cipriana lingered. "Do you still have the stud?"

"Of course."

"Oh." Her expression changed. The stud hadn't

liked her much. Hadn't liked any of them, once the loki had climbed inside.

"He'd be different, now," I told her.

"He bit me," Massou said.

"Yes, well, he had his reasons. He's bitten me, too, and I was never a loki."

Adara's color deepened. "I wish we could forget that."

"It wasn't you," I told her. "I know that, and so does Del. We don't blame you for any of it."

"We could have *killed* you."

Or worse. But I didn't say it. "Let it go," I said quietly. "Don't let it eat at you."

"Can I see Del?" Massou asked.

As always, I looked to Adara. There had been a time when she'd wanted her children to avoid us.

Adara, comprehending my hesitation, nodded at once, as if to dispell any hint of her former reluctance. "Of course you may go, but only if invited."

"Del won't mind," I said. "I'm sure she'll be glad to see him."

"I want to go," the boy declared.

I gestured. "Two streets over, third house on the left."

Massou darted away.

Cipriana murmured something about finding Garrod and went away. Adara smiled at me and stripped wind-teased hair out of eyes. "You look a little tired. Would you care for something to drink? Eat?"

"Just ate." I was oddly ill at ease. "How long will you be staying?"

"Until Garrod is ready to leave." She shrugged a little, hearing how dependent it sounded. "He is a good man and treats Cipriana well. They care for one another. And it's easier for Massou and me to stay with them. I can help with the baby."

I smiled. "First grandchild."

Her eyes glowed. "Yes. Kesar's blood will be carried on."

She had buried her husband on the road from the border to Kisiri. A strong woman, Adara; as strong, in her own way, as Del. Borderers have to be.

Wind blew grit in our faces. It gave me an excuse. "Best go inside," I said.

Adara nodded absently, looking into my face intently. As if she sought an answer. I don't know what she saw. I don't know what she wanted. All I could do was wait.

She smiled a little eventually, sensing my unease. She put a hand on my forearm. A callused, toughened hand. But its touch was somehow tender. "A good man," she said gently. "We will never forget you."

I watched her turn toward the house. Watched her walk through the door. Saw the quiet swing of hips; the flicker of windblown skirts; a glint of bronze-colored hair. Heard the lilt of a woman's voice lifted in soft song.

Don't ask me why. I've never been one for music. But it touched something inside me, and I followed it anyway.

Adara turned, startled, as I stepped into the doorway. The song broke off in her throat; one hand was spread across it.

She was suddenly vulnerable. And something in me answered. "Are you all right?" I asked. "Do you need anything?"

Adara swallowed heavily. "Don't ask that," she said. "You might not get the answer you want."

I glanced at a broken wall.

"They're somewhere else," she said, interpreting the glance.

"No, I just meant—" I broke it off. "It could be awkward, if they misunderstood."

Adara smiled a little. "Yes."

Shadows crept into the room, softening her face. Snow or no snow, a storm was brewing. The light had changed.

"I wanted to say something," I told her.

Adara's color altered.

It was harder than I'd thought. I've never been a man for really talking to a woman of things that have substance, of things to do with feelings, except for Del. And even that is sometimes uncomfortable, because we think so differently. But something about Adara made me want to help.

I drew in a deep breath. "It's none of my business. But I'll say it anyway."

"Yes," she said faintly.

"A woman like you needs a husband. You've been alone too long. Del might disagree . . . she'd probably say a woman is often better without a man—maybe, for some, she's right—but I don't think you're one of them."

"No." It was a whisper.

"You shouldn't be alone. I know there's Garrod to help, but that's not what you need. You need a man of your own. Someone you can tend; someone who can tend you."

Adara said nothing.

I shifted a little. "All I mean is, there might be a chance for you. Here, in Iskandar. There will be plenty of men."

A brief, eloquent gesture indicating herself. "I'm no longer a young woman, and I have two children."

"Cipriana has her own life now. Massou will be a man soon enough; for now he needs a father. He's quick-witted. A man could do much worse than to take you and the boy."

She stared at me a long moment. Her eyes were full of thoughts. Of possibilities.

She shut them a moment. Then looked straight back at me and carefully wet her lips. "I think you'd better go."

It took me aback. "What?"

Her mouth trembled a little. "This is not what I want to hear, this talk of other men. Not from you. Not from *you*."

It wasn't what I had intended. Somehow I'd made it worse. And for both of us; after too many weeks without Del in my bed, I was very aware of Adara. I'm not made for abstinence. I didn't *want* Adara . . . but part of me wanted a woman.

Most of me wanted Del so bad it confused the rest of me.

Adara's smile was bittersweet. "I didn't think I could say this: I won't be a substitute."

It was cold water. The wind blew through the room, rippling the gauze of her skirts. Stripping the hair from her face, so I could see her pride.

I wanted to touch her, but couldn't. It would only make things worse.

"For someone else, you won't be." I turned and went out of the house.

Four

Sarad the swordsmith was one-eyed. The blind eye was puckered closed behind a shrunken lid. The good eye was black. Matching hair was twisted into a single braid and bound in dyed orange leather at the back of his neck. He wore an ocher-colored burnous and a leather belt plated with enameled copper disks. The colors were bright and varied.

Sarad showed me his smile. He sat cross-legged on a blanket with swords set out before him. Steel glowed sullenly in the dying light of the day. "These are my best," he said. "I can *make* better, of course . . . but that would take time. Have you the time to spare?"

Well, yes and no. I could spare the time for him to make a blade to order, but only if I was willing to use my *jivatma* in the meantime.

Squatting across from Sarad, I thought about Kem, the swordsmith on Staal-Ysta. It had taken days to fashion Samiel, and with my help. But mostly because of rituals; Kem rushed nothing. And while Sarad probably wouldn't hurry either—not if he wanted to forge a good sword—he had no elaborate rituals to eat away extra hours.

The swords all looked fine. They felt fine, too; I'd already handled six, trying them out on simple and intricate patterns. Two had a balance I found to my liking, but they were only halfway measures. I'd spent more than half of my life using a sword made specifically for *me*. I didn't like the idea of dancing with a ready-made blade created for anyone with the coin to buy it.

But I liked even less the idea of dancing with Chosa Dei lying in wait in my steel.

Sarad gestured, indicating a sword. "I would be pleased to offer the Sandtiger my best at a very good price."

I shook my head. "Your best isn't here. Your best is still in your hands."

Something glittered in his eye. "Of course. A sword-dancer such as yourself appreciates true skill and creativity; I can make you a perfect sword. All I require is time."

I picked up one of the two swords I thought would do. The steel was clean and smooth, with keen, bright edges. It had the proper weight, the proper flex, the proper grip, the proper promise.

"This one," I said finally.

Sarad named his price.

I shook my head. "Too much."

"It comes with a scabbard—see? And I am a master, Sandtiger—"

"But this isn't the best you can do. Do you expect me to pay full price?"

He thought it over. Considered what it might do for business if the Sandtiger carried his sword. Named a lower price.

I counted out the coin.

Sarad pocketed it. "Have you a tanzeer yet?"

"Not yet. Why?"

The swordsmith gestured casually. "I have heard tanzeers are looking for sword-dancers."

"I heard that, too." I frowned a little. "Do you know *why* the tanzeers are hiring so many all at once?"

Sarad shrugged. "I hear things . . . things about the tribes, and the jhihadi." He glanced around, then looked back at me. "I think the tanzeers are afraid. So they unite in the face of a powerful enemy and hire men to fight."

I looked at Sarad gravely. "If this rumor is true, it would indicate the tanzeers believe this jhihadi exists

—or *will* exist. And I've never known tanzeers to believe in much of anything except their own greed."

Sarad shrugged. "It's what I have heard." He eyed me thoughtfully. "I thought surely a man such as the Sandtiger would be sought by many, and hired immediately."

I sheathed the new-bought sword and thought about how best to attach it to my harness, specifically made for another sword. "I only got here at midday."

"Then you are slow." Sarad smiled. "Your son arrived a week ago."

I stiffened. "Where *is* this person?"

He shrugged. "I've seen him here and there. He visits the circles, lingers, then goes to the cantinas."

"Which ones?"

A flick of his hand. "That one. And that one. And the other one street over. There are many cantinas here. Sword-dancers like to drink."

I rose. "I think it's about time I paid 'my son' a visit."

"He will like that," Sarad said. "He's very proud of you."

I grunted and walked away.

He had, I'd been told, an old gray mare with a white splash on her face and three white legs. He was dark-haired and blue-eyed. Young; maybe eighteen or nineteen. No sword. A necklet of claws at his throat. And a tongue busy with my name. All of which meant it shouldn't be hard to find him.

Except I couldn't find him.

Oh, people knew of him. I went to each of the three cantinas Sarad had mentioned, plus two more. None of them were *real* cantinas, being little more than broken buildings where a Southroner with liquor had set up hasty shop, selling cups of aqivi and *amnit* at premium prices. But no one seemed to mind. It was a place—or places—to gather, swapping tales and seeking work.

Yes, men said, they knew him. And they described him in the fashion I'd grown accustomed to hearing.

But none of them had a name. Everyone knew him only as the Sandtiger's cub.

I found it disconcerting. *Anyone* could claim the same, since no one knew any different, and do all sorts of nefarious deeds, thereby harming my reputation, which I'd been at some pains to establish. It had taken years. And then some boy fancying himself my son appropriates it without my knowledge.

I didn't like it much.

Even if he *was* my son.

After a while, I gave up. But I cautioned everybody to point him out to me if he ever showed his face where I could see it.

Which gave them all something to laugh at: a grown man—the *Sandtiger*—had mislaid his own son.

I went "home" with my new-bought sword and thought bad things about the man who claimed my blood; by inference, also my name. I didn't like it at all. My name was *mine,* won at a very high cost. I didn't want to share it. Not even with a son.

I woke up because of the stud. It was very late and very dark, and everyone else was asleep, bundled up in blankets because of the temperature. Alric, in the other room, snored gently in Lena's arms.

Del, in our room, slept alone in her personal bedding. As I did in my own.

The stud continued to stomp, paw, snort. If I let him go much longer, he'd wake up everyone else. And since I didn't much feel like making excuses for a horse, who wouldn't have any, I decided to shut him up.

I sighed, peeled back blankets, crawled to my feet. Alric's makeshift roof dipped down from rotting rafters, but it cut out some of the wind. It also cut out the light. I had to strain to see.

It was cold outside of my blankets. Here'd I'd been saying how nice it was to be back home again where it was warm, and it had to go and get cold. But I shut it out of my mind—glad I'd slept in my clothes—and went out to see to the stud.

Del's blue gelding was tied in one of the corners of the room Alric had deemed the stable. He'd been roused by the stud's noise, but stood quietly enough. The stud, however, did not; tied out of reach of the roan, he nonetheless warned him away.

Alric's blanket-and-skin roof did not extend to the "stable," but the light was little better. There was no moon, no stars. It was all I could do to see through the damp gloom. Wind brushed my face, crept down the neck of my tunic. I put my hand on the stud's warm rump, then moved around to his head. Promised to remove his *gehetties* if he didn't quiet down; meanwhile, I tried to interpret his signs of unease.

It wasn't just the gelding. The stud didn't like him, but he tolerated him well enough. He'd learned to over the weeks. And I doubted it was the packhorse belonging to Alric, an old, quiet mare. He'd already proved uninterested in her, which meant it was something else entirely. Something I couldn't see.

Wind scraped through the broken wall, spitting dust and bits of grit. The stud laid back his ears.

I put a soothing hand on his neck. "Take it easy, old son. It's just a little wind. And the wall's breaking most of it; let's hear no complaints out of you."

There was, in the dimness, the faint shine of a single eye. Ears remained pinned.

I thought briefly of Garrod. He'd tell me he knew what it was just by "talking" with the stud.

Who wasn't talking to me.

Then again, he was. He stomped a foreleg smartly and came very close to my toes.

"Hey. Watch yourself, old man, or I *will* cut off—"

A quick sideways twist of his head and he shut teeth upon my finger.

I swore. Punched him in the eye to make sure I had his attention; he'd ignore me otherwise, and I might lose the finger. Then, when he paid attention, I retrieved my hand from his mouth.

And began to swear in earnest.

I backed up a prudent step, out of the stud's reach, and squinted at the finger. It was ugly.

I swore some more, gritting the words in my teeth, and then proceeded to hold the entire hand out—torn finger included—and tell myself, repeatedly, it didn't hurt at all.

I wrung the hand a little. The finger didn't like it.

I walked around in a jerky circle, thinking mean thoughts about the stud. Wished briefly I was a woman so tears wouldn't be disapproved of; I didn't cry, of course, but thought it might be nice to have that kind of release. But a man, with others near, doesn't show that much of himself.

"Let me see," she said.

I jerked around, swore some more, told her I was fine.

"Stop lying," she said. "And stop trying to be such a *man*. Admit the finger hurts."

"It hurts," I gritted promptly. "And now it *still* hurts; admitting it didn't help."

"Is it broken?"

"I can't tell."

"Did you look?"

"Not very long."

Del came closer. "Then let me see."

The hand was shaking. It didn't want to be touched.

"I'll be gentle," she promised.

"That's what they all say."

"Here, let me see." She took my wrist into one hand.

"Don't touch it," I said sharply.

"I'll *look*, I won't touch. Of course if it *is* broken, the bone will have to be set."

"I don't think it's broken. He didn't bite that hard."

Del inspected the finger as best she could in poor light. "Hard enough to shred the skin. You're bleeding."

"Blood washes off—*ouch*—"

"Sorry," she murmured.

Her head was bent. Pale hair obscured her face; fell softly over her shoulders; lingered on her breasts. I couldn't see her expression. Only hear her voice. Smell her familiar scent. Feel her hands on mine.

Arousal was abrupt.

Oh, hoolies, bascha—how long can this go on—?

"It's raining." Del glanced up, peering at the sky through the place where the roof had been. Lips parted. Hair fell away from her face. A sculpted, flawless face made brittle by years of obsession. By months of determined *focus*.

I thought suddenly of Adara, who'd be more than pleased to have me. But wasn't a substitute; for Del, what woman could be?

"So it is," I said tightly.

Raindrops crawled through her hair, running with pinkish blood, the blood from my bitten finger resting, like my hand, unquietly on her shoulder. Wanting to cup her jaw; wanting to touch her face; demanding to lock itself tightly in slick pale hair—

Del swallowed visibly. "We should get under cover."

I didn't even blink as water ran down my face. "Yes, we probably should."

Del looked at me. Neither of us moved.

Rain fell harder yet. Neither of us moved.

My voice was unsteady. "I can think of better places."

Del didn't say anything.

"I can think of *dryer* places."

Del didn't say anything.

Tension exploded between us. "You'd better go back," I said harshly. "I don't know how much longer I can respect your precious focus."

Del touched my face. Her sword hand trembled.

Oh, Delilah—*don't*—

In the darkness, her eyes were black. *"To hoolies with my focus."*

Five

By dawn, we were back in bedrolls. This time we shared one, spreading blankets and pelts in the chill of a too-damp morning, trying to hide from the breeze curling down through dripping blankets.

"Too long," I murmured weakly. "Can we forget your focus more often?"

Del, pulling hair from beneath my shoulder, twisted her mouth a little. "Sidetracked already; I told you men can't keep their minds on anything if a woman is at issue."

It didn't sting at all, because she didn't mean it to. I found it a welcome respite. "Have I destroyed your concentration?"

"Last night, certainly. But not today."

"No?"

"No," she answered lightly. "I'll ask my sword for it back."

For some strange reason, it disturbed me. "Bascha—you don't mean it."

"Of course I mean it."

I twisted sideways, putting room between us, so I could look at her clearly. "Do you mean to tell me you plan to shed all the humanity you just regained?"

Del's brows arched. "And do *you* mean to tell me I should forget who I am in the name of a single night's bedding?"

I scraped at a stubbled cheek. "Well, I sort of thought it might lead to *more* than a single night's

bedding. Like maybe *lots* of single night's bedding all
strung together, until we can't tell them apart any
more."

Del thought about it. "Possibly," she conceded.

I was moved to protest, but didn't. Couldn't. I saw
the glint in her eyes. "Hoolies, I think she's thawed!"

But the amusement faded away. "Tiger, I dismiss
nothing about last night. But neither can I dismiss
what I came here to do."

I sighed, stretched out again, scratched at an eyebrow. "I know. I wish I could ask you to forget about
Ajani, but I don't suppose it would be fair."

"I'd never ask it of you."

No, maybe not that. "But you *did* try to sell my soul
to Staal-Ysta for a year."

Del stiffened beside me. "And how many years will
you remind me?"

I lay there not breathing. Not because of her tone,
which was a combination of shame, distress, irritation.
And not because of her posture, which bespoke the
deep-seated pain. But because of the words themselves.

"Years," I echoed softly.

"Yes." She *was* irritated. "Will you bring it up once
a year? Twice? Even once a week?"

I swallowed heavily. "Once a year, I think."

"Why?" The cry was instinctive. "Haven't I said I
was wrong?"

"Once a year," I repeated, "because it means we
have that year."

Del lay very still. She didn't breathe, either. "Oh,"
was all she said, after a time of consideration. Of
self-interpretation.

The prospect was frightening. But also strangely
pleasing.

I'm not alone anymore.

You could argue I hadn't been, not really; not since
Del and I had first joined up, except for a couple of
enforced separations. But we had not, until this mo-

ment, explored anything past the moment. Sword-dancers never do.

Men and women must.

Which led me to other things. "I wonder if he *is* . . ." I let it trail off.

Del shifted beneath blankets. "Wonder what? About who?"

"If he really is my son."

She smiled. "Would it please you if he is?"

I thought about it. "I don't know."

"Tiger! A *son*."

"But what good is it to discover you have a grown son you never knew existed? And that if he *does* exist, it's only because of a bedding you can't even remember."

Del's tone was dry. "Have you had so many as that?"

"Yes."

She eyed me askance a moment, then rolled her head straight again and stared up at the lightening sky. "Well, a son is a son. It shouldn't matter how he was gotten, just that he was."

"How Kalle was gotten matters."

I thought she might snap at me, as she can. I thought she might swear at me, as she can; I taught her most of the terms. I thought she might even withdraw altogether; she's very good at that, if she's of no mind to share. Del hides herself very well.

But this time she didn't try.

Del sighed heavily. "Kalle was never Kalle. Kalle was a cause. Kalle was an excuse. She justified the pain. She made it easier to hate."

"So you could give her up."

"Yes. So I could fulfill my oaths."

"Which were made *before* you even knew you were pregnant."

Del frowned. "Yes. I made them even as my kinfolk died; even as Jamail burned; even as Ajani broke my maidenhead. Does it matter when? They were made. Well worth the doing. The honor is worth the strife."

Like Del, I stared at the sky. "You gave up a child. Why should I acknowledge mine?"

After a lengthy, painful silence, Del turned her head away. "I have no answer for you."

"There isn't one," I told her, and rolled over to pull her close.

I had fully expected, when Del discovered it, she would say something about the new sword. But not that it was broken.

I turned from arranging bedding to dry in the sun. Except there wasn't any; clouds still choked the sky. *"What?"*

"It's broken," she repeated.

"It *can't* be!" I stepped across bedding and stopped dead by the new scabbard. It lay precisely where I had left it: on a blanket by Samiel.

The sword was spilled out of the scabbard. The blade was broken in half.

"Bad steel," she said.

I shook my head. "It wasn't. I'm sure of it. I examined it carefully."

Del shrugged; the weapon, being plain, unmagicked sword, held no interest for her. "When pressed too hard, it can break. Who did you dance against? Alric?"

"Del, I didn't dance. Not against anyone. All I did was buy this sword. I've never even *sparred* with it."

"Bad forging, then."

"I'd never buy a bad sword. You know that." Now I was irritated. It shouldn't matter that it wasn't a Northern *jivatma*, only that it was a sword I was entrusting my life to. Or would have, had it been whole. I inspected the sword closely. "The hilt and this half look perfectly normal. Let's see the rest of it."

I picked up the scabbard, turned it upside down, shook the rest of the blade out. It landed on the hilt half with a dull, ugly clank.

Del's indrawn breath was loud.

"Black," I said blankly.

"Just like your *jivatma*."

We locked eyes for only an instant. And then I was grabbing harness, grabbing scabbard, closing a hand on the hilt. And jerking it from the sheath.

Samiel was whole. Samiel was unchanged. Steel shone bright and unblemished—except for black charring stretching fully a third of the blade.

"There's more," I said. "More discoloration."

Del didn't say a word.

I looked at the broken blade. "He unmade it," I said plainly.

She knelt down beside me, looking more closely at the *jivatma*. "He's trapped in your sword."

"He *unmakes* things," I declared. "Don't you understand? The new sword was a threat. He wants me on his own terms, not risking a loss by default."

Del's tone was carefully modulated. "Tiger, I think you're— "

"—sandsick? No." Somehow, I was certain. Don't ask me how. I just *knew,* deep in my gut, deep in my heart, deep in the part of me no one else could share. "I'm beginning to understand. I think I'm beginning to know him."

"Tiger—"

My look cut her off. "You said he'd come to know me. Why can't I come to know him?"

Alric stepped into the doorway. "Do you want to spar?" He asked. "They're betting on matches at the circles . . . there are wagers to be won."

Del and I looked at him. Then we looked at the sword.

Thinking of Chosa Dei.

"When?" I asked aloud, of anyone who might know. "When is this jhihadi supposed to arrive?"

Del and Alric were equally uncertain of the question, and why *I* would ask it. They exchanged glances, then looked at me, shrugging.

"I know as much as you," Del said.

I shot a glance at Alric, still plugging the doorway between our two rooms. "You've been here longer."

"The Oracle's coming," he answered. "I imagine he's supposed to get here first. Since he's the one foretelling the coming of the jhihadi, I'd think he'd want to do it from Iskandar instead of just tribal gatherings."

Something sounded odd. "Tribes," I said intently. "Are you saying this Oracle is aiming his foretelling *only* at the tribes?"

Alric shrugged. "I imagine his foretelling includes everyone; wouldn't it have to, since he's talking about the South? But all anyone knows for certain is he's moving among the tribes." He paused. "Or else they're coming to him."

I thought back to the discussion Abbu Bensir and I had had with Del regarding tanzeers, jhihadi, tribes. "I don't know how much of this is real, or how much of this is some ambitious man's attempt to gain himself a name," I said slowly. "You'd think if he wanted the obvious kind of power, he'd go straight to the tanzeers. They rule the South . . . parts of it, anyway."

"But they're corrupt," Alric remarked. "Tanzeers are bought and sold all the time. Domains fall overnight."

"There are people who aren't corrupt," I said evenly. Southron people whose only interest is in surviving, in keeping alive their own way of life. They owe nothing at all to tanzeers, and they ignore the petty pacts and power struggles. All they do is live, drawing strength from their homeland."

"The tribes," he agreed.

"I should know," I said. "I grew up with one."

Del shook her head. "I don't understand."

I frowned, trying to put it into words that meant something. "The tribes are all little pieces of the South. Different races, different customs, different religious beliefs. It's why no one can really rule the Punja . . . the tribes are too fragmented, too difficult to control. And so the tanzeers content themselves with the pieces they *can* control, and the people . . . the tribes are left alone."

Del nodded. "You said something like this before, with Abbu."

"*Now* I'm wondering if this jhihadi nonsense has nothing whatsoever to do with the tanzeers—at least, directly—but is aimed instead at the tribes." I chewed my bottom lip. "The tribes, put together, outnumber the rest of us. No one really knows how many there are—they live in all parts of the South, and almost none of them stay put. Which makes it impossible for anyone to deal with them, even if they wanted to."

Del nodded. "So?"

"So, if you were a man who wanted absolute power, what is the surest way of getting it once and for all *without* involving tanzeers?"

She didn't waste any time. "By uniting the tribes."

I nodded. "Which might explain why so many tanzeers are leaving their domains to come to Iskandar. Not because of the jhihadi. Because of the *tribes*. They're hiring sword-dancers to mount a defense of the South."

Alric shook his head. "Impossible," he said. "I'm a Northerner, yes, but I've lived in the South for years. I don't think anyone *could* unite all the tribes, for all the reasons you've given."

My turn to shake my head. "It's a matter of language," I said. "All you have to do is find the sort of message that appeals to every individual tribe, and then use the proper language."

"Religion," Del said flatly.

Now I nodded. "Religion, stripped of faith, of belief, is nothing more than a means to enforce the will of a few upon the many. Don't you see? Tell a man to do something, and he may not like the idea. He refuses. But tell him his *god* requires it, and he'll rush to do the task."

"*If* he believes," Alric cautioned.

"I don't know about you," I said, "but I'm not a

religious man. I don't think there's much use in wor-
shiping a god or gods when we're responsible for our
own lives; relying on something—or some*one*—you
don't know is a fool's game. But a lot of people disagree. A lot of people arrange their lives around their
gods. They talk to them. Make offerings. Ask them for
aid." I looked at Del. "They make oaths in the names
of those gods, then live their lives by those oaths."

Color flared in her face. "What I do is my own
concern."

"Yes," I agreed. "I'm not arguing that. What I'm
saying is, the tribes are full of superstitions. If a nanny
bears twin kids, the year is supposed to be generous.
And when it isn't, *if* it isn't, something else is blamed."
I sighed and scratched at scars. "If a man discovered a
way of uniting the tribes in a common goal, he could
claim the South for himself. That's what I'm saying."

Alric was frowning, considering implications. Thinking about tanzeers, who would want the jhihadi dead.
Who would want the Oracle dead. And all the sword-
dancers they could hire in order to win a holy war.

Del shook her head. "Would it matter? How do you
know it wouldn't be better for the South if one man
did rule it, instead of all these tanzeers?"

"Because who's to say what this one man will do?" I
countered. "For one, if he's got the tribes on his side
he wouldn't need to hire sword-dancers. We'd be out
of a job." Del's expression was sardonic. "All right," I
conceded, "aside from that, what if the tribes decided
the rest of us didn't deserve to live? That we profaned
the South? What if this jhihadi declared holy war and
made the rest of us his enemies, fit only for execution?"

"He wouldn't," Del declared. "An entire people?
An entire land?"

Alric's tone was odd. "The Vashni are killing
foreigners."

Del's color faded.

"If the sand is changed to grass," I said, "the South
becomes worth having."

Del frowned, thinking. "But if the South is changed so drastically, it alters the way the tribes live. Would they want that? You yourself said they're trying to protect their way of life."

"There is that," I agreed. "But there's also the knowledge that, for his god—or gods—a man will do many strange things."

Alric nodded slowly. "The *khemi*, for instance. How many men do *you* know would willingly give up women?"

Del's tone was disgusted. "I know about *khemi*," she said. "Giving up women is one thing . . . claiming we are excrescence and not worthy of speech, of touching, of *anything* is carrying things too far."

"They interpret the Hamidaa'n a bit too literally," I agreed. "Those scrolls don't really say women are completely worthless, just inferior to men. If you talk to anyone of the true Hamidaa faith—not the *khemi* zealots—they'll tell you how things are."

Del's brows rose. "And that makes the opinion right?"

"No. What it does is prove what I've been saying: religion is a method of control."

Del tilted her head. "If you allow it to be. It can also offer security, a focus for your life. It can make your life worth living."

I looked at her harness, lying next to mine. At the intricate, twisted hilt of a dangerous, spell-bound sword. "You worship *that*. Does it make your life worth living?"

Del didn't even blink. "What it promises does."

Alric dismissed our argument. "If what you've said is true, something should be done."

Del overrode me before I could get started. "What if what the *Oracle* has said is true? Do you mean to argue with a messiah?"

"Right now," I said, "I need to go buy another sword."

Alric shook his head. "I have the Vashni sword. I would be pleased to loan it."

Del waited until he went in the other room. "You are a fool," she said. "You're avoiding your *jivatma* when you should be learning to control it."

"That's *right,*" I said sharply, and bent to pick up the sword. "Here. You won the wager. The sword is now forfeit."

"Tiger, *no*—"

"You won, bascha. You said I couldn't last." I put the sword in her hands. I knew she was safe; Del knew his name.

She closed fingers over the blade. Knuckles shone white.

I frowned. "You know better, bascha. You'll cut your fingers like that."

Del said nothing. Her eyes were wide, and black; color drained out of her face.

"Bascha—?" I thought again of how Sarad's sword had been broken. "Here, let me have—"

"It wants me—"

My hands were on the sword. "Let go, Del . . . let *go*—"

"It *wants* me—"

"*Let go*—"

"Boreal," Del whispered.

It shocked me. It turned me to stone.

"He wants us *both*—"

I took one hand off the sword and stiff-armed her in the chest.

Del fell away, releasing my sword, hands springing open. She tripped over the bedding, landed sprawled on her back, gazed up at me in horror.

Not because I'd hit her. She understood that. But because of what she'd learned. Because of what she'd *felt*.

"You have to kill it," she said.

"How can I—"

"Kill it," she repeated. "You have to discharge it. You have to strip it of Chosa Dei. You have to—"

"I know," I said. "I know. Haven't I been saying that?"

Del gathered herself, rearranged herself, remained sitting on the damp dirt. "He wants me," she said. "Do you understand? He is a man; he is a *sword* . . . do you realize what that means?"

It was a hideous thing to consider. Bile moved in my belly.

"Kill it," she said again. "Before it does worse to me."

Six

Del didn't like the idea. "It should be watched," she declared. "It should never be left alone."

Quietly I continued wrapping the *jivatma* in a blanket, wincing as I jarred my swollen little finger. We had determined it wasn't broken, but it hurt like hoolies. Tight wrapping protected torn flesh, but didn't do much for the pain.

I set the bundle aside, next to the wall, and rose. "I'm not taking it with me. I've got the Vashni sword to use; this one can stay here."

"You saw what it did."

"When you touched it. If no one knows it's here, it can't do anything."

"The girls—"

"Lena has them well trained. They won't come in here because they've been told not to, and they respect privacy."

Del was unconvinced. "It should be attended to."

I sighed. "Yes. Why do you think I asked about the jhihadi?"

Eyes widened. "But you don't *believe*—"

"Right about now, I'll try anything. I think this messiah is probably nothing more than an opportunist, but why not give it a try? The tanzeers will demand proof of his divinity . . . they'll ask for specific signs, give him specific tasks. Why not ask him to 'cure' my sword."

"Because maybe he can't."

341

"Maybe he can't. Maybe he can." I shrugged. "I figure it's worth a try."

Del frowned at me. "This isn't like you, Tiger."

"What isn't? My unwillingness to agree with you, or my willingness to let the jhihadi try?"

"You're almost *never* willing to agree with me; that's not what I mean. I mean the latter. You're the one who claims religion is nonsense."

"I used to say the same about magic, too, and look where it got me." I hooked arms through my harness, settled my borrowed Vashni sword. "Look, bascha, I'm not saying I believe in religion—I really don't think I could—but who's to say this jhihadi, if he's real, isn't something more than a messiah?"

"More?"

"If he's supposed to change sand to grass, I'd say he's got something more than divine charm going for him." I grinned. "Maybe he's a sorcerer. Maybe he's Shaka Obre."

It startled her. "The *jhihadi?*"

"Well? Isn't Shaka Obre the one who once held the South? Who made it green and lush? Doesn't it make sense that if he really did create the South, he might want to restore it to what it once was?"

"Chosa Dei imprisoned him."

"And he imprisoned Chosa. But Chosa's out now—sort of—and maybe Shaka is, too. *He* could be the jhihadi. *He* could be the man the Oracle's spouting about."

Del considered it. "If he is—"

"—then he owes me."

She raised a skeptical brow. "And you think he'd be so grateful he'd do you a special favor."

"Chosa Dei was on the verge of destroying the wards. He had who knows how many *jivatmas* he was collecting magic from, as well as a few other tricks. Given a bit more time—or your sword—he'd have broken through. I may have sucked him into *my* sword, but at least he's not roaming free. If I were Shaka Obre, I'd be grateful to me."

Del sighed wearily. "It makes as much sense as anything else."

"And if this jhihadi *isn't* Shaka Obre, what does it matter? He might still have the ability to discharge my *jivatma*."

She glanced at the tightly rolled bundle. The sword was completely hidden. "It deserves to die," she said flatly.

"I sort of thought you'd agree . . . once you saw my point." I resettled the harness and turned toward the door. "Do you have plans for today?"

"Seeking out word of Ajani."

Something pinched my belly. "But not the man himself."

Del shook her head. "I need to learn about him. I need to learn who he *is;* what makes him think. It's been six years, and I never really knew him. Just what he'd done." She shrugged. "I need to see him without him seeing me. Then I will talk to my sword."

"You don't mean—-ask for your focus again? *Now?*"

Del smiled. "You had last night, didn't you?"

"*We* had last night. And I'd like for it to continue."

The smile went away. She was calm, controlled, commited. "It will . . . if I win."

I left the stud behind because trying to pick my way on horseback through the increasing throngs of people would try my patience, and might even result in a fight if the stud decided to protest. And besides, you can overhear gossip better if you're on foot with everyone else; if I wanted to learn the latest about the Oracle or the jhihadi, I'd do better to mix with the others.

By the time I'd fought my way through the alleys, streets and bazaar, I knew a little more. The Oracle, it was said, was busily foretelling the jhihadi's arrival soon. Of course, soon is relative; by oracular reckoning, it still might take a year. And I sincerely doubted anyone would wait that long.

But the Oracle was also foretelling a few other

things. He was mentioning specifics, things about the messiah. Things like *power:* a power newly gained. A revelation of *identity:* a man of many parts. And an unwavering commitment to make the South what it was.

No wonder the tanzeers were worried.

I approached the tribe side of the city with a twinge of foreboding. Generally an individual tribe, on its own, can be dealt with one way or another, through trades, gifts, agreements. Some tribes, like the Hanjii and the Vashni, tend to be a bit more hostile, and are generally avoided. Except when you're riding through the Punja—where the tribes, being nomads, go wherever they feel—sometimes it's hard to avoid them. But it was very unusual to have so many different tribes all clustered together. It changed the rules of the game.

I wasn't certain my visit would do any good. For one thing, the Salset might not be present. For another—even if they were—they might simply ignore me. The adults all knew very well what I'd been. And none of them let me forget it.

Certainly not the shukar, who had his reasons for hating me. But maybe he was dead. If the old man was dead, I might have an easier time.

But the old man wasn't dead.

I found the Salset mostly by accident. After picking my way through goats, sheep, danjacs, children, dogs, and chickens, winding through the clusters of hyorts and wagons, I came to the end of the hyort settlement beside the city. I wavered uncertainly a moment, thinking about approaching another tribe, then swung around to go back. And saw a familiar red hyort staked out beside a wagon.

The Salset had settled behind a cluster of blue-green Tularain hyorts. Since there were more of the Tularain, it wasn't surprising the Salset were hard to see. So I wound my way through the Tularain cluster, then stopped at the shukar's hyort.

He was sitting on a blanket in front of his open

doorflap. His white hair was thinning; his teeth were mostly gone; his eyes were filmed and blind. Not much life left in the old man. But he knew me anyway, the moment I said a word.

"We gave you horses," he snapped. "We tended your ailing woman. We gave you food and water. You have no more claim on us."

"I can claim courtesy. You owe that to anyone. It's a Salset custom."

"Don't tell *me* what Salset custom is!" The quaver of his voice came from age and anger, not fear. "It was you who revoked custom and sought aid from an unmarried woman."

My anger rose to meet his. "You know as well as I do that was Sula's decision. She was free, bound to no man; Salset women take who they will, until they accept a husband. You're just jealous, old man—she took a chula, not the shukar."

"You forced her to say *you'd* killed the beast—"

"I did kill it," I said flatly. "You know it, too . . you just don't want to admit a chula succeeded where you'd failed." A glance at the shabbiness of clothing and hyort told me times were no longer easy. Once he'd been a rich man. "Is your magic all used up? Have the gods turned their eyes from you?"

He was old, and probably would not last a year. A part of me suggested I not be so bitter, so harsh, but the greater portion of me remembered what life with the Salset had been like. I owed him no courtesy. I owed him nothing but honesty; I hated the old man.

"You should have died from the poison," he said. "Another day, and you would have."

"Thanks to Sula, I didn't." My patience was at an end. "Where is her hyort, shukar? Direct me to Sula, as you are required to do in the name of Salset courtesy."

He peeled back wrinkled lips and showed me his remaining teeth, stained brown by beza nut. Then spat at my feet. "When the jhihadi comes, you and others like you will be stripped from the South forever."

It confirmed my foreboding, but I said nothing of it to him. "Where's Sula, old man? I have no time for games."

"I have no time for *you*. Find Sula yourself." Filmed eyes narrowed. "And I hope you *like* what you find, since you are the cause of it!"

I didn't waste my time asking futile questions, or trying to decipher his purposely vague pronouncements. I just went to find Sula.

And when I found her, I knew she was dying. Clearly, so did she.

"Sit," she said weakly, as I lingered in the doorflap.

I sat. I nearly fell. I couldn't say a word.

Sula's smile was her own. She hadn't been robbed of it yet. "I wondered if the gods would grant me the chance to see you again."

The day was dull and sullen. Fitful light painted a harsh sienna patina against the ocher-orange of her hyort. It washed the interior with sallowness, like aging ivory. To Sula, it was unkind.

This was my third Sula. The first had been in her early twenties, a slim, lovely young woman of classic Salset features: wide, mobile face; dipped bridge of nose; black hair so thick and sunkissed it glowed ruddy in the daylight. At night it was black silk.

The second had been over forty, run to fat; lacking former beauty, but none of her generosity, the kindness I'd come to crave. She had saved Del and me from the ravages of the Punja. And now I'd see her die.

The third Sula was not much older, but the plumpness had melted away. There was nothing of Sula left except hide stretched over bones. The hair was lank and lifeless. The eyes dulled with pain. Lines graven in flaccid flesh bespoke a constant battle. The hyort smelled of death.

All I could manage was her name.

I don't know what she saw in my face. But it moved her. It made her cry.

I took her hand in mine, then closed the other over it. Brittle, delicate bones beneath too-dry, fragile flesh. The woman of my manhood was a corpse in Salset gauze.

I swallowed heavily. "What sickness is it?"

Sula smiled again. "The old shukar says it's not. He says it's a demon put inside to punish me. It lives here, in my breast—eating away my flesh." She was propped against cushions. With one hand, she touched her left breast.

"Why?" I asked harshly. "What have you ever done?"

Sula raised a finger. "Many years ago, I took in a young chula who was no more a boy, but a man. And when he killed the sandtiger—when he won his freedom—I made certain he was given it. For that, I am being punished. For that, I host a demon."

"You don't *believe* that—"

"Of course not. The old shukar is jealous. He has always wanted me. And he has never forgiven me." She made a weak gesture. "This is his punishment: he tells people about the demon, so none will give me aid."

"*No* one—"

"None," she said raggedly. "Oh, I am given food and water—no one will starve me to death—but none will aid me, either. Not where the demon can see."

"He's a dangerous old fool. And he's a *liar*—"

"And he's been shukar forever." Sula sighed and shifted against her cushions. "But now he has lost even that."

"*Lost* it . . ." It stunned me. "How?"

"His magic was bad. Ever since you left, his magic has been weak. And so when the summons was made—when the Oracle called our names—the old shukar was replaced with a younger, stronger man." Black eyes were sad. "The old man sits in the sun. The young man speaks of power."

"Gained from the jhihadi."

Sula nodded weakly. "The Oracle says the South will be given back to the tribes. There will be no more need for lengthy journeys from this oasis to that one; from this place to another. The sand will be changed to grass and water will run on the land."

I cradled her hand in mine. "Is that kind of change what you want?"

She was very tired. Her voice was a travesty. "All I have known is the desert . . . the heat, the sand, the sun. Is it wrong to long for grass? To ask the gods for water in plenty?"

"If war is the cost, yes." I paused. "Let me get you a drink."

Sula lifted a hand. I sank back down at her side. "You see only one side," she said. "You, of all people."

"I don't understand."

She smiled, but very sadly. "Why did you stay with us?"

"Stay—?" I frowned. "I had to. I didn't have any choice."

"Why not run away?"

"Water," I said at once. "I couldn't carry enough water to get me far enough. The Punja would have killed me. At least with the tribe, I was alive."

Stiff fingers curled in my hand. "If the land were lush and cool, no one could keep any slaves. It would be easy to run away, to survive a day unsheltered, with water in abundance."

I had run away once. I had been caught. As punishment, I was tied to a stake in the sand and left for a second full day with no water to slake my thirst. Left there, and ignored, all of ten paces away from the camp so I would know what it was to realize the Salset were my deliverance; that I owed my life to them.

I had been nine years old.

I drew in a painful breath. "I came for information. You've already given me some . . . but I need to know about the jhihadi. About what the tribes are planning."

Sula held onto my hand. "They are planning a holy war."

"But no one worships the same gods!"

"It doesn't matter. We are to have the jhihadi."

"And *this* is what he wants? To destroy the South completely?"

"To make it new again. To make it what it was, before the land was laid to waste." She rolled her head against her cushions. "I am only a woman . . . I don't sit in councils. All I am told is the jhihadi will unite all the tribes. The Oracle promises this."

"So, this man is just supposed to *arrive* one day, wave his hands and declare everyone friends, then send them out to kill?" I shook my head. "Not a peaceful kind of messiah."

"The young men don't want peace." Sula closed her eyes. "They have listened to the Oracle, but have heard what they want to hear. When he foretells the ascendancy of the tribes, they think it can only come at the cost of other lives. They think nothing of living in peace with the tanzeers. They forget how our lives will change . . . how crops will grow on the land, how water will come to the tribes instead of the tribes following it." She dragged in a laboring breath. "He says nothing of a war, but that is what they hear."

"You've heard him? The Oracle?"

"He has gone to a few of the tribes. Word is being carried."

"And they accept him without question, believing what he says."

Sula rolled her head. "They believe what they choose to believe. The Oracle speaks of a jhihadi who can change the sand to grass. A man need only walk out into the Punja to know what that could mean."

I knew. I'd lived there. Hoolies, I'd been *born* there.

Which reminded me of something.

"Sula." I shifted closer. "Sula, there's something I have to know . . . something I have to ask. It has to do with how I came to be with the Salset—"

Sula's eyes were glazed. "—histories say the South and the North were one . . . divided between two brothers—"

I hung on to my patience. I owed this woman too much. "Chosa Dei," I said. "His brother was Shaka Obre."

"—and that after a final battle one half would be laid to waste—"

"Shaka Obre's wards. Chosa Dei tripped them."

"—and after hundreds of years the brothers would be freed to contest for the land again . . . to make whole the broken halves—"

"Sula," I said sharply, "is the jhihadi Shaka Obre?"

Her lips were barely moving. "—only a small favor—a single small favor . . ."

"Sula—"

"Let me die free of pain."

"*Sula*—" I bent over her. "Sula, please—tell me the truth . . . did the Salset find me? Or did they *steal* me?"

Pain-graved brow creased. "Steal you?"

"I was told—they always said—" I stopped short and tried again. "It would mean something to me to know how I came to the Salset."

Tears rolled free of her eyes. "I heard what they told you. The children. How they taunted you."

"Sula, was it true? Was I abandoned in the Punja? Exposed and left to die?"

Her hand closed on mine. The voice was but a thread. "Oh, Tiger . . . I wish I knew . . ."

It was all she had left to give. Having given it, she died.

I sat there and held her hand.

Mother. Sister. Bedmate. Wife.

All and none of those things.

I hung on to my patience. I owed this woman too much, "Bone Dog," I said, "the native was almost blind."

Seven

The man stepped out in front of me. I checked, moved aside; he blocked me yet again.

Not a man: a Vashni.

"Not now," I said clearly, couching it in Desert.

Dark eyes glittered. He didn't move a muscle, didn't say a word, made no indication he intended to step aside.

Three others came up behind me; this wasn't coincidence.

The day was gray. Dull, sullen sunlight gave way to heavy clouds. Rain stained the ground.

Vashni wear very little. Brief leather kilts with belts. No boots, no sandals. Jewelry made out of bone, claimed from enemies' skeletons. In the rain, bare torsos were slick, smooth as oiled bronze. Black hair was plaited back from fierce desert faces in a single long braid, hanging clear to belted waists in sheaths of gartered fur.

Bone pectoral plates chinked and tinkled as they breathed.

I wore a knife and a sword. I touched neither of them.

Oddly, I felt tired. Too weary to deal with this on the heels of Sula's death. "If it's foreigners you're killing, why start with me? There's a whole city full of them all of ten paces from here."

The warrior facing me smiled, if a Vashni can do such a thing. Mostly he bared his teeth, very white in a dark face. His Desert was quick and fluent. "Your time will come, Southron . . . for now your life is spared."

"Generous," I applauded. "So what is it you're after?"

"The sword," he answered calmly. Behind me, the others breathed.

Hoolies, how had word of Samiel gotten around already? I hadn't killed anyone. Hadn't displayed his magic. Only Del and I knew of the broken sword and its blackened, discolored half. And the Vashni, as far as I knew, weren't partial to any weapon other than their own, with its wicked, curving blade and human thighbone hilt.

Slowly I shook my head. "The sword is mine."

Color stained his face and set black eyes aglitter. "No one but a Vashni carries a Vashni sword."

A Vashni—oh, a *Vashni* sword . . . like the one hanging from my harness.

Vashni aren't quite like anyone else, and they don't judge outsiders by anything but their own customs. They don't engage in socially unacceptable behavior like the Hanjii, who eat people, and they don't condone outright murder. But they do have a habit of provoking hostilities so the death meted out to an enemy is considered an honorable one.

And then they strip away flesh, muscle, viscera and distribute the still-damp skeleton in a lengthy celebration.

Right about now an engagement of hostilities might be what I needed, but I was angry. Too angry to think straight: this Vashni had no right to interfere with my life out of a perverse tribal whim, regardless of the cause.

Not right after Sula—

I cut it off. Knew better than to protest, or to say anything he might interpret as rude. I had no intention of becoming anyone's pectoral. "Take it," I said flatly.

He flicked a finger. I stood very still. I felt the touch of a hand on the hilt, the snap of a blade sliding free. Weight lessened across my back; all I wore now was the harness.

The Vashni's black eyes showed only the slightest hint of contempt. "A Vashni warrior also never gives up his weapon."

I clenched teeth together. "We've already established I'm not Vashni. And I don't see the point in trying to protect—or in dying over—a sword that was only borrowed."

Eyes narrowed. "Borrowed."

"My own sword broke. This was loaned to me."

"A Vashni never *loans* his sword."

"He does if he's dead," I snapped. "Call it a permanent loan."

Clearly the warrior had not expected such a response. Vashni are accustomed to cowing frightened people into instant acquiescence, and I wasn't cooperating. He glared at me through the rain, then glanced past me to the others. One hand was near his knife; was the insult enough to repay? Or would he have to work harder?

Deep inside, anger rose. Instinctively I called to memory my recollection of our immediate surroundings and situation: tribal hyorts clustered but a pace or two away—rain-slick ground—poor footing—no sword —four Vashni—no support—the city entrance ten paces away—chickens and dogs and goats—

And then something occurred to me. It made me forget about fighting. "What part of the South are you from?"

The arched nose rose. "Vashni are from everywhere. The South is ours to hold."

"So the Oracle says." I smiled insincerely. "But it isn't yours quite yet, so why don't you answer my question?"

He contemplated my attitude. "Answer mine," he countered. "Why does it matter to you?"

"Because the mountain Vashni down near Julah have been 'hosting' someone I know. I just wondered if you knew him."

He spat into the mud. "I know no foreigners."

I continued anyway. "He's a Northerner—blond, blue-eyed, fair . . . he's also castrate and mute, thanks to Julah's former tanzeer." I shrugged offhandedly so my real concern wouldn't show, which might give them a weapon. "His Northern name was Jamail. He's sixteen now."

He assessed me. Black eyes didn't blink. "Is this boy kin to you?"

I could have said no, and been truthful. But lying has its uses; in this case, I'd get my answer. "I'm blood-bonded to his sister."

Kinship. Such a simple, obvious key to unlock Vashni secrets. To force the warrior's hand.

He looked past me again to the others. But I knew he'd have to tell me what he knew, no matter how he felt. They are a fierce, ferocious tribe, but the Vashni have their weaknesses just like anyone else. In this case, it was kinship. They won't tolerate bastards or half-bloods, but full-birth kinship or blood-bond takes precedence over pride.

His eyes were not kind. "There was such a boy."

"A Northern boy—sixteen?"

"He was as you describe."

I kept my voice even. "You said 'was'?"

The Vashni didn't play diplomat to try to soften the blow. "The Northern boy is dead. This is a holy war, Southron—we must purge our people of impurities to prepare for the jhihadi."

I tried not to think of Jamail—or Del—as my own contempt flowered. "Is that what the Oracle said?"

I expected offense to be taken. I expected to have to fight. But the Vashni warrior smiled.

It was open, unaffected, and utterly genuine. Then he turned and went into the rain.

*   *   *

How do I tell Del? How in hoolies do I tell her? *Sula's gone, chula. Salvation no longer exists.*

How am I to tell her she's the only one left of her blood?

How do you thank Sula for all that she was and did?

I can't just walk into our borrowed bedroom and say: "Your brother's dead, bascha."

You can't go to the gods of valhail and ask to have Sula back.

It would kill her. Or *get* her killed; she'd immediately go after Ajani.

How do you tell a childless woman that she still gave birth to a son?

She's only just now coming to realize there's more to life than revenge.

How do you tell a dead woman she's the one who gave you life?

Is her freedom worth the price?

Is my freedom worth the price?

*　　*　　*

Something was wrong. I knew it immediately as I got closer to the house Del and I shared with Alric and his brood. There is a feeling, a *sound* . . . when a crowd gathers to witness death, everybody knows.

Too much dying, I thought. First Sula, then Jamail—who was dying now?

The death-watch was on. It took all I had to break through, trying to reach the house. And then all I had to stop.

Oh, gods—oh—*hoolies*—

All the hairs stood up on my body. My belly began to churn. The street stank of magic.

Oh, hoolies—no—

Someone had my *jivatma*.

No—my *jivatma* had him.

But I put it away. I wrapped it up, set it aside, put it away—

And someone had stolen it.

Now it was stealing him.

He dug in mud with his feet. Sprawled on his back, he dug. Because the blade had gone in at his belly and threaded its way through his ribs to peek out at the top of a shoulder.

Showing a blackened tip only slightly tainted by blood.

No one kills that way. A clean thrust through ribs, through belly; a slash across abdomen. But no one threads a sword through ribs like a woman weaving cloth.

Except for Chosa Dei.

He lay on his back in the rain, digging mud with his feet. Trying to shred the cloth of his flesh so he could unstitch the hideous needle.

How can he be alive?

Because Chosa Dei wants the body.

I thrust my way through the gathered crowd and knelt down at his side. His eyes saw me, knew me; begged for me to help.

Slowly I shook my head: he'd known what the sword was. He'd told me about Chosa Dei.

"Why?" was all I asked.

His voice was wracked by pain. "She wouldn't have me—have me . . . Xenobia wouldn't have me . . ."

"Is she worth dying for?"

"They wouldn't have me—have me . . . they said I was a bastard . . ."

From whom I had come, I knew. "Vashni," I said grimly. "That's your tribal half."

Nabir didn't nod. Black eyes were wide and fixed. *"My brother,"* he said. *"My brother; yes? I must unmake my brother."*

"Nabir!" I shut my hand on his arm. "Give him up, Chosa."

"I must unmake my brother."

"But I'm here, Chosa. How do you plan to win?"

Nabir dug mud with his feet. "I knew what it was—I knew . . . with this sword, they might have me . . . with this sword, *she* might have me . . . the sword of the Sandtiger—"

There was very little blood. Chosa Dei was taking it all.

"Nabir—"

"I tripped . . . he made me *trip* . . . he took my feet away—"

Immediately, I looked. Nabir still dug mud, but there were no feet to do it. Only mud-coated stumps.

"—and I fell . . . and it turned . . . without a hand on it, it turned—"

"Nabir—"

"CHOSA DEI—don't you know who I am?"

I put a hand on the hilt. Felt the virulence of his rage.

"Don't you know WHAT I am?"

Only too well.

"I'm sorry," I said. "I'm sorry . . . I've got no choice, Nabir."

"I'll give him back his feet—"

"No, Chosa . . . too late."

"I'll unmake YOU—"

"Not while *I* hold this sword."

"You don't want this sword—"

Two hands on the hilt. "And you can't have this body."

Nabir's body arced. *"SAMIEL!"* it shouted. *"The sword is Samiel—"*

Eight

He wasn't quite dead. But I knew I'd have to kill him.

"Nabir," I said, "I'm *sorry*—"

—unthreaded the deadly needle—

Nabir was mostly gone. Chosa used what was left. "Sam—Sam—Sami*el*—"

"No good, Chosa. Now it's just me."

—blood and breath rushed out.

Unfettered rage exploded.

Hoolies, but this *hurts*—

I was aware, if only dimly, of the crowd gathered around. For the moment, what they saw was a dead man on the ground and another man by his side, holding on to the sword that killed him. What they *heard* was a low, keening wail like the moan of a stalking cat. They didn't know it was steel. They didn't know it was Chosa. They only knew the boy was dead in messy, spectacular fashion.

Faces: Alric. Lena briefly, with the girls; she hustled them back inside. Garrod, braids and all, working his way out of the crowd to the inside perimeter. And Adara, staring mutely, trying unsuccessfully to send Massou away. And many, many strangers.

No Del. Where's De—

Chosa Dei was angry. Chosa Dei was *very* angry— and he took no pains to hide it.

It wasn't unexpected. But the power was overwhelming.

I knelt in bloody mud while the rain ran down my

358

back, wishing I knew what to do. Wishing I had the strength. Wishing I had the ability to unmake my perverted *jivatma*.

Heat coursed down the sword. In cold rain, steel steamed.

I shook. I *shook* with it, trying to suppress the raw power that strained to burst free of the sword. Chosa Dei was testing all the bonds, attempting to shatter the magic that bound him inside the steel. I knew better than to wonder what could happen if I just let him go, let him free—if he left the sword entirely, he'd be nothing but an *essence,* lacking face or form. In order to be what he wanted to be he'd have to have a body. He'd tried to take Nabir's. He'd take mine if I let him.

In rain, the blood washed away, leaving the blade free of taint . . . except for the discoloration reaching nearly to the hilt.

If Chosa ever touched it—

No.

My bones ached. They *itched*. Blood ran hot and fast, *too* hot and too *fast,* surging toward my head. I thought my skull would burst.

Samiel was shrieking. The sword was protesting Chosa.

If we could work *together*—

Light flashed inside my head.

Go to hoolies, Chosa . . . you're not beating me.

The blade began to smoke. .

You're not beating *me*—

Rain stopped falling. Mud began to dry. The ground beneath me steamed.

If it's a song you want, I'll sing it . . . I can't sing, but I will . . . I'll do what I have to, Chosa . . . whatever it takes, Chosa . . . you're not going to beat me, Chosa . . . you're not going to have my sword . . . you're not going to have *me*—

Parched mud began to crack.

I got off my knees and stood. Clutching the hilt in my hands. Watching the black creep forward, licking at the hilt.

I'm a Southroner, Chosa—you're in *my* land, now.

A wind began to blow.

Do you really think you can *win*—?

The wind began to wail.

This is *my land*—

A hot, dry wind.

—you're not welcome here—

A wind from off the Punja.

—*I don't want you here*—

Blasting down through the alleyways, the streets, shredding silk burnouses, stripping makeshift roofs, drying eyes and mouths.

Go away, Chosa. Go back into into your prison.

Dried mud broke and crumbled, blown northward out of the city.

Go back to sleep, Chosa. I'm too strong for you.

The sun ate into flesh.

Don't be stupid, Chosa . . . you're no match for *me*—

Black flowed down the sword and lodged again in the tip.

No, Chosa—away—

Chosa Dei refused.

No, Chosa—*away*—

Chosa withdrew a little . . . and then the firestorm engulfed me.

I came around to voices.

"Keep him covered," someone said.

"But he looks so hot," another protested.

"He's sunburned. What he feels is cold."

Sunburned? How could I be sunburned? The last I recall, the day had been full of rain.

I shivered beneath the blanket.

"I wish we could get him to let go of that sword."

"Do *you* want to touch it?"

"After what it did? No."

"Neither do I."

Nothing was very important. I let it all drift away.

And then came back again, trying to make sense of the words.

"—what they're saying about the Oracle . . . do you think it's true?"

Alric's voice now; I was beginning to tell them apart. "It's why most of the people came here . . . to see the Oracle and the jhihadi."

"But they're saying he's coming *now*." That was Adara.

Garrod's tone was dry. "Right this very moment?"

"No. But any day. Maybe even tomorrow."

Lena's quieter voice: "I heard he's already here, but being hidden by the tribes."

"Why would they hide him?" Garrod asked. "He's what the people want."

Alric's tone was crisp. "There are those who'd like to kill him—or *have* him killed. And besides, would you show off your holy oracle before things were ready?"

Adara sounded puzzled. "What do you mean: things?"

Garrod understood. "If there really is a jhihadi, it would be more dramatic to have the Oracle appear not long before the messiah. If he arrived too soon, everyone would get bored."

"People are already bored," Alric observed. "The tanzeers—who are perhaps the most bored of all, and yet have the most at stake—have already taken to challenging one another. They're pitting sword-dancer against sword-dancer, wagering on the outcome . . . I was at the circles earlier, trying to earn a wage. They're talking about the Oracle there, as well—wagering on him, of course, and what kind of person he is. Rumor says he's neither man nor woman." Alric's tone changed. "I'll go back as soon as I know Tiger is all right."

"Is he?" Adara asked.

Something I wanted to ask myself.

And then Del's voice, raised, from a little distance

away, responding to Massou's treble comment in the other room. "What do you mean, he's sick?"

I peeled open an eye. Saw Lena, Alric, Garrod, Adara—and Del, pushing through. The eye closed again.

"It's the sword," Alric told her. "It's done something to him."

She knelt down next to me. I realized, somewhat vaguely, I was lying on my own bedding in the room Del and I shared.

She stripped away blankets. "Done *what* to him?"

Alric shook his head. "I can't tell you exactly what happened . . . I don't think anyone really knows. But it was the sword. The *jivatma*—and Tiger. In the middle of some kind of battle."

I cracked the eye again.

"Chosa Dei," Del said softly, creases marring her brow. Fingers were gentle and deft, then she stopped examining me. "Tiger, can you hear me?"

I opened the other eye. "Of course I can hear you," I answered. "I can hear *all* of you—now."

"What happened?"

"I don't know."

She pressed the back of her hand against my cheek. "You're sunburned," she said. "And the day is blazing hot."

I blinked. "It was raining."

Del lifted her hand and pointed straight up.

I followed the direction of her finger. Realized Alric's makeshift blanket-and-skin roof had come down—or been torn down, since shreds were left to dangle—and saw the sky clearly. The blue, burning sky, full of Southron sun. No rain. No clouds. No wind. It was still, very still; my skin quailed from the sun.

I moved a little. Felt weight in my right hand. Realized it held a hilt, with the blade still attached. "What in hoolies—?" I frowned at Del.

Alric answered instead. "You wouldn't let go. And no one dared to touch it."

Well, no; it was, after all, a *jivatma*—

I stiffened. Then wrenched myself off the bedding into a sitting position. "Hoolies, that was *Nabir!*"

"It was." Garrod's face was solemn. "Whoever he was, he's dead."

I stared at the sword. Slowly, very slowly, I unlocked stiffened fingers and set it down beside me. "He unmade Nabir's *feet*— " I swallowed heavily, realizing I was dizzy; that my belly was none too content. "Then put himself into the boy. First the sword, then himself . . . he nearly got what he wanted."

Adara's voice was puzzled. "I don't understand."

Del barely glanced over a shoulder, watching me instead. "Do you remember the loki, Adara?"

"*Yes.*"

"Something very like one is trapped in Tiger's sword."

"Not a loki," I said. "Something far worse."

Adara shuddered. "Nothing could be worse."

Garrod's brows rose. "You saw what Tiger did . . . and what it did to Tiger."

Something began to concern me. "What *did* it do to Tiger?"

Garrod was very succinct. "Tried to burn you up. Except you wouldn't let it do it . . . you stopped it cold—in a manner of speaking." He grinned. "The rain went away, the mud dried up, the sun came out for good."

Lena's voice was hushed. "It was a simoom."

Simoom—or samiel.

I looked at Del. Neither of us said a word.

Lena's face was troubled. "The young man came after Alric was gone to the circles, saying he wanted the Sandtiger. When I explained you weren't here, that you'd left for a while, he asked what sword you wore." She lifted wide shoulders. "I told him: Alric's Vashni sword. And then he went away."

"Only to come back later when Lena and the girls were gone." Alric's voice was heavy. "Who would steal a *jivatma*?"

"A young, proud man trying to impress his first woman. An outcast Vashni half blood trying to buy his way into the tribe." I rubbed at my cheek, then wished I hadn't. Del was right: I was sunburned. "He probably got word to the warriors that I had the Vashni sword, knowing it would create a diversion so he could steal the *jivatma*." I sighed. "I'm sorry Nabir's dead, but I can't say he wasn't warned."

Del looked at the sword lying naked beside the bedding. "Tiger—the black is higher."

So it was: discoloration reached nearly halfway up the blade. "Less than there was," I told her. "It almost touched the hilt." I glanced around, saw the harness, stretched out an arm to reach it. Del dragged it closer, then put it into my hand. I sheathed the discolored sword, then set it back on the ground. "Do you think—" But whatever it was started to ask slid off my flaccid tongue.

Del's voice was startled. "Tiger—? *Tiger*—"

"What is it?" Adara cried.

Cramps wracked me the length of my body. Toes, calves, thighs, then through abdomen and chest, until it reached my back. Pectoral muscles knotted, stretching the flesh of my shoulders. Pain crawled up into my neck, then reached out and snared my jaw.

Hoolies, but I *hurt*.

"What *is* it?" Adara repeated.

"Reaction," Del explained crisply. "It's because of the magic—it's happened before . . . it will pass, in time; Lena, have you any huva weed? If not, could you send Alric to fetch some? I can brew a tea that will help."

"I have some," Garrod said, and took Adara and Massou with him.

I found it somewhat discomfiting to be discussed as if I were not present, but since basically I wasn't—only my spasming body—I didn't bother to protest. I just lay there tied up in knots, trying to breathe in and out through the cramping of midriff and back.

Alric, catching Del's twitch of the head, herded Lena and the girls back into the other room.

"Bascha—I can't—*breathe*—"

Del moved the sheathed sword aside, out of the way. "I know. Try to relax. Try to think about something else."

"*You* try it."

Her tone softened. "I know," she said again.

It took effort to speak an entire sentence. "Has this—happened to you?"

Del was busy trying to knead out the worst of the cramps. Trouble was, I was cramping all over, and she only had two hands. "Not like this," she answered. "A bit, yes, the first time I invoked my *jivatma*. But never again, and nothing like this . . . this is the worst I've ever seen."

Trust it to happen to me. "If these swords are supposed to be so *helpful*—" I broke it off and ground my teeth. "Oh, hoolies . . . this hurts."

"I know," she said yet again. "It must be because of Chosa Dei . . . if it were only the *jivatma*, it wouldn't be so painful. I don't know what you did, but it roused too much of the wild magic. And now you're paying the price."

"I don't know what I did, either." Oh, hoolies, it hurt. Sweat ran off my body, stinging sunburned skin "I just—I just tried to stop Chosa Dei from taking Nabir's body—from trying to take *mine*."

Del dug into my neck, trying to loosen a locking jaw. The pain was exquisite. "You changed the weather, Tiger. You called up a storm."

She sounded so certain. "How do *you* know?" I demanded through locked teeth. "You weren't even here."

"Because with mine I call up a banshee-storm, which is known only in the North. Your storm is a samiel . . . a hot desert wind blasting straight out of the Punja." She paused. "Don't you understand? You have the strength of the South in your sword. The strength, the power, the magic . . . your sword *is* the South, just as mine is the North."

It took some thinking about. "Since when—*ouch*—has this been so clear to you?"

"Since you used the sword against Chosa in the mountain."

"So why wait until now—*ouch!* . . . hoolies, bascha, be gentle . . . you sent Garrod for huva?"

"Yes."

"Huva weed is a narcotic."

"Yes."

"It will muddle up my head."

"No more muddled up than it is when you drink too much aqivi . . . ah—here is Garrod now. Lena will brew some tea."

Lena brewed tea. Del kneaded. I sweated and cramped. By the time the tea was ready, *I* was ready for anything if it meant the pain would go.

"Here." Del held the cup. "It will be bitter because it hasn't been properly brewed or steeped as long as it should be, but drink. It will help."

It was worse than bitter. It was *horrible*. "How long does it take?"

"This concentrated, not long. Try to relax, Tiger."

"I think I've forgotten how."

She worked the rigidity of my shoulders. "Give it a little time."

I gave it time. I gave it a lot of time. And then when I wasn't looking, the tea snuck up on me.

"Bascha—?"

"I'm here, Tiger."

"The room is upside down."

"I know."

"And you're floating in midair."

"I know."

"And *I'm* floating in midair."

"I know."

Pain diminished a step. Relief tapped at my consciousness, but I wouldn't let it in. I was *afraid* to let it in. If I let it in, and it didn't stay, I'd never be able to bear it.

Drowsily, I said: "He unmade Nabir's feet."

"And tried to unmake *you.*"

"He wanted Nabir's body . . ."

Her hands still worked sore flesh. "Do you see now, Tiger, why you must be vigilant? Why you can never set it aside, or sell it, or hide it, or give it to anybody? Why the sword is yours to ward?"

I didn't answer.

"You are right to seek out Shaka Obre. He may be the only one who can aid you . . . the only one who understands Chosa Dei well enough to defeat him."

I slurred everything together. "If things keep going the way they've been going, Chosa may get to know *me* well enough . . . he wants my body, you said?"

"You are strong enough for Chosa Dei. You are his match, or better . . . he cannot defeat you."

The words were getting harder to say. "You don't know that, bascha . . . he nearly beat me today . . ."

"But he didn't. You stopped him. You fought him, and you beat him. You have every time, and you *will* every time."

More pain flowed away. With it went much of my sense. "I have—to get rid of . . . it . . ."

"Then have it discharged properly."

"Shaka Obre," I mumbled. "Maybe the jhihadi . . may *be* the jhihadi . . ."

Del smiled a little. Through the veil of my lashes, the tense Northern features softened. "If the jhihadi has time for such."

"Hoolies . . . tea . . . *strong* . . ."

Cramps began to untie. I let the relief wash in, denying it nothing now. It could take me, it could *have* me . . . and its gift was akin to bliss. "Oh, better . . . *better* . . ." I drifted drowsily, letting the huva take me. And then words fell out of my mouth. "I asked Sula," I slurred. "I asked her about the truth."

Del's fingers slowed, then resumed their steady kneading. "What did she say?"

It was hard to stay awake. "She didn't know the truth . . . she said she didn't know . . ."

The fingers now were gentle. "I'm sorry, Tiger."

My tongue was thick in my mouth. "And then—she died. She *died*."

The hands stopped altogether.

My eyes were too heavy to open. "I'm sorry—bascha . . ."

"Don't be sorry for *me*."

"No . . . because—because of Jamail." The world was sliding away.

"Jamail! What *about*—" She broke off.

It was harder to make the effort. "I didn't—I'm sorry—I meant . . ." Vision was slowly fraying.

Del said nothing.

I walked the edge of the blade. *One—more—step—*

"That's not—that's not how—" I licked dry lips "—I meant it to be different—"

Del sat like a rock.

One more tiny *step—*

I was nearly incoherent. "I'm . . . sorry . . . bascha—"

The rock moved at last. Del lay down beside me, one hip jutting toward the sky. I felt the angle of her cheekbone against the loosening flesh of my shoulder.

So—close—now—

She rested her arm on my chest and put the flat of her hand over my heart, as if to feel its beating.

"—*Del*—"

She locked her feet around mine. "I'm sorry, too," she whispered. "I'm sorry for us both."

—over the edge—

—and *off*—

Nine

Del's face was white. "This is *serious*."

After a moment, I nodded. "That's why I brought it up."

"If the name is freely known—"

"It wasn't my fault, bascha. Nabir said the name."

"But—how did he know?" She waved the question away before she finished the intonation. "No. He knew because Chosa Dei told him. Chosa Dei was *in* him . . . the *jivatma* had no secrets."

"You're saying if my blade ever cuts into someone, he'll know all about the power?"

Del's tone went dry. "While he's dying, yes. But I don't think it will do him much good."

Alric came into the doorway. "I couldn't help overhearing . . . and anyway, I heard the boy scream it out yesterday." He shrugged. "If you're worried about the blooding-blade's name being known, I don't think it's as serious as all that."

Del scowled at him. "You're Northern. You know better—"

"*Because* I'm Northern, yes." Alric shook his head. "Named blades aren't known down here, Del. Not by very many. And the people I saw in the crowd yesterday were Southron, most of them; the name won't mean a thing. Certainly they won't realize that to know the name means they can freely touch Tiger's sword—and even if they did know it, I doubt they'd do anything about it." His expression was grim. "You weren't here yesterday. You didn't see what happened."

"No, but I know the results." Del still looked concerned. "Southroners may be no threat, but if there were Northerners present—"

"—then they know it, too." Again, Alric nodded. "But even in the North *jivatmas* are mostly legend. Unless you've trained to be a sword-dancer, you don't hear so much about blooding-blades."

"Hoolies," I said wearily, "what I'd give for a Southron sword."

Del's tone was implacable. "That, you can never have. Not while Chosa lives."

It irritated me. "What do you mean? What if I went out and bought *another* sword?"

"Like the one from Sarad the swordsmith?" Del's contempt was delicate. "Like the one you borrowed from Alric?"

I didn't say anything.

She sighed. "Don't you understand? He won't *let* you have another. He'll break it, like the first one."

Alric nodded. "Or see that it's taken away, like the Vashni sword I loaned you."

"That was probably Nabir . . . I think he went to the Vashni and told them, hoping it might buy him goodwill." I peeled dead skin off a forearm. For some odd reason the sunburn was already fading, sloughing off dead skin two days quicker than usual. I stared at the curl of skin; at the pattern of flesh and hair. "I can't risk another Nabir. I can't risk another—fight."

"Another storm, you mean." Alric's mouth twisted. "I don't know, Tiger—you controlled that one well enough. And if *I* had the ability to call up a simoom any time I wanted—"

"I *don't* want," I stated clearly. "All I want is to go back to the kind of life I had before, when I hired on with local tanzeers, or made money on circle wagers."

"You can't have it," Del said. "That is over for you."

Alric's brows rose. "Maybe not. I mentioned to the others earlier . . . there is wagering at the circles.

Tanzeers are hiring, so the sword-dancers are showing off. Some of the tanzeers are pitting their sword-dancers against one another for the hoolies of it. Some are settling scores. Those dances are real."

I shook my head. "I'm in no shape for dancing. Everything hurts too much."

Alric shrugged lightly. "That will pass soon enough."

"Will it?" Glumly I picked at dead skin. "I'm not as young as I once was."

"In the name of *hoolies!*" Del cried. "You're only thirty-six!"

Only. She said *"only."*

How generous of her.

Alric slouched against the doorjamb. "*I'd* bet money on you."

"On me, or on my sword?"

He grinned a Northern grin. "A little of both, I think."

I shook my head slowly. "I don't know, Alric . . . I'm not so sure anyone around here will ever risk a coin on a dance with me involved. If as many people as you say saw what happened yesterday . . ." I let it trail off.

"You're sandsick," he answered pleasantly. "Do you know how many people will pay just in case you *might* key that sword again?"

I twisted my mouth briefly. "Maybe. People *are* bloodthirsty—they might like that sort of thing. But how many sword-dancers would be willing to risk their lives against a possessed sword? I'll have no opponents."

Alric straightened hastily and moved aside as Lena thrust immense belly between man and doorjamb. "Tiger," she said, "someone is here to see you."

"See me?"

She nodded. "He asked for you."

I glanced thoughtfully at Del a moment, then gathered aching muscles and harness and made myself get up. The huva disorientation was gone, but not the aftermath of the cramping. I hurt all over.

"Shall I send him through?" Lena asked.

"No, I'll go outside. It's time I got some sun." With a glance at the blatant sky, uncluttered by blanket or skin.

Outside, the day was as bright. So was the man waiting for me, swathed in blinding silks. Baubles flashed on his fingers

"Lord Sandtiger," he said, and grinned at me happily.

Dumbfounded, I stared. And then reached out to slap a plump shoulder. "Sabo. *Sabo!* What are you doing here?"

The eunuch's grin was undiminished. "I've been sent to fetch you."

My answering grin died. "Fetch me? Fetch *me?* I don't know, Sabo—the last time you were sent to fetch me it was to play me right into Hashi's palsied hands . . . and nearly under the gelding knife!"

Some of his gaiety faded. "That is over," he told me. "My lord Hashi, may the sun shine on his head, died two months ago. You need have no fear of his retribution now."

I hoped not. Sabo's master, tanzeer of Sasqaat, had proved a very inhospitable host. Of course, he claimed retribution because his intended bride's virginity was missing, so I suppose he had a right . . . except no one else had ever accused Elamain of being a virgin— *ever*—so the so-called retribution had been little more than an old man's jealous spite. But it nonetheless nearly got me gelded. Only Sabo's help had freed Del and me.

The round-faced eunuch still smiled. "I have a new master, now."

"Oh? Who?"

"Hashi's son. Esnat."

"Esnat?"

"Esnat. *Lord* Esnat."

I nodded deferentially. "And is Lord Esnat anything like his father?"

"Lord Esnat is a fool."

"So was Hashi—excuse me: *Lord* Hashi. Was a fool."

"My lord Hashi, may the sun shine on his head, was an old, bitter man. Lord Esnat is a fool."

"Then why are you serving him? *You've* never been a fool."

Sabo's tone was bland. "Because the lady asked me to."

Deep in my belly, something twitched. "The lady," I echoed ominously. "You don't mean—"

"—Elamain," he finished. "May the sun shine on her head."

"And other parts of her anatomy." I chewed at my bottom lip. "Then am I right in assuming it's Elamain who's sent for me?"

"No. Lord Esnat sent for you."

"Why?"

"Elamain asked him to."

I decided to say it straight out. "I'm still with Del, Sabo."

The eunuch smiled. "Then you have retained your good sense . . . and your taste."

"But—don't you see? I can't go to Elamain."

"Elamain won't care."

"About Del? She certainly will. I'm not *that* stupid, Sabo."

"The lady wants to *see* you."

"She'll want to see *all* of me."

Sabo's pale brown eyes were guileless. "That didn't stop you before."

I shifted uncomfortably. "Yes, well . . . maybe not—"

"Come tell her yourself," he suggested. And then his face brightened. "Ah, the Northern bascha . . . may the sun shine on your head!"

Del, in the doorway, glanced skyward. "I think it already is."

I stared at her. Thought back on the topic Sabo and I had discussed; on my invitation from Elamain. Found I had nothing to say.

Del's smile was slow. "Don't keep the—*lady*—waiting."

I wet my lips. "I don't suppose you'd want to come."

Her smile stretched wider. "You sound almost hopeful, Tiger."

Yes, well . . . maybe so. But I wouldn't tell Del that.

I shrugged. "Just a thought," I mentioned. "I thought maybe you'd want to gossip. Two women, after all—"

Gravely, Del shook her head. "I'd sooner step into a circle . . . at least *there* I know the rules."

I started to answer, then remembered something. "Wait. You went to find out what you could about Ajani."

Del was expressionless. "So I did."

"And did you?"

She shrugged. "It can wait."

"Maybe it can, but will it?" I shook my head. "I know you, bascha . . . you'll tell me nothing, then go off all by yourself."

She smiled. "Go off to Elamain."

"Del—"

"Go," she said plainly.

Irresolute, I offered a promise: "I'll come straight back."

Her tone was perfectly bland. "And perhaps I shall be here."

Hoolies, she can be difficult.

I looked at Sabo. Saw the gleam of amusement in his eyes. Knew I couldn't delay any longer without giving myself away.

You're a grown man, I told myself. And Elamain's only a *woman*.

Hoolies, what a fool.

Esnat wasn't alone.

Ten

Elamain *was* alone. "Hello, Tiger," she purred.

Oh, hoolies. Del.

And then wondered what I was thinking. I mean, I was a grown man. One who makes his own decisions, needing no woman to do it for him. Needing no guidance, no suggestions, no commands. I could make my own way in the world, with or without a woman, and therefore didn't even need to *think* of Del right at this very moment.

Elamain shed her burnous. "Remember how it was?"

Hoolies, hoolies, *hoolies* . . . where's Del when I need her?

"Which time?" I asked. "In your wagon? Or in Hashi's cell?"

Elamain pouted. Elamain pouting is enough to move all the sand out of the Punja.

Except I didn't want to.

Elamain had set up housekeeping in one of the buildings that still had a roof; Esnat was, after all, a tanzeer, and Elamain the widow of one. The room she inhabited had been much improved by rugs and silks and gauzes, draped and piled here and there. She reclined on fat cushions tumbled invitingly on thick rugs.

Her golden eyes were sorrowful. "Do you blame me for that?"

Golden eyes; black-silk hair; smooth, dusky skin. The woman was made for bedding.

The woman *enjoyed* her bedding.

With studious care, I kept my eyes above the artful droop in the silk of her underrobe, falling away from her breasts. "You *did* have something to do with it. Wasn't it you who offered Del as a wedding present to Hashi, so he'd give me to you?"

Lids lowered minutely. Black lashes veiled her eyes. "I didn't want to lose you."

"Maybe not. But that's a pretty nasty way of trying to *keep* me, wouldn't you say? It nearly got me castrated."

She sat upright stiffly. "*That* wasn't my fault! How was I to know Hashi would be so annoyed?"

Annoyed. Interesting word: annoyed. I'd have put it more strongly, considering the penalty Hashi demanded in retribution for me sleeping with a woman who slept with whomever she liked—and was widely known for it. Hashi *himself* had known.

I lifted eyebrows. "Are you sleeping with Esnat?"

"Of course I am." Elamain's tone was matter-of-fact. "Hashi's *dead* . . . I had to retain my position somehow."

"Sons don't often marry their father's wives."

"I don't have to marry him, Tiger. I only have to sleep with him. Esnat is—" She paused.

"A fool?" I supplied.

She made a gesture of casual acknowledgment with one graceful hand. Then stretched the hand toward me. "I was hoping you were in Iskandar. Come to me, Tiger. Let us rekindle what we once shared."

So much for Sabo's assurances. "I can't, Elamain."

Silk slid lower. "Why not? Have I gotten old and fat?"

She knew better. Elamain was no fatter than she'd been a year and a half before, when I'd helped rescue her caravan from borjuni. And though she was that much older, it didn't show anywhere. She was a lovely, alluring woman.

And I'm not made of stone.

I cleared my throat hastily. "Sabo said *Esnat* sent for me."

Elamain pouted again. "Because I told him to."

"Sabo said that, too. So, now I'm here. Was it business you wanted, Elamain . . . or something else entirely?"

Elamain stopped pouting. Her eyes lost their seductive cast and took on another expression. Elamain was thinking.

A woman like Elamain—*thinking*—can often be dangerous.

"There is someone else," she said.

"Maybe," I agreed warily. "Maybe it's just that I don't *feel* like—"

Elamain didn't let me finish. "No man has ever not *felt* like it," she snapped. "Not with me."

The situation took on an entirely new complexion. Now I was curious; women are often baffling creatures. "Are you serious?" I asked. "No one? Ever? No matter the circumstances?"

"Of course I'm serious." Elamain wasn't amused. "No man—not a single man—has ever said no to me."

"And that means something to you."

Color bloomed in her cheeks. Lovely, dusky cheeks. "How would you feel if you ever lost a sword-dance?"

"We're not talking about a sword-dance, Elamain . . . we're talking about you sleeping with men. One has nothing to do with the other."

"One is very *like* the other," she retorted, "and not in the obviously vulgar sense, either."

"Elamain—"

She rose. Straightened flowing silks. Crossed the carpeted floor to me. "There's someone else," she declared. "A man like you would never say no otherwise."

It intrigued me. "A man like me? What is a man like me like?"

"A man like you is *all* man; why should he say no?"

Elamain had a point, although it didn't please me. "Are we all so predictable?"

"Most of you," she agreed. "Not a single man I've ever met—except Sabo, and other eunuchs—has been blind to the bedding, and what it might be like. *You* certainly weren't."

No.

"And no man," she went on, "whom I have invited into my bed has ever refused the chance. Even men with sworn women, or men with wives at home."

No, I imagine not. She's that kind of woman.

Elamain frowned. "Except you."

"I'm not blind," I told her. "I'm not even deaf. And I'm *certainly* not a eunuch."

"But you won't go to bed with me."

I sighed. "Elamain—"

"Because there is someone else."

I said it clearly: "Yes."

A faint crease marred her brow. Then, abruptly, it cleared. "When you rescued my caravan, there was a woman with you . . . a Northerner. You don't mean *her,* do you? That woman who thinks she's a man?"

I cleared my throat. "First of all, Del doesn't think she's a man. She doesn't *want* to be a man; why should she? She's more than adequate as a woman . . ." I paused. "*More* than adequate."

Elamain was shocked. "She's nearly as tall as you! *Much* taller than me!"

"I like tall women." I thought about where I was, and whom Elamain could call on: a tanzeer with authority. "But I like shorter women, too."

"She's *white-haired.* She looks old."

"She's not white-haired, she's blonde. It bleaches out, down here. And she certainly isn't old; she's several years younger than you."

Uh-oh. Shouldn't have said that.

Elamain glared. "I've *seen* her, Tiger. She looks like a man with breasts."

Unfortunately, I laughed.

Hands went to hips. "She does. She's huge. *And* she carries a sword . . . do you know what that means?"

It took effort not to laugh more. "No, Elamain. Why don't you tell me?"

"It means she hates men. It means she wants to kill them. She probably wants to kill *you*."

"Sometimes," I agreed. "She nearly did, once."

Golden eyes narrowed. "You are teasing me."

I grinned. "A little. And you deserve it. Haven't you learned by now not all men appreciate hearing a woman yowl?"

Elamain lifted an eyebrow. "I'd rather hear the Sandtiger *growl*."

I smiled. "Not this time."

"You did before."

"That was before."

The crease in her brow came back. "Is she really that good?"

Patiently, I explained, "There's more to it than that."

"Oh?"

"But you wouldn't understand."

Elamain considered it lengthily. And then smiled—as only Elamain can smile—shook back her silky, sooty curtain of unbound hair, took a single smooth step forward to merge her body with mine. And Elamain knows how to merge.

"Then," she said huskily, "I will have to *apply* myself."

Hoolies, she's making it hard.

I was four steps away from the doorway when a man came out of an alley and stepped into my path. A slender, youngish man with dust-colored hair straying out from beneath a wilted turban. He wore plain white gauze, now smudged and soiled. There were spots on his chin, which tried to bury itself in his neck. His eyes were a medium brown. His manner hesitant.

"Sandtiger?" he asked. When I nodded, he looked relieved. "I'm Esnat," he said.

Esnat. *Esnat.* Guilt made me hot. Or maybe it was the sunburn.

"Esnat," I answered; a stupid sort of answer.

He didn't seem to mind. "Esnat," he agreed. "I'm tanzeer of Sasqaat."

Elamain's sleeping with *this?*

Well, Elamain would.

I cleared my throat. "So Sabo said."

"Yes. I told him to."

Esnat was not the sort of man I expected Hashi to sire. He was diffident, polite, altogether too unassuming for a man in his position. Which meant, I thought resignedly, Elamain had free rein. He only *thought* he ruled.

I thought about Elamain. "So," I said, "can I help you?"

Esnat glanced pointedly past me to the doorway, which made me feel even hotter. Then gestured for me to follow.

I did not, at first, intend to. After all, I'd just come from Elamain, and who knows what Esnat might do. He *was* Hashi's son; appearances don't always count.

But his manner remained much the same: hesitant, polite, almost too unassuming. He was a very humble man—or else a clever one.

I stayed where I was. "What is it?" I asked clearly.

Esnat stopped, came back a few steps, looked worriedly past me again. "Will you *come?*" he hissed. "I don't want her to hear."

I didn't move. "Why not?"

He fixed medium brown eyes on me and glared. It was the first expression of any passion I'd seen on his face. "Because, you lumbering fool, how am I supposed to plot in secret if I'm not *in* secret?"

Lumbering fool, was I? Well, at least it sounded more like a man who really was tanzeer. Or believed he was.

I remembered I had my *jivatma.* I went with Esnat. Not far. Only around the corner, where he sheltered in a deep doorway. It left me out in the street, but since I wasn't yet part of the secret I decided it didn't really matter.

Esnat cast quick glances around the street behind me. "All right," he said finally, "I sent for you because—"

"*Elamain* sent for me."

He only nodded, clearly impatient. "Yes, yes, of course she did . . . *I* wanted you, too, but I've learned it's easier to let her think she runs things." His manner was matter-of-fact, very like Elamain's when speaking of Esnat's status. "And I know what she wanted, too . . . but you don't know what *I* want."

I shifted stance a little.

Esnat saw it; smiled. "That's what I want," he said.

I froze. "You want *what?*"

"You," he said plainly. "I want to hire you."

I relaxed a little. For a moment . . . hoolies, the moment wasn't yet gone. "Why do you want to hire me?" And delicately: "What for?"

"Your sword," Esnat said.

I wasn't born yesterday. "Excuse me," I said. "What sword are we talking about?"

Esnat scowled at me blankly. And then understood, and gaped. "Not *that*, you fool . . . I want to hire a sword-dancer to do sword-dancerly things."

I wished he'd stop calling me a fool. Particularly since it was what everyone called *him*—and I didn't think Esnat and I were anything alike.

"Sword-dancerly things," I echoed. "What sort of things are those?"

Esnat blinked at me. "Don't you know?"

We were, I began to think, talking at cross-purposes. Time for plain speech. "What do you want me to do?"

"Help me win a woman."

"I thought you were already sleeping with Elamain."

"Not *that* woman . . . a woman I can marry."

I grinned. "Then send Elamain away."

Esnat laughed. "No, not quite yet—Elamain serves

a purpose. For now. And besides, how else would a man like me get a woman like that in my bed?"

He wasn't *that* bad . . . well, maybe he was. But still— "You're a tanzeer, Esnat . . . you can have any woman." I amended it quickly, thinking of Del. "Almost any woman."

"Any I bought, yes . . . even *Elamain* is bought." His smile wasn't amused. "The issue isn't Elamain. The issue is Sabra."

I nodded slowly. "And I'm supposed to help you win her. How?"

"By dancing, of course."

With effort, I retained my patience. "Esnat, my dancing isn't going to help you marry this woman."

"Of course it will," he assured me. "She'll know I'm serious about courting her." He paused, observing my frown. "Don't you see? It used to be when a man wanted to impress a woman, he fought her other suitors. Whoever won, won the woman. Well, I'm a tanzeer, and we don't do those things. It's stupid to risk ourselves when there are sword-dancers to do it for us."

I ignored the implication. "You said something like that before."

"And I meant it. This will be a proxy dance. A way of getting her attention, of making her see my point. So she'll accept me as a suitor."

Maybe this was the way tanzeers got married. At any rate, it wasn't really my business. Something else was. "How much are you offering?"

Esnat told me.

"You're sandsick!" I exploded.

"No. I'm serious."

I stared at him. "That much for a woman?"

Esnat looked right back. "Isn't a woman worth it?"

He was as bad as Del. "You're putting a lot at stake," I told him. "What if I lose? Will you want my *gehetties*, then?"

"Your *gehett*—oh." He laughed out loud, which

didn't amuse me much. "No, no—that was my father's style. I'd just as soon you kept your *gehetties*, Sandtiger . . . I don't need any more eunuchs."

"What if I lose?" I repeated. "You're offering a lot if I win. What happens if I lose?"

Esnat's smile died. "You won't lose," he said. "I saw that sword."

I began to understand. "You're not such a fool after all."

Esnat's eyes glinted. "I let them think I am. It makes it easier. If they have no expectations, I don't have to waste my time trying to live up to them. I can do what I want. What I want is Sabra." He shrugged. "I am not the sort of man women notice. You know that by looking at me; *I* know that by looking at me."

"Oh, I don't know—"

"Don't try to be kind, Sandtiger." He shrugged a little, tucking hands inside wide sleeves. "A woman like Sabra will not notice me, either, unless I find a way to make her look. She's wealthy herself; coin will not impress her. I need help. I need an advantage. I need a way of making her *see* me, to see what I can offer." He looked a little above my left shoulder. "That sword," he said plainly, "can give me my advantage. News of it is all over Iskandar. Every tanzeer will want it, and you. But if *I* hire the man who carries that sword . . . ." Esnat smiled happily. "I can win Sabra's regard."

Men have done more for less. "You knew," I said, "You knew if you baited the hook with Elamain, I'd come at once. And you would buy my service before anyone else could offer."

"I have learned," Esnat said, "to strike before anyone else. To do the unexpected. To *anticipate* certain things . . . things like magical swords."

"You couldn't have anticipated this sword."

"Well, no, not exactly," he agreed judiciously, "but I have made it a practice to be *aware* . . ." Brown eyes were shrewd. "Will you hire yourself to me?"

It would be easy enough, I thought, even with a possessed *jivatma* I didn't want to use. I am good, very good; if I wasted no time at all, fighting to win instead of dance, it could be over immediately. And I wouldn't risk hurting anyone, meanwhile making a huge profit.

But I *liked* Esnat. Slowly, I shook my head. "I admire your intentions, but you're offering too much."

Esnat's eyes took on anxious appeal. "Don't you think you're worth it?"

I shrugged. "What I'm worth doesn't really matter. I just think this is too much. I don't want to beggar you. There'd be nothing left over for Sabra."

Esnat grinned. "If you want to *win* the game, you have to be willing to lose it."

Hoolies, this was ridiculous. But if that's the way he felt . . . "All right," I agreed at last, "I'll accept your terms. You make it hard not to."

Esnat smiled happily. "I'll see to sending the challenge. The dance will be in two days."

There was nothing left to say. I turned to walk away.

Esnat's voice stopped me. "Did you find the bait to your liking?"

I didn't bother to look around. "Ask Elamain."

Eleven

The walk back through Iskandar's teeming bazaar was odd. There were still hundreds of people, all jammed together in the alleyways and streets, but the feel of it was different. The *smell* of it was different.

At first, elbowing my way through clusters of people gathered here and there at stalls, or talking together in groups, I thought it was simply that there were more of them. And then I realized, as I worked my way more deeply into the center of the city, it had nothing to do with numbers. It had to do with emotions. I could actually *taste* them: anticipation, impatience, a tense expectancy.

Puzzled, I glanced around. And knew almost at once what part of the feeling was.

The city was empty of tribes. It hadn't been so the day before. People of the desert had walked freely throughout the city, doing much the same as the others: looking, talking, buying. But now the tribes were gone. Only the others remained.

Also tanzeers, and their guards, filling narrow streets.

"This isn't right," I muttered, pushing my way through the crowd.

Nearby, someone spoke of the Oracle, discussing divinity. A listener disagreed; an argument ensued. I don't know who won.

Nearby, someone spoke of the jhihadi and the changes promised the South. That a man with a new-born power could unite the Southron tribes, then change the sand to grass.

I shook my head as I walked. It was impossible.

At last I made my way through and went to find Del, to tell her about Esnat and the dance I'd accepted. But discovered she was gone.

Lena looked up from cooking. "Some men came by earlier, looking for you."

"Oh?"

"They said they represented a tanzeer named Hadjib, who wanted to hire you."

I shook my head. "Don't know him."

Lena's expression was odd. "They said their employer had heard about your sword."

So it began. Everyone wanted the power. "Where's Del?"

"She went to the circles, with Alric. She said she had a sword-dance."

Foreboding was swift and painful. "She said she'd wait here for me."

"No, she didn't." Lena grinned. "She said she *might* be here."

I glared down at her. "It isn't fair," I complained. "You women always protect one another."

Lena's brows rose. "Is that what Elamain does?"

I blinked. "She *told* you about Elamain?"

"A little." Lena's smile didn't waver. "I've known her kind before."

I had no more time for Elamain or her kind. "Never mind, it doesn't matter—" And then I broke it off as something occurred to me. "Hoolies—she wouldn't. Would she? *Would* she?" I stared at Alric's wife. "She wouldn't challenge Ajani without telling me."

Lena looked right back. "Why don't you go and see?"

But I was already gone.

He was big. He was blond. I'd never seen him before.

Oh, hoolies, bascha . . . you said you wouldn't . . . not with *him*—he wasn't worth a circle . . . you said he wasn't worth it . . . you said you wouldn't do it—

Maybe it isn't Ajani.

Don't let this be Ajani.

As always, she'd drawn a crowd. Most were sword-dancers, which was to be expected; many were tanzeers; the rest were simply people. Southroners mostly, with a Northerner here and there.

Don't tease him, bascha . . . just get it over with.

My belly knotted up. My hands itched for a sword. My eyes wanted to shut; I wouldn't let them do it. I made myself watch.

He was not particularly good, but neither was he bad. His patterns were open and loose, lacking proper focus, but he was big enough to do damage if he ever got a stroke through. I doubted that would happen; Del's defense is too good.

Hurry up, bascha.

I wet dry lips. Bit into a cheek. Felt the tickle of new sweat under arms and dribbling down temples.

Oh, bascha, please.

I thought again of Staal-Ysta. Of the circle. Of the dance we'd had to dance, before the watching *voca*. Before the eyes of her daughter. No one was there for me. No one thought of me.

Except for the woman I faced.

Then, I hadn't felt helpless. Used, yes; tricked, certainly. But not helpless. I knew Del would never go for the kill, any more than I would. And we hadn't; not really. That had taken the sword. A thirsty, nameless *jivatma* demanding to be blooded.

Now, I felt helpless. I stood on the rim of the crowd watching Del dance and was conscious only of fear. Not of her skill, not of her grace, not of her flawless patterns. Only of my fear.

Would it always be like this?

Someone moved next to me. "I taught the bascha well."

I didn't look. I didn't have to. I knew the broken voice; the familiar arrogance. "She taught herself, Abbu. With help from Staal-Ysta."

"And some from you, I think." Abbu Bensir smiled as I chanced a quick glance at him. "I won't deny your skill, or sully my own in the doing. We learned from the same shodo."

I watched Del again. She had recovered quickness, timing, finesse. Her strokes were firm and sure, her patterns artlessly smooth. But she wasn't trying to kill him.

I frowned. "Then this can't be Ajani."

Abbu, startled, looked at the man in the circle. "Ajani? No, that's not. I don't know who that is."

I turned sharply. "You *know* him?"

"Ajani? Yes. He rides both sides of the border." He shrugged. "A man of many parts."

The phrase stopped me a moment. *"A man of many parts."* I knew I'd heard it before. It had to do with the jhihadi; something the Oracle had said—

No time for that now. "Is he here? Ajani?"

Abbu shrugged. "Possibly."

The sound of the forgotten sword-dance faded. "Abbu—is he *here in Iskandar?*"

Abbu Bensir looked straight at me. Saw how intent I was. "Possibly," he repeated. "I haven't seen him yet, but that doesn't mean he's not here. No more than it means he *is*."

"But you'd know him if you saw him."

Abbu frowned. "Yes. I told you; I know the man."

"What does he look like?"

"He's a Northerner. Blond, blue-eyed, fair . . . taller even than you and heavier in bone. A little older, I think. And a little younger than me." Abbu grinned. "Do you want to ask him to dance? He's not a sword-dancer."

"I know what he is," I retorted, staring grimly out at Del.

Abbu looked also. "If I see him, I'll tell him you want him . . . *ah*—there, she's won. And no disgrace in the doing."

Blades clashed a final time. The Northerner, patterns destroyed, reeled out of the circle, which meant the dance was forfeit. He stood on the ruined perimeter and stared in shock at Del.

Who was, as always, contained, not glorying in her win.

Relief was a tangible thing. "I don't want him," I said. "And don't tell him anything."

Abbu studied me. "Is this an old hatred?"

Now I could give him my full attention. "I said: it isn't anything."

He rubbed thoughtfully at the notch in the ruined arch of his nose. "We are not friends," he said, "this Northerner and I. I *know* him; that is all."

It didn't really matter. Even if Abbu was lying and he and Ajani *were* friends, advance warning would do very little. One way or another, Del and I would find him.

I looked out at Del, who was tending to her sword. "What would you call a man," I began, "who raids the unguarded caravans of families, killing everyone he finds except those he can sell as slaves. Those who are only children, because they offer less trouble. Those who are *Northern* children, because they fetch a higher price on the slaveblock in the South."

Abbu looked also, and for a long time. Dark eyes were fathomless, masking what he thought. When he did speak, his voice held no emotion. "What I would call *him* doesn't matter; what matters is what I call her."

Something moved deep in my belly. "And what is that, Abbu?"

"Sword-dancer," he said huskily, then shouldered his way through the crowd.

I turned back, intending to go to Del; was stopped by a hand on my shoulder. "Sandtiger!" the hand's owner cried. "I didn't know you had a son. Why didn't you tell me? And such a fine speaker, too—the boy was born to be a *skjald*."

Red hair, blue eyes, flowing mustaches. "Rhashad,"

I said blankly. Then, with exceptional clarity, "Where —is—he?"

He jerked a thumb. "Over in that cantina. He's right in the middle of a story about his father, the South's greatest sword-dancer . . . I didn't offer to argue, since the boy's proud of you, but he might recall there is *me*, after all, and Abbu Bensir—"

I cut him off. "—and your mother, no doubt." I scowled briefly out at Del, who was taking her own sweet time. "Over in that cantina, you say. . . ? Well, I think it's time I met this son." I sucked air. *"Del!"*

She heard me. Saw me. Made her way across the circle. Her face was a trifle flushed and pale hair was damp at the temples, but she appeared no worse for wear. "What is it?" she asked quietly, as if to reprove me for noise.

I had no time for it. "Come on. Rhashad says this fool who's been going around telling everyone he's my son is over in that cantina." I waved a hand in the proper direction.

Del looked over at it. "Go ahead," she suggested. "I have to claim my winnings."

"Can't they wait?"

"Yours never do."

Rhashad beamed at Del. "Won the dance, did you? A delicate girl like you?"

Del, who is not precisely delicate, knew the manner for what it was. And since she liked Rhashad—don't ask me why—she was less inclined to argue. "I won," she agreed. "Do you want to dance with me next?"

Blue eyes widened. "Against you? Never! I'd hate to crack those fragile bones."

Del showed him her teeth. "My bones are very hardy."

"Talk about your bones some other time," I suggested. "Are you coming with me?"

"No," Del said. "I told you that already. Go ahead; I'll catch up."

Rhashad made a grand gesture. "I'll show her the way."

Hoolies, it wasn't worth it. I went off to see my son.

The cantina was small. It was, after all, culled from the rest of the ruined city, which meant it offered little in the way of amenities. There was a makeshift blanket roof, which gave its customers shade in which to drink, but that was about it.

I lingered in the doorway, looking for my son.

Dark-haired, blue-eyed, nineteen or twenty. Who couldn't ride very well, judging by his mount. Who didn't carry a sword, having a tongue instead, and liking to use it more than was good for him.

Not much to go on. But I thought it would do, under the circumstances.

There were men gathered in the cantina. No chairs, but hastily-cobbled stools and benches were scattered about the room. In the center, on a stool, sat a man with his back to the door; never a good thing. But plainly he wasn't concerned about who might come through. He had an audience.

The voice was young and accented. He obviously reveled in the attention his story gained; everyone was enthralled. "—and so I, too, found myself the destroyer of a great cat, just as my father was, the Sandtiger—you all know of *him*—and so I marked my victory by taking the cat's claws and making myself this necklace." A hand went to his neck, rattled something briefly. "It was, I thought, a most opportune and appropriate meeting between this great cat and the Sandtiger's cub—such is in the blood—and when at last I meet my father I will be most pleased to show him the claws and tell him what I've done. Surely he will be proud."

The listeners nodded as one: surely the Sandtiger would be.

Except I wasn't. Not *proud*. What I was, was—hoolies, I don't know what I was. I felt very odd.

"Of course," the boy added, "I kept my face pretty."

The men in the cantina laughed.

Is this my son? I wondered. Could I have sired this mouth?

I left the door and moved quietly into the room, saying nothing, pausing behind the young man. There wasn't much to see: dark brown hair brushing his shoulders; a vivid green-striped burnous; eloquent, graceful hands of a different color than mine. He was tanned, yes, but the sun marked him differently. Darker than a Northerner. Lighter than a Southroner; lighter even than me. And there was the foreign accent, coloring his Southron.

Why wait any longer?

I drew a steadying breath. "Where I come from," I said quietly, "a man doesn't name a father unless he's certain of the truth."

He started to turn on his stool, swinging around easily. His face was young, open; a bit, as he'd said, on the pretty side. "Oh, but I *am* certain . . . I am the *Sandtiger's* son—" Dark blue eyes abruptly widened in belated recognition.

"Oh?" I asked softly.

The young man rose in a single smooth movement. I didn't even see it coming.

"Do you *know*," the boy cried, "how long I've been waiting for this?"

I am big enough and strong enough to withstand most single punches, especially when they come from a smaller, slighter man. But there was a stool behind me, and as the blow connected with my jaw I spread both feet for balance and promptly fell over the thing.

It wasn't a graceful fall. It was an *embarrassing* fall. And Del was there to see it.

I sat up, dragged my sheathed, harnessed blade into a more comfortable position, sat there swearing. Ignored the staring audience and looked around for the boy, who'd headed for the doorway. He was gone, but she wasn't.

Del drifted into the cantina. Her arrival did have one advantage: now they gaped at her instead of gaping at me.

"Fatherhood," she commented, "can be a painful thing."

I got up, untangling my legs from the stool and kicking the thing aside. "That lying Punja-mite isn't my son . . . what he is, is a charlatan!" I scowled at her. "*You* saw who he was!"

"Yes," Del agreed.

"I'll kill him," I promised.

One of the men spoke up. "You'd kill your own son?"

I glared at him. "He isn't my own son. He isn't even Southron."

The man shrugged a little. "*You* don't look Southron, either." And then reconsidered it. "Maybe a half, or a quarter. But you're not a full Southroner. There are other things in the stewpot."

For some reason, it offended me. Usually I don't much care what I look like, or what people think of me. In my business it doesn't matter where I was born, or to how many races. Just that I can dance. And win; I'm paid to win.

I glared. "At least I was *raised* here. The Punja is my home; *that* boy's from somewhere else. He's a lying, scheming foreigner, using my name to gain *him* one."

The Southroner shrugged. "No harm in that."

No harm. No *harm*. I'd give him "no harm."

"Tiger," Del said quietly. "Is it worth fighting over?"

No. Not here. And not *him;* who I wanted was Bellin the Cat.

"Panjandrum," I muttered disgustedly, and stalked out of the cantina.

Twelve

Del's tone was quiet. "Are you angry because he lied? Or because it isn't true?"

We sat in one of the broken rooms in one of the broken buildings doubling as a cantina. Because there was no proper roof the full moon had free rein, painting the room silver. Dripping candles and smoky lanterns added illumination. There were no proper tables, either, and nothing resembling chairs; merely bits and pieces of odds and ends appropriated for things on which to sit, or on which to put the liquor. It was very much like the cantina in which I'd discovered Bellin.

Masquerading as my son.

I had known all along there was nothing to it. While it wasn't *impossible* I'd sired a son of his age, it was a bit unlikely. At least, unlikely that the boy would know enough to tell everyone the Sandtiger had sired him. It seemed more likely that if there *was* a sandtiger cub wandering about the South, he wouldn't know who he was.

He wouldn't know who *I* was.

I sighed. "I don't know."

Del smiled a little. "It bothers you now, doesn't it? You had begun to think what it might be like to have a son . . . begun to think how you'd feel, seeing your own immortality; it's what a child is." She hunched a shoulder, looking at liquor instead of at me. "I know what it was for me, seeing Kalle, but I *knew* I had a daughter. For you, it was different."

Different. One might say so.

I sighed again, sipped slowly, let aqivi slide down my throat. The familiar fire was muted; I was thinking of something else. "He shouldn't have done it, bascha. That kind of lie is wrong. If he wants so badly to become a man of repute—a *panjandrum*—he might look for a better way than borrowing someone's name."

"Or someone's other than yours."

Dull anger stirred. "It took me too long to get it . . . I won't share it with anyone, certainly not with a liar."

"He must have had a reason."

"That foreign-born Punja-mite doesn't need a reason for anything, remember?" I said testily. "All he wants is fame. So he decided to borrow mine."

Del's tone was dry. "You have more than enough to share."

"That's not the point. The point is he's been riding around the South for hoolies knows *how* long telling hoolies knows *how many* people he's my son." I heard the passion in my voice and purposely damped it. "I just don't like it."

Del sipped her wine. "If you find him, you can tell him."

"*I'll* find him," I promised. "He can't hide from me."

Her mouth twitched slightly. "He seems to have done a good job of it for the last several weeks. I doubt you'll find him again unless he wants you to."

"I'll find him," I repeated.

A body arrived at our low "table." "Well, Sandtiger," he said. "I hear you've been hired to dance the day after tomorrow."

I glanced up: Rhashad. "The word's gone around already?" Thinking Esnat hadn't wasted much time bragging about his suit.

The red-haired Borderer grinned. "All over Iskandar. Doesn't take long when the Sandtiger is involved." He sat down on the floor, not bothering with a "stool," and leaned against the crumbling wall. A sun-spotted hand, waving, signaled for more aqivi. "I plan to put money on it."

I shrugged. "Nothing to bet on, yet . . . I don't have an opponent."

Rhashad displayed big teeth in the shadow of ruddy mustaches. "Could even be me."

I didn't even blink. "Your mother wouldn't like it."

"Why not?"

"She wouldn't want you to lose."

"Hah!" Rhashad had played this game before. "I wouldn't be so certain of winning, Sandtiger . . . word is also making the rounds that you're not the dancer you once were."

I drank sparingly. "Oh?"

Rhashad waited until the recently summoned aqivi jug arrived, then splashed a measure into a cup. "Oh, yes. It's quite well known. The Sandtiger, rumor says, hasn't danced in months. He's lost his speed, his edge . . . lost a lot of his fire. Because of a wound, I hear . . . a cut not fully healed."

I smiled insincerely. "You've been talking to Abbu. Or *listening* to him; that's worse."

Rhashad shrugged. "You know Abbu Bensir. Part of the reason he's who he is, is because of the dance up here." The Borderer tapped his head. "You've never been a victim; you don't know what it's like."

"Abbu says whatever he likes." I drank more aqivi. "You know rumor as well as I, Rhashad. How many times have we heard how old and slow someone is—or how young and undisciplined—and discovered how wrong we were?" I grinned, showing teeth white as his own. "Sounds to me like someone—Abbu, maybe?—is trying to force better odds."

The Borderer nodded. "Not a bad attempt, since you *don't* look as healthy as I've seen you look." He grinned back pointedly. "And yes, I know rumor . . . like the ones about this Oracle fellow and the jhihadi."

I sighed. "What now?"

He shrugged. "Just that this Oracle fellow is supposed to show up here in the next couple of days. Tomorrow, maybe the next day. Maybe the day after that."

"They've been saying that for days."

"This time the rumors are a bit more specific." Rhashad sucked down aqivi. "I figure it doesn't matter. Except, of course, it'll have some effect on our coin-pouches."

"Why?" Del asked. "What has the Oracle—or the jhihadi—have to do with money?"

"There's likely to be a war." He sat against the wall with legs splayed, combing mustaches with his fingers. "Haven't you seen the change? The tribes have all but disappeared—the warriors, that is . . . word is all the tribesmen have gathered in the foothills to welcome this Oracle fellow. And then they're supposed to bring him down into Iskandar, so he can name the jhihadi."

I nodded thoughtfully. "I noticed things felt different. The tanzeers are hiring armed men."

"And a few assassins." Rhashad's teeth showed briefly. "That's never been my style, but it didn't stop him from asking."

I frowned. "Who asked what?"

"A tanzeer asked me to help assassinate the Oracle." Rhashad gestured. "Not in so many words, of course, but that was the gist of the talk."

I rubbed at gritty eyes. "I thought it might come to that. They can't afford to let him live . . . *especially* if he's rousing the warriors like this. They'll try to kill him before he does any more harm."

Del shook her head. "That will *cause* a war."

Rhashad pursed his lips. "A small one, yes . . . but without the Oracle to rouse them, the tribes will never remain united. They'll end up fighting themselves."

"And the tanzeers will win." I nodded. "'So, they're hiring sword-dancers to fill out their guard, planning to send them against the tribes."

"Seems likely." Rhashad drank. "I'm not an assassin. I told the tanzeer's man I'd hire on to dance, but not to murder a holy prophet. He wasn't interested in that, so I still don't have a job."

Del looked at me. "You have a job."

"I hired on to *dance*," I emphasized. "Believe me, bascha, the last thing I'd do is get myself tangled up in a holy war, *or* an assassination. I don't mind risking myself in a circle—since it really isn't a risk—" that for Rhashad's benefit, "—but I won't hire on to assassinate anyone. Let alone this Oracle."

Rhashad's blue eyes glinted. " 'A man of many parts.' "

Del frowned. "What?"

"Oh, that's one of the things they're saying about the jhihadi. That, and his special 'power.' Since nobody knows who—or what—he is, they're making up anything."

I looked at Del. "That's how Abbu described Ajani."

"*Abbu* described him . . ." Del let it go, interpreting other things. "So, Abbu knows Ajani. And does he ride with him, too? Both sides of the border?"

"I don't think so, bascha."

"How do you know? *I* danced with him; I have learned a little about him. Abbu could be—"

"—many things, but he's not a borjuni. He's not a murderer, or a man who sells children." I kept my tone even. "He said he knew Ajani. He also said they were not friends. Do *you* claim everyone you meet as a friend? Or are they all enemies?"

Rhashad, not much of a diplomat, didn't sense the danger. "*I'm* not an enemy, bascha . . . I'd much rather be a friend."

Del's tone cut through his laughter. "Do you know Ajani?"

Rhashad stared at her. Amusement died away. "I don't know him. I know *of* him. What's he to you?"

Del was very succinct. "A man I plan to kill."

Ruddy brows arched up. "Oh, now, bascha—"

"Don't," I said clearly.

He is slow, but he gets there. "Oh," he said at last. And then went off in another direction. "You danced with Abbu Bensir?"

"Sparred," she answered briefly.

I grinned. "That's what *she* calls it. Ask Abbu about it: he'll tell you he was teaching her."

"Abbu wouldn't teach a woman." Rhashad eyed her thoughtfully. "*I* would, though. Do you still need a shodo?"

Del's tone was cold. "What I need is Ajani."

I set down the jug of aqivi. "What *I* think you need—"

But I didn't finish it. Something intruded.

It was, at first, unidentifiable. It was noise, nothing more; an odd, alien noise. I thought immediately of hounds, then dismissed it impatiently. It didn't sound like that; besides, there *were* no hounds any more.

Rhashad stirred uneasily, leaning forward from the wall to alter posture and balance. He did it without thinking; ingrained habits die hard. "What the hoolies is *that?*"

I shook my head. Del didn't move.

The noise renewed itself in the silence of the cantina. No one spoke. No one moved. All anyone did was listen.

It was a high-pitched, keening wail. It echoed in the foothills, then crept onto the plateau and into the city itself.

"Tribes," I said intently, as the noise abruptly changed.

The keening wail altered pitch. Hundreds of voices joined in exultant ululation.

Rhashad's eyes were fixed. "Hoolies," he breathed in awe.

Del looked at me. "You know the tribes."

It was an invitation to explain. But there was little I could say. "If I had to guess," I murmured finally, "I'd say it's the Oracle. They're paying tribute to him . . . or else preparing for an attack."

"Foolhardy," Rhashad muttered. "They'd have to come up the rim trail. The plateau is too easy to defend."

I flicked a glance at him. "Who's camped at the head of that trail?"

"Tribes," Del murmured. "But still, I think they're outnumbered."

"We don't even know their numbers. Some of the warriors may have come through here every day, but most have camped elsewhere. The *families* have been here . . . with a few men to protect them."

Rhashad nodded. "To make things look normal."

I rose and kicked back my stool. "I think we should go back. Alric's probably with Lena and the girls, but you never know."

Even as we moved, the ululation died. The absence was eerie and strangely unsettling. Then everyone in the cantina was heading out the door.

"Come on, bascha," I said. "I don't like the way this feels—like something's going to happen."

Del followed me into the street.

Something did happen. It waited until we were almost all the way back to the house we shared with Alric, giving us time to breathe, but then it grew impatient. The time for waiting was done.

Del and I heard it before we saw it. Hoofbeats, then frenzied shouting. About four streets over.

"The bazaar," Del said, unsheathing Boreal. In the moonlight, the blade was white.

I unsheathed my own, hating it all the while.

In the bazaar, people gathered. They hugged the shadows of empty stalls and dwellings uneasily, disliking uncertainty, but not knowing what else to do. In the middle of the bazaar, in the city's precise center, tribesmen had gathered. Not many; I counted six, all mounted and ready to ride. We outnumbered them vastly.

A seventh horse was mounted, but not in the usual way. The man who rode it was dead.

"What are they?" Del asked.

"A couple of Vashni. A Hanjii. A Tularain. Even two Salset."

"Do you know the Salset?"

"I knew *them*. They didn't know a chula."

A stirring ran through the crowd. One of the tribes-men—a Vashni—continued his harangue, pointing at the body, then gesticulated sharply. Clearly, he was unhappy.

"What is he saying?" Del asked, since he spoke pure Desert in the dialect of the Punja.

I released a noisy breath. "He's giving us a warning —no, not *us;* he's warning the tanzeers. The man—the dead man—crept up to their gathering and tried to murder the Oracle, just as Rhashad predicted. Now he's telling the tanzeers they're all fools; that the Ora-cle will live to present the jhihadi to us, just as he has promised." I paused, listening. "He says they don't want war. They only want what's rightfully theirs."

"The South," Del said grimly.

"And the sand changed to grass."

The warrior stopped shouting. He gestured, and one of the others cut the ropes binding the body on the horse. The body fell facedown; it was turned over roughly, then stripped of its wrappings to display the bloody nakedness and its blatant mutilation.

I must have made a sound. Del looked at me sharply. "Do you know him?"

"Sword-dancer," I answered tightly. "Not a very good one—and *not* a very smart one—but someone I knew nonetheless." I drew in a deep breath. "He didn't deserve that."

"He tried to kill the Oracle."

"Stupid, stupid Morab." I touched her on the arm. "Let's go, bascha. The message has been delivered."

"Will the tanzeers listen?"

"No. This just means they'll have to look to their

own men to find another assassin. No sword-dancer will take the job; I'm surprised Morab did."

"Maybe he wanted the money."

I slanted her a disgusted glance. "It'll be hard to spend it now."

Even as Del and I went back into the shadows, the hoofbeats sounded again. I knew without having to look: the warriors were riding out. And Morab was dead and gone, lost to greed and stupidity. Someone would bury him; already the gawkers gathered.

The darkness was thick and deep in the caverns of recessed doors. Del and I knew better; we avoided those we could without exposing ourselves too much by using too much of the street. A compromise was best. Compromise—and a sword.

And yet the sword didn't help much when the *thing* slashed across my vision and thunked home in the wood of a doorjamb but two feet from my face.

"Sorry," a voice said. "I just wanted a little practice."

He should have known better. Not only did the voice tell me who he was, it told me *where* he was. And I went there quickly to find him.

He grinned, stepping smoothly out of a doorway directly across the street. In each of his hands was an ax; the third was stuck in the wood.

"Ax," Del said quietly, inspecting the planted weapon as I moved to cut off its thrower.

"Oh, I know," I answered lightly, and teased his chin with my blade.

"Wait," Bellin said.

"*You* wait," I suggested. "What in hoolies do you think you're doing?"

Bellin's tone was disingenuous. "Practicing," he declared.

"Not any more." A flick this way and that; axes spilled out of his hands. "No," I said plainly, as he made a motion to scoop them up.

In the moonlight, his face was young. Almost too

young, and too pretty. The grin bled away from his
mouth. "I knew what I was doing."

"I want to know: *why?*"

He stared back at me unflinchingly, ignoring stinging hands. "Because I could," he told me. "And because you're *you.*"

Del jerked the ax from the doorjamb and brought it
over to me. "He might have sheared off your nose."

Bellin the Cat smiled. "I just wanted your attention."

I eyed him assessively, disliking his attitude. Then
reached out my left hand and caught a wad of cloth at
his throat, jamming him back against the wall. "You,"
I said, "are a fool. A lying, conniving fool who's lucky
to be alive. I should give you a spanking—with three
feet of Northern steel."

With my fist tucked up beneath his chin, Bellin's
face was less than happy. But he didn't sound repen-
tant. "I hit you in the cantina because I had to."

"Oh? Why is that?"

"If I *hadn't,* they might have begun to suspect me."

"Who is that?" I asked.

"The men I'm riding with."

"The men you're riding with would have required
you to hit me? I find that hard to believe."

"You don't know them." He swallowed awkwardly.
"If you'd remove your hand from my throat, I might
be able to breathe . . . and then I could explain."

I let go all at once. "Explain," I said harshly, as
Bellin staggered his way to regained balance.

He rubbed gingerly at his throat, then set his green-
striped robe into order. "The story would sound better
over a jug of aqivi."

I lifted my blade slightly. "Or over three feet of
steel."

Bellin looked past me to Del. Smiled weakly, eyeing
the ax in her hand, then glanced back at me. "It was
your idea."

"*My* idea—" Abruptly I stepped close, forcing him
to back up. The doorway behind him was open; Bellin

fell in, then through. I followed silently with Del on my heels. "My idea, panjandrum?"

"Yes." He stopped and stood his ground. "My axes," he said plaintively.

Del and I didn't move.

Bellin, seeing it, sighed. Rubbed vigorously at his head, which hurt his cut hand and mussed his hair, then glared back at me. "You said I could ride with you if I found Ajani for you."

Now it was Del's turn. "Have you?" she asked. "Or is this another trick?"

"No trick," he assured us. "Do you know how many months it took me to find him?"

"Less than me," she snapped. "What about Ajani?"

Bellin sighed. He was, I realized all over again, no older than nineteen, maybe twenty, and a stranger to the South. I didn't know much about him except he was seeking fame, and he had a smooth way with his tongue. I was surprised he was still alive, that no one had killed him yet.

And then I remembered the axes.

"We're waiting," I said grimly.

Bellin nodded. "Not long after meeting you, I set out to find Ajani. It was the condition, you said; I decided to fulfill it."

The ax in Del's hand flashed. "Don't waste time, panjandrum."

He eyed her. Eyed the ax. Considered what it might be like to die by his own weapon; at least, I *think* he did. But it got him talking again.

"You can't just walk into countless towns and settlements asking for Ajani," he explained, even though Del, so straightforward, had. "It takes more than that. Cleverness, guile, a hint of ingenuity." Briefly, he smiled. "What it takes is a man who knows how to fit a story to suit his needs."

"The Sandtiger's son," I murmured.

Bellin nodded. "Who was I, but a stranger? A foreigner, to boot. No one would tell me the truth if I said what I really wanted. So I fed them a story. The best one I could think of." He touched a shadow at his neck; strung claws rattled. "I said I was your son. People talked to me."

"Why?" Del asked harshly. "Why go to so much trouble? You must know we want no part of you."

It was blunt, but true. Bellin only shrugged. "But if I told you what you wanted to know, you'd think more kindly of me. Stories would make the rounds. My name might be mentioned in them."

"Oh, *your* name is known," I said, "except you stole it from me."

He grinned. "Besides, I might grow on you. I grow on a lot of people. Once they get to know me, they're rather fond of me."

Pointedly, Del and I said nothing.

Bellin cleared his throat. "'Using your name made me known, with some claim to fame, so I could get some attention. It bought me into places, gave me a card to play when—*if*—Ajani became aware of me, or was *made* aware of me." Bellin shrugged. "It got me what I wanted: hired by Ajani. And it got *you* what you wanted . . . but more than you ever expected."

Del's tone was curt. "What is that, panjandrum?"

"Ajani is the jhihadi."

Thirteen

"What?" I blurted.

Del managed more. "If you think for one moment we will believe such nonsense—"

Bellin merely smiled. "It doesn't matter what either of *you* believe, only what everyone else does."

That silenced us a moment; it was too true to ignore.

Then Del got angry. "I don't care what he calls himself. I know what he is—I know what he's *done*."

Bellin interrupted. "But it matters. Can't you see? Ajani is setting himself up as the jhihadi. He will make people believe he is; if they believe hard enough, he *will* be the jhihadi, because they'll make him so."

"Do you mean . . ." I trailed off a moment, thinking about everything that had happened since we'd first heard about the jhihadi. "You're telling us this entire charade was Ajani's idea? The Oracle and everything?"

"Impossible," Del said curtly. "Not with the tribes involved. Not with so many people ready to name him messiah."

Bellin shrugged. "I don't know anything about Oracles and jhihadis—I'm a foreigner, remember? All I know is, Ajani's manipulating the city for his own benefit."

I shook my head. "Not the whole city. Not everyone who's here. Not all the tribes, the tanzeers, the people who need a god. He *can't* do all that . . . it just isn't possible."

Bellin sighed. "He's hired men to spread the rumors. I'm one of them. We've been going out among all the people dropping hints here and there, making them think about it. It was Ajani's idea to say the Oracle would arrive in two days. Because then he can point out the jhihadi—"

Del took it up, nodding. "—who really will be Ajani."

Slowly I shook my head. "There's too much to it. Too many people involved . . . a man can't just decide one day he wants to be a messiah, and then proclaim himself one. It doesn't happen that way."

"Of course it does." Bellin laughed. "Religion is an odd thing. A *very* odd thing—and Ajani understands that. He understands that if one very strong man surrounds himself with equally ambitious men, he can create his own religion, or set himself up as a king. All he requires is a core of loyal followers willing to do as he asks, *no matter* what he asks, and then have them spread the word." He gestured. "He has that already. And we've all been working the crowds."

"Sula," I said intently. "She spoke of the histories . . . of a promised jhihadi supposed to change the sand to grass."

Bellin merely shrugged. "If you want to make something seem real, you borrow from real things."

It was utterly impossible. Not the idea, which I could understand very well, but that he could manage to rouse so many people willing to name him messiah. "He's only a borjuni—a Northern-born renegade. He kills people. Kidnaps children and sells them into slavery. Are you telling us Ajani has the wherewithal to create a new religion and make himself a *messiah?*"

Bellin's expression was odd. "Have you met Ajani?"

"I have," Del said coldly.

He spread his hands. "Then you know."

"Know *what?*" she snapped. "How much he enjoys his job?"

Bellin didn't flinch. "If you met him, you know."

"Tell *me*," I suggested. "I don't know anything."

The young man gestured fluidly with eloquent hands. "In islander-talk we'd call him a *musarreia*, a man who shines very brightly, like the biggest star in the sky. I am a sailor also; he could be called the polestar, by which we navigate." He frowned, seeing our faces. "Do you understand? He shines more brightly than anyone else. He is the flame, we are the moths . . . Ajani attracts us all. And for those who are not wary, the flame will burn us to death."

I couldn't say anything. Del, however, could.

"He's a *murderer*," she declared. "He killed all of my kinfolk and sold my brother to slavers. I was *there;* I know."

Bellin looked at her. His voice was very quiet, but no less convincing for it. "No one else knows that. And by the time he's proclaimed jhihadi, no one will believe it."

Del's expression was odd, almost painful to see. It was obvious she wanted to call Bellin a liar, to refute everything he'd said, because to admit he might be right gave Ajani additional power. She had spent six years of her life building a prison for him, some place to keep him whole, until she could deal with him. There, he was simply Ajani, the man who'd destroyed her life.

Now he was someone else. Someone no longer in prison. Someone she had to deal with in terms other than her own.

It hurt me to see her. It hurt me to see the pain, the struggle to comprehend. To confront Ajani again before she ever saw him.

I slid my sword back home, deep into the sheath. "I'll get the axes." And went out to retrieve them.

By the time I was back, Bellin was seated on the ground, leaning up against a crumbling brick wall. Del paced in silence: pale-haired, black-eyed cat, protesting imprisonment.

I gave Bellin his axes. He already had the other. "Are you sure?" I asked quietly. "Are you very sure?"

In the moonlight, he looked younger. "I don't know everything. Only what he's told us." Axes clinked together as he handled them nimbly. They weren't heavy chopping axes, but smaller, more balanced weapons. Deadly all the same. "I am a pirate," Bellin said quietly, "a fortuitous mariner. I know how to spot good fortune, and I know how to steal it. I've made my way in the world on quick wits and a quicker tongue; you've seen the result." His boyish smile was lopsided. "I've learned to judge men under their skin. Ajani's is thicker than most."

I squatted down nearby. "Go on."

Bellin sighed. "I don't *know* this—now I'm only guessing. But I've been here for a while, and I think I understand a little about how the South works." He glanced briefly at Del, who stood listening cloaked in shadows four paces away. "To have power in the South, a man must be a tanzeer."

"That's obvious," I said. "Everyone knows that."

"Could a Northerner claim a domain?"

"Probably not," I replied. "Even if he had enough men to win himself a small domain, the people would never accept him. Someone else would come along—someone *Southron,* and with more men—and depose him forcibly. He'd lose his domain, and probably his life."

Del moved into the light. "He's a borjuni," she said. "He has been for years. Why would he change now?"

Bellin shrugged. "Ajani is forty years old."

It hit home. I rubbed a scar thoughtfully. "Time for a change," I said. "Time for something more permanent." Scowling, I rose and began to pace myself, walking out speculation. "All right. Let's say Ajani is ambitious; we know he is. Let's say he's greedy; we know that, too. And let's say he's gifted in the ways of inspiring—and controlling—men; *you* say he is." I shrugged. "Then let's also say he wants more than a simple domain. Maybe he wants them all—or at least a large portion."

" 'Let's say,' " Bellin echoed, by way of agreement.

I went on, still pacing. "But how does he go about it? By killing the enemy; in this case, enem*ies*." I thought it over. "We know killing is an obvious means for Ajani—he's done it often enough—but he also needs a weapon. A particular kind of weapon no one else can oppose. And I don't mean a sword."

"People," Del declared, understanding too well.

"People," I agreed. "So many people the tanzeers are forced to give in."

She came farther into the light, leaving the shadows behind. "He wants the tribes. But he knows nothing can unite them. Nothing can make them willing to stand together to defeat the Southron tanzeers. You've said that often enough."

I nodded. "So he uses religion. The tribes are incredibly superstitious . . . he makes himself a messiah, whom the tribes will revere utterly, because he tells them the things they most want to hear: he can change the sand to grass." I stopped pacing abruptly. "If he is as compelling as Bellin suggests, they'll do anything Ajani asks, even start a holy war."

Del's protest was desperate. "He's only *one man*."

Bellin's tone was soft. "His burning is very bright."

Silence was loud. Then I stated the obvious: "This changes things."

Del shook her head. "I still intend to kill him."

Dryly, I suggested, "Then you'd better do it in secret."

It stung. "I am not an assassin, Tiger. What I do, I do in the daylight, where everyone can see."

"Fine," I agreed. "Go ahead, bascha, but you'll start a holy war."

Del made a sharp gesture. "But there *is* no messiah! There *is* no jhihadi. All of it is a lie!"

"Didn't you listen to Bellin? Didn't you hear what he said?" I jabbed a thumb in his direction. "It doesn't matter what we know or what we think . . . only what *they* believe. If you kill the jhihadi, they'll be after your blood. They'll be after *everyone's* blood."

"Tiger—"

"Do you want that on your head?"

"Do you want me *not* to kill him?"

"After swearing all those oaths?" I shook my head. "I only want you to think."

"I've thought." She looked at Bellin. "Where *is* Ajani?"

The boy didn't hesitate. "Somewhere in the foothills. I don't know where."

Her eyes narrowed. "And yet you are working for him."

Bellin shrugged. "All I was hired to do was ride into Iskandar and help spread rumors. He met with us near Harquhal and told us what to do. Then he went to ground to prepare for his divine arrival."

"Can you find out where he is?"

"He'll be *here* in a day or two."

"You heard Tiger," she said. "For once he's making sense."

How nice of her to say so.

Bellin stood up, tucking axes underneath his robe. He snugged them into a belt at the small of his back, where they didn't show at all beneath the billowy fabric. "I can try," he said. "But Ajani went to ground on purpose. He doesn't want to be found. He wants to remain hidden until the jhihadi can appear."

I thought about the warriors, gathered in the foothills. Likely they knew where he was; possibly he was *with* them.

Then I thought about dead Morab, lacking so much of his skin and all of his genitals.

Not worth the risk.

"We'll think of something," I muttered.

Bellin grinned at me. "So will the Sandtiger's son."

Fourteen

Del was silent all the way back to the dwelling we shared with Alric. There wasn't much I could think of to say, to shake her out of the silence; and anyway, I was too busy thinking myself.

Ajani. The *jihadi?* It just wasn't possible.

And yet Bellin's explanation made perfect sense. Made too much sense; if all of it were true, Del's oaths were in serious trouble.

Clearly, she knew it.

We did not go into the dwelling because Del stopped short of the door. Then twisted aside and half collapsed against the crumbling wall, arms folded tightly beneath her breasts as she leaned.

"Six years," she said tightly. "Six years they've been dead—six years *I've* been dead. . . ." She rolled her head against the wall in futile, painful denial. "A messiah—a *messiah* . . . how can he do such a thing?"

"Del—"

"He's *mine.* Always mine. It's what I stayed alive for. It's *how* I stayed alive. It's why I didn't give up."

"I know. Del—"

She wasn't listening. "All the way to Staal-Ysta, I fed myself on hatred . . . on revenge promised to me in the name of Northern gods. When I had no food, I had no hunger, because there was the hate . . . when I had no water, I had no thirst, because there was always the *hate*—" She broke it off sharply, as if hearing herself and the lack of control; Del dreads loss of control.

More quietly, she went on. "And when I knew there would be a child, I feasted on the hatred . . . it gave me a means to live. It wouldn't let me die. I wasn't *allowed* to die, because I had sworn my oaths. The child would bear witness, even inside my womb."

I said nothing.

Del looked at me. "You understand hatred. You lived on it, as I did . . . you ate and drank and slept it . . . but you didn't let it consume you. You didn't let it *become* you." She put both hands to her face. "I am—warped. I am *wrong*. I am not a woman, not a person, not even a sword-dancer. I am only hatred— with nothing left to eat."

The echo of Chosa Dei: *"Obsession is necessary when compassion undermines."*

Del raked splayed fingers through her hair, stripping it from her brow. The moonlight bared her despair in the travesty of her face. "If Ajani is taken from me, there is no more 'me' left."

It hurt too much. I made my tone hard. "So, you're going to let him win after all. After six years. After all those oaths."

"You don't underst—"

"I understand very well, Delilah. As you yourself said, I lived on hatred, too. I know its taste, I know its *smell*—I know how it is in bed. And I know how seductive it is, how completely all-consuming . . . how *satisfying* it is in place of a human partner."

Del's face was bone white. "All of the things I have done were done in the name of that hatred. I bore a daughter and gave her up . . . I apprenticed myself to Staal-Ysta . . . I killed many men—" she swallowed jerkily. "—I tried to usurp the freedom of a man I care about—and then I nearly killed *him*."

It took me a moment. "Well," I said, "he survived."

Del's gaze didn't waver. "If he had not, I would have allowed myself no time to grieve. I would have

set aside the pain and gone on, seeking Ajani . . .
alone, as before: a woman fed on hatred, sleeping
with obsession—'' The voice cut off abruptly. And as
abruptly, came back. "Why are you here, Tiger? Why
do you stay with me?"

I wanted to touch her, but didn't. I wanted to tell
her, but couldn't. I have no skill with words. This
particular sword-dance required more than what we
both knew. Much more than what we had learned, in
the circle with our swords.

When I could, I shrugged. "I kind of thought you
were staying with *me*."

Del didn't smile. "You have sworn no oaths. Ajani
is not your duty."

Idly, I kicked at a stone, rolling it aside. And then
moved against the wall, next to Del, letting it hold me
up. "I think there are times when no oaths *have* to be
sworn. Some things just—happen."

Del stared at me. Then drew in an unsteady breath.
"You make it too hard."

I stared steadfastly across the alley. "You're afraid,
aren't you?"

"Of Ajani? No. I've hated too much for fear."

"No. You're afraid of what comes after."

Del shut her eyes. "I am afraid," she said, "that I
won't feel the things I know I should feel."

"What are those, bascha?"

"Pleasure. Satisfaction. Elation. Relief. Fulfillment."
Her eyes opened; the tone was edged with bitterness.
"The things that should come with bedding unencum-
bered or colored by hatred."

I frowned down at the ground. "When I was young,"
I told her, "I swore to kill a man. And I meant it
utterly; there was no room in my soul for anything but
hatred, for anything but this oath. Like you, I lived on
it. I drank it. I went to bed with it each night, whispering to the stars the oath I swore to keep: that I would
kill this man. I was a boy; boys swear things, and
never keep them. But I *meant* it . . . and that oath

helped me survive until the time a sandtiger came into camp and killed some of the children. That oath made me take my crude spear and go out into the Punja by myself to kill that sandtiger. Because I knew that if I succeeded, if I killed the sandtiger, I could ask for a boon, and then I would get the one thing I most wanted."

"Freedom," Del murmured.

Slowly I shook my head. "A chance to kill the shukar."

She stiffened. "That old man?"

"That old man did more to destroy what was left of my life than anyone else in the tribe. And he was what made me survive."

"But you didn't kill him."

"No. I was sick for three days from the poison. Sula spoke for me, saying I was owed my freedom." I shrugged. "I thought killing the shukar would give me a freedom—of mind, if not of body. It was the only kind I knew."

"But they sent you away, instead."

"They gave me physical freedom. No more was I a chula."

"What are you saying, Tiger?"

"That in the end I won. That what the old man most wanted was me *dead*, not free . . . and I cheated him."

"Tiger—"

I kept my voice quiet. "Sometimes what we want is not what's best for us. No matter how much we want it."

Del made no answer. She leaned against the wall, as I did, staring into darkness. And at last spoke. "Do you think I am wrong?"

I smiled wryly. "It doesn't matter what I think."

Del looked at me. "It matters," she said. "I have always cared what you thought."

"Always?"

"Well, perhaps not at first . . . not when we first

met. You were insufferable then, so cocksure and Southron and *male*." Del smiled a little. "I thought what you needed was a kick in the head, to knock some sense into you . . . or maybe castration, so you wouldn't think with your manhood instead of with your brain."

"You have no idea what you can do to a man, Delilah, when he first sets eyes on you. Believe me, no man—no *whole* man—can think with anything else."

Del grimaced. "I never asked for that. It is a burden, not a gift."

"Funny," I said idly, "*I've* never found it a burden."

She slanted me a glance. "Vanity doesn't become you."

"Everything becomes me."

"Even Chosa Dei?"

I scowled; the game was over. "As far as I'm concerned, he has no stake in this. He's not part of me. He's not even part of the sword; he's merely a parasite."

"But deadly. And now that we know Shaka Obre is in no way linked to this jhihadi . . ." She let it trail off. "I still can't believe it. Ajani—a messiah?"

I shrugged. "He's an opportunist. Maybe there really is something to this jhihadi business—after all, it was the old holy man in Ysaa-den who first mentioned the Oracle and jhihadi—and Ajani concocted a plan based on what he'd heard."

Slowly, Del shook her head. "I can't reconcile the man I knew with the man Bellin knows."

I gave it a moment, then spoke carefully. "Are you so sure you can reconcile him with anything? What you remember is brutality and murder . . . you saw Ajani and his men kill your entire family. You saw Jamail on fire. You suffered Ajani's—*attentions*. At fifteen years of age—and under those circumstances— you could never judge a man. Never see his potential for anything as complex as this. All you could do was *feel* . . . and emotions—or the lack of them—don't allow for much objectivity."

Del's tone was flat. "What they allow for is the ability—and the desire—to kill a murderer."

"And so we are back where we began." I straightened. "But maybe not."

"Maybe not? Tiger, what are you—"

"Come on," I said intently, "there's someone I have to talk to."

"Now? It's late."

"Come on, bascha. This won't wait."

Elamain, of course, thought I'd come to see her. Until she saw Del.

"Esnat," I said succinctly.

Sabo, who had greeted us at the door, went at once to fetch his master. This left Elamain standing in the room swathed in the silk of her hair as it poured down the front of her nightrobe. Delicate feet were bare. I found it oddly erotic; then recalled that to Southroners, any part of a woman was, since she hid it under so much.

"Esnat?" she echoed.

"Business," I said briefly. "You may as well go back to bed."

Elamain flicked a glance at Del, then looked back to me. "Only if you're in it."

"Don't waste your time," Del suggested. "He is a man, Elamain, not a tame cat . . . and I, unlike you, believe he has more sense and integrity than you give him credit for. Teasing and tricking a man is no way to win him."

Elamain's eyes widened. "Who is teasing? Who is tricking? I hide nothing of what I want. No more than you do what *you* want, wearing a man's weapon—"

But she didn't get to finish, because Esnat came into the room.

He'd been asleep and was not yet fully awake. He blinked as he saw us, pulled his robes into order, raised brows at Elamain's presence. Thin dust-colored hair, now unencumbered by a turban, hung lankly to narrow shoulders. The spots on his chin were worse. I realized all over again I was supposed to dance for this man, so he could impress a woman.

Except his courtship might have to wait.

"I want honesty," I said. "Why are you here?"

Sabo, Elamain, and Esnat stared. It was not what they'd expected.

"Why?" I asked again. "Sasqaat is clear across the Punja. It's a small domain. Why would you come all the way to Iskandar? Why, for that matter, would *any* tanzeers come? What's in it for them?"

Something flickered in Esnat's eyes. Now I knew I had him.

"Don't waste my time," I said. "You're a tanzeer, and not a stupid one, no matter what you've led Elamain and others to believe. The masquerade is over, Esnat. I want the truth. Then I'll give you mine."

Esnat glanced around. Then gestured at cushions and rugs. He sank down on the nearest one even as Del and I found seats. "The Oracle," he said.

Elamain, who had opened her mouth to protest the situation, now closed it. A crease marred her brow. Clearly Esnat's answer was unexpected and baffling; she'd believed they'd come to Iskandar for another reason entirely.

Esnat gestured irritably, "Oh, Elamain, sit *down*. It would do no good to send you to bed—you'd only listen at the doorway. So sit down and keep your mouth closed; maybe you'll learn something." He glanced now at Sabo. "You, too, Sabo. You know this man better than I."

Elamain sat. Sabo sat. Esnat looked back to me.

"You view him as a threat," I said. "All his foretelling of a jhihadi has every tanzeer frightened he might be telling the truth."

Esnat nodded. "There is no doubt the Oracle has roused the tribes. When word came he was foretelling the coming of the jhihadi here in Iskandar, no one could believe it. But the tribes did, and they left the Punja en masse. That made us nervous."

"So you came up here to kill him before this jhihadi can appear."

Esnat shook his head. "*I* don't want to kill him. I think that would touch things off. There are other tanzeers who believe as I do, and we want to avoid a holy war, not start one by killing the Oracle. We came to Iskandar hoping to convince the others."

"The other tanzeers want war?'

He shrugged. "Hadjib and his followers consider it unavoidable. They believe nothing will calm the tribes now, unless the Oracle is killed. Without a leader to unify them, the tribes will fracture again." Esnat scratched his chin, leaving red streaks. "They have brought as many men as they can hire, and are hiring more. They fully believe they can smash this rebellion before it occurs—or else consume the tribes in war." He grimaced. "These men are accustomed to absolute power. They have no conception of religion, or what it can do to unify men . . . even desert tribes."

Hadjib. *Hadjib.* Somehow I knew the name . . . and then I recalled how. Lena had told me about a tanzeer who'd come looking for me. Now I knew why.

"But you *do* understand it," I said. "You understand, you and a few others, what could happen."

Esnat didn't hesitate. "It would be a bloodbath."

"And you don't want that."

"No. Such a thing would be harmful." Esnat frowned, glancing briefly at Sabo, Elamain, Del. "The tribes are no threat to us if they remain as they have been for decades: insular, independent races with no specific home, simply traveling about the South. But if they unite in a common goal motivated by faith, they become the greatest enemy we could know. They will gladly die in the name of their jhihadi, believing what they do is for divine favor . . . that sort of fanaticism can destroy the South. For us—for everyone—it is better left the way it is."

"The tribes might not agree."

Esnat shrugged. "They have been content with their lives, as you well know . . . had the Oracle not appeared, they would not now be here."

"They believe," I said quietly, "this jhihadi will change the sand to grass."

"It doesn't matter," Esnat said. "You and I know such a thing cannot occur."

"Magic," Del said quietly.

Esnat glanced at her. He assessed her quickly, then smiled. "You have your own share of magic, bascha, and so does the Sandtiger. But surely you must see what it would take to alter the South. I don't think such magic exists any more, if it ever did."

"Never mind the magic," I said. "There's something else we have to think about." I shifted on my cushion. "Esnat, what would you and the others say if I told you there was no jhihadi?"

He smiled wryly. "That we are all of a like mind. But what good will it do? Hadjib and his followers don't care if the jhihadi is real or not."

I leaned forward slightly. "What if I told you a man *was* behind this holy war, but not a true jhihadi? Merely a man, like you and me, but a very clever one. A man who has very carefully manipulated the tribes into believing he is the jhihadi, so he can gain power."

Esnat's eyes widened. "A single man?"

"A single Northerner with a gift for inspiring others."

He sat stunned, thinking about it. Thinking of what it could mean. "But the *magnitude* of it . . ." He let it trail off. "It's impossible."

"Is it? Think about it. A man hires another and calls him an 'Oracle.' He sends him out to a few of the tribes well-primed with the kind of words that would appeal to nomadic peoples. This jhihadi, the Oracle says, can change the sand to grass, so that the tribes will know comfort again. The tribes will know *power* again."

Esnat said nothing.

"After a while, the tribes themselves carry word throughout the Punja; eventually throughout the South. Bit by bit by bit this 'Oracle' seeds his ground, and eventually it takes root. Eventually it bears fruit."

"One man," Esnat murmured.

"Ajani," I said. "A Northern borjuni—a man who burns very brightly."

Frowning, Esnat rubbed his chin. "Hadjib wouldn't listen," he murmured. "We have tried, all of us; they ignore the wisdom we offer. They are angry, powerful men unwilling to think of compromise when war is another way." He stared blankly at me. "They want this war, Sandtiger. They want it contained in Iskandar so no domains are threatened."

"More than domains are threatened," I declared. "Things are bad enough in the Punja for caravans, what with borjuni and a few hostile tribes. If the tribes went into full revolt, they could cut off all the caravan routes. *That* would destroy the domains as well as anything else." I shook my head. "Some would survive, yes, but not the small ones so dependent on trade. What about Sasqaat? You supplement your people with outside trade, don't you?"

"Of course. Sasqaat would die without trade."

"Well, then?"

"Well, then," he echoed. "What is there to do when the other tanzeers won't listen? We can't just send them home, though it would be the best thing."

"Challenge them," Del suggested.

Esnat blinked at her. "What do you mean: 'challenge'?"

Her voice was very quiet. "This is the South, is it not? Where things in the lives of tanzeers are often decided by a sword-dance. Two men hired for a single purpose: to settle differences. To make a ruling by the sword. To declare a single winner."

"Southron tradition," I said, "can be a very powerful thing."

Esnat stared at us. "They have already tried to assassinate the Oracle."

"*If* there's an Oracle," I agreed. "Ajani may have already relieved him of his duties. And I have no doubts that if he's shown himself as the jhihadi to the tribes—or is planning to—he's surrounded himself with guards." I shook my head. "Already tonight we've seen what the tribes will do to protect their Oracle. For the jhihadi, they will do worse. I don't think the tanzeers will find another man willing to risk that."

"But there are other ways. And they will look for that way."

I shook my head. "Not if a ruling based on the outcome of a traditional sword-dance won your side the chance to defy them openly, to declare the Oracle and jhihadi safe. If all the tanzeers attended—from both sides—and agreed to abide by the outcome, you could end the war before it began."

"*If* we won," he said.

"That's always a risk," I agreed. "If Hadjib's faction won, you'd have to let them do whatever they wanted. You'd have no say in their plans, even if it included assassination."

His tone was thoughtful. "But if they *lost,* we could send them home."

"And probably prevent more violence."

Esnat frowned. "But the *tribes.* No one can be certain what they'll do."

"No. But if Ajani's behind this thing, and all the tanzeers go home, he'll lose some of his power. If they left, I doubt Ajani could keep the tribes reconciled long enough to march all over the South capturing domains for himself. Eventually, the tribes would fall to quarreling." I shook my head. "For all we know, it was Ajani's idea to lure as many tanzeers as possible here to Iskandar. Contained, tanzeers are controllable; scattered, they are not. Much like the tribes."

Esnat studied me intently. "He is playing one against the other."

"The trick is to dilute Ajani's plan. Forcing the other tanzeers to withdraw would do it. If your side won the dance and all the other tanzeers went home, half the battle would be won without a sword being drawn, except for those in the circle." I shrugged. "Maybe the whole war."

Esnat considered it. "If I talked with the others who feel as I do and they agreed . . . we'd have to find the proper words, the kind of words that will cause the other tanzeers to accept such a challenge . . ."

I interrupted. "Make it a formal challenge to Hadjib. If he feels he's in control of the pro-war faction, his pride will require that he answer the challenge personally. I can give you the ritual phrases that will demand an acceptance."

Esnat continued, easily incorporating my suggestion into his plan. "—then hire a sword-dancer worthy of the dance, one worthy of the risk, because it wouldn't *be* a risk, if we were certain he could win—" Brown eyes sharpened. "Will you do it, Sandtiger?"

I smiled. I've never been the kind of man to ignore an opportunity as golden as this one. "You already hired me to dance in hopes of impressing a woman. For that, you offered a very generous—"

Esnat didn't bother to hear me out. "Coin," he said dismissively. "For this, you will have a domain."

Elamain gasped. "You can do such a thing?"

Esnat smiled at her. "I can do many things."

"But—an entire *domain?*"

He raised a dust-colored eyebrow. "I think stopping a war might be worth the cost."

Elamain looked at me. Then she looked at Esnat Sabo merely grinned.

May the sun shine on his head.

Later—actually, *late*—I sat contemplating my future, scratching idly at a kneecap. I guess the scratching was loud, because Del rolled over.

"Tiger, can't you sleep?"

"No. I'm sitting here thinking about what it will be like to be a tanzeer."

" 'Will'?" she asked ironically. "*You're* sure of yourself."

"Why shouldn't I be? I'm the best sword-dancer in the South."

"Who hasn't danced for months."

"I danced against Nabir."

"You *sparred* against Nabir."

"Besides, I've got this sword."

"Which you swore not to use in a dance."

I decided not to answer. Seemed like every time I said anything, Del had a retort.

Which meant we were back to normal.

I sat against the crumbling wall in our private room. Del was snugged up in blankets next to me, nothing much visible except a little hair, pale luminescence in the light of the moon. Next door, Alric snored. I'd tried to sleep, but couldn't; too many thoughts in my head.

Me: a tanzeer. A sword-dancer-turned-tanzeer. It seemed impossible to consider, in light of my origins. A baby, left to die in the desert, born of people no one knew. And then a slave, in bondage to the Salset. And finally, a killer. A man who lived by the sword.

Me: a tanzeer. It made me want to laugh.

I stretched out legs and carefully adjusted the arrangement of my knees from the inside, shifting tendons and cartilage through interior muscle control. I heard the dull chatter, the snaps; felt the catch, the pop into place. I'd need my knees to dance. I wished they were a bit younger.

Del, whose head was close to my legs, peeled a blanket back. "That sounds terrible."

"You should hear the rest of me."

"*I* don't sound like that."

"You're not old enough to." Not an encouraging thought; except, maybe, for Del. "Be silent as long as you can."

"I have a finger that cracks." Del demonstrated. "I broke it on Staal-Ysta."

"Hoolies, I've broken fingers and toes so many times I don't even remember which ones." I looked at the still-wrapped little finger the stud had tried to eat. "Except for this one. This one I remember."

"That one's not even broken." Del shifted and rolled over onto her back. "Maybe it will be a good thing, this domain. Maybe it's time you settled down. No more traveling, no more dancing—no more broken bits."

Settled down. Me. I hadn't thought of it that way. I'd just been thinking about the things that came with the title. Coin. A place of my own. A stable for the stud. People to cook and clean. Aqivi whenever I wanted it. Maybe even a harem.

I slanted a glance at Del.

Maybe not a harem.

I scooched down the wall and stretched out on my bedroll again, pulling a blanket over me. Del lay very close; her hair caught on my stubble. I picked it away, then moved a little closer. Thought about how it had been for so many years, sharing nothing with no one.

The question occurred again. "Bascha, what are you going to do once Ajani's dead?"

"Ask me when he's dead."

"Del—"

"I'm hunting him tomorrow. Ask me tomorrow night."

Her tone of voice was definitive; she wanted no more questions, especially about Ajani. I watched her shut her eyes.

"Bascha—"

"Go to sleep, Tiger. You're older than me; you need it."

I lay there in aggrieved silence for long moments, trying to think of an appropriately cutting retort. But by the time I did, Del was sound asleep.

So then I lay there wide awake and wide-eyed,

glaring into darkness, thinking uncharitable thoughts about the woman by my side, and snoring Alric, and sleeping Lena and the girls.

Why do people who have no trouble falling asleep think it's easy for everyone else?

It just isn't fair.

If I were tanzeer, I'd make everyone stay awake until *I* was asleep.

If I were a tanzeer?

Hoolies . . . I just might be.

If I managed to win the dance.

Fifteen

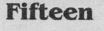

I went out to inspect the circle, and that was where he found me.

His words were mostly ritual. "I'm sent to tell you my lord Hadjib accepts Lord Esnat's formal challenge. His personal sword-dancer will meet you in the circle when the sun is directly overhead."

Which didn't give us much time; it was already mid-morning. "Does your lord Hadjib understand the challenge fully? That should I win the dance, he and his followers must leave Iskandar at once and return to their domains?"

"He understands the challenge fully. My lord Hadjib swears not a drop of blood shall be spilled, should he and his fellow tanzeers be required to leave Iskandar. And he asks in return if your lord Esnat understands his part in the challenge should *you* lose the dance."

"Lord Esnat understands the challenge fully. Should I lose the dance, Esnat and his followers will join battle as Hadjib commands."

Simple terms, spelled out. It wasn't a dance to the death, simply to victory.

The ritual was finished. No more need for formality.

"So," I said expansively, "care for a jug of aqivi?"

He smiled. "I don't think so."

I looked at the dark eyes; at the lines carved deep in his face; at the notched arch of his nose. Remembered what I'd felt when I nearly crushed his throat.

"Too bad," I said lightly. "You might have enjoyed the time spent retelling our tall tales."

Abbu Bensir's smile widened. "Oh, I think we'll have a new and better tale to tell when this day is over. And so will the rest of the South."

I shook my head a little. "This isn't your sort of dance. What did they promise you?"

"Any dance is my sort of dance; you know better, Sandtiger." He grinned. "As for what they promised me? A domain all for myself."

I blinked. "You, too?"

A silver-flecked eyebrow arched. "A popular gift, this domain. I wonder if it's the same one."

"They wouldn't."

"They might. Do you trust your tanzeer?"

"Do you trust yours? He tried to hire *me*."

"Not for this."

"No. He wanted an assassin."

"Ah. I see." Abbu rubbed his nose. "I think we've gone beyond that, judging by this dance. Was it your idea?"

I frowned. "What makes you say that?"

"You lived with the Salset. You know what the tribes are like. I'd be willing to wager you'd want to avoid a holy war, since you have a very good idea how messy one would be."

"Messy," I echoed. "A good way of putting it."

"I, on the other hand, don't really care. As far as I'm concerned, the tribes are nothing but parasites stealing water out of our mouths. It's better left to us, what little there is of it."

"So, you'd just as soon *win* this dance so you can kill a few warriors."

"I'd just as soon win *any* dance, Sandtiger. But I must admit meeting you will make it all the sweeter."

"Finally," I said.

"Finally," he agreed.

Which left us with nothing much else to say; both of us went away.

* * *

I sat outside in the shade, leaning against the wall. The sun climbed the sky; everyone watched it closely. Once it was overhead, we'd all adjourn to the circle.

Massou watched me. "Are you going to die?"

Adara, of course, was aghast. I waved her into silence.

"It's an honest question," I told her, "and I don't blame him for asking it. He's only curious."

Adara's green eyes were transfixed by the motion of hand and arm as I carefully honed my sword. "He has no *business*—"

"At his age, I'd have asked the same thing." If I'd been allowed to ask anything. "No, Massou, I'm not going to die. It's not a dance to the death. Only to victory."

He thought about it. "Good. But I'd rather see Del dance."

It stung a little. "Why?"

"Because she's better."

Del, who leaned against the wall not so far away, smiled, then tried to hide it behind a mask of cool neutrality.

I shot her a scowl, then looked back at the boy. "That's only because when you saw me spar, I wasn't at my best."

Del's tone was dry. "You're not at your best *now*."

"Sound enough for Abbu."

Alric stood in the doorway. "Are you?" he asked seriously. "Abbu Bensir is good."

"I'm not exactly *bad*."

Del's voice again: "But not as good as you were."

"And besides, it's not like I've never danced against him before. I'm the one who gave him that throat."

Del, once more: "With a wooden sword."

I stopped honing the blade. "All right, what is it? Do you *want* me to lose? Is that why you're being so pointed about doubting my confidence?"

Del smiled. "I have *no* doubts about your confidence. What I have doubts about is your willingness to recognize that you are not in proper condition."

"I'm fine."

"Fine is not fit." Del straightened from the wall. "I don't want you to walk into that circle thinking Abbu stands no chance. He is good, Tiger—I have sparred with him myself. You are good, also—I have *danced* with you myself. But if you refuse to acknowledge the truth of the matter, you've lost before you've begun."

"I have no intention of stepping into the circle without being careful, if that's what you're afraid of. Hoolies, bascha, you'd think I'd never danced before!"

Del looked directly at me. "How many times have you been wounded in the circle?"

"More times than I can count."

"How many times have you been *seriously* wounded in the circle?"

I shrugged. "Two or three times, I guess. It happens to all of us."

"And how many times have you come very close to death in the circle?"

"All right," I said, "once. You know that as well as I."

"And you have not danced a proper dance since then."

The defensiveness was abrupt. "I'm not afraid, if that's what you mean."

Del didn't smile. "Of course you're afraid."

"Del—"

"I saw it, Tiger. I was in the circle, remember? The last time you tried to dance, the fear drove you out."

I forgot all about Massou and Adara and Alric. "That was fear for *you!* It had nothing to do with me." Angrily, I glared. "You have no idea what it was like for me seeing you sprawled on the ground with steel in your ribs. You don't know what I felt. You don't know what I thought. When I stepped into that circle on our way to Ysaa-den, I was on Staal-Ysta again.

All I could think about was that dance, and I was afraid it might happen again."

Del drew Boreal. "Then dance with me now."

"*Now?* Are you sandsick? Besides, you're supposed to go meet with Bellin, remember? He'll have information about Ajani."

"Now," she said coolly. "A warm-up will do you good. It will loosen all your muscles . . . quiet your noisy knees."

"Oh, *good*," came from Massou, before Adara could hush him.

Hoolies, hoolies, hoolies. I don't want to do this.

So tell the bascha no.

Not so easy to do.

Especially when she's right.

I wiped the blade clean. Glanced up at the sun. Knew we had the time. "Alric?"

He nodded. "I'll play arbiter."

Adara, muttering, forcibly dragged Massou to the end of the alley. He protested, of course, but she didn't let him go. Eventually he subsided, since she threatened to take him away entirely if he didn't shut his mouth.

There was no need for a circle, so we didn't bother to draw one. We just faced one another in silence, took the measure of each other, thought our private thoughts.

Mine were not happy ones. I don't know *what* hers were.

"Dance," Alric said.

Hoolies, but I don't want—

Too late, Tiger. Nothing to do but dance.

Nothing to do but *sing*—

No—don't sing—

Don't give Chosa Dei the chance—

Northern steel clashed. The sound filled up the alley.

Get looser, I thought. Get *looser*—

Del's blade flashed. In and out of shadow, slicing

the sun apart. Shattering the daylight with the brilliance of magicked steel.

Gods, but she can dance—

Well, so can I.

Of their own accord, my feet moved. I felt the acknowledgment of muscles too long kept from the circle; the sharpening of eyes. Focus came back quickly, blocking out the alley, the sun, the others gathering. All I saw was Del. All I heard was Del: the sloughing of her feet, the keening of her steel, the breathy exhalations.

This is the true dance, where two perfectly balanced halves come together at last and form a perfect whole. This is a dance of life, of death, of continuity; the world within seven paces. Nothing else exists. Nothing is as important. Nothing can fill the need the way a proper sword-dance can, danced with a proper opponent.

There is no other for me.

Ah, yes, bascha . . . show me how to dance.

And then, abruptly, my sleeping sword awoke. Chosa Dei awoke. I felt him swarm through the blade from wherever it was he lived. Felt him test my strength. Felt him gather himself. Knew what he meant to do.

Confusion diluted the focus, seeping through concentration: But I haven't sung. I haven't even *thought* of singing.

Chosa Dei didn't care. Chosa Dei was awake.

Oh, bascha—*bascha*—

She felt it in the swords. Tasted it in the air, in the acrid stink of magic. And jerked her blade from mine, falling back two steps. "Control it!" she cried. "Control it! You have the power; *use* it!"

I could feel it—feel *him*—trying to leave the sword. Trying to creep up the blade to the hilt, where he could make contact with my hands. Once it was made, I was lost, because the flesh is much too weak. He'd nearly taken Nabir—he *had* taken Nabir—he'd unmade Nabir's feet—

What would he do to me?

I stood in the center of the alley clutching the blooding-blade, wondering how to fight it. How to *beat* it, before it beat me.

"Control it," Del repeated. "You have the strength; use it!"

Power, she'd said. Strength.

The blade was turning black.

Use it, she'd said. *Use* it.

Do I know how to do that?

Hoolies, of course I do. I'm *the Sandtiger*.

No one defeats me.

Not even Chosa Dei.

"Yes!" Del shouted. *"Yes!"*

I must be doing it right.

Samiel, I whispered. But only inside my head. Nabir had said it aloud. Nabir had put me at risk.

Or was it Chosa Dei?

Samiel, I repeated. But only inside my head.

Del's face swam into my vision. A sweat-glossed, laughing face. "I *told* you you could do it—but you never want to believe me!"

I was panting. Breathing like a bellows. I felt the twinge in my midriff: knurled scar tissue had been pulled. Hands still clenched the sword, clamped around the grip. Knuckles shone white.

"It's—done?" I looked down at the sword in my hands. "Did I do it?"

She nodded, still grinning. "You drove him back down, Tiger. This time without the simoom. This time without the heat. This time with just yourself. With the strength from inside here." She put a hand to my heart. "And you have it in abundance."

I frowned, looking at the blade. "But it's still black. The tip. Chosa Dei's still in there."

She nodded, withdrawing her hand. "He's not banished. Only beaten. Banishment will take time. We have to discharge it properly."

And for that, we needed more magic. We needed Shaka Obre.

"Tiger?" Alric's voice. "Tiger—can you come? Something's upset your stud. He's trying to tear down the house."

Now I could hear it. He was stomping and pawing and kicking, squealing his displeasure.

"It's the magic," I muttered resignedly. "He hates it as much as I do."

I sheathed my defeated sword and went in to see the stud. He was indeed trying to tear down the house; he pawed chunks of crumbling brick and ancient mortar out of the wall, grinding it into the dirt.

"All right," I said, "you can stop now. I've put the sword away." I stepped in through the door, entering the "stable." "You're not going anywhere, so you may as well be qu—"

He let loose with both hind hooves. One of them caught my head.

Voices.

"Alric—get him *out*—"

"I can't, Del—the stud's broken his tie-rope . . . he won't let me near him—"

A spate of unintelligible words in a language I didn't know, or else I had forgotten.

The same male voice. "I know, Del—I *know* . . . but how can I drag him out if the stud won't let me near him?"

A woman's voice answering: frightened, angry, impatient."— need a horse-speaker—" Then, abruptly, "Get *Garrod*—"

A boy's voice: "*I* will!"

"Then hurry, Massou—hurry!"

I was flat on my back in the dirt.

Why am I in the dirt?

Tried to sit up. Couldn't. All I could do was twitch.

The woman's voice again. "Tiger—stay still! Don't try to move."

Eyes won't open.

Everything sounds distorted.

"Tiger—don't *move* . . . don't give him a second chance."

Give who *what* second chance?

"Is he bleeding?"

"I can't tell."

Why would I be bleeding?

Sharply: "Don't try it, Del. I don't need two of you down."

"I can't leave him there, Alric. The stud's liable to stomp his head in."

Someone was moving around me. No—some*thing*. It breathed heavily. Pawed. Moved around me again.

Now a new voice. "Where is—oh. Here, give me room."

"Tiger, don't *move*."

Don't worry, I don't think I can.

"Talk to him, Garrod. Tell him to let us in so we can get Tiger out."

Silence, except for nearby scraping. I tasted dust. Felt it. It feathered across my face. I tried to lift an arm to brush the dust away, but nothing did what I wanted. All I did was twitch.

The scraping stopped. I smelled the tang of sweat and fear. Something was afraid.

"Now," said a quiet voice.

Hands. They touched me, grasped me, dragged me.

Hoolies, don't *drag* me—my head will fall off my neck—

"Here," someone said, and they put me down again.

"Is he alive?"

Hoolies, yes, I wouldn't be anything else.

Something pressed my chest. "Yes." Relief. "*Yes,*" I tried to open my eyes. This time I succeeded.

Not that it did much good. What I saw wouldn't stay still.

"Bascha?" My voice was weak. "Del—what happened?"

"The stud tried to kick your head off."

"He wouldn't—"

"He almost *did*."

Memory snapped back. "Hoolies—" I blurted. "The dance—"

"Tiger—Tiger *no*—"

I lurched into a sitting position, thrusting away the hands. "I have to go—the dance—" And then clutched my head.

Del sounded exasperated. "You're not going anywhere."

Through the pain, I gritted it out. "Abbu will be waiting. *All* of them will be waiting—"

"You can't even stand up."

It even hurt to blink. "Too much depends on the dance . . . they *agreed*, all the tanzeers . . . if I don't dance, Hadjib and his followers win—there'll be *war*—oh, hoolies . . ."

Everything went gray around me. I lingered on the edges, wondering which way I would fall.

"Tiger?"

I yanked my senses back. "—have to get up," I mumbled. "Someone help me up."

"Postpone the dance," Del said. "Do you want me to see to it?"

"They won't—there's no—I don't think—" Hoolies, it was hard to think. Harder yet to talk. "I won't forfeit this dance."

Del's face was tight. "They won't expect you to dance when you're in this kind of shape."

"Doesn't matter . . . Abbu will claim victory, and there'll be no chance for peace—"

She took her hand from my arm. Her tone was very cold. "Then if you *must* do this, get up and walk out of here. Now. Waste no more time on weakness."

I rocked forward, slopped over onto an elbow, tried to gather legs. It took me two tries. Then I staggered to my feet.

Only to fall again. This time to my knees. And eventually to a hip, levered up on an elbow. I shut my eyes, shut my teeth, tried to wait it out. Begging the pain and sickness to wane.

"I'll postpone it," she said.

I was sweating. "You can't . . . bascha, you *can't* . . . they'll claim forfeit—they have the right . . . Abbu would win, and Hadjib would win . . . we can't afford to lose—"

"We can't afford to lose *you*."

"—sick—" I muttered tightly.

"You've been kicked in the head," she said curtly. "What do you expect?"

Maybe a bit more sympathy—no, not from Del. Too much to hope for.

And then another voice intruded. A husky, male voice, asking after me. Mentioning the dance.

He came through the doorway. I blinked up at him dazedly, trying not to vomit. It was very hard to think clearly.

"Ah," Abbu remarked, "one way of avoiding the truth." He glanced at the others, then looked back at me. "I came over to see what was keeping you. Everyone is gathered. Everyone is waiting." He smiled. "Your lord Esnat came close to forfeiting, but I said I would come here myself. It's very irregular, of course . . . but I want this dance too badly. I've waited too many years."

It was all I could do to lift my head high enough to see the sun without spewing my belly across the floor. "I'll be there," I mumbled; the sun glared balefully down from directly overhead.

Abbu Bensir laughed.

Del's tone was deadly. "Will you accept another dancer in his place?"

"Oh, bascha—"

Del ignored me. "Will you?"

"—South," I slurred. "Do you think Abbu or anyone else will accept a woman in my place?"

Del only looked at Abbu.

He was, above all, a Southroner: old habits die very

hard. But every man can change, given reason enough to do so.

Abbu Bensir smiled. "It's the Sandtiger I want—but that can wait a little. You are no disgrace to the circle."

Del nodded once.

Abbu glanced at me. "Another time, Sandtiger . . . first I will beat your bascha."

"Go," Del said coolly.

Abbu Bensir went.

Time to protest again. "—can't—Del . . . *Del*—" I sucked in a breath. "You have to go look for Ajani." The world was graying out. "You have to go meet Bellin, to find out where Ajani is . . . bascha, you have to go . . . you've waited too long already—"

Del knelt down by me. She put a hand to my temple and drew away bloody fingers. The look in her eyes was odd.

I squinted through the fog. "You have to find Ajani."

Her tone was very fierce. *"To hoolies with Ajani."*

"Dell—*wait*—come back—"

But Del didn't wait.

And Del didn't come back.

Sixteen

He knelt next to me. I looked him in the eye. "Am I dying?" I asked. "Is there something I should know?"

Alric smiled. "No. You only feel like it. Here." He gave me a bota. "Drink a little of this. It'll make you feel better."

I drank. "Hoolies, that's aqivi!"

"It'll help settle you. I got hit over the ear once . . . it takes away your balance."

"Is that why I keep falling down?"

"That, or clumsiness."

Gingerly, I touched the tender place. It was, as Alric said, right over my ear. It was swollen, matted, a little crusty; no new blood. It also hurt like hoolies.

It was too quiet. "Where is everyone?" I asked. "Where did everyone go?"

"To the dance. They wanted to wager on Del."

"Oh, hoolies . . . it's *my* dance—"

"You're in no shape for dancing."

"Maybe this will help." I drank more aqivi. Tried to uncross my eyes. "I have to go," I said. "Do you think I can sit here while she's out there dancing?"

"I don't expect you to, no. But I also don't expect you want me to carry you."

I drank yet again, then hitched myself to my feet. Stood there wavering, trying to maintain balance. "Why are there two of you?"

Alric stood up. "Two of *me?*"

"Yes."

He took the bota away. "I think you should go to bed."

"After I see about Del."

"Tiger—"

"I have to see about Del."

Alric sighed. Put away the bota. Took me under one arm. "We'll never make it to the circle."

It took great effort to speak. "Certainly we will."

"Then why don't you show me the way?"

"First just show me the door."

Alric steered me toward it.

By the time we made it through the alleys and out to the circles, I was more than ready to lie down and pass out. But I didn't dare do either, in any particular order, after what I'd said.

"Hoolies," I mumbled, "the *people*—"

They thronged around the circle. Behind us lay the city, broken walls and rubble now serving as steps and platforms from which to watch the dance. People hung out of the windows of crumbling second stories and lined the fallen rooftops. Others rimmed the circle itself, forming a human perimeter. Someone had drawn a second circle around the first as a line of demarcation. The three paces between the true circle and the second one was meant to serve as a buffer zone, to keep the people back.

I swayed. Alric's hand tightened. "What did you expect? This is a dance between two of the best sworddancers in the South—even with you out of it—and a lot depends on it."

I squinted against the sunlight. "I wonder where Esnat is. He ought to be here. He *better* be here . . . him and all his friends . . . and Hadjib, too."

"They're probably watching from the city."

Someone jostled me. Unbalanced, I nearly fell. Only Alric kept me upright.

"Everything's moving," I muttered.

I shouldn't have had the aqivi. Or maybe it was just that I shouldn't have been kicked in the head. Nothing fit together. I saw faces, heard talk, felt the press of the crowd. But everything seemed to exist at a very great distance from me.

I squinted through the rising thumping in my head. "Where's Del? Can you see her?"

"Not through all the people."

"Then let's get closer. I have to see Del."

"Tiger—wait—"

But I wasn't waiting for anyone. Not when I had to see Del.

It's not easy trying to *walk* when your balance isn't right, let alone push your way through a crowd. I stumbled, staggered, nearly fell, ignored oaths and insults, shouldered my way through the throng as Alric brought up the rear. A few people tried to stop us, but Alric and I are big. They didn't try for long.

We broke through at last and nearly fell over the line. People protested, complaining about my pushiness, but a few were sword-dancers who recognized me. The word went around quickly: I was given room. It gave me a chance to breathe.

All right, I'll admit it. I had thoughts of forcing Del out of the circle by claiming the dance mine; after all, it was. But just as I broke through, nearly falling flat on my face, someone told them to dance.

"Wait—" I blurted.

Too late.

It was a true dance. Both swords lay in the precise center of the circle. Abbu's back was closest to me; Del stood across from him. He blocked her view of me, but it didn't really matter. Now that the dance had begun, Del would see nothing at all except the man who danced against her.

At the word, they ran. Scooped. Came up. Swords flashed, clashed; screeched away to clash again.

All around us the people hummed.

Hoolies, my head hurts.

"Are you all right?" Alric asked. "You're looking kind of gray."

I didn't bother to look. I knew where he was: on my right.

"Tiger, are you—"

"Fine," I snapped. "*Fine* . . . just let me watch the dance.

The dance was mostly a blur. Abbu's back was still to me. He wore only a suede dhoti, as is customary, bare of legs, arms, torso.

The crowd muttered and hummed. Talking about the man. Talking about the woman. Discussing who would win.

To a man, they said Abbu.

I squinted, spreading feet in an attempt to maintain balance. "Watch his patterns," I muttered. "Bascha— watch his patterns."

Alric's voice was calm. "She's doing all right, Tiger."

"She's letting him tie her up."

"Del knows what she's doing."

Abbu blurred into two people. I scrubbed a hand across my eyes. "She has to take the offensive."

Blades clanged and scraped.

"Bascha—drive him back. Bring him across to me."

When he moved, I could see her. She wore only the ivory tunic and a relentless ferocity. She didn't want to kill him; she most certainly wanted to beat him beyond the hope of redemption. It was what she'd have to do in order to force his hand. Abbu wouldn't yield unless he knew she could kill him.

Unless he knew she *might*.

Del's patterns were flawless. His better still.

"Come on, bascha, watch him . . . don't let him draw you in— "

She drove him across the circle. Behind me, the spectators moved, fearing a broken circle. I knew better. They'd neither of them break it.

"Yes, bascha—*yes*—" The dance blurred again. I tried to squint it away. "Hoolies, not *now*—"

Abbu Bensir's turn to move. I nearly moved with him.

Alric's hand clamped around my right arm. "This isn't your dance."

Someone bumped my left elbow. He'd come in close, moving across the outer circle, usurping the little space left to me and Alric. I reeled, nearly fell. Scrubbed my eyes again. "Two of everything . . ."

"Aqivi," Alric remarked. "I should have given you water."

I felt drunk. I felt *distant*. Noise increased, then receded. The clamoring hurt my head. Around me, the world squirmed. Even Alric squirmed.

"Stay in one place," I suggested, as he moved closer on my left. "Come on, bascha—*dance*—"

Everything was gray. The steelsong hurt my ears.

"What's that?" Alric asked.

I chanced a glance to my right. Waited for vision to still. "Will you stop switching sides?"

"What's that sound?" he asked.

All I could hear was the steel. It cut my head right open.

Del broke through Abbu's guard and stung him in the elbow. Abbu skipped back, but the trick was a telling one. The woman had drawn first blood.

"Better, bascha . . . better—"

"What's that *noise?*" Alric asked.

I heard the clang of steel, the screech and scrape of blades. What did he think it was?

"Come on, bascha—*beat* him—"

"Tiger—look at that."

All I saw was the dance. Two moving bodies: one male, one female. Both perfectly matched. Both moving easily to a rhythm no one else heard. A desire no one else felt.

Come on, bascha—

"Tiger!"

Alric's voice got through. It stole my wits from the dance, from Del; it made me look beyond.

Across the circle from us, behind Del's back, the crowd abruptly parted. Lines of spectators peeled away like bark from a willow tree.

Leaving Vashni in their place.

Vashni. *Vashni?*

"Tiger," Alric repeated.

In the circle, the dance went on. Steel rang on the air.

The ululation began.

Softly, first; then rising. It swallowed. It swallowed the song of the swords. It swallowed the murmuring. It swallowed the whole world.

I rubbed at aching eyes. "Too much noise," I complained.

Alric, having moved again, now stood on my left. He smiled down at me. And odd, triumphant smile.

Smiled *down* at me; but we are the same size. "Wait—" I began, but the world grayed out again.

"Tiger. Tiger?"

Now from my right. "Two of you," I muttered, "trading places with one another."

In the circle, Del danced. But no one watched any more.

"Oracle!" someone shouted. "Show us the Oracle!"

The ululations stopped. Vashni divided and flowed aside, leaving the middle open.

"Oracle," someone murmured. The word threaded its way through the crowd until all I could hear was the whisper. The sound of the syllables.

I squinted across the circle. Saw the hair, the eyes, the skin. "Alric," I said in disgust, "how did you get over *there?*"

He sounded startled. "What?"

"There." I tried to point. "One minute you're over there—the next you're here on my right—the next you're on my *left*. There aren't three of you, are there?"

Alric didn't answer. "He's a *Northerner*," he blurted.

Northerner? Northerner?

What is he talking about?

Del and Abbu danced. I heard the steelsong threading through the humming, the shouts from everyone else.

Not shouting for the dance. Shouting for the jhihadi. So many Northerners. So many Alrics.

I looked right: Alric.

I looked left: Alric.

Across the circle: Alric.

Hoolies, I must be sandsick.

"Aqivi," I muttered. "It's muddled up my head."

My muddled head swam.

I squinted again across the circle. "Alric—is that you?" I swung my muddled head and stared at the man on my left. "Or is *that* you . . . no, neither one . . . then who's *that* man?"

The Alric on my left looked at me out of piercingly bright blue eyes. No, not Alric—Alric's smile is different. Alric's *eyes* are different. He doesn't cut you with them.

These eyes were cold. These eyes were icy. These eyes waited for something.

"The Oracle," repeated Alric—the Alric on my right, mimicking everyone else.

I stared across the circle. Blond, blue-eyed Northerner: Alric was right in that. He looked a lot like Alric. He looked a lot like Del. Maybe it's just that Northerners all look alike to me—

My mouth dropped open. "Hoolies, that's *Jamail*—"

Alric's voice: "Who?"

"Del's brother—but the Vashni said he was dead!"

"He doesn't look dead to me. He looks like an Oracle."

Oracle. Oracle?

In the circle, in the dance, swords scraped and clashed and screeched.

"Wait—" I said, "*wait* . . . I don't—this isn't—*he* can't be the Oracle . . . Jamail doesn't have a tongue!"

Jamail opened his mouth and began to prophesy.

Now *my* mouth dropped open. "Am I awake?" I asked numbly, "or did the stud really kill me?"

Alric didn't answer.

"Del!" I shouted. *"Del!"*

But Del was busy dancing. Her back was to her brother.

"Hoolies, bascha—can't you hear? That's your brother talking!"

That's her brother—*talking?*

A flash of salmon-silver blade; the cry of magicked steel.

"He has no tongue," I protested.

Hoolies, everything fit. A mute who wasn't a man, but wasn't a woman, either.

Oh, bascha, *look.*

Steelsong filled the air, punctuating the Oracle's words as he lifted an arm to point.

"Jhihadi!" someone shouted. "He's naming the jhihadi!"

The crowd behind me surged forward. Jostled, I nearly fell. A hand on my left arm steadied me, another hooked into my harness; Alric was on my right.

Alric was on my *right.*

"*Jhihadi!*" the crowd roared, as the Oracle made it clear.

The man on my left laughed. It was a wild, exultant laugh filled with surprise and gratification, and an odd sort of power. "All that money spent on a false Oracle, and now the real one picks me anyway . . ." He tightened his grip on my harness. "Now all I need is this."

I knew as I turned to look. By then it was too late.

Ajani wasted no time. He locked one hand around the hilt and jerked my *jivatma* free, shoving me back as he moved. I very nearly fell.

He watched me out of pale, icy eyes. Saw me stagger. Saw me struggle. Saw me gather flagging wits. Saw me open my mouth to protest.

And smiled. "Samiel," he whispered. The blade flared to life.

Oh—hoolies—*Ajani*—

Ajani with Samiel.

Ajani with Chosa Dei.

Who now was pointed at me.

I heard Alric's curse. Saw Ajani's eyes. How could I have confused them?

"Thank you," Ajani said. "You made it easy for me."

I sucked in a breath, trying to hold off disorientation. "You don't know what you have. You don't know what that sword *is*."

Ajani's voice was smooth. Incongruously soft. "Oh, I think I do. People are talking about it . . . even my own men, who saw what you did with it and remembered what the boy said." The smile was brief, but warm. "I know what a *jivatma* is. I knew what to do with the name. It will be very useful for a man just named jhihadi."

I kept my tone steady. "If your men were there, you know. You know what else it can do. What it can do to *you*."

All around us the people fled.

Ajani lifted the sword. I thought about what it would be like for Chosa Dei to have me at last. And what it would be like when he—in my skin—tore Ajani to pieces.

It might be interesting. But I'd rather just be *me*.

Beyond me, Alric shouted. Said something about men: borjuni.

I looked only at Ajani, who held my *jivatma*.

And then heard Delilah's song, cutting through the circle.

Oh, bascha, bascha. Here is your chance at last.

The song rose in pitch. The circle was filled with Northern light so bright even Ajani squinted.

I pointed a courteous finger toward the woman who approached. Politely, I told Ajani, "Someone wants to see you."

By the time he turned, she was on him.

Seventeen

I knew she should be tired, after dancing with Abbu. But this was Ajani at last; I knew it didn't matter. Del could be on her deathbed and Ajani would get her off it.

So she could put him on his.

She drove him back, back, into the crowd; the crowd scrambled away. And then surged close again, surrounding Alric and me, murmuring about the jhihadi and the woman who tried to kill him.

Hoolies, they believed it! They thought he was the jhihadi!

Which meant if Del killed him, the crowd would tear her apart.

"Don't kill him," I said. "Oh, bascha, be careful—think about what you're doing."

I didn't expect an answer. Del didn't give me one.

They'd kill her. They'd shred her to little pieces.

Bascha, don't kill him.

Unless I could get to Jamail. But I knew better than to try. I could barely stand, jostled this way and that. And even if I could, the Vashni would kill me outright for daring to approach their Oracle, no matter what the reason. Already things had gone wrong; the Oracle had spoken, and a woman was trying to thwart him.

The Oracle's own sister.

Jamail, remember me?

No. He'd only seen me once.

Jamail, remember your sister?

But between Jamail and his sister were hundreds of Southerners: tanzeers, sword-dancers, tribesmen. Even the Oracle might have trouble getting through the crowd, now the jhihadi was named.

Jamail no longer mattered. His part in the game was done.

The crowd closed up tight. Hoolies, Del, where are you?

The crowd abruptly parted.

"Tiger—*down*—"

Alric's hand on my harness jerked me to the ground. Then his sword was out and slicing through someone's guts.

What?

What?

Ajani's fellow borjuni. Now become holy bodyguards warding the jhihadi.

Oh, hoolies—not *now*. My head hurts too much and my eyes won't focus.

I rolled through screening legs, scrabbling away, cursing as fingers got stepped on. Wished I had a sword.

Above me, battle commenced. Alric was all alone.

Hoolies, where's Del?

And then I saw the light. Heard the whistle of the storm. Felt the sting of flying dust. With the power of *jivatmas*, they built a private circle. They created a fence of magic made of light and heat and cold.

"I need a sword," I muttered, staggering to my feet.

In the circle, the wind howled. Ajani had my sword.

"Tiger! Tiger—*here!*"

I turned; caught the weapon. An old, well-known blade. I stared in muddled surprise.

Through the brief gap, Abbu Bensir grinned. "You're mine," he called, "not theirs." And was swallowed by the crowd.

More of the new jhihadi's borjuni friends arrived with weapons drawn. Alric and I didn't count them;

we knew they outnumbered us. But we also knew how to dance. All they knew was how to kill.

Time. Too much, and the tribes would reach the circle Del shared with Ajani. They couldn't break through until the dance was done and the magic muted, but in the end they'd reach her. In the end they'd kill her.

If she was still alive.

Too much time, and Ajani's borjuni bodyguards would wear down Alric and me. Too little, however, and we might be able to get away, if we had a bit of luck.

Luck decided to call.

"Duck," a voice suggested. I didn't wait; I ducked. The thrown ax divided a head.

Bellin laughed aloud. "Practicing," he said.

Now we were there. The fourth was still in the circle.

Come on, Delilah, *beat* him.

Fire flared in the circle. People began to scream.

At first I assumed it was in the natural course of fighting, since by now others had joined in as well. And then I realized it had nothing to do with fighting, and everything to do with magic.

Chosa Dei wanted his freedom. Others would pay the price.

Even Del might.

Not again, bascha. You already paid it once.

Ajani was shouting something. I couldn't understand him; my head pounded unmercifully and my vision still was muddled. But I heard Ajani shouting.

He said something about Shaka Obre.

Ajani didn't know Shaka Obre.

I cut down a borjuni. "Hold him, bascha—*hold him*—"

Boreal keened. A cold wind burst out of the circle, shredding silk and gauze. It frosted hair and eyebrows. Those who still could, fled.

I sucked in a breath and jerked my borrowed blade from a body. "Sing up a storm, bascha . . ."

In a mad dash to escape, people fell over one another. I saw their breath on the air.

Winter came into the circle. Summer drove it back. The blast of heat baked us all; I blocked my eyes with an arm.

Samiel burned white-hot. The air was sucked out of lungs.

The hostility around us turned abruptly to fear. Even Ajani's borjuni exuded a different stench.

Ajani. Ajani in the circle.

With Del.

Hoolies, bascha, where are you—?

Shouting died away. Light corruscated. All the rainbows danced, though there was no rain to form them. No moisture in the air. Only scorching heat.

Ajani was shouting still. Del stalked him in the circle. Back, back, back; Boreal teased Samiel, salmon-silver on black.

"Dance," Del invited. "Dance with me, Ajani."

Back. Back. Back. He tried to parry, couldn't.

I saw the bared teeth, the strained face. Saw the fear in piercing eyes. It wasn't fear of Del, but of what he felt in the sword.

He was a very large man, a man of immense strength as well as strength of will. But he didn't know Samiel. He didn't know Chosa Dei.

"Too much for you," I muttered.

Ajani shouted something. Tendons stood up in his neck.

Heat exploded from the circle. Nearby, a blanket roof caught on fire. Then another. People began to scream. People began to run. Iskandar was on fire.

Wind ripped through the streets, spreading flame in its wake. Now burnouses caught fire, and people began to burn.

"No," Del declared.

Boreal's song-summoned banshee-storm howled out of the sword, shredding Samiel's flame. Winter came at Del's call. Fire doesn't burn in sleet.

It was abrupt and unpleasant. It doused Iskandar completely, then wisped into nothingness. I was wet, cold, sweaty. But so was everyone else, even Ajani's borjuni.

With renewed vigor, they attacked. With renewed vigor, I repulsed. Next to me, Alric fought; behind me Bellin counted Ajani's supporters they moved in to surround us. He called out greetings to each, naming them to their faces, which served to startle them. For Alric and me, it was an infallible way of knowing which man meant us harm.

Bascha, I said, I'm coming.

Something stung a rib. I smashed the sword away, then buried my own in a belly. Ripped it free again to turn on another man, but a misstep sent me by him. I staggered, tried to catch my balance, was swallowed by heat and cold and light and all the colors of the world.

Bascha, bascha, I'm coming—whether I want to or not.

I broke through, swearing, and fell into the circle, landing hard on a shoulder. Abbu's sword spilled free.

Hoolies, my head hurts . . . and the world's gone gray again.

Inside, the storm was raging. A hot rain fell. Steam rose from the ground. The breath of winter blew, whistling in my ears. Numbing nose and earlobes.

Boreal was ablaze with all the colors of the North, all the rich, vivid colors. Samiel was black.

A new thought occurred: If Chosa Dei takes Ajani, Del can take Chosa Dei.

But Del didn't wait that long.

Sprawled on the ground, I saw it. Hatred. Rage. Obsession. The memory of what he'd done; of what had shaped her life. Of *who* had shaped her life, bringing her to this moment; bringing her to the edge, where balance is so precarious, so incredibly easy to lose. She teetered there, on the edge, looking just beyond. Acknowledging the price, because she'd paid it so many times.

Paying once more would change nothing. And also change everything.

Delilah's long song would end.

Wind screamed through the circle. It caught on blades and tore, shrieking an angry protest. Ajani's face was stripped bare. An unforgettable face; an assemblage of perfect bones placed in impressive arrangement. A Northerner in his prime: taller than I, and broader, with a lion's mane of hair equally thick and blond as Del's, flowing back from high brow. The magnificence of a woman made masculine for a man.

Bellin had summed it up: his burning was very bright.

His burning was *too* bright—Chosa Dei looked out of his eyes.

Pale, piercing eyes alight with unholy fire. With the knowledge of promised power.

Time to extinguish him, bascha—before he extinguishes us.

Del stopped singing. Del lowered her sword. And stood there waiting for him.

Waiting? Waiting for *what?*

Was she blinded by his burning?

No, not Delilah. This was the man who had made her, the way I made my sword. In blood and fear and hatred.

Ajani bared his teeth. *"We meet again,"* he said. *"This time to end it, yes?"*

Del, like me, stared. His features were softening. The perfect nose, the set of his mobile mouth; the upswept angle of Northern cheekbones, slanting down his face. Ajani was being *unmade.*

Hoolies, bascha, *kill* him!

She slashed the blade from his hands. Her own was at his throat. "Kneel," she said hoarsely. "You made my father kneel."

Bascha, that isn't Ajani—

My sword lay on the ground. My clean, silver sword made of unblemished Northern steel.

My *empty,* unblemished sword.

Oh, bascha—wait—

"Del—" I croaked.

Ajani bared teeth at her. Chosa Dei stared out of his eyes. *"Do you know what I am?"*

"I know what you are."

Ajani shook back his hair. The shape of his jaw was changing. He was wax, softening. Light a candle; he would melt.

Del's voice was deadly. "I said: *kneel.*"

Around us, beyond the circle, hundreds waited and watched, too frightened to attempt escape. I lay on the ground and panted, trying to clear my head. Thinking: If I can get to the sword—

But Ajani was too close. He had only to pick it up. He *would* pick it up—

"Del—" I croaked again. It was all I could manage.

Ajani did not kneel. Chosa Dei wouldn't let him.

"I am power," he said. *"Do you think you can defeat me? Do you think I will do* your *bidding, after waiting so long to do mine?"*

Hoolies, he didn't need a *sword.* All he needed was himself.

Bascha—bascha, *kill* him—don't play games with this man—not even in the name of your pride—

Ajani spread his arms. There was no wasted flesh on him, nor a pound out of place. He was taut, fit, *big.* He made me look puny. His magnificence rivaled Del's.

"Do you know what I am?"

And I wondered, as I watched him, which man asked the question.

Del shifted her grip. The sword scythed down from above. She sliced a hamstring in two.

He fell, as she meant him to. It wasn't a proper posture, but no longer did he stand upright to tower over her. To tower over *me* as I staggered to my feet.

His burning was very bright.

"Now," I whispered intently.

Del began to sing.

Chosa Dei was in him, but some of Ajani was left. Northern-born, he knew. I saw it in his eyes; in Ajani's still-human eyes, as the flesh of his face loosened. I saw it in his posture as he slumped before the sword, wearing a bloody necklace. Boreal was thirsty. She tasted him already.

Del sang a song of the kinfolk she had lost. Father, mother, grandfolk, brothers, aunts, uncles, cousins. So many kinfolk murdered. Only two of them spared: Jamail and Delilah, the last of the line. The man could never sire a son; the woman could never bear one.

She would kill Ajani. But in the end, he would win.

Delilah ended her song. Stood there looking at him. Did she feel cheated, I wondered, that Ajani wasn't alone? That when the moment came, she would kill more than the Northerner?

Chosa wasn't stupid. He reached out. Touched the sword. Closed slack fingers on the grip. Dragged it up from the ground. Black flowed into the blade; better a sword than useless meat.

Pale hair tumbled around his face. His magnificent Northern face, with no hint of softness about it. Chosa Dei was gone.

Ajani shook back his hair, holding the blackened *jivatma*. But he didn't try to use it, with Boreal kissing his throat. All he did was stare at the woman who held Boreal, progenitor of storms.

"Who are you?" he asked.

Del didn't bother to tell him. "You have a daughter," she said.

And then she took his head.

Eighteen

The body slumped to the ground. Del, set free at last, staggered back and fell.

Oh, hoolies, bascha . . . don't pass out *now*.

She tried to get up, and couldn't. Exhaustion and reaction stripped her of her strength. All she could do was gasp, clinging to her sword.

Hoolies, Tiger, *move*—

The private circle was gone, banished by banished magic. Anyone who reached us now would find us easy to touch.

Del had killed Ajani. To the rest, he was the jhihadi.

I heard the ululations, the shouts of angry tanzeers. The clash of Southron steel.

"Sorry, Esnat," I mumbled. "I think Hadjib will get his war."

Samiel, I knew, was the answer . . . before they got to Del.

Bellin got there first. "Don't touch it!" I shouted.

He dove, thrust out with his axes, scooped up the blade. As I took an unsteady stride—Del and I were a pair—the sword came flying to me. I plucked it out of the air.

Southroners stirred, shouted. They saw the headless jhihadi; the woman with the sword; the Sandtiger with another. And a foreign boy with axes.

Bellin grinned at me. "Do something," he called. "You're supposed to be good with that thing."

Do something?

Fine.

How about a song?

The crowd surged forward en masse. But I cut the air with a reblackened sword and the crowd lurched back again. Across from me stood Alric, teasing the air with his swordtip. Promising violence.

Alric. Bellin. Me. And Del, but she was down. For now we had stopped the crowd, but that wouldn't last long. We needed more help.

Samiel might give it. All I had to do was sing.

Sing. I hate singing. But how else do you call the magic?

Bellin juggled axes. It was an impressive feat; also a useful one. They'd all seen how he used them. Everyone hung back as Bellin moved easily around Del and me, building a fence of flying axes.

"Just curious," he mentioned, "but why are you singing *now*? Especially when you do it so badly?"

I just kept on singing. Or whatever you want to call it.

"Jivatma," Alric said briefly, as if it answered the question. For some, it might; for Bellin, it answered nothing.

"Get Del," I said, and went right back to my song. Samiel seemed to like it.

Behind us, far behind us, the ululation increased. The tribes were coming in.

We edged toward the city. Hoolies, if they got through they'd cut us down in a minute. Samiel would take a few, but eventually we'd lose just because of sheer numbers.

Bellin, being helpful, started to sing along. He had a better voice, but he didn't know my song.

Samiel didn't seem to mind.

"Alric—have you got Del?"

"I've got her, Tiger . . . come on, we've got to go."

"Tiger?" It was Del. "Tiger—that was *Jamail.*"

The keening wail increased. Moving this slowly wouldn't gain us any time. We needed something special.

All right, I said to my sword, let's see what you can do.

I thrust it into the air over my head, balanced flat across both palms, as I'd seen Del do. And I sang my heart out—loudly, and very badly—until the firestorm came.

It licked out from the blade, flowed down my body, spilled across the ground. I sent it in all directions, teasing at feet and robes. It drove everyone back: tanzeers, tribesmen, borjuni.

Magic, I thought, can be useful.

I called up a blast of wind, a hot, dry wind born of the Punja itself. It tasted at sand and sucked it up, then spat it at the people.

The tribes, if no one else, would know what it was. Would call it samiel, and give way to its strength. You can't fight the desert when it rises up to rebel.

"Go home!" I shouted. "He was a false jhihadi! He was a *Northerner*—is that what you want?"

In the sandblast, they staggered back. Tribesmen, borjuni, tanzeers; the samiel knows no rank.

"Go home!" I shouted. "It's not the proper time!"

The wail of the storm increased.

"Now," I said to the others, as the crowd, shouting, scattered.

I peeled the storm apart, forming a narrow channel. With alacrity, we departed.

Garrod met us with horses: the stud, and Del's blue roan, "Go," he said succinctly. "They're watered and provisioned; don't waste any time."

The thought of riding just now did not appeal to me. My head was not very happy. "He'll dump me, or kick me again."

"No, I've spoken to him. He understands the need."

It was, I thought in passing, a supremely ridiculous statement. He was *horse*, not human.

Ah, hoolies, who cares? If Garrod said he would . . . I pushed away a damp muzzle come questing for reassurance.

Del sheathed her sword. "Jamail," was all she said.

That decided me. "Don't be sandsick," I snapped. "Jamail's the Oracle; do you think anyone will hurt him?"

"I thought he was dead, and he's not."

"So be happy about it. Let's go."

Garrod handed her reins. "Waste no time," he repeated. "I can hold the other horses, but not for very long. There are far too many of them . . . the sandstorm will only delay them, not stop them—once they've recovered their courage they'll come after you again. If you want a head start, *go*."

Del swung up on the roan and gathered in her reins, staring down at me. "Are *you* coming, then?"

I took the pointed hint. Sheathed my sword. Dragged myself up on the stud, who stomped and pawed and snorted. I clung muzzily to the saddle. "Which way is out?"

"This way," Del said, pointing, as Alric slapped the stud's rump.

"What about me?" Bellin called. "Aren't I supposed to come? I found Ajani for you!"

I held the stud up a moment. "I can think of better ways of becoming famous than riding with the woman who killed the new jhihadi. Certainly *safer* ones; it's no good being a panjandrum if you're not alive to enjoy it."

"True," Bellin agreed. "So I guess I can still be your son. You look old enough."

I called him a foul name and sent the stud after Del.

We clattered through the ruined city with no respect for its inhabitants. Garrod was absolutely right: now that I'd banished the sandstorm and Del and I were gone, there was nothing to prevent the crowd from solidifying its deadly intention. No matter what I'd shouted about Ajani being a false jhihadi, he was still the only one they knew, thanks to planted rumors and Jamail's misinterpreted gesture. The crowd, fired by bloodlust, wouldn't listen to the truth no matter who gave it to them. Not even the Oracle.

Through the city and out, then bursting through colored hyorts huddled together on the plateau. And over the rim and off, swarming down the trail. Behind us, as we fled, the shouting slowly died, shredded by canyons and distance. And Iskandar was gone.

We rode as long and hard as we could, knowing we needed the distance. Del eventually called halt as we traded border canyons for border foothills, and scrubby, tree-clad ridges carved out of Southron soil. I wasn't so certain it was a good idea to stop yet, but she said I looked like I'd fall off if the stud so much as sneezed.

I held my head very still. "If he so much as *blinks*."

"Can you follow me?" she asked.

"As long as you don't go fast."

Del took us off the trail and over a snaky line of ridges and foothills closer to Harquhal than Iskandar. Trees were low and twisted and scrubby, but plentiful, providing decent cover. Behind a sloping, tree-screened hillside well off the new-beaten trail, Del dismounted her roan.

She reached out to catch the stud. "Do you need help?"

With great care, I dismounted, clinging to the stirrup. "Help doing what?"

She just shook her head. "Go sit down somewhere. I'll tend the horses.

I did. She did. And eventually came back, carrying saddle-pouches, bedrolls, botas.

In the hollow of the hill, we ate, drank, stretched out. Thought about what had happened. Thought about what we'd done.

Del was close beside me. I could hear her breathing. "Well," I said, "it's done."

She didn't say anything.

"You sang the song for your kinfolk, the one you swore to sing, and collected the blood-debt he owed for murdering everyone."

She still didn't say anything.

"Your song is over, bascha. You sang it very well." She drew in a lengthy, noisy breath.

"You said I should ask you after Ajani was dead." I waited a moment. "What will you do now?"

Del's smile was sad. "Ask me in the morning."

"Bascha—"

"Ask," she said softly. "And then ask me the next morning, and the next . . ." She rubbed at eyes undoubtedly as tired and gritty as mine. "If you ask me enough times, maybe one of these days I'll know. And by then it won't matter, because years will have passed, and I'll have forgotten why I never knew what I would do once Ajani was dead. I will have simply *done* it."

It was, I thought, convoluted reasoning. But at that particular moment it didn't really matter.

I released a sigh. It felt so good just to *stop*. "Busy day," I observed.

Del only grunted.

The sun dipped low in the west. "Who won the dance?"

Next to me, Del shifted. "Nobody won the dance. The dance was never finished."

I attempted to summon outrage. "Do you mean to tell me you threw away my chance at a domain? My chance to be a tanzeer?"

Unimpressed, Del shrugged. "You'd be a bad tanzeer."

"How do *you* know?"

"I just do."

My turn to grunt. "You're probably right."

"*I'd* make a better tanzeer."

"You're a woman, bascha."

"So?"

"So we're South, remember?"

"Aladar's daughter is a tanzeer."

"That will never last."

She sighed. "You're probably right. The South is still too backward."

The sun dipped lower still. "I think instead of a sword, I'm going to get a new horse."

Del grinned briefly. "The old one might protest."

"The old one can protest himself right into the stewpot, for all I care. I'm not about to put up with him taking pieces out of my head just because he hates magic."

"You hated magic, once."

"I still hate magic. It doesn't mean I'm going to kick somebody's head off if they use it."

"You used to *bite* mine off."

I grunted. "Long time ago, bascha."

"Hours ago, maybe."

I sighed. "Why are we arguing?"

"We're not arguing. We're delaying."

"What are we delaying?"

"Discussing what we're going to do."

"What *are* we going to do?"

"Go north?"

"No."

'Go south?"

"We have to. There's Shaka Obre to find."

Del didn't answer at once. When she did, her tone was odd. "You're certain you want to do that?"

"I have to. How else am I going to discharge this sword?"

"You've already learned to control it better."

I frowned. Rolled my head to look at her. "You sound like you don't think it's such a good idea to go hunting Shaka Obre."

She chose her words carefully. "I just think it will be very difficult to find him. His name is shrouded in myth—he's part of children's stories."

"So was Chosa Dei, but that didn't make him any less real. *I* can attest to that."

Del sighed, picking at the thin blanket she'd thrown over her long, bare legs. "It isn't easy, Tiger."

"Nothing much is, but what do *you* mean?"

"Looking for a man very difficult to find. I had reason, I had *need* . . . but the task was no easier."

"You're saying you don't think I'll stick with it."

"I'm saying it will be a very difficult quest."

"I don't have a lot of choice. Chosa Dei's presence will provide a good enough reason, I think."

Del sighed. "It will be complicated. We are wanted now, more so than anyone in the South—we killed the jhihadi. They will track us without respite. We killed the *jhihadi*, the man who intended to change the sand to grass."

"The man they *think* was the jhihadi."

Del considered it, then laughed a little. "Jamail was very clever, doing what he did. I wouldn't have thought of it."

"What did Jamail do?"

"Pointed at Ajani. He must have known someone would try to kill him . . . if not me, then the tanzeers. He got his revenge after all."

I grunted. "He wasn't pointing at Ajani. And it wasn't Alric, either; I know: I was there."

"Who *else* was he pointing at? I saw him do it, Tiger."

"So did I, bascha."

"Well, if it wasn't at Ajani—" Then, lurching up out of blankets: "You're *sandsick!*"

"Oh, I don't think so."

Loud silence.

"He wouldn't," she said at last. "He *didn't*—you know he didn't. Why would he do such a thing?"

I didn't offer an answer, thinking it obvious.

Del stared at me. "That horse kicked you harder than I thought."

I yawned. "I might make a bad tanzeer, but I think I can handle messiah."

Louder silence.

Then, in pointed challenge, "Can you change the sand to grass?"

Another yawn. "Tomorrow."

Del's tone was peculiar. "He didn't *really* point at you. You were right there, yes, but it was *Ajani* he pointed at. I saw him. I saw him point. It was Ajani, Tiger."

I just lay there and smiled, blinking drowsily.

"Swear by your sword," she ordered.

I grinned. "Which one?"

"The *steel* sword, Tiger; don't be so vulgar."

I put out a hand and caught the twisted-silk hilt. "I swear by Samiel: Jamail pointed at me."

I knew she wanted to admonish me not to speak the name aloud. But she understood what it meant. She understood the oath.

Del thought about it deeply. Then made a careful observation. "You know better than to swear false oath on your *jivatma*." As if she wasn't certain; maybe, with me, she wasn't.

Through yet another yawn, "Yes, bascha. You've made it very clear that's a bad thing to do." I paused. "Would you like me to swear on *your* sword?"

Very firmly, "No."

I drifted off toward sleep. The edge was so very close. All I needed to do was take that final step and slide myself off the horizon, in concert with the sun—

Del lay down again. Said nothing for several long moments.

I just drifted, aware of her nearness in an abstract, pleasing way. Legs and elbows touched. My temple brushed her shoulder.

Drowsily, I thought: A good way to fall asleep—

Then she turned a hip, shifting closer to me. Her breath in my ear was soft. "Do sword-dancers-turned-messiahs have bedmates? Or are they celibate?"

I cracked open a gritty eye. "Not tonight, bascha. I have a headache."

The sun fell over the edge. Laughing, so did I.